Advance Praise for

"Boykin, a retired lieutenant general and founding member of the Delta Force, an elite special operations unit, teams up with adventure-travel author Morrissey (In High Places) for a hair-raising international military suspense thriller. Blake Kershaw goes undercover inside an al-Qaeda camp in Pakistan to foil a plot to set off a nuclear device in the United States. The novel offers a fascinating, even sympathetic look into the brotherhood behind radical terrorism while showing how an operative narrowly stays alive to thwart disaster. Blake says to his 'brothers' in the terrorist cell, 'My government is corrupt. We say we believe in freedom of religion, but we do not.' The plot is underdeveloped compared to the amount of attention paid to the hardware of military operations, which will satisfy readers who connect guns and religion. With descriptions of the hero killing in at least three scenes, the story contains more violence than most Christian fiction, but it's a vivid portrayal of spy work and the inner workings of a terror cell."

"A phenomenal book by a man of great courage and an inspiring faith."

— Joel C. Rosenberg, *NYT* bestselling author of *Inside the Revolution*

"A powerful and moving chronicle of courage, commitment, and devotion by an audacious soldier and gifted leader."

— Lt. Col. Oliver L. North, USMC (Ret.), *NYT* bestselling author of *American Heroes*

DANGER CLOSE

A NOVEL

William G. Boykin,
Lieutenant General (Retired)

and Tom Morrisey

A FIDELIS BOOKS BOOK
An Imprint of Post Hill Press
ISBN: 978-1-64293-276-8
ISBN (eBook): 978-1-64293-277-5

Danger Close:
A Novel

Cover Design by Jomel Cequina

Post Hill Press
New York • Nashville
posthillpress.com

Published in the United States of America

Today you are
driving me from the land,
and I will be
hidden from your presence;
I will be a restless
wanderer on the earth,
and whoever finds me
will kill me.

Genesis 4:14

CHAPTER ONE

❑ ❑ ❑

The Hindu Kush, Afghanistan, 2006

The satellite moved with the steadiness and speed of a tiny white pencil point being drawn across the deep, black bowl of the sky. It crossed the seven burning pinpoints of the Pleiades, skimmed the edge of the Milky Way—a billowed, luminous cloud in this dark place—and continued, unblinking, on its steady journey south.

Blake Kershaw watched as it crossed the sky, wondered whose satellite it was and what it saw as it looked down—whether it was gauging drought or counting troops, whether its visit was just one more entry in a climate survey or the prelude to an attack, to mayhem and destruction.

It was his job, always, to assume the latter.

Turning so his back was to the valley beyond, Blake flipped the night-vision goggles down from his helmet and examined the object before him. It was not large—about the same width as the netbook computer in his tent back at the compound on Bagram Airfield. Across the device's curved surface were raised block letters: "FRONT TOWARD ENEMY." He opened the two scissor-legs on the bottom, turned them so they supported the three-and-a-half-pound device like the legs of a miniature sawhorse, aimed it in the general direction of the sloping terrace in front of him, and placed rocks behind and to the side of it to lessen the chances of something knocking it over.

The object was a Claymore mine, “M18A1” in the military catalog. It was old-school—Vietnam era—but remained a reliable means of defense, capable of firing seven hundred steel ball bearings across a sixty-degree, fan-shaped kill zone at something like three-and-a-half times the speed of sound. When an operation called for a half-strength, six-man Special Forces team to defend a fairly exposed position, it was a reliable, low-tech way to protect a perimeter. Old-school or not, Blake liked the Claymore mine.

Working by the green glow of the night-vision image, he unscrewed the cap on the mine’s top and attached one end of a cable. On the other end was a small radio receiver, duct-taped to the plastic-wrapped circuitry out of the mine’s usual clacker-type trigger. The whole thing, marked with a hand-painted yellow “6,” looked jerry-rigged and homemade, which it was. But when he and another weapons specialist tested the multifrequency system back at Fort Bragg, it proved to be an excellent way to defend a broad perimeter with devastating firepower.

Blake switched the receiver on. A small, low-power LED began glowing, a bright nova in his night-vision goggles, and he covered the tiny light with a piece of electrical tape. Then he set the receiver on the ground next to the mine.

Flipping up the goggles, Blake stood and inspected his work, nothing more than a dim, black oblong in this dark place. He stretched to get the kinks out of his back and looked once again at the cloudless, moonless sky.

Where he was, the mountains of southern Afghanistan, near the Pakistani border, was nearly the same latitude as the southern Virginia farm where he’d grown up, so the autumn constellations were all familiar. And what they were telling him right now was that it was early—still another five hours to go before dawn. Blake exhaled, the fog of his breath curling and dissipating in the cold air of high altitude.

Wouldn't want to live here. Having placed six Claymores in twice as many minutes, Blake stooped, carried his long-barreled rifle at quarter arms, and kept his silhouette hidden as he made his way back up the ridge to his team.

"Blue," he half-whispered as he drew within hearing range of the first man.

"Moon," came the reply.

Blake straightened up a bit and joined the other seven men positioned around the ridge.

"Fifty percent alert, Blake." The team's captain, Puerto Rico born and bred, was a West Point graduate and spoke English—as well as five other languages—like someone from the heartland.

"Sir." Blake flipped the night-vision goggles down again. His team had already prepared rudimentary "hasty fighting positions"—shallow, body-size fortifications, made from low walls of stacked rock and whatever natural cover they could find. The team's master sergeant, its engineer, and the medic were already curled up on thin foam pads in these small trenches, using poncho liners to conserve what heat they could as they slept. Blake walked up the hill to where Harry Chee, the communications specialist, was working with the two Signals Intelligence people—the specialists the Special Forces team was escorting on this night mission.

The SigInt men brought two pieces of gear with them. The first, a signals survey unit, had immediately been dubbed "the sniffer" by the rest of the team. The term was descriptive; the unit continuously sampled airwaves across all frequencies and stored what it found on a built-in, ruggedized hard drive.

The other piece of electronics, not nearly as exotic, was a much more sophisticated version of a police scanner, designed to allow the team to listen in on any voice transmissions in the radio and wireless phone spectrums.

Other than Pakistani Army traffic from across the border, any signals intelligence in the region was assumed to be Taliban; the local people were goatherds, for the most part—strangers to radios and satellite phones. They lived in huts devoid of electricity, primitive homes even by Third-World standards. As an American officer once quipped when someone mentioned bombing this part of Afghanistan back into the Stone Age, "That wouldn't be much of a trip."

The two Signals Intelligence soldiers were hunched over the scanner unit as Harry tinkered on it with his field kit.

"There," the junior of the two SigInt men was saying as he pressed a pair of stereo headphones to his ears. "That fixed it. Strong signal, five by five."

Harry nodded wordlessly, put his tools away, and moved off into the darkness. Blake was walking away as well when he heard one of the SigInt solders—the one wearing the headset—whisper to the other, "Old Sitting Bull don't say much, does he?"

Blake turned, came back, leaned close to the man, made a "come here" motion with his finger.

"Yeah?" The man lifted one side of the headset away from his ear.

"Four things, soldier," Blake said, his voice low. He began to count on his fingers. "One, Sitting Bull was Lakota Sioux; the man who just fixed your equipment is a member of the Navaho Nation and third-generation Army—fact, his granddaddy was a code talker in the Pacific. Two, you probably talk a little louder than you think you're talking when you've got those cans on your ears. Three, the people on this team probably hear better than most."

Blake fell silent.

"That's three," the SigInt guy finally said. "What's the fourth thing?"

Blake leaned closer. He was almost whispering in the other man's ear.

"Special Forces are tight, soldier," he said. "We know one another's families, know one another's houses. We even know one another's blood types. So if you go talking crap about one of us, there are people here who will take it as a reason to open up a giant-size can of whoop-ass. Me, I'm prone to give a man a second chance, let him say he's sorry."

The younger man straightened up and glanced at his partner.

"Hey." The more senior man held up both hands. "You want to dance with the Green Berets? Sorry, dude. You're on your own."

The guy with the phones glared at Blake. Then his face softened in the starlight.

"I'm sorry," he said.

"Don't sweat it." Blake picked up his rifle and moved off down the ridge.

The rifle Blake Kershaw carried was an M21—technically, the "M21 sniper weapon system," the highly accurized, rifle-scoped version of the M14. Like the .45 on his hip and the Claymores down the slope, it was a decades-old design, long since superseded by modern, more sophisticated weapons. But, like the .45 on his hip and the M18A1 Claymores, the M21 was extraordinarily robust and would function perfectly even in environments like the mountains of southeastern Pakistan in midautumn, which was pretty much like the dead of winter anywhere else. While it could not reach out and touch someone at the extreme ranges of the bolt-action rifles used by conventional army snipers, the M21 was semiautomatic, meaning Blake could engage several targets in rapid succession—a necessary ability for a weapons specialist in a Special Forces team deployed in open country.

One concession to the nocturnal nature of this mission was that Blake replaced the rifle's usual Leupold riflescope with a bulkier Bushnell nightscope. The optics weren't as good, but it was still able to pick out objects almost to the limits of the rifle's usual range, and it could do that under dim starlight.

Sitting down, he draped a poncho liner over his head and shoulders; the viewing end of the nightscope put out a soft green glow—not much but enough to illuminate a man's face and give him away to a careful observer. Then he switched the scope on and canvassed the slope below him, moving the rifle in discrete, ten-degree arcs.

Stones and rises. That was all it showed. But that didn't make Blake relax. To a soldier with his training, stones and rises were cover. And there was enough cover on the mountainside beneath him to conceal a well-trained platoon.

"Kersh?"

Blake switched off the scope and emerged from beneath the poncho liner. He turned, nodded wordlessly at the team's engineer.

"Your turn to stand down." The six-man unit, half of a conventional Special Forces team, was itself operating at 50 percent alert—three people on watch and looking for possible threats, the other three asleep or resting for two-hour shifts.

Blake nodded again. He pointed to a distant yellow spark, perhaps five kilometers distant. It flickered as someone or something walked past it. "Nothing but that fire down on the flats, probably goatherders. Got me wondering, though. Doesn't feel right."

Tony glassed the distant spark through his nightscope. "I'll watch it."

He looked at Blake, his head tilted. "Kersh . . . you have never been much into fire, have you?"

Blake shrugged. "Seems to me a fire comes with bad news more often than it comes with good."

Rather than getting into his fighting position, Blake put his sleeping-pad against a shelf of rock and leaned back, the rifle at his side and within reach.

He tried to close his eyes but kept opening them and gazing out at the distant campfire that was the only light in the landscape, the only thing glowing other than the stars. After about ten minutes, a thin stream of orange sparks shot up from it: *somebody just threw on another piece of wood, goat dung, or whatever they're burning.*

He watched it for more signs of activity, but it remained nothing other than a tiny, flickering, yellow point of light.

Five minutes later he sat up and gave up—he wasn't going to sleep. Not this shift. He grabbed the M21 and walked up the ridge to where the junior SigInt guy sat alone, headphones on his head. Blake touched him on the shoulder and he looked up, lifting one phone from his ear.

"Sorry I walked on you back there, soldier," Blake said.

"I deserved it, Sergeant." The SigInt man shook his head. "Running my mouth before my brain's engaged."

Blake sat. "Listen; I'm not doing any good grabbing zees. If you want, I'll listen to that for you, let you rest."

The other man brightened.

"Really?" Then his face straightened. "Any traffic'll be in Urdu. You speak it?"

"*Kuch*," Blake said. *A little.* "Did the language school before we deployed."

"You certain you don't mind?"

"Give me something to think about besides the cold."

The SigInt man handed the warm headphones to Blake, who put them on and settled back to listen.

Every ten seconds or so there would be a soft, fuzzy *shtick* as the scanner crossed to a frequency with distant, faint, background static. But that was it. If there was traffic out there, it was data, not voice. After fifteen minutes or so, he understood why the SigInt guy was so eager to hand over the phones.

Then five minutes later he heard a single word over the headphones.

"*Tayyar.*"

Ready.

Ready for what? Blake sat up, noted the frequency and the signal strength, and turned up the volume.

"Intezar kama huku dayna mayra. Yaad radhna . . . Zindaa ek. Hukm dayna sarbaraah."

Wait for my command. And remember—take one alive. Commander's orders.

Blake nudged the sleeping SigInt man with the toe of his boot.

"Wha—?" The groggy man stretched. "What's the sit?"

"Balloon's going up." Blake handed him the headset.

He grabbed his rifle and crab-walked swiftly down the hill. The captain was sacked out, but the master sergeant was up, scouring the slope beneath them with night glasses.

"Traffic, Phil," Blake told him. "Real clear signal, right in the neighborhood. Said to hit us, take one for intel, whack the rest."

"How soon?" The master sergeant was already shaking his captain awake.

"Any time. The signal was . . ."

A brilliant white flash erupted, as if the fabric of the night was being ripped in two, and a wall of noise flung Blake headlong down the slope.

CHAPTER TWO

❏ ❏ ❏

Blake flinched. A dozen points of searing, burning pain radiated torment from places up and down his right leg. He blinked at the dirt in his eyes and swallowed the coppery taste of blood. The ground beneath him quivered; white light fogged the sky about two hundred meters down the ridge. But he barely heard the explosions.

He blinked more dirt away. Then he put together the white light, the burning wounds, and the fact that, even though he could now hear automatic weapons firing all around him, they seemed distant, muffled.

Mortar. I've been mortared. By the freaking Taliban.

If it didn't hurt so much, it would almost be funny. The joke around Special Forces was that the safest place to be when a Taliban fired a mortar was wherever they happened to be aiming. This guy had put his first round right on target: What were the odds?

Blake worked his shoulders, his hips. Everything seemed connected. His M21 was lying at an awkward angle underneath him, and he fished it out, checked it over by feel. Reaching for the night goggles on his helmet, he touched gritty forehead and hair.

Helmet's gone. Blake rolled over onto his stomach and reached for the switch on the nightscope. But he didn't need it. Automatic weapons fire, the distinct metallic staccato of a Klashnikov, muffled by his now-ringing ears, echoed off the rocks around him; and the attacking force was near enough that he could make out the muzzle flashes less than a hundred yards away. Red tracer rounds flashed against a rock fifty feet to his right and ricocheted into the midnight sky. A steady rhythm of return fire drummed above him, the team's M249 Squad Automatic Weapon painting the landscape with rounds.

Blake gritted his teeth. The M249 SAW fired a 5.56-millimeter round, and a 5.56 round was the same size as a .223 Remington, the kind of ammunition he would have used for picking off hedgehogs back home. People were another story. When the team expected to fight, they brought the bigger M240G, chambered for the larger 7.62 millimeter. But this mission was clandestine.

At least it was.

Twin white flashes strobed far to his right and his left, and the ground shook again.

Somebody's been teaching these boys. The attacking force was lifting and shifting its mortar fire, moving it to either side of the team's position, creating an avenue through which to attack.

Time to move. Ignoring the searing barbs of pain in his leg, Blake scrambled to his feet and bolted up the hill.

"Blue! Blue! Blue!" Blake shouted, resorting to the running password. "Me! Blake! Don't shoot!"

Crossing the perimeter, he stumbled over something, fell, touched an arm in fatigues.

Body. He didn't know who. Sniper rifle at quarter-arms, Blake hurled himself into his hasty fighting position. He flipped on the rifle scope and took a look at the slope below, where all the shooting was coming from.

Men in pairs were running up the hill, crouched low: *two there . . . six . . . twelve.* He sighted on the left man in the lead pair, squeezed the trigger, and felt the butt of the stock shove back against his shoulder. Then he shifted to the man on the right and fired again.

Both went down, but nobody behind ducked for cover. The other ten were still charging uphill like the Light Brigade, so he fished the radio trigger out of its cleft in the rocks, turned it on, and set the selector dial to "1."

His first mine placement was far down the slope, aimed into a shallow ravine a running man would naturally see as partial cover. They did; all ten Taliban hustled into the kill zone. Blake lifted his eye from the nightscope and popped the first Claymore.

Red fire erupted into the night, shook the ground with a resonate *thump*. Over the ringing in his ears, Blake could hear the screams of the two or three people who did not die instantly in the wall of shrapnel. He swallowed and swiveled his head. All fire from directly in front of him abruptly stopped. But it picked up off to his left.

Flanking attack. Probe. Rifle in one hand, radio trigger in the other, Blake got halfway to his feet and limped toward that side.

In the center of their position, the senior SigInt man was sprawled on his back; in the sporadic light of the distant mortar rounds, Blake could just make out a dark, wet stain covering his entire chest. The younger SigInt soldier was crouched over his equipment, hunkered down.

Blake ignored him, crouched low, and dashed past, falling in next to the team engineer, who was sending three-round bursts downrange. The engineer glanced at Blake.

"Clacker?"

Blake held the radio trigger up.

"Two and four—now!"

Blake popped both Claymores, one right after the other. He raised his rifle scope: clouds of dirt and mine fragments were billowing downhill. But farther to his right there was movement—riflemen popping up from under cover, taking a snap-shot, and then dropping back down. One was a little too regular in his prairie-dogging; Blake sighted on his position and squeezed as the man's head was coming up. The rifleman dropped, and when one of the Taliban's comrades rushed to his aid, Blake led him with the reticle of the scope, squeezed off a round, and heard a scream.

Not clean. Up a click next time.

He barely heard the *tink* of a grenade bouncing off the rocks below him; both he and Tony ducked as it detonated harmlessly downslope.

They're close. Grabbing two hand grenades off his own web gear; Blake laid them on the ground next to his shoulder and checked through the riflescope. Sure enough, five people were threading uphill through boulders, not a hundred feet away.

Rising to his knees, Blake pulled the pin on both grenades and threw them, one in front of the running men, one behind.

The lead attacker jumped back as the grenade bounced before him. It slowed the runners, gathering them together just as both grenades went off.

More screams. The incoming fire died off.

"I'm checking the other side," Blake said. "You good?"

The engineer nodded and Blake fell back. An M16 was lying on the ground, and he slung his own rifle and picked it up. The younger SigInt man was still cowering over his gear. Blake shook his shoulder and handed him the rifle.

"Man down there needs supporting fire," Blake shouted, nodding in the direction of Tony.

The young soldier just looked at him.

"Now!" Blake shouted. "Move!"

The SigInt man got to his feet and ran toward the engineer. Crouched over, Blake sprinted the other way and dropped in next to his captain. But before he could say a word, the officer stiffened, his head popping back, as if punched.

Something warm, wet, and thick slashed across Blake's face. He put his hand there and found a thin splinter of bone lodged in his cheek.

He crabbed right to where the team sergeant was. The medic was there, bending over him.

Blake swallowed—had to work to do it.

This is going in the fan. We are running out of rounds, and we are running out of people and this is going in the fan.

He froze for a second. Took a breath.

Radio.

Harry, the communications man, was dug in on the side of the perimeter with the best shot at the communications satellite. It was right next to the ridgetop, just a few feet from the steep drop-off. So Blake scrambled back there. Got there. Stopped.

The radio was gone.

So was Harry.

CHAPTER THREE

❑ ❑ ❑

Harry's helmet was lying on the ground. Blake picked it up, felt blood, sticky but still warm on the side. He put it on—the odd feeling of wearing someone else's gear—and tried the night-vision goggles. They worked.

Blake looked around. The team had two men dead, the captain and the senior SigInt man; and the medic had stopped working on the master sergeant and was returning fire on his side. The SAW was still raking the slope in front. Tony and the younger signals man were side-by-side, holding off the disrupted force on their perimeter.

No Harry.

The only place he could possibly have gone was over the back. But that was one step short of a cliff. He thought about it just a moment and then ducked down next to the medic, handed him the Claymore trigger.

"Three, five, and six are still good to go," he told the medic. "Pop 'em if you need 'em."

The medic nodded, not questioning Blake: the intrinsic trust of men who'd trained together.

Blake put a fresh magazine into the M21 and went back to the edge of the ridge, peering down through the night-vision goggles.

It took ten seconds for him to pick out the movement, four men moving as a unit. It took even longer to realize they were on a barely visible goat-trail that snaked its way through a series of switchbacks down the extremely steep ground. And they were half-carrying, half-dragging something as they went.

Harry.

"Take one alive."

What would I do if I were them? Get Harry back behind my probes and then . . .

And then what?

And then shift my mortars back on center. Get heads down. Use the mortar fire to get close. And throw every grenade I had in there.

Kill everything. That was the only end-game to this. One side was going to annihilate the other.

Blake plunged down the slope, rock rolling ahead of him, slipping and sliding until his heels hit the level ground of a foot-wide path. He was being too noisy, and he knew it, but the Taliban had too much of a head start. He needed to make up ground, and all he could do was hope the weapons fire up on the ridge masked the sound of him moving.

He was halfway down the slope when he realized it hadn't. One Taliban, his hair and beard a mass of darkness even in the night-vision goggles, stepped out from behind a boulder and fired one shot. Blake fell.

Arm. Left. He tried moving his left hand: nothing.

A click. The Taliban was reloading.

Blake sat up, drawing his .45, right thumb snapping off the safety as he brought the pistol to bear, lined the softly glowing Tritium sights up, put them center-of-mass on his attacker, and fired two shots, one right after the other.

The Taliban collapsed without a sound.

Blake sat, the pistol in his lap.

Arm useless. Can't hold the rifle. Three of them left.

He thought of the team sergeant, unconscious last he'd seen him.

That means I'm in command. Team needs me.

But they have Harry.

More small-arms fire from up above on the far side of the ridge.

Lord, I need wisdom.

There was a pause in the fire on the other side of the ridge. Maybe three seconds, then it started up again.

Take one alive.

And then his strategy became clear. Once the enemy had Harry back and clear, there would be no reason to leave anyone alive on the ridgetop. To help his team, he had to get Harry back.

Blake pushed himself to his feet with his good hand.

He didn't follow the switchbacks this time. Half-scrambling, half-sliding, he stayed high on the slope and worked in the direction the Taliban was going. He came to a gap in the ridge, crossed it, and realized he was now coming out off to the side, but in front, of his team's position.

He checked through the goggles. The goat path was about forty feet below him. And nobody was on it.

I'm ahead of them.

Holding his left arm, he slid down to the path, raced ahead on it, and found a low boulder he could lie behind. He looked around its base, felt for a new magazine for the pistol, and then stopped.

People were coming. Coming down the trail toward him.

Three people. Six rounds left in the pistol. Double-tap each one?

He thought about it a second and rejected it.

One apiece. Three in reserve if I need it.

The Taliban were all wearing the long vests and soft pillbox hats men wore in this region. None spoke. They were grunting with the effort, two dragging Harry with a hand under each of his armpits, and one carrying the radio and all three men's rifles.

That made things simpler.

Blake waited until they were less then ten feet away. Then, without moving from his prone position, he put two rounds in the man carrying the weapons: head and chest.

The dead Taliban's friends moved faster than Blake would have imagined, dropping Harry and reaching for the rifles on the ground. But Blake was the one with a gun already in hand, and he shot each one once. The first dropped silently. The second screamed.

Blake shot the screamer in the head, the shriek stopping like someone hit the "Mute" button.

Pushing up off a rock, he scrambled to Harry and pinched his ear until the Navajo came around.

"Huh? What's . . ." He blinked, trying to focus. "Situation?"

"It's Kershaw, Harry. Stay down."

Harry blinked. "Where are we?"

"Around the ridge. Three hundred meters below our perimeter."

Harry sat up, tried to get to his feet, but collapsed on a broken leg.

"Harry, take it . . ."

The Navajo's eyes opened wide. "You need to be on the move. Now."

"What?"

"Go. Get back up the ridge."

"What . . ." Then Blake stopped, understanding. "Air strike?"

Harry nodded. "Team sergeant called it. 'Danger close.' Inbound now. Pilot said ordnance was cluster bombs."

Cluster bombs. Capable of punching a thousand thumb-size holes through armored personnel carriers. For people in the open . . .

Blake scrambled back to the radio. It was in pieces, struck by one of the rounds he'd fired in the ambush.

Time for Plan B. Whatever that is.

Blake thought for a moment. Then he began unclipping and unbuckling, shedding his web gear. He opened the first aid kit as he lightened his load, taking out something small and hiding it in the palm of his good hand. Stooping over Harry, he offered the Navajo his forearm.

"On your feet, Harry. Now."

Gripping Blake's arm, Harry got up with the resolve of a man accustomed to obeying orders, groaning as he did it. Then, once he saw Blake without his gear, he shook his head.

"No way, Kersh. Can't take us both. No time."

Blake popped the cap off the object in his hand.

Harry backed up, gritting his teeth involuntarily. "You stupid cracker. Get moving."

"Will do."

Neck's exposed. Just don't hit the artery; you'll stop his heart.

In one quick movement Blake jabbed the morphine syrette into the exposed skin at the base of Harry's neck and squeezed the plastic bulb, injecting the entire contents. He bent and put his good shoulder at the Navajo's waist, catching the 180-pound soldier as he sagged. Wounded leg and shoulder roaring, Blake straightened up and started back up the hill.

Running was out of the question. *Walking* was virtually out of the question. The only viable way back was the goat path, and it was uneven, covered with deep sand in some places and loose rock in others. The best Blake could manage was a staggering shuffle, and even then he dropped to his knee once. As he struggled back to his feet, his vision narrowed.

No, Lord. Please. I cannot black out right now.

Blake staggered up the goat path, aiming toward the gap. The scream of jet engines sounded in the valley behind him.

Go. Go. Go.

He staggered faster, slipping, almost falling again but using the inertia to pick up a little speed. The sound of the engines got louder.

The gap in the ridge loomed ahead, dark sky behind it. Blake lurched through, spilling Harry and himself into a depression, back of a boulder.

Behind them the sky lit up, orange and white, with a sound like a building falling, the sound of the world coming to an end.

CHAPTER FOUR

❑ ❑ ❑

Interstate 495, Virginia, 2006

Light rain streaked the windshield, and Grant Reinbolt toyed with the pickup's intermittent wiper settings, trying to find a speed that could keep things clear but wouldn't make the wipers squeak over dry glass. There didn't seem to be one.

He punched the knob on the stereo and hit "Find." The first station to come up was playing "Do I Make You Proud" by Taylor Hicks.

Grant scowled. If you asked him, Taylor Hicks had a squeaky, whiney voice. That and the gray hair made him look old. True, *American Idol* raised the age limit to twenty-eight, but Taylor Hicks did not look twenty-eight. The dude looked forty, easy.

Not everybody thought so. Grant's last girlfriend thought Hicks looked "sexy, like George Clooney." Which didn't help Grant's opinion of Taylor Hicks any.

Then again, she hadn't really been a girlfriend. They'd only gone out three times before she'd dropped him. With a text message, no less. Said that she was looking for someone with "more maturity."

Like Taylor Hicks, maybe, with his old-man gray hair.

Well, if that was what she was after, Grant was definitely the wrong one for her. His hair was sandy brown, not a strand of gray in it yet. He pushed his hand back through it, and his hand came away slightly damp.

And besides, who listened to that soul-pop stuff Taylor Hicks sang anyhow? Old black women, maybe. Grant hit "Find" again, and the radio went to the next station up: Brooks and Dunn singing "Neon Moon." He settled back in his seat. They were a little old-school for his tastes, but at least they were country.

He lifted the Mountain Dew bottle and shook it.

Empty.

That was the problem with doing meth. It gave you dry mouth. He knew he shouldn't be doing the stuff anyhow. He'd heard about a guy in Norfolk who snorted it so often the cartilage in his nose dissolved. So he didn't really have a nose anymore, just this flap of skin in the middle of his face. And depending on who was telling the story, it bled all the time. This pasty flap of skin hanging in the middle of his face, dripping watery blood.

Gross.

But he'd gotten the call right as he was getting off his shift at the Home Depot, and he'd been out partying the night before, and besides, he owed Diego—that was the dude's name. Grant owed Diego money from the five hundred he'd fronted him to get the CV joints fixed in Grant's girlfriend's Taurus.

The girlfriend who'd dropped him like a hot potato after the third date.

Which made him wonder if she had only gone out with him because the front end on her Taurus was thumping and bumping in the turns. But how would she have known he was going to do that? Then again, she was way hotter than any woman he'd ever asked out before, and hot women seemed to have a radar for suckers.

One thing was sure; he'd texted her back and said okay, that was cool, she could go look for somebody with more maturity, but in the meantime, when was she going to pay him the five hundred back? And when she hadn't replied, he called her, and some guy answered the phone.

Game over. The five hundred was gone, and this Diego didn't seem like the type who wanted to wait too long for his money, and you didn't necessarily have much cash laying around if you earned it an hour at a time, mixing paint down at the Home Depot.

So when Diego called and said, "Hey man, how'd you like to make that five bucks I floated you go away and get another ten on top of it?" . . . When Grant heard that, he was all for it, lack of sleep or not; and besides, he knew where his roommate kept his meth.

Fifteen hundred bucks to drive a pickup truck to Baltimore. And he was already almost to Silver Spring. Drive it up, leave it locked in a McDonald's with the keys in the ashtray, and catch a Greyhound back. Diego even gave him an extra hundred for the bus.

Sweet.

Of course it wasn't legal. No one in the whole world gave you fifteen hundred—sixteen hundred with the bus fare—to take a little drive if it wasn't illegal.

Drugs was Grant's first guess. After all, this Diego dude was Columbian, and it didn't take a lot of imagination to put "Columbian" and "illegal" together and come up with "cocaine." And it wasn't as if Grant was all that antidrug. He was doing the crank, wasn't he?

But when he'd asked Diego, straight out, if he was running drugs, the dude laughed and said, "Naw. Not this trip, bro."

So then Grant figured maybe the pickup was hot, but Diego showed him the lease papers, and they were in the name of a car wash Diego owned. So finally Grant just asked him what the deal was. Diego took a key out of his pocket, opened the hard tonneau on the pickup bed, and then he'd opened up a seabag lying in there; and it was packed tight, full of money—twenty-dollar bills in thousand-dollar wrappers, shrink-wrapped into bricks of fifty thousand. It was one of those take-your-breath-away moments.

"Counterfeit?" Grant asked when he could finally talk again. But then Diego gave him one of those pens like the chicks had at the 7-11, and he drew on one, and it marked it in yellow, rather than black, just like it was supposed to. And when Diego held one up to the light, Grant could see the little polyester strip running through it.

"It's just freakin' money, man," Diego told him. "And I got to get it up to Baltimore. And you won't have no key to the bed cover; and besides, it's all counted; and if there's even one bill missing, man, even one . . . Well, I mean I know where you live, you know? You're driving money to Baltimore, man. That's all. You're like, you know, one of those Brink's dudes. Nothing more. Except you don't ever want to tell no one about this. Not ever. Because if you do business with me, I expect you to keep it quiet; and besides, like I said, man: I know where you freakin' *live*."

Which rattled Grant a little. So he drove the truck back to his trailer first and—keeping the trailer door open so he could keep an eye on the truck—he went back into his roommate's dresser drawer and got out the nine-millimeter Ruger the dude kept there.

After all, that was one big seabag, and he wasn't sure about how many shrink-wrapped twenties it took to fill one, but he was thinking a couple million, easy, maybe more. Maybe a lot more. And Grant Reinbolt might have been just a dumb, down-home white boy from rural Virginia, but he sure wasn't no dumb white boy that was going to go driving around with two million dollars in a pickup truck and no way to protect himself. So he got the gun and stuck it in his waistband, under his shirt, and pointed the pickup north, toward Maryland.

Static began crowding in on the country station, and Grant pushed "scan" on the radio. A contemporary Christian station came up, and he cursed before pushing the button again. This time it came up vintage metal, which was not really Grant's style, but it fit him better than soul-pop and Taylor Hicks with his old-man hair, and it certainly fit him better than contemporary Christian.

"Hypocrites," Grant muttered under his breath. It was an unusual word for him, one he might have been challenged to define back when he was in school, but he was pretty sure it fit when it came to

Christianity—at least the brand of Christianity Grant Reinbolt grew up with.

He shook the Mountain Dew bottle again. Nope. It hadn't miraculously replenished itself. And now he was getting really dry-mouthed. An exit was coming up on the right. He took it.

Methedrine was supposed to be an appetite suppressant, and Grant Reinbolt wasn't the least bit hungry, but as long as he was in the 7-11, he picked up some pork rinds and a big bag of Reese's Pieces along with the Mountain Dew—a two-liter out of the cooler section. The meth wasn't going to last forever, and he figured he'd get the munchies eventually, and besides, he wasn't sure how often he'd be able to find pork rinds in Maryland. The fact he was headed for a McDonald's didn't enter into the equation at all because Grant didn't eat at McDonald's; he was a Burger King man.

At the counter in the 7-11, Grant wound up going through all of his pockets, looking for change, which struck him as semi-hilarious because Diego gave him the hundred for the Greyhound up-front, and it was sitting in the console of the pickup, and besides, there was enough cash to stock a hundred ATMs under the tonneau, in the bed of the pickup. That got him snickering. The gun almost fell out of his waistband while he was digging for the last quarter, which stopped his snickering because showing a gun in a 7-11 would have brought everyone there to the wrong conclusion.

Still, he was chuckling a little as he left the carry-out, and that was when he saw the Maryland state trooper in the parking lot, looking over the pickup.

Grant's chuckle evaporated.

"This your truck?"

Just like that, Grant was sweaty under his arms. "Uh, I'm driving it, sir. It belongs to my . . . boss."

The trooper nodded, squinting at the back plate. "Southern Virginia, huh? What brings you to Maryland?"

"Uh, my boss. The dude runs like, a car wash, you know? Needs parts for it. Gotta go to Baltimore to pick 'em up."

The trooper lifted his head, the brim of his Smokey-bear hat coming level as he did it. "Running for parts? At eleven o'clock on a Saturday night?"

Grant felt hotter. "Car wash can't run without 'em, officer. Dude's losing money. People like to wash their cars on the weekend, you know?"

The trooper nodded. "Got your license on you, sir?"

Grant nodded and dug the wallet out of his hip pocket, conscious of the gun sagging under his waistband in front. He fished out his license and handed it to the cop.

"Well, Mr. Reinbolt, I was keeping pace with you for about a quarter mile there, just before you got off at the exit, and I was showing you running eighty-one, eighty-two miles an hour there."

"Was I?" Grant's mind raced. "Sorry, sir. I was needing to get to a restroom."

"Understood," the trooper told him. "But just bear in mind that, while most law enforcement will give you five, ten miles an hour over the limit, nobody *has* to do that. And I'm pretty sure the fine would wipe out anything you're making doing this parts run tonight, even if you're on overtime."

Bet not, Grant thought. But what he said was, "I'm sorry, sir. I really should have stopped a couple exits back."

"Keep 'er down to the limit." The cop handed him his license. "Roads are wet from these rains that've been passing through. Real easy to lose it if you're runnin' even a little too fast."

"Yes, sir." Grant slipped his license into his shirt pocket and buttoned the flannel flap.

By the time Grant got back into the truck, set the Mountain Dew and the pork rinds and the Reese's Pieces on the passenger seat, and buckled his seat belt, he was feeling half-ready to hurl.

Man! A couple million bucks he couldn't account for in the pickup bed, a gun that wasn't his in his waistband, and he'd almost blown it by getting stopped for speeding.

Not cool, man. Not freaking cool at all.

Grant wiped his hands on his shirt, opened the Dew and took a swig of it, and then put the top back on the bottle and started the pickup. He backed out of the spot in front of the 7-11, crept to the entrance, put his signal on, and turned onto the road.

He looked at the mirror. Sure enough, the trooper was leaving the carry-out as well. Then again, he said he had followed Grant off the interstate. Maybe he was just going back to work.

Maybe.

The gun was the real problem. If he got stopped again and the police searched the truck, he could just tell the truth. Sort of. Say that he had been hired to drive the truck up to Baltimore for a friend. Fudge on the amount he'd been promised to do it. Say he didn't know anything about no seabag in the pickup bed. Say he didn't even have the key to the tonneau. Which he didn't.

But there was nothing he could say that would explain the gun in his waistband. And he'd already carried the piece across a state line, which he was pretty sure made it worse. A lot worse.

So he needed to get rid of the Ruger. Sure, his roommate would get torqued, but he could pay him for it. Or maybe even not pay him for it because as far as he could remember, the dude won it in a poker game. If things worked out right, he might not notice it was missing for a while, and Grant could just replace it with another one just like it. Or not replace it and just play dumb when the dude mentioned it.

But right now he had to get rid of the stinking gun, and it wasn't as if he could just toss it out the window because the Maryland trooper was rolling about a 150 yards behind him, and if he saw a pistol come out the window, he'd arrest Grant for illegal transportation, illegal possession, carrying without a license, and littering to boot.

So the next exit he had to pull off and toss the gun.

No. Not the next exit. The trooper had just seen him pull off at the last exit. If he got right off at the next, what would be his excuse? It wasn't as if he'd have to stop to pee twice in eight miles.

Stay on for an exit or two. That would be the ticket. State troopers didn't usually patrol that many miles of roadway; maybe in a mile or two, the dude would drop down into the median and turn back or something.

But he absolutely had to get rid of the stinkin' gun.

A dumpster, a trash can outside a Mickey D's, a Goodwill collection bin, a mailbox that wouldn't be collected from for a while, a bridge over some country creek, undergrowth, weeds, a sewer grate with wide enough openings . . . any of that stuff would work. It didn't have to stay gone forever, and he didn't care if it got found tomorrow, as long as it couldn't be tied to him.

Man. Why did he bring the stinkin' gun?

He glanced at the rearview mirror.

It looked as if he was catching a break; the state trooper's headlights were receding in his mirror, like maybe the dude was slowing down to do a turn-around in the median.

Yeah, man. Do it. Turn around. Go back. Go write somebody a ticket.

If the cop turned around, all Grant had to do was wait for a gap in traffic and toss the pistol into the wet grass in the median. He wondered what the chances were that the gun would go off when it landed, because that would not be cool.

Grant pulled the pistol out from under his shirt. He'd never shot it; his roommate told him not to touch it. The dude could be a jerk like that. Which was a load because Grant's roommate never even had weapons training, was never in the military.

Grant, on the other hand, was a Marine. At least, for a few months he was. Long enough to get some sidearms training.

In the darkness of the pickup cab, he felt around for the magazine release on the pistol. But the Ruger was different from the Beretta he'd been trained on, and he couldn't find a way to drop the mag.

Not a prob. He could just cycle the slide, eject the rounds one at a time until the mag was empty. Keeping his finger well clear of the trigger, Grant pulled the slide back and then released it.

Nothing happened. Either the gun was already unloaded, or he had just loaded it.

Grant worked the slide again, and this time a bullet flew out and hit the passenger's-side window with a loud *click*.

Oh, man. The ejector in this thing was like a catapult.

Grant wasn't sure if being found with bullets in the car was as bad as being found with the gun, but he didn't want to take a chance. He fished around and found the bullet on the passenger's seat under the pork rinds.

Tilting the gun so the next bullet would land in his lap, Grant cycled the slide again. Another bullet.

He worked the slide five more times, and each time a bullet, small and heavy, fell into his lap.

Man! How many rounds are in this sucker, anyhow?

Forget it. He was just going to toss the gun and the bullets. If they landed in the grass, it'd be soft. Sort of. He didn't think there was much chance anything would go off.

The cop was way back now. Two sets of headlights were coming up behind Grant in the passing lane.

Let them pass. Then toss the piece.

The vehicles went by: a gray Ford Fusion and a black GMC Suburban. Grant hit the button and lowered the window; a cold, fine spray of rain blew in. How hard would he have to toss the pistol to be sure it landed in the median? He hefted it in his hand.

He paused. That Suburban that passed: there was something hinky about the wheels, the tires.

Ahead of him, taillights flared as both vehicles hit their brakes and began sliding on the wet pavement. Grant hit his brakes as well, nine-millimeter ammunition spilling out of his lap and onto the floor mat.

Lights! Lots of flashing lights. Blue. Red. In the rear windows of the two sliding wheels ahead of him. In the taillights. Atop the trooper behind him, who was coming up fast, his spotlight playing bright, blue-white all over the interior of the pickup.

Oh.

Man.

The two vehicles ahead were sliding to a halt, cocked toward the centerline, forming a "V" in the road. Grant slid to a stop twenty feet behind them, the gun still in his right hand.

Behind him a loudspeaker blared: "STAY IN YOUR VEHICLE. PUT BOTH HANDS OUT THE WINDOW."

Trees crowded the roadside. Grant would only have to cross fifty feet of shallow ditch to reach them. He released the seat belt.

Run.

Grant threw the door open and hit the pavement in a sprint, feet scrambling in the wet. Men in ballistics vests were pouring out of the two unmarked vehicles. The trooper was outside his patrol car as well, gun trained on Grant.

Everyone was shouting at once, terse commands: "HALT! DROP THE WEAPON! ON THE GROUND!"

Grant ran.

Feet pounded the pavement behind him.

The surface turned from asphalt to gravel. Then grass. Headed downhill. Grant ran, gun still in his hand.

He tripped over a clod of earth, came up running again, looked back at the jumpsuited man closing in on him. Grant extended his hand, aiming the gun.

From somewhere behind Grant's pursuer, a pair of white-orange flashes lit up the night. His left arm felt as if he had been struck with a crowbar. Grant spun, and the nearest of the two agents hit him with the kind of flying tackle that reminded Grant why he'd never gone out for the football team back in high school.

He had the briefest glimpse of a gloved fist flying into his face.

Blackness dropped in like a heavy blanket.

CHAPTER FIVE

❑ ❑ ❑

Hampden-Sydney, Virginia, Present Day

Both hands on the pistol, Blake focused on his front sight and squeezed off a double tap—two shots in rapid succession. The report of the .45 sounded hollow through the foam and plastic of his hearing protection—more like a nail gun than a handgun.

He dropped his left hand to his belt and did the next two shots one-handed. Then he switched the pistol to his left hand, fired until the slide locked back on the pistol, removed the empty magazine, set the .45 on the shelf before him, and flipped the little silver switch on the wall of the shooting station. The paper target bowed, like a sail, as it rode the wire trolley back to him. In its center ring, only slightly low and left, the seven shots formed one ragged, oblong hole.

"That's good shooting."

Blake turned. Behind him, carrying a handgun case, and wearing a set of plastic earmuffs nearly identical to those on Blake's head, was a broad-shouldered, square-jawed man well over six feet tall. He was dressed in khaki slacks and a polo shirt, but he had the bearing and posture of someone who'd spent a lifetime in uniform, his white hair the only clue he was well into his eighties.

His was a familiar face. General Sam Wilson was more than the head of the leadership program at Hampden-Sydney College. He was unofficial mentor to most of the men at the school.

"General! Good morning, sir," Blake wiped his hand on his jeans to get the gun oil off, and then the two men shook. "Didn't know you shot here."

The older man hefted his gun case. "Perishable skills, son. Have to keep 'em up."

"Exactly."

General Sam tapped his earmuffs. "I'm headed out. You about finished?"

"Yes, sir." Blake held up an empty cartridge box before dropping it in the trash. "Only shoot a hundred rounds a week—student budget."

He dropped the paper target into a trash bin at the shooting station and cased up his pistol. The two men stepped out into the prep area and took off their headsets. The general nodded at Blake's pistol case.

"Don't see many of the younger fellas shooting one-handed. Then again, I suppose you've learned the merits of practicing that way."

"Sir?"

"I read your commendation. Two years back when you applied for admission. How's that shoulder doing?"

Blake moved it without thinking about it.

"The bone's grown back pretty close to 100 percent, sir. I'm using it, and I've got close to the full range of motion. Took a while, though—just glad it was my left."

Muffled gunshots tapped hollowly on the range they'd just left.

"You're a brave man, Blake."

"Sir, I was just scared—scared and trying to save my . . . my skin. You ask me, our master sergeant deserved the Distinguished Service Cross more than I did."

The general raised a single eyebrow. "You ask me, you deserved the Medal of Honor. But Congress doesn't give them out to young men who live through their actions these days. The people on the Hill vote pork until they're blue in the face, but when it comes to giving a hero a special pension and taking the chance they'll have to send his kids through one of the academies, it seems to scare them silly."

Blake laughed. Then he shook his head. "I'm no hero, sir."

"The real ones always say that." The general smiled. "Had lunch yet?"

"No, sir."

"Me either. How about keeping an old man company?"

The River Hunt Inn was on the Appomattox River, the border between Prince Edward County and Appomattox County—site of the famous battlefield. The Inn looked old enough to have followed that battle by less than half a century, and both it and the surrounding woods and hills looked as if they were meant to go together; the place at once both gentile and rustic.

As he swiveled the kickstand down on his Harley and set his helmet on one of its rearview mirrors, Blake took in the antique, multipaned windows, weathered shingles, and slate roof of the building. A bronze fountain, its metal faded green with age, burbled in the forecourt; and more than a few Jaguars and Range Rovers were resting in the parking spaces. He took the card case out of his left front pocket, checked to make sure his debit card was there, and then locked the fork on the bike.

The inside of the restaurant looked every bit as upscale as the exterior: lots of dark wood paneling and a décor that leaned toward paintings of Irish setters, Labrador retrievers and Springer spaniels, and fine old shotguns displayed in gilded shadow boxes. Blake took off his sunglasses and stood in the lobby for a moment, letting his eyes adjust to the darkness. A squeeze on his shoulder brought his head up.

"Booth all right with you? I have one in the back: better view of the river there."

Blake turned and smiled. "A booth is fine, sir."

General Sam nodded and the two men walked, the general leaving his hand where it was, steering the younger man gently.

"First time here?"

"Yes, sir."

"Most of the college men save this place for when they're trying to impress a girl. As for me, I just come because I like the quiet."

The general stopped them at a booth in a niche on a slightly raised platform. It looked out over one end of the dining room, and the north-facing windows lining the far end offered just a hint of a river view worthy of a nineteenth-century landscape artist. The two men sat.

"How about you?" The general took a napkin from its ring as he spoke and smoothed it on his lap. "No girl serious enough for the River Hunt?"

Blake grinned. "No girl at all, sir. Not at the moment."

"Strapping young fellow like yourself? What's the story on that?"

Blake opened his hands, clasped them. "There used to be a girl, sir. Lasted through my first deployment but not my second. I think she loved the idea of a man in uniform but not where the uniform took him."

The general nodded, keeping his eyes on Blake. "That's too bad. Better to find that out when you did, though. I've seen too many men get married and watch it all go into the fan later on."

"Way I looked at it, sir. I figure the best thing for me to do right now is concentrate on my studies, get my degree."

The general nodded again, two quick nods. "I remember reading your application. You're going back into Special Forces, becoming an officer. That your plan?"

"Yes, sir. If they'll have me."

"They will. I watched you last semester in the leadership class. Men who've seen combat usually do better there, but you're beyond that. You've got a good head on those shoulders."

Blake glanced down for a moment. When he looked up, the general was smiling at a middle-aged woman. Like all of the River Hunt staff, she was dressed in a white shirt with a dark vest and bow tie.

"You a beef eater, Blake?" When Blake nodded, the general turned to the waitress. "Two prime ribs on the rare side of medium, Minnie. Loaded baked potatoes and the asparagus. Leave the sauce off, please. Sweet tea. Oh, and two cups of French onion soup."

He turned to Blake. "Sound good to you?"

"Lot more than I'm used to for lunch, sir."

"What'd you have for dinner last night?"

"Leftover pizza."

"I rest my case. Two prime ribs, please, Minnie." The general smiled as the waitress left. Then he turned back to Blake. "Tell me something. . . . Been wondering about this ever since we admitted you. Man with your goals, seems as if West Point would have been a natural first choice. Your aptitude, not to mention your decorations, I'm sure they would've put down the red carpet. Why Hampden-Sydney?"

"West Point was my first choice, sir. But my injury kept me from passing the physical." He touched his shoulder for a moment as he said it, then realized he was doing it and stopped. "They said they could start me when I'd recovered, but that would have been two, maybe three years. I didn't want to wait."

"Sounds familiar." The general crossed his arms and nodded. "I was in the 5307th Composite Unit in Burma during the war . . ."

"Sure—Merrill's Marauders." Blake fell silent for a second, realizing he interrupted a general officer. He covered up by continuing. "You got the DSC there as well, didn't you, sir?"

General Sam laughed. "Sure did. Got malaria, too. And that's why I couldn't enroll in the Academy. Wound up going to Colombia instead, majoring in Russian language and culture. It all worked out."

He tapped on the table. "That still doesn't answer the question of why here, though."

Blake lifted his hands, dropped them. "Three reasons, really, sir. One, it's an all-male school and after Carla—that was the girl—I figured there'd be fewer distractions. Second, I'd heard about the Hampden-Sydney code of honor."

General Sam rubbed his chin. "Other schools have student courts, student justice systems."

"Yes, sir. But at other schools, it's based on a rule book. Here, it's based on integrity: 'I will not lie, I will not steal, and I will not tolerate anyone who does.' That tells me any degree a man gets here is more than just a line on a résumé; it's a symbol of something greater. It means you have not only been educated; you have been judged by other men of character to be a man of character yourself. And that means something."

"Indeed it does." General Sam cocked his head just a bit. "That's two things, Blake. What's the third?"

Blake looked down for a moment. Looked up. "It's you, sir. I'd heard about your leadership class. Many of the officers I've known have spoken highly of it."

An uncomfortable two seconds passed before Blake added, "And they were right. Best time I've ever passed in a classroom."

"I'm flattered." The general leaned forward, hands clasped, on the table. "But if that's the case, why haven't I ever seen you on the applicant list for Introduction to National Intelligence?"

"Tough class to get into, sir."

"True." The general tapped the table again. Lightly. "But you wouldn't have a problem. I've got to think you know that."

Blake glanced at the windows as if looking for something outside, on the river. He turned back to the general.

"Sir, you probably know that course has a nickname among the students."

"'Spying 101.'" The general chuckled. "Yes, I've heard that."

"And the guys here see it as a fast track to a job at Langley. There or Bolling. I mean, you were high up in both agencies—director of the DIA, deputy director for military affairs when the president was heading up the CIA . . ."

The general nodded, saying nothing.

"And the work those folks do there is important, sir, but I don't see myself at a desk. Not for quite a while. It's just not . . . I don't know; it's not on-mission for me. I see myself back in the field, leading people I can trust, folks I know really understand their jobs, not that the people at Langley don't . . ."

Blake looked up, wondering what he'd just stepped in. The general lifted a hand.

"It's okay. I get you."

"I'm just trying to get back to the teams, sir. And I want to take the fastest route."

The iced tea came and the general sipped his.

"Being a team player is good, Blake. Never met a Special Forces man who wasn't. That doesn't mean you're not competent on your own, though."

"Sure, sir. I went through several levels at Camp Mackall . . . that's where they teach Survival, Evasion, Resistance, and Escape . . ."

"SERE," the general said.

"Yes, sir. Yes. SERE: that was probably the toughest course I went through—but also the most valuable. But SERE's a bridge. It's doing what you have to do until you can get back with your team, be effective."

The general showed the beginnings of a smile. "An effective team is just effective individuals multiplying their effect, Blake. Ah—here's Minnie with the soup."

The soup came and went, followed by the prime rib, which Blake finished, asparagus and all. Then they ordered coffee—regular for Blake and decaf for the general. General Sam waited until Minnie cleared the dishes away. He turned the cup on his saucer before him and settled back in his seat.

"How's your mother doing, Blake?"

"She's well, sir." Blake tried to think of when he had ever mentioned his mother to the general; he came up blank. "I was just home last weekend. I'm hoping she'll come up for Parent's Day. I'd like you to meet her."

"Already have."

Blake straightened. "Sir?"

The general smiled. "It was a long time ago. I came to your folk's wedding. Your grandpa, Ted, invited me."

"Grandpa Ted died before I was . . ." Blake looked up. "How did you know him?"

"Knew him when I was young. Not kids, but young. He was a Pittsylvania County boy and I was Prince Edward, but we knew each other. Both enlisted in the Guard at the same time." He looked up. "Both lied about our age to do it, in fact. We did basic together. He went to Europe when I was in the Pacific, but we stayed in touch. And after, we'd get together for a bottle of stumphole whiskey from time to time, talk about the war."

The general pursed his lips. "Sure missed him when he left. Farming accident, wasn't it?"

"Yes, sir. I think a tractor rolled while he was mowing ditches."

"Same farm your mom has now?"

"Yes, sir. We don't farm it. She rents the acres out." Blake looked up. "Wow. It's just . . . nobody ever said you knew our family."

"On your dad's side. Your mother probably barely remembers me. And your father . . . he died when you were small, didn't he?"

"Yes, sir. He was in the Guard, too. Got killed in a SCUD attack in Kuwait during the first Gulf War."

"That's rough. It's what a man always worries about when he's deployed and he has small children at home."

The two men fell silent for a moment. Then Blake said, "He wasn't really deployed sir. He volunteered. We . . ."

Blake took a breath. Swallowed. "We had a fire, sir. Tobacco barn. Lost it, the crop. Insurance didn't pay for everything. So Dad figured he'd volunteer. He was a motor pool mechanic; we thought he'd be safe. And he didn't figure the war would last long. Just enough to get us some overseas pay."

Blake found his gaze attracted to the river outside. He had to concentrate to look the general in the eyes. "But that's not . . ." His voice trailed off.

The general lifted his cup to the waitress across the room. She smiled and brought over two carafes and left them. He refilled both cups.

Blake looked out the windows at the river again. It looked timeless: the same river that had been there in 1865 when Lee surrendered to Grant near the courthouse named after the river. The same river had been there when only the Powhatan and the Shawnee roamed these valleys.

"That must have been tough on your mother, Blake."

"It was, sir." Blake nodded.

"She doing okay now?"

Blake sat. Tried to brighten. "Yes, sir. In fact, she's seeing someone, finally. One of the trauma surgeons who worked on my shoulder."

"You okay with that?"

Blake nodded. "It's about time. Dad passed a long time ago."

He looked down, then up again.

"Good. Good." The general handed a credit card to Minnie and smiled as she walked off. He rearranged the cards in his wallet for a moment, then put it in his pocket. "Listen, my missus has some ladies' deal in Alexandria this weekend, and I've got a little fishing cabin on the Roanoke River, down by Brookneal. How would you feel about getting on that motorcycle of yours and coming down for an early dinner on Saturday night?"

Blake looked at the table and opened his hands. "Two dinners in one week?"

"This was just lunch." The general grinned. Then his smile lessened a bit. "And besides, I've got somebody you need to meet."

CHAPTER SIX

❑ ❑ ❑

Blake's Harley was not the biggest one the Motor Company made—just a Sportster 1200 Custom, a lighter motorcycle that combined pleasant travel with good mileage. He'd bought it used in the economy intrinsic to traveling soldiers, a Green Beret, coming home from Afghanistan, buying surplus transportation from an MP about to be deployed to Iraq.

He hadn't been able to ride it at first—not with the damage from a 7.62mm round in his upper left arm and shoulder. But that was part of the reason for the purchase. He'd had a friend park the bike in the carport of the apartment he rented near the college. He went out and polished it a little every morning before going to the guest room, which he'd converted into a rudimentary gym with a used Bow-Flex machine (also picked up from a recently deployed infantryman) and an assortment of free weights. After the surgeries and the initial therapy at Walter Reed, it took two months working out on his own just to regain enough strength to hold in the clutch lever reliably on the spotlessly clean Harley-Davidson. Now, after more than two years of working out six days a week, he could use his left arm alone to lift the entire motorcycle up and set it back on its kickstand, if he needed to.

The bike came tricked out with saddlebags, a windshield, and passing lamps: all things he'd originally planned to take off. Then a weekend trip to Virginia Beach convinced him those miscellaneous extras were actually useful, so he left them on; they made the motorcycle comfortable for travel.

It was forty-eight miles from the apartment to the general's cabin: an easy one-hour ride on the Harley. Blake passed through Brookneal and went several miles further before slowing, looking at numbers on the infrequent mailboxes. Within a tenth of a mile of where his odometer said it should be, he got to one with "S. V. Wilson" on its ridge in simple, metal-cutout letters.

The drive from the main road to the cabin was nearly a quarter-mile long and downhill the whole way, but it was also paved—professionally crowned and smooth asphalt. And when the trees gave way so he could see it, the "cabin" turned out to be a two-story log home with an attached guesthouse.

Conscious of the deep *potato-potato-potato* rumbling from the Harley's chrome pipes, Blake shifted into neutral and killed the engine, silently coasting the last two hundred yards. He parked next to the general's old Jeep Cherokee and a late-model Lincoln Town Car with Maryland plates, left his helmet on his seat, and walked up onto the porch. There was a yellow Post-it note on the glass of the front door.

"We're in back, on the river," it read. "Go around to the deck—follow the path down." And it was signed with initials: "SVW."

Blake walked around the log home. In the side yard he came upon a swing set—the kind with wooden supports and crossbeams. It was not out of place with the surroundings, but seemed odd in the yard of an octogenarian.

The deck behind the house looked out on a small and simply landscaped yard, separated from a meadow by a split-rail fence. But there was a gap in the fence and a curving path mowed though the waist-high meadow grass—not just brush-hogged but finish-cut down to the same height as the grass in the yard.

Blake followed this and after a minute of walking, glimpsed a wisp of yellow, like a strand of spider's web tracing a momentary, greatly elongated "C" against the green of distant trees. Moments later he rounded a turn and saw the general standing on a spit of exposed gravel bar at the edge of the river, expertly laying the line on the surface of the water while a middle-age man in a tweed sport coat watched from the shore.

The sport-coated man said something, and General Sam turned, a smile on his face.

"Blake! Right on time. Have any trouble finding the place?"

"No, sir. Right where it was supposed to be."

The general stripped in his line, reeled it up, and walked back to the riverbank.

"Colsun, this is Blake Kershaw, the young man I've been telling you about. Blake, meet Colsun Atwater."

Blake shook the man's hand. With steel-rimmed glasses and graying black hair parted bookishly close to the center, Atwater didn't look like a man with much of a handshake, but his grip proved surprisingly substantial. His eyes, pale blue behind his glasses, twinkled as if at some shared joke, and he smiled, showing teeth so white and straight Blake wondered if they were real.

"It's good to finally meet you, Blake," Atwater said. "I've heard a lot about you."

He didn't say in what context. Blake didn't ask.

"Colsun's been kind enough to watch me cast," General Sam said, "although I think he secretly believes that angling is semi-barbaric."

"Never said such a thing, Sam."

The general grinned. "Sometimes you don't have to."

Blake found himself smiling as well. The two men were obviously old friends.

"What about you, Blake?" The general held out the rod. "Ever wet a line?"

"Mostly spin-casting," Blake said, accepting it. "Wouldn't know what to do with one of these."

"Oh, it's the simplest thing in the world. Get out on that bar, there, where you're closer to the water."

Blake did as he was told.

"Go ahead and strip out about twenty feet of line," the general told him. "Just let it float on the water there, next to you. Now raise the rod up, and then bring it down smartly in front of you."

Blake did that, and a hoop of line rolled across the water. He remembered doing a similar trick with a garden hose when he was a kid. A bit of the line didn't pay out, and he held it loosely in his left hand, the way he saw the general do it.

"Big difference between this and a spin-casting reel is that with spin-casting it's the lure that has the weight, and with fly-fishing it's the line," said the general. "Now just lift that line back up off the water with the rod tip, bring it back over your right shoulder, hold it there until it's pretty much behind you, and then smoothly bring it back forward, and let loose of that coil in your left hand."

Blake did it, and the line paid forward and then settled gently on the moving river. For the briefest of moments, he remembered an afternoon in a rowboat when he was five, casting a bass plug with his father. Then he blinked and began to mend line.

"Fine cast," said General Sam. "You're a natural. Maybe the two of us can convince Colson to take this up."

The general looked at his wristwatch. "But right now we'd best get back to the house. Dinner's in five minutes."

Dinner was served by a gray-haired housekeeper the general addressed as "Mrs. Murphy," and it made the previous week's lunch at River Hunt Inn look like fast food; there were game hens in a leek-and-mushroom sauce, potatoes au gratin in puff pastry, and something green, buttery, and wonderful that Blake was surprised to learn was spinach. The dessert, by contrast, was so simple it could have come from his mother's kitchen back on the farm—cinnamon-sprinkled apple pie with ice cream on the side.

Throughout the dinner the conversation remained casual. Blake complimented the general on the property, and General Sam explained that it had been in his family since the second Adams administration, adding, "We had family on both sides in the Civil War."

Atwater mentioned he first met the general in Vietnam, ". . . when I was with the Agency. Sam was seconded to State with the rank of minister."

The word *agency* caught Blake's attention. But before he could ask about it, Mrs. Murphy came in and started clearing away some dishes.

Atwater launched into a rambling discussion about another State Department representative he worked with in Saigon.

Finally, the three men retired to the library where the elderly housekeeper had cups and a tall carafe of coffee waiting.

"That was wonderful, Mrs. Murphy," the general told her. Blake and Atwater echoed his compliment.

"Oh, 'tweren't a thing," the woman said, setting out cream and sugar. It turned out there was a hint of an Irish accent in her voice. She looked up and added, "I've got the kitchen ready for morning and set the timer on the dishwasher, general. Will there be anything else?"

"Thank you, Mrs. Murphy. We're all set. You get on home to Andy."

The woman smiled and left.

"'Andy,'" Blake said. "Is that Mr. Murphy?"

"Oh, no," the general shook his head and laughed. "Clara's a widow. Andy's her great-grandson. Five years old. Her granddaughter is deployed with the Air Force in Iraq. Clara usually brings him with her, but she gets a sitter when I have guests for dinner."

"Ah . . . so that's who the swing set's for."

Atwater chuckled. "Sam's probably got a college fund set up for the little guy."

The general said nothing, and the room fell silent for several seconds.

Finally General Sam cleared his throat. "Well, Blake, I guess you're wondering what this is all about."

"I am, sir. That was a pretty thorough background check you gave me this week."

The old officer tilted his head. "Background check?"

Blake nodded. "Yes, sir. You seemed to be making sure I wasn't involved with anyone at the moment. You . . ." He shrugged. "I mean, I know you used to know my mom and all, but the conversation. . . . It's the kind of talk you have to figure out if a guy has anything tying him down. I'm just trying to figure out why."

The general raised an eyebrow and looked at Atwater. "Didn't I tell you he was sharp?"

"That," Atwater said, tamping his pipe, "or your technique's gone to pot."

The general turned to Blake. "See what a caustic old grouch I'm getting you involved with here?"

Blake looked from one man to the other. "Sir, what exactly *am* I getting involved with here?"

General Sam looked at Atwater, who nodded.

"You're right, Blake," the general said. "I was feeling you out along those lines. And maybe I should just ask you directly: how would it be if you were put in a position where you wouldn't see your mother for a while?"

Blake sat up a little straighter.

"How long, sir?"

He looked at the general, who looked at Atwater.

The other man lit his pipe, three puffs of flame rising up to engulf the match before he finally exhaled a small, blue cloud of smoke. When he looked at Blake, his eyes were kind yet discerning, like the eyes of a hunting animal looking at one of its pack.

"I'm not going to lie to you, son," he said. "Possibly forever."

CHAPTER SEVEN

United States Penitentiary, Marion, Illinois, Present Day

"Subhaana rabbiyal 'Alaa."

Kneeling on his prayer rug in the large, open space at the back of the stark prison chapel, toes bent and facing toward the Qibla, bent prostrate so his palms, forehead, and nose touched the ground, Grant Reinbolt paused.

"Allahu Akbar," he half-spoke, half-sang into the short-clipped fibers of the rug. When he breathed, he could smell the wool of it. Around him, other men, most of them Middle Eastern, were bent prostrate as well, reciting the Arabic prayer along with him.

"Allahu Akbar," they all repeated as they rose to a seated kneeling position, left feet sole up, the heels of their right feet raised. Together they chanted the *Fatiha*, the first surah of the Qur'an:

"Bismillaah ar-Rahman ar-Raheem
Al hamdu lillaahi rabbil 'alameen
Ar-Rahman ar-Raheem
Maaliki yaumid Deen
Iyyaaka na'abudu wa iy yaaka nasta'een

Ihdinas siraatal mustaqeem
Siraatal ladheena an 'amta' alaihim
Ghairil maghduubi' alaihim waladaaleen
Aameen"

Remaining on their knees, the men around Grant began to recite *At-Tashahhud*, a prayer based on the conversation between Muhammad and Allah on the Night of Ascent. Grant had not yet memorized *At-Tashahhud* all the way through, so he recited just the first few words and then fell silent while the sounds of Arabic filled the chapel around him. As often happened at this time during prayer, tears welled in his eyes and he blinked them back, not wishing to touch his face during this holy moment.

Looking over his right shoulder at the angel recording his good deeds, Grant said, *"As Salaamu 'alaikum wa rahmatulaah"—may the peace and blessings of Allah be upon you.* Then he looked over his left shoulder and pronounced the same blessing on the angel recording his sins.

Hands cupped at chest level, he said his personal prayers; and then, finally, he could wipe his face with his palms. He stood and turned to the men on either side of him saying, in English, "May God receive our prayers."

They each returned the salutation.

Grant stooped and rolled up his prayer rug.

"You got farther into At-Tashahhud than you did last night at evening prayers," said a voice behind him.

Grant turned, grinning sheepishly. "Thank you, Ibrahim, but my Arabic su- . . . uhm, stinks. I hear you and the others praying and, man . . . I almost want to give up."

Tall, slender, just a hint of gray in his black beard, a plain cloth cap sitting squarely on his head, Ibrahim smiled and put his right hand on Grant's shoulder. "Your Arabic is poorer today than it will be tomorrow, yet better by far than it was yesterday. Come sit with me at the midday meal, and we shall practice."

Grant smiled. "I'd like that. When I say my own prayers, I say them in English, and like . . . I wonder sometimes if God can even understand them."

Ibrahim laughed. "God understands all the tongues of men and angels, my son. We pray in Arabic because it was the language of the prophet. But rest assured that God hears your every prayer . . . even as he hears your every thought."

The two men picked up their prayer rugs and walked out the main door of the chapel. A hundred yards away a guard tower cast its shadow toward them. When Marion was a supermax facility, it would have held a trained sniper. Today USP Marion was medium security, and the tower was closed and empty.

"Your probation hearing on Wednesday . . ." Ibrahim looked straight forward as they followed the sidewalk. "Did you pray about that today?"

"Yes. I sure did."

"The letters I told you about . . . I have received confirmation that they have been sent. There is one from a man named McNamara, whom no one will suspect is Muslim. He will tell the board you have a job waiting for you as a taxi driver, which is true. Another is from the head of a nondenominational charity, which we support. That letter will assure the board an apartment has been secured for you and that the first month's rent has been paid in advance. This, also, is true. So be confident; you have people from outside this place speaking on your behalf."

Three men with the powerful arms and broad chests of bodybuilders were standing on the sidewalk ahead, talking. When the largest one looked up and saw that it was Ibrahim coming, he said something to his companions, and all three stepped aside, eyes averted, letting the mullah and his companion pass.

"After you are released, joining our . . . our community in Washington—you are still comfortable with that idea?"

Grant nodded.

"And our cause? You still wish to make it your cause?"

Grant swallowed. "Ibrahim, you saved my life."

The older man laughed. "From those ruffians? Those infidels? They are nothing. Greedy men who sell poison to children and use their gains to defraud others. The man who put you here—this Diego—he gave you what? A thousand dollars to transport five million dollars in Colombian supernotes? The least detectable counterfeits in the world? Did he tell you that his was the Secret Service's most-wanted operation and that they had been watching him for months? Even my people knew of this; they considered buying some of this man's goods because, at fifty cents on the dollar, we could have used it to purchase more . . . supplies for our cause. But we did not because the stink of an investigation was all over it. And obviously the agents knew you were coming: they even waited until you were across a state line so the FBI could participate with them in a joint stop. His threat was nothing but an attempt to cover his error. I was pleased to warn his people away.

"If anything, it is they who owe you." Ibrahim touched Grant lightly on the upper part of his left arm. "A man who takes a bullet for another man's folly has certainly paid more than anyone ever should."

"Yes." Grant moved the arm unconsciously. It was still stiff from the wound even though years had passed. "And yet, if I go home, away from you and the others, Diego and his people would just as soon grease my . . . would just as soon kill me as look at me."

He glanced at the older man. "I am sorry, Ibrahim. I know you do not approve of street talk."

The mullah dismissed the thought with a wave of his hand. "It is a subject that is quite emotional for you. I understand completely."

Grant took a deep breath. "I have no home back there . . . back where I came from. You have . . . all of you have. . . . My home is with Islam. My life is with Islam. And I will do whatever Allah wishes me to do."

"As long as that, too, is your wish," Ibrahim said. "Allah loves those who give without regret."

They got to the entry to their cell block and waited as, one by one, the officers checked their prayer rugs and then frisked them; chapel services were known to be good places to exchange drugs or other contraband. Not that Grant would dream of such a thing now—Islam forbade drugs; not even the occasional doobie was allowed. And alcohol, even beer and wine . . . all of it was *hadd*.

The corrections officers released the inmates one by one into the cell block; procedures called for them to go to their cells and wait for the morning count.

Grant went to his cell, a seven-by-ten room with two bunks, a stainless-steel commode with a sink built into its top, a plastic storage bin and a steel shelf designed to hold a TV, although it was empty because no one on the outside cared enough about Grant to buy him one and he had not earned enough in the prison shop to buy his own. He had no "bunkie"—no cell mate—and that was unusual in Marion, but Ibrahim had somehow fixed that with the guards. It allowed Grant to sleep at night, secure that none of Diego's homeys had gotten to someone and bribed the guy to put a shiv into him in the middle of the night.

Grant put his prayer rug away in his storage locker and got out his Qur'an. It was a bilingual edition, Arabic on one page and English on the facing page, but he was finding he needed the English less and less. The men in Ibrahim's congregation were always willing to help him learn. All in all, they were the most generous people he had ever met.

And what he told Ibrahim was true. They had saved his life. Diego's crew in Marion was extensive, and they cornered him the first week he'd been there. Only Ibrahim's intervention—all he had to do was say a few words—kept Grant from dying painfully right on the spot.

Ibrahim hadn't even recruited Grant into his congregation. Once Grant saw the potent blend of peace and power surrounding the Middle Eastern Muslims in the penitentiary, he had willingly asked to learn more. And they, always generous, taught him.

Following the Arabic across the page, Grant thought about his dead-end job in the paint department at the Home Depot, which would probably never hire him back now that he'd been inside. He thought about the girl who'd used him just to get her car fixed, about the predators like Diego who would put him in mortal danger and then threaten to kill him when things backfired.

That wasn't living. And he could care less if he ever went back to southern Virginia and its dead-end everything.

He looked at the words of Muhammad on the printed page.

They were telling him he found a new life. One worth living.

One worth dying for.

CHAPTER EIGHT

❏ ❏ ❏

Virginia, Present Day

Blake leaned into the turn, the headlamp of the Harley painting the dark, wooded shoulder of the two-lane road. He looked deep, far through the turn, but he also stayed alert for the glowing, double yellow spots indicating deer—their eyes reflecting his headlamp back at him.

The thought dredged up memories of being small—five or six years old—riding along with his father in the old Ford pickup and shining a handheld spotlight, the kind that plugged into the cigarette lighter. They never brought a rifle along on those outings because the purpose was not to conduct a lazy man's hunt. It was an educational exercise, playing the yellow-white beam into the brush at the side of the road and up into the trees, picking out the glowing eyes of deer and raccoons and learning how they moved about at night.

And then the following year, his father took him on his first hunt, the two of them up in a makeshift stand watching a game trail as the first light of dawn crept over a ridge. It was a trail his father watched for months; and, sure enough, less than an hour after they'd climbed up to the stand, an eight-point buck came up the trail and stopped at a turn, standing in perfect profile, and that was when Blake's dad put the Model 70 in his hands and gave him the nod that said, "You know what to do."

That buck put so much meat in the freezer Blake and his mother were still eating it after his father left for Kuwait, on the deployment from which he never returned.

Blake slowed a bit as the motorcycle exited the turn, shaking his head. The first rule of riding a motorcycle was that you don't ride it distracted. Yet a motorcycle was what he had for the ride home, and after the conversation at General Sam's, how could he be anything but distracted?

The night before his team flew to Germany, on the first leg of their deployment to Afghanistan, Blake was back home at the farm, on the last evening of a three-day leave. Before leaving for the farm, he carefully cleaned, sorted, and packed his equipment. Not a thing was out of place; every piece was ready to go. As he'd sat across the kitchen table from his mother, he could picture it all, stacked and waiting at Fort Bragg, waiting for him to return, ready to fly halfway around the world with him: the tools of his vocation.

That was the night they had the conversation: the conversation he'd known would one day be coming, ever since the morning when, with her blessing and—once they'd talked it over—her encouragement, he'd enlisted.

But on the eve of his deployment, there was no telling her she had nothing to worry about. Even his father never tried saying that before he went to Kuwait, because military women have seen and heard too much to be placated by false assurances. They know that—even in peacetime, and even at home, and on a base during peacetime—things can happen. And in a theater of war, that risk went up, and it went up considerably; it was simply the nature of the beast.

The shoulders of the road opened up a bit, fields now on either side, the treeline a hundred yards distant or more, just a darker shadow under the star-strewn country sky. Blake twisted the throttle a fraction of an inch, came up to the speed limit, and stayed there, the Harley growling its low, throaty song into the cool night air. He pulled the zipper all the way up on his leather jacket and hunched just a little to stay out of the slipstream running back over the top edge of the windshield. His eyes searched the farthest edge of the headlamp pattern, and his mind wandered again, back to the night before deployment.

They were sitting at the kitchen table, the same table, with its chrome legs and Formica top, Blake ate nearly every meal of his boyhood on, the same table he had used for doing homework, for building model planes. And it was the same table his mother and his father had sat at the night before his father went to Kuwait.

"A man from the judge advocate general's office helped me put this together," Blake had said, sliding an envelope across the table to her. "It makes clear that any stake I might have in the farm would go to you, as well as my insurance. You know, just in case."

"A will." His mother hadn't touched the envelope. "Twenty years old and you're making a will."

"Well, I figured . . ."

"Yes." She'd nodded. "I know."

It was one of those moments when there didn't seem to be anything left to say. But there was one thing left Blake decided he had to say, and he did that next.

"Mom." He'd looked down at the speckles in the Formica tabletop as he said it. "I'm the reason Dad died."

"Blake, don't talk foolishness. Sure, your father wanted to take care of you. He wanted to take care of me, this farm, as well. That's why he went. But it's not your fault."

"You don't understand." His eyes welled as he got ready to tell her, and he willed the tears back because tears would bring sympathy, and that was not what he wanted. "That fire. In the tobacco barn. I was in there, playing with matches before dinner. One of the heads broke off and went shooting away, and I couldn't find it. So I figured it must have gone out. But obviously it didn't. It kept on burning and

I didn't notice, and it set off a fire that took the barn with it. That fire was my fault, Mom. I caused it."

For a long moment his mother said nothing, her mouth slightly open, her eyes searching his. The compressor in the refrigerator whirred softly to life, ran for a bit, and then stopped. Then his mother cleared her throat and told him, "That's nonsense, Blake. The fire marshall said it was the old wiring. If we'd been able to afford insurance back then, the policy would even have paid for it."

"But we didn't have insurance and it wasn't wiring. I was playing in the corner, by the fuse box. That's why the fire marshall thought it was wiring; it started by the fuse box. But it was me. And I never told Dad, never told you. At first I was afraid. Then later I was too ashamed. I've been ashamed all these years."

"Oh, Blake . . ." His mother wept then, and it was nearly another minute before she reached across and put her hand atop his. "You were just a little boy. And a body can't take blame for what a body does as a child. I thank you for telling me, son, but you put this thing right out of your mind. Those matches never killed your father. An Iraqi missile did."

That's what she said. But it was the beginning of a new distance between Blake and his mother.

And while he told himself he did it to come clean, so just in case he was lost in combat he wouldn't die with that truth untold between them, he'd become aware there was another reason as well.

It was in Afghanistan, at the mess hall one late afternoon. He was having his supper with Niikura, a Hawaiian guy whose folks were both from Okinawa; and Niikura told him that, sometimes, when samurai were going to war, particularly when the battle was apt to be desperate, before they left home they would kill their entire household—wives, children, servants, everybody.

"That's crazy," Blake said. "Why would you kill the very people you're fighting for?"

"Because they weren't fighting for their families, man," Niikura told him. "They were fighting for their shogun, their warlord. And if there was somebody back home they were thinking about, they knew were thinking about them, they knew they might hesitate in battle, might put self-preservation over duty. So they eliminated the possibility by eliminating their entire households. We are talking some heavily committed dudes, you know?"

Blake knew. And while he had not severed his ties with his mother by any means, he distanced himself from her ever so slightly with his admission. He made himself a person who she could mourn for a bit and then move on.

Blake downshifted, leaned into a curve, accelerated past the apex and out of it, and then brought the bike upright again.

It was messed up. The thing with his dad. The thing with his mom. But it was what it was. And by telling her about the matches, he'd at least squared one account: it took better than a decade, but he came forward with the whole story, with the thing that had to be said. And now he could say with a clean conscience he never lied to her.

Never ride distracted? Blake was disappointed with himself when, with no memory of either coming into Hampden-Sydney or of passing through the little town, he turned down an open side street and then into the parking lot of his apartment building.

In the unit next to his, some students from Longwood had set up folding chairs in the carport and set a keg in a trash can full of ice.

"Yo," one of them called. "Pull up a chair, man. Have a brewski."

"Thanks," he'd said. "I've got an early morning coming up."

"It's Saturday, dude." One of the others had reached that stage of early drunkeness that brings on a sort of jovial belligerence. "The weekend. Have a brew."

"Thanks," Blake said again. "I've got church in the morning."

"Church!" The belligerent drunk started laughing, saw Blake was serious, and caught himself. "Well, okay. But next time, dude. Alright?"

"You bet."

Blake let himself into his apartment. The front room held nothing but a sofa, an end table with a lamp, and a TV. The guest room had the Bow-Flex machine, nothing more. And in his bedroom he had a double bed—which was luxury to a man accustomed to cots—and a desk with a chair, lamp, and a laptop. The whole thing looked as if it could be packed away into a U-Haul in about ten minutes, which it could. It was a temporary place, a place to stay while he finished his education, after which he intended to move on.

Would he be able to do that—finish his education? Colsun Atwater—whoever Colsun Atwater was—sounded as if the government needed him right away.

And then there was the elephant in the room: never seeing his mother again. True, he'd moved her away from him a bit a few years before with the confession about the tobacco barn. And true, she had the surgeon in her life; if Blake wasn't mistaken, that was probably headed, sooner or later, to marriage. So his mother could probably have a life without him.

The problem was he distanced her from him, but he never distanced himself from her.

Church in the morning; he needed it. And after that maybe some time with General Sam, just the two of them.

Blake got a soda out of the refrigerator, carried it into the living room and set it on the end table. He picked up the remote for the TV and then set it down again.

Church in the morning wasn't soon enough.

Blake knelt on the hardwood floor next to his couch and bowed his head.

CHAPTER NINE

❑ ❑ ❑

On the second day of classes at Hampden-Sydney College, all entering freshmen don coats and ties and report to Johns Auditorium on Via Sacra, one of the older roads on the campus. There they take the oath that officially enters them into their class: an oath to support and obey the fundamental codes of the college.

Blake remembered that day. His sport coat was not as smart as those on some of his classmates; he'd last worn it to a wrestling banquet in high school, spending the intervening years in uniform. The upperclassmen were cordial but somber, a contagious attitude. Any horseplay, any suggestion that the occasion was anything less than completely serious, was left outside the door.

While the college had a student manual spelling out its regulations in detail, the codes—a tradition stretching back almost two-and-a-half centuries—contained everything necessary to guarantee the college produced men of character. The two oaths embodied the essence of student comportment.

There was the Code of Conduct, sixteen words: "On my honor, I will behave as a gentleman at all times and in all places."

And then there was the Honor Code, identical to those used at the nation's military academies: "I will not lie, cheat, or steal, nor tolerate anyone who does."

Enforcement of the codes was rigorous, unequivocal, and conducted by the students themselves. As cochair of the Student Court, Blake had, the previous fall, presided over the trial of a sophomore who took another man's umbrella from the dining hall one stormy evening. Two students saw him do it, and the sophomore's roommate turned in the umbrella as evidence. The sentence was suspension for the rest of the academic year; the umbrella carried a value of perhaps fifteen dollars.

As a decorated veteran, Blake was excused from the obligation to live in college housing, even during his freshman year, and to conserve funds he leased the apartment in neighboring Farmville for nearly four years. It was eight miles from where he lived to the school: an easy fifteen minutes on the motorcycle, even on a weekend, when downtown Farmville was dotted with SUVs towing U-Haul trailers—homeowners from Lynchburg, Richmond, and even Washington, DC, in for the day to shop the dozen warehouses of Green Front Furniture.

There were people parking in the lot on College Road and walking along the shoulder; it was a home-game day for the baseball team. Blake throttled the motorcycle down, reducing its exhaust note to a low burble so as not to disturb the families walking to the game. He rolled past, hit the kill switch on the engine, and made the turn silently into the parking lot next to the Packer House.

A two-story white clapboard structure with a modest front porch, the Packer House looked like what it once was—an early twentieth-century residence for a university official. Only the signboard in front distinguished it as the "Wilson Center for Leadership" . . . that and the gravel parking lot, which held only the Ford Focus belonging to Ms. Arlton, the administrative assistant. Helmet still on his head, Blake fished in the inside pocket of his leather jacket and took out a notebook and a pen. He wrote a short note and then unbuckled his helmet, settling it onto the mirror of the Harley, fastening the strap so it would not fall off. He walked to the front door of the Center, tried the door handle and, when it opened, stepped inside.

General Sam's office was the first room on the left off the entrance hall, the former dining room of the old house, accessed by double glass-front doors. Blake was surprised to see that one standing open . . . surprised further still to see General Sam sitting at his desk, writing something in longhand. When Blake knocked, the old soldier looked up, smiling.

"You look startled, Blake."

"I was going to leave a note—didn't see your car in the lot."

"Mrs. Wilson got back late last night, about the same time I did. I let Colsun have the cabin to himself. My missus dropped me off on her way into town."

"Not like you to be in the office on a Sunday, sir."

"Nor is it like you to come around on the last day of the week. The Lord knew what he was talking about when he said man had to rest. Besides, I'm not working today. I'm just catching up on some correspondence while I wait for you."

Blake cocked his head. "You've been waiting for me?"

General Sam nodded. "Ever since church. And now you are here, so you may as well come in, my friend. Have a seat."

The General's office was a microcosm of his career: scenic photographs from places where he had been posted—Tower Bridge, the Brandenburg Gate, the Kremlin, military histories and memoirs of world leaders, a walnut desk that appeared to have seen as much of the world as its owner, and, on a broad shelf near one windowsill, two copies of the American Standard Version of the Bible, one considerably less worn than the other.

Blake did as he was told and sat.

"I trust you will excuse us for being obtuse in our discussions last evening," the general said. "Colsun asked for my discretion until we felt you out on your willingness to work clandestinely. As you have probably surmised, he is CIA—in fact, he is the agency's deputy director of Operations."

That opened Blake's eyes an additional notch. "DDO? That's what? Fourth highest in the agency? Pretty big hat to be out recruiting in the colleges. I'd think he'd send one of his staff."

"That would be logical," the general agreed. "But by law, CIA must inform both Congress and a variety of intelligence committees on any significant efforts. If a mission involves only the deputy director and one or two other people, he can plausibly claim it did not meet the legal criteria to be considered significant—although in terms of intelligence value, I can assure you Colsun would not be personally involved unless the stakes were considerable."

The general paused there for a moment, and from the playing fields next door, Blake heard the distinct *tunk* of a ball being struck by an aluminum bat and the ragged sound of people cheering.

"I have been cleared for top secret information by seven presidents, including the most recent," General Sam said, setting aside his pen. "But Atwater hasn't told me much more than that he selected your file after a review of current and recently discharged Special Forces men. He contacted me as part of his review. We spoke, but it was he who asked the questions, not I. I vetted what your records suggested. All I know is the mission he has in mind for you is clandestine, that it will take you away from here, and possibly from this country, for a considerable length of time, and that it may take all of your skills and all your training to have a hope of success."

General Sam sat back in his chair. "But you already understand that I wouldn't have any of those answers, Blake. You have done enough clandestine work to understand need-to-know. And the peril Atwater hinted at would not deter you; you have faced danger—mortal danger—before."

Blake said nothing, listening.

"You have also faced the possibility of leaving your mother alone before," General Sam continued. "And Atwater confirms what you told me about your mother and the doctor who worked on you: that your mother may be considering remarriage."

"He's a good man," Blake said.

"As you have told me. So you would have no hesitation in that regard." General Sam took off his glasses. He chuckled. "You know what I've said about the true intelligence hero, do you not?"

Blake nodded. "That he's Sherlock Holmes, not James Bond."

The general nodded back. "The continuing conundrum of intelligence: young men want to *be* James Bond. Recruiters spend 90 percent of their time weeding those folks out. Now, finally, CIA has a role in which they need a James Bond. And that's it; you are hesitant about becoming a spy, are you not?"

Blake shifted in his seat. "It's not where I've ever seen my life, sir."

"I do not know the particulars." General Sam folded his hands. "But I can tell you with a fair degree of certainty that Colsun Atwater will be asking you to live a lie. For the past three years here at Hampden-Sydney, we have required you to live as a gentleman among gentlemen, and truth—truth in all things and truth without omission—has been at the heart and core of that philosophy. Yet if you had to tell an untruth to save a life . . . if you told a gunman that there was no one else in the house, even though you knew that there was . . . you would do it, would you not?"

"Yes, sir."

"Then you have answered that question for yourself, as well."

General Sam looked down at his desk and then looked up.

"There is more to consider, Blake. You have been a soldier . . . *are* a soldier. And that means you have lived with the possibility that your mother would one day receive word that her son has perished in the line of duty. Should you take this assignment, she will receive that word."

Blake blinked. "Sir?"

"This assignment will require you to go deeply under cover, Blake. So far, you may not emerge for months, even years. Your decoration for valor, the publicity associated with it, means you are a person who will be missed unless there is a means of accounting for your absence. And Colsun is not willing to take a large number of people into the nation's confidence on this. Not even your mother. So if you agree to participate in Colsun's action, the Agency will have to stage your death. Your mother will lose you, will experience grief, as certainly as if you have been killed in action."

Blake clung to the arms of his chair while trying not to appear as if he was clinging to the arms of his chair. The room seemed to tilt ever so slightly.

"That seems a hard and cruel thing, Blake. I know that. I understand that. But again it is no more than the possibility you lived every day when you were in Afghanistan. It is a great deal to ask. But the mission requires that it be asked."

Blake looked down at his hands, soaking in what the general just told him. When he lifted his head, General Sam's eyes met his.

"There's more," Blake said. "Isn't there?"

The general nodded once, gravely.

"Blake, there come times in battles when men must decide to risk their own lives—sometimes to sacrifice their own lives—for the greater good of their comrades, their unit, their nation. I won't insult you by asking if you understand it because your military record proves you do. It is not something most soldiers like to talk about, but it is something all soldiers—all good soldiers—understand."

Now it was Blake's turn to nod slowly.

"And as you have chosen to seek a commission as an officer," the general continued, "I know you understand that commanders have an additional responsibility in this regard. Commanders must often decide to risk the lives of their men, or even to sacrifice the lives of good soldiers, to achieve a worthy objective. Many of our young men here at Hampden-Sydney are students of the Civil War, Blake. Would you count yourself among them?"

Blake straightened in his chair. "I suppose I would, sir. It's hard not to take an interest; so much of it was fought right here."

"Indeed it was." The general gestured to his left, in the direction of Farmville. "There is a house here, not far from my own, that still bears the scars from the minié balls that struck it."

The general leaned forward, arms on his desk. "Tell me, then, Blake. Grant and Lee; who would you see as the superior military strategist?"

Blake thought for a moment. "Lee was the first choice to command the Army of the Potomac, sir. He even considered taking it but could not fight against his home state. And I'd say that I agree with that sentiment; Lee had the better military mind."

General Sam smiled. "Spoken like a true son of Virginia. So tell me, Blake; why did Lee lose the war?"

"Well, sir, he became overextended from his supply lines, and . . ."

General Sam shook his head. "That is Appomattox Station; that's the end-game, not the war. Why did Lee lose the *war*?"

Blake sat silently and shook his head.

"It was because of attrition, Blake. Grant did not hesitate to sacrifice entire units to achieve strategic ends. Many military historians now believe it was Grant's philosophy that bloody battles make for shorter wars; he was willing to let men die so the Union could heal more quickly. And as a military officer that is the sort of decision one must be prepared to make every second of every day: to balance the value of individual human lives against the good of an entire nation."

Both men were silent for a moment. It was the sort of pause in which Blake found it easy to imagine battle cries and screams, the sound of musket fire and the sulfuric stink of black powder.

When the general spoke again, his voice was lower, more somber. "Many have said this is the most difficult decision a human being can make, Blake: the decision to risk or sacrifice the life of a subordinate in order to achieve an objective. But there is a decision more difficult."

Blake found himself scowling. "What is that, sir?"

The general sat back. "Colsun has not shared your mission with me, son. But from what he has said, it bears all the signs of infiltration. When one infiltrates, one becomes a double agent—one campaigns on behalf of one side while appearing to campaign for another. And that presents a conundrum. What if, in order to appear to campaign for the other side, you were required to sacrifice one of our own?"

"Sir?"

"A member of a cobelligerent force. An American soldier. Possibly even an American civilian."

"Sir, I don't think I could ever . . ."

"Think it through, Blake." The interruption was rare for the general, and Blake fell silent. "The greatest current threat America faces today, and I believe the threat Colsun Atwater intends to use you against, is extremist Islamic terrorism. The most significant terrorist attack from that quarter to date would be that of September 11, which took in excess of three thousand lives.

"To make a resonant statement, their next attack must trump that, and trump it significantly. I did not ask Colsun to take me into his confidence, and I doubt that he would have, had I asked; he is a seasoned intelligence professional. But you may be in a position to thwart an attempt to take not only thousands, but hundreds of thousands or possibly even millions of American lives. And if, in the process of gaining the opposition's confidence, you must sacrifice one of our own, it raises a positively Damocletian quandary.

"There is the command imperative—the officer's imperative—to place the good of the many above the life of an individual. Yet if you exercise that imperative and take that life, you will be outside every law of this country. You will have committed what would be, in the mind of any court, murder. And you have my assurance the act will haunt you to the end of your days. Do you understand this quandary?"

Blake nodded. He was glad he was not standing because the thought of what the general just said left him shaken.

"Nor will you have the solace of knowing you have ended something for good, Blake." The general looked straight at him as he said it. "At most, all you can buy with your actions is time. We are not fighting an enemy who answers to a prince, a potentate, a government in any usual sense of the term. They will not surrender because they lack the command-and-control structure an organization must possess in order *to* surrender. It is the myth of the Lernaean Hydra, brought to life; sever one head, and another grows in its place. But while it is growing, there is respite. Respite, and perhaps a semblance of peace."

All this. Blake thought about what the general just said. *All this, just to buy time.*

"Those who labor in espionage are the sewer workers of international affairs, Blake. What they do is absolutely essential for the continuation of society. But it is the dirtiest sort of livelihood imaginable, and the lives they save are never aware of the perils from which they have been rescued. You will not be thanked, and you may suffer repercussions for your actions. You may never be able to return to the life you have enjoyed in the past. You may not even be able to return to this country. In the event information about your activities becomes known to the public, you could wind up being scourged and reviled by some of the very people whose lives you have saved. It is conceivable you could be indicted, tried, and imprisoned. You could pay an extraordinary penalty and to what purpose? To win a single round in a hundred-round fight." The general sat back in his chair. His usual smile was gone; he looked weary. "I don't like saying all these things, Blake. But I would not have you contemplate any of this without being fully informed."

In the silence that followed, a cardinal called, somewhere in the trees outside the old house.

The general looked at his watch. "They are setting lunch at Pannil Commons. And I did not wake Mrs. Wilson to make breakfast before church today; we both had a late night. Shall we go up?"

Blake startled back to the present.

"I don't have a car. . . . I'm on the motorcycle, sir." Blake knew the general wasn't as ambulatory as he had been; the Wilson Center had a wheelchair ramp for him to help on the bad days.

The general dismissed the concern with a wave of his hand. "I woke feeling fairly spry this morning, Blake. I can't sprint up, but if we take our time, we can walk up. Excuse me, please, while I make one call, and then we can go."

Settle Hall, the building containing the dining commons and a student lounge, was a fairly new building, opened in 1991. But it was built in a style reminiscent of the other Federal-style buildings that dotted the campus.

Blake held the door open, and General Sam, wearing the garnet-and-gray Tiger warm-up jacket—his preference when the occasion did not require coat and tie—entered. The general doffed his porkpie hat, putting it under his arm, the habit of an old soldier. They crossed the lobby and went down the broad stairs to Pannil Commons, the dining hall.

Blake carried both the general's tray and his own, simply getting whatever the general got, because eating was the last thing on his mind.

The high ceiling of Pannil Commons dining hall was lined with flags: the national flags of more than two centuries of international students. Every table had at least two students at it; the Tigers were undefeated in Old Dominion baseball, and almost the entire student body had returned to campus early to catch the game. Only seven or eight of the diners were women; some were students from Longwood, taking classes not offered at their home university, and some were the daughters of faculty members—the only exceptions allowed to Hampden-Sydney's all-male tradition.

Blake led the two of them to two vacant spots at a table that held some faculty members, knowing it was going to eliminate any chance he might have of asking the general the questions burning in his head. He picked at his lunch as the general ate his own, even offered to run and scoop the old soldier some ice cream at the end of the meal. Blake didn't allow himself to show his confusion or his frustration; years of training had proven to him that all that did to a person was make him more mistake-prone. He tuned the room out for a moment and asked God for clarity.

The buzz of scores of conversations came flooding back in. The general talked about the restoration work going on at Slate Hill Plantation, the historic building where the school was founded while Virginia was still a British crown colony. He chatted with another faculty member about the due dates for upcoming budgets and listened with interest as an associate professor described a photograph he had just taken of an antebellum tobacco barn.

Finally General Sam nodded to Blake, and the two men left the dining hall, the old soldier mounting the steps slowly, one at a time. In the lobby he paused and turned to Blake.

"I'm going to stop for a moment," he said, glancing in the direction of the men's room. "It's a pleasant spring day; why don't you wait for me outdoors?"

"Sure." Blake turned and was about to walk away when the older man took him by his shoulder, his grip surprisingly strong.

"Blake," the general said, "two things . . . I know you have a month and a half to go on your senior year, but Colsun sounded as if he may need you before that. And I want you to know that, in case of national need, there is a precedent for graduating a senior early."

"There is?"

The general nodded. "April of 1861, when Virginia joined the Confederacy. The entire senior class was given diplomas and released to enter the service. I have spoken with the president and enough of the trustees, and we can do the same for you. The official story is you have been requested as an officer by Special Forces. I made a call to a friend at the Pentagon last night: a lieutenant's commission will be cut to back the story up. Your mother will have the honor of knowing her son graduated from an estimable school and received a commission as an officer and a gentleman. You shall make her proud."

Blake glanced at his feet. Graduation, commissioning, and getting his lieutenant's bars . . . he'd always thought there would be ceremony, his mother there, perhaps some of his old team. That was vanity; he nodded his head. Then he thought of his mother and pushed the dread from his mind.

"That's very good of you, sir," he said, rallying back into the moment. "Thank you. What's the other thing?"

"Your mother. Should anything . . . untoward . . . happen, I give you my word she will be cared for and comfortable for the rest of her life. I shall personally intervene if necessary."

This time Blake's words failed, but he nodded again.

General Sam's faced softened. "I can see it in your eyes. You have made a decision already, have you not?"

Blake swallowed. "Yes, sir. I have."

"You are a good man, Blake, and I am proud to be your friend." The general patted Blake's shoulder. "Go ahead and take the air; I won't be but a moment."

It was a beautiful spring day. Any hint of the mild southern winter was banished. New leaves were out on the trees, and the sky was a cloudless, clear blue, with only the barest hint of a breeze blowing.

"General Wilson's wife will be picking him up in a few minutes. We can take a walk without him."

"Mr. Atwater," Blake said without turning. He glanced at his watch. "The general made his phone call less than fifty-five minutes ago. I assume it was to you. And you made good time if you drove all the way here from Brookneal."

"Came up earlier this morning. Been watching batting practice and warm-up over at the ball field. You boys have a junior pitcher who could play the majors if his arm doesn't blow out beforehand."

Atwater fell in next to Blake, and the two men walked, exchanging greetings, as was the custom, with other students as they encountered them.

"I won't insult you by asking you to sign a confidentiality statement," Atwater said.

"If this is a matter of national security, I imagine that talking about it would violate more than a few federal laws, anyhow."

"You're right, there," Atwater said. He reached into his jacket pocket, took out a white handkerchief, dabbed at the corner of his mouth, and put the handkerchief away. "So let me give you the background on this thing. . . ."

CHAPTER TEN

It was one of those episodes where Blake was aware he was dreaming, yet everything seemed real. Beyond real, actually. The oak trees in the front yard of the farmhouse were detailed beyond description, and when his mother answered the door, every feature on her face was in deep relief, as if under harsh theatrical lighting.

The conversation they had was the same conversation they actually had just a week before—the long lie: how his former Special Forces commander contacted him about coming back to oversee the training of two new teams, that he would be sequestered at Fort Bragg while that was happening. He wasn't sure where he'd be posted once that assignment was over.

And she wept with joy when he gave her the diploma from Hampden-Sydney and wept again, her joy not as apparent, when he presented her with his lieutenant's commission. Yet she put both of them on the mantle in the old farmhouse's front parlor, in places of honor, right next to her wedding photo.

And then the dream shifted, and he saw himself through his mother's eyes. He saw himself begin to fade, the wallpaper pattern of the parlor visible through his face, through the Carhartt jacket he wore on that cool spring day. As he faded, his presence was replaced by a scent, a wonderful, complicated heady smell, yet not overpowering. It reminded him of something he'd read once, that in Oriental cultures the presence of ghosts is indicated not by anything visible, or the cold spots so common in Western folklore, but by a scent. And in the dream, within his mother's body, Blake tried to reach out.

He couldn't. His arms were restrained. He tried to free them. Couldn't.

Darkness engulfed him. He struggled again.

"Shhh. Be still." The voice was soft, feminine. Just the barest hint of an accent—possibly Middle Eastern, maybe just the slightest hint of British. Saudi, or Egyptian, by way of London. "Your eyes are bandaged. The medical staff put you in wrist restraints so you cannot harm yourself as you come out of the anesthetic. They'll take them off when you're fully awake."

Bandages. Anesthetic. Yes. Of course. The surgery. Blake remembered being readied for the surgery.

"Wh—" It hurt to talk. His jaw wouldn't move. Above and below his teeth, his mouth felt as if it was lined with ropes. And his entire face had this wooden feel he recognized as pain being masked by drugs. He tried to speak again.

"Who are you?" It came out as a barely intelligible mumble.

"My name is Alia." *All-eh-yah* was the way she pronounced it. "I work with Colsun Atwater. I am here to help you with your Arabic, to teach you about Islam."

Blake was coming more awake. The wonderful smell was still there. The woman. Her perfume. "You're . . . Muslim?"

It really hurt to talk.

"I am Christian." There was hurt in her voice. Blake could tell that she was trying to hide it, but it was there. "My family was Muslim."

"Was?"

"Is. The doctors say we are not to encourage you to talk. Not yet. Rest. Sleep. I shall be here when you wake."

It seemed to Blake he slept for mere minutes, but when he awoke, the right side of his body was warmer than his left.

Sunlight. I am next to a window. That was the case when he awoke before, so either he had been sleeping for hours or the bed was moved. He lay quietly, listening. The sound of a heart monitor, the distant, continuous sigh of an air-conditioning vent, the faint, barely audible buzz of a florescent light: these were all sounds that were present earlier. So he had been asleep for hours.

He tried moving his arms. The wrist restraints were gone. He turned his head to the left, to the right. No visible change in the darkness, despite the warmth of the sunlight. He lifted his right hand to his eyes and a light touch, an uncalloused hand, smaller than his own, encircled his wrist.

"There are eyecups—aluminum—over your eyes. You mustn't disturb them. Nor move your head overmuch. The surgeons have altered your retinae so they correspond to your new identity. You have also had facial surgery. Do you remember?"

"Yes." Speaking was easier now, but his jaw was wired, so it was like speaking through a straw. "Plastic surgery. Make me a better match."

"Are you hungry? I have broth. It's *halal*. Everything you will eat from now on will be halal."

"I guess honey-roasted ham is not on the menu?"

"The honey, perhaps. But not the ham."

Blake tried to smile. It hurt. As if his cheekbones had been broken and re-sutured, which he supposed they had.

"Your name—Alia. Do I have that right?"

"You do." The woman's voice sounded pleased. "And I have been instructed to refer to you as 'Grant.'"

CHAPTER ELEVEN

❏ ❏ ❏

Ten days went by. Blake's eyecups were removed daily but always in a completely darkened room; all he ever saw was the examining light. Most of the sutures in his mouth had dissolved, as they were supposed to, and the doctors restored enough mobility to his jaw so he could eat soft foods and brush his teeth. But he still wore what felt like a hockey mask over most of his face, cushioned by layers of gauze.

And he was learning.

Blake had not been ignorant of Islam—of the *halal* dietary laws, of ritual purification, of the times and order of prayer, of the basic rules of dress and comportment—but Alia taught him more in ten days than he learned during two tours in Muslim countries. The difference was one of perspective. His experience was that of an observer viewing the culture from without. But Alia was able to tell him what it looked like from within. To an extent, at least.

When he asked her what it was like to be a woman in that culture, she at first said, "That is not something you need to know. You are coming from prison, from an all-male population. All you would know about women under Islam would come from the men who taught you, and they would have told you little. The life of a woman would not be a matter of great importance to them."

She fell silent then for a moment. Blake became conscious of the faint buzzing of the room light—a noise that had mostly subsided into the background for him over the course of days. Then she spoke again.

"You have seen Muslim families here in America, Grant," she said, employing the name she'd been instructed to use. "The men are dressed like peacocks, very modern, very *GQ*. But the women? They are veiled. They are humbled. Muslim women—conservative Muslim women—exist to bear children and to serve Muslim men. Nothing more. All they lack is the yoke over their shoulders for carrying water."

She made a sharp intake of breath, then, as if it had taken a great effort to speak.

"Is that why you turned Christian?" Blake kept his voice soft and sympathetic.

"No." The retort was immediate and curt. "Now let us speak of the hierarchy of surahs within the Qur'an."

So they did just that, and it was not until the next day that Blake, who had not shared anything about his own background, asked Alia, "So why did you decide to become Christian?"

He was sitting up in a chair by then. They even walked a bit in the corridors with the help of an orderly, who steered Blake by his shoulders. Sitting in his chair, Blake turned his head to listen for her breathing because she fell so silent he was beginning to wonder if she had slipped out of the room.

"I'm sorry," Blake said. "I'm getting too personal here."

"No, Grant," she'd finally responded. "It is a reasonable question. Your enemy is Muslim. I *was* Muslim. You need to understand why I would comply with you in this mission, why I would assist you in infiltrating the culture into which I was born."

Blake nodded silently. The young woman was intuitive; that had been precisely his thought.

"My father is Arab," Alia told him. "My mother is from Indonesia. These are both Muslim nations, but in the eyes of the people in Cairo, where my father worked as an oil executive and where I grew up, this made me, my sister, and my brothers . . . white—outsiders. I did not mind; I went to an American school. It was always my mother's wish that I would one day go to America. Yet the distinction made my siblings and me . . . less than full members of society. There was a certain measure of . . . separation. Does this make sense to you?"

"Sure it does." Blake nodded, the bandages heavy against his face. "I grew up in southern Virginia. Brown versus Board of Education? That case was tried practically in my backyard. Before my time, but I grew up aware of it."

The room went silent for a moment again, and Blake understood why. In four sentences Blake gave Alia more background on himself than he had divulged in the previous week.

"It's okay," he added. "What I just said; it also fits my cover."

"All right." There was a rustle of clothing as Alia shifted in her seat. She was across from him, and he sensed she was leaning forward. "One of us—my younger brother—was more of an outsider than the rest of us. Baasim was born with Down syndrome. He could speak, dress himself, wash himself, care for himself after a fashion. The intelligence of a Down syndrome child varies from case to case, but it quickly became apparent to us that Baasim would never mature intellectually beyond the level of an eight- or nine-year-old. Yet he was a beautiful child. Let's test your Arabic; do you remember what *Baasim* means?"

Blake thought for a moment. "'Smiling.' Did I take too long?"

Alia laughed. "Your legend says you learned Arabic in prison. No one is going to expect fluency."

"Baasim was like . . ." Alia's voice became somber again. "You know how some special-needs children are so lovable and sweet? He was exactly that way. A beautiful boy, and yes, someone would have to care for him for the rest of his life, but I was more than willing to do that. Even before I found Christ, I would have been much more than willing to do that."

She fell silent then, and Blake did not speak either. It was curious. He felt drawn to her, a bond with her. Yet he had never laid eyes on her. *Is this what it is like when the blind are drawn to someone?*

Alia sniffled. Blake heard the distinctive sound of a tissue being pulled from a box, of her blowing her nose.

"I'm sorry," she said.

"Nothing to be sorry about."

Another tissue. This time only a sniffle.

"There is a charity," she said. "The name of it would translate as 'The Prophet's Hands.' Our mullah brought it to the attention of my father. He said Baasim had been a burden on us long enough. I was fifteen when Baasim was thirteen, and the mullah told us no man would court me, no man would marry me, if they thought they would be getting a . . . a 'mental deficient' is how he put it . . . that no man would marry me if he thought he would be saddled with such an obligation. Because, if something were to happen to my parents, caring for Baasim would become my duty. The mullah said the Prophet's Hands could care for Baasim for the rest of his life, and it would cost us nothing. It was a charity funded by a great number of mosques."

She took a deep breath.

"But the Prophet's Hands was not in Egypt. It was in Iraq. Baghdad. I wept when I heard that. And when he heard me weeping, Baasim came to my room, and he smiled that wonderful smile of his. He was a child with no darkness within him at all. He said, 'Don't cry, Alia. They are taking me on an airplane. I get to fly on an airplane.' He had never flown before, and to him it was a great adventure. He did not know he was moving away for good, and I did not have the heart to tell him. So I dried my tears and pretended to be glad."

Another audible breath.

"Three years passed. About this time I began to hear about Jesus. Different from Muhammad. Consistent. God and man both, which troubled me at first because to a Muslim the idea of God coexisting in something as base and sin-prone as a man . . . well, it is almost unthinkable. But a girl in my class at the American school . . . she told me about her experience with Christ. We were nearing graduation, but even so we had to be secretive about it. Some of the teachers and most of the staff were Muslim. In Islam, you know, once you are Muslim you are supposed to be Muslim forever. To denounce the faith in a Muslim country can carry with it a death sentence. Yet I was on the edge of doing just that. And then it happened."

This time she fell silent for a long time. The faint buzz in the florescent light seemed to grow louder. Finally Blake asked, his voice low, soft, "What happened, Alia? Tell me."

"It . . ." Her voice faltered for a moment. "It was a restaurant in Baghdad. One known to be favored by opponents of Saddam. This was after the city fell, after the coalition occupied it. A customer leaving the restaurant saw Baasim and spoke with him. The poor child . . . he was embarrassed. He had a package addressed to the maître d', and he didn't know what a maître d' was, so he asked the customer, and the man pointed out the owner."

Blake tensed then. He knew what was coming.

"The bomb went off a minute later," Alia said. "Thirty people near the center of the restaurant were killed. More than a hundred injured. Even the man who spoke with Baasim was badly injured when the windows blew out. . . ."

Blake knew he had to say something. He didn't know what. But just as he was about to talk, Alia was speaking again.

"I know Baasim could not have done that, Grant. Not willingly. He was an innocent; he probably thought he would be given a sweet for running the errand. One time, when my mother scolded a servant for putting the wrong wax on a piece of furniture, Baasim wept for the woman, told her he was sorry if we hurt her feelings. He was that gentle. I am certain someone handed him the device, lied to him about what it was, and then detonated him. Like a car bomb. Like a trash can at the side of the road."

"I'm so sorry." Blake finally got the words out.

"That is not why I am a Christian, Grant. The reason I am a Christian is because when the mullah came to our house to tell us the news, he did so as if Baasim had become a *jihadim*, a fighter in the name of Islam. Him—the same child before whom one could not swat a fly. Yes, he was a man without, but completely a child within; and when that supposed man of God sat there in our parlor, eating figs, drinking tea, and telling us how my brother was now enjoying a warrior's reward of virgins in paradise, . . . I ran screaming from the room.

"The next week I sold some of my mother's jewelry, went to a place in Cairo where one can have a false passport made, and I flew to London. I found the name of a Christian charity on the Internet, a charity that helps Muslim women, and I went to them. I was eighteen by then, old enough to be considered emancipated in Britain, and they took me in, found money to send me to college, gave me a new start. Confessing Christ was the easiest decision I ever made. Do you know the Bible?"

"Yes." When Blake said it, there was another pause. They both realized Alia just got another small piece of his background.

"There is a place in the Gospels that talks about how, when an unclean spirit is driven out of a person, it's important that a clean spirit take its place. I understood that intuitively, Grant. And when Islam went out of me, the Holy Spirit had to come in. I asked Christ into my life in London."

Blake resisted the temptation to say "amen." He'd said too much already.

"I made money waiting tables at an Indian restaurant, saved my money, and came to America," Alia continued. "Colsun met me when he was lecturing in one of my graduate classes at Georgetown.

He needed someone fluent in Arabic, versed in Islam. About two months after his lecture—I know now he was running a covert background check at that time—he hired me. Special assistant."

"You're special assistant to the CIA's deputy director of Operations, and you're teaching me about Islam and helping me eat?"

Alia laughed. Blake was taken with the sound of her laughter.

"Your situation is . . . highly compartmented, Grant. Everything is on a need-to-know basis, and few people have a need to know what you are doing. Even I only know a small piece of it, and Colsun trusts me implicitly. This is for everyone's safety; a person cannot be made to divulge that which she does not know. Even so, a tutor or a nurse's aid would be potential weak points in our security. So, as I had to know some of this anyhow, I was the logical person to fill in."

"Spending all your time with me—what must your husband think of that?"

In the pause that followed, Blake sensed—not saw, but sensed—that Alia cocked her head.

"Grant, I do not know what your mission will be, but if it involves the clandestine gathering of information, I certainly hope you can be more subtle than that."

He laughed. It was the first time since his surgery he had been able to laugh without pain.

"Okay. In plain, then, Alia. What's your situation? Married? Engaged? Seeing someone?"

"None of that is pertinent to your assignment, Grant."

He waited.

"No to all three," she'd finally said. "Unless you call *this* 'seeing someone.' In which case I suppose I am seeing you."

CHAPTER TWELVE

❑ ❑ ❑

She is going to *weigh four hundred pounds. She is a toothless hag with a mustache. She chews tobacco. She has green teeth.*

When Blake was in Afghanistan for his first tour, he knew a guy, an armorer on the air base, who got one of those "To An American Soldier Overseas" letters. Most of those were from school kids. But this one was from a nineteen-year-old girl, so he wrote back, and the two struck up a correspondence. She even sent him a photo, with a note of apology, saying it was shot when she was sixteen and she didn't have anything more recent.

That should have been a clue right there, what with just about every cell phone having a camera built-in these days.

And he sent her a photo of him looking all studly behind a 50-caliber sniper rifle, which was blatant exaggeration. He was qualified to clean and lubricate the weapon, but he never actually fired one.

Then, when they finally met in New York, the first words out of her mouth were, "You're short." And the armorer, being something of a gentleman, resisted the urge to say, "And you've gained about a hundred pounds since that photograph, babe." So the romantic hookup, which the two of them had been looking forward to for months, dissolved in about thirty seconds because reality has a hard time matching up to long-held expectation.

Blake knew that. He'd seen it time and time again. And today the bandages were coming off of his eyes.

She has twisted, ugly feet. She has big, hairy man-hands.

He knew the last one couldn't be true. He'd touched Alia's hands, or rather, her hands had touched his. The first time they'd checked his eyes, even the subdued light they'd used had been painful. He flinched and she'd held his hand. He remembered every detail of that moment; her hands were small, delicate, soft—perfect.

Still, low expectations are rarely disappointed.

She has European habits. She doesn't shave . . . anything. She wears big, thick, Coke-bottle glasses.

What did he know for certain about her, other than the hands? She was about a full head shorter than him; he knew that much from hearing her speak as they walked. And her footfalls were light, making the four hundred pounds highly unlikely.

The door to his room hissed open, the sounds of the corridor seeping in behind it.

That scent again. Her scent. It had become like an old friend. And there was another smell, like the smoke of pipe tobacco absorbed into wool. But the sound, although greatly muted, was of three distinct footfalls.

"Alia," Blake said. "Colsun. . . . Who's your friend?"

"You hear that?" It was Atwater's voice. "I told you the kid was sharp. 'Grant,' meet the artist who did your new face: Commander Tyler Brooks."

"Commander?"

He was answered by a deep, baritone chuckle.

"Let me guess." The voice was vaguely African-American, the Mississippi delta by way of Harvard. "Army?"

Blake nodded.

"Well then, your worst fears have all come true, soldier. You've been carved up by a squid."

Blake moaned. "Probably made me look like the little Dutch boy."

He held his hand out. "Nice to meet you, sir."

The handshake was firm, warm. "You, too, son. Want to lean your head forward a bit?"

Blake did. He felt and heard Velcro straps being separated.

"The technique we used on you," the surgeon said, "was developed to treat massive facial trauma on Marines in Iraq. Concussive damage, mostly. Typical scenario: an IED goes off and the shock wave sends a Marine face-first into an armored Humvee. Hit at the right angle and there'll be few deep lacerations—facial skin is actually fairly thick—but the Marine might wind up with every bone in his face broken."

Blake wondered how Alia was feeling, hearing the reference to an IED—an improvised explosive device. So far she had not said a word.

"Injury like that," the naval surgeon continued, "typically you either re-arrange things as best you can by feel—sort of like putting together a jigsaw puzzle wearing ski gloves—or you open up the face, which leaves some pretty obvious scarring. My team pioneered a third technique. We use the same sorts of tools employed in arthroscopic surgery, and we go in through incisions made between the edges of the gums and the inner lips. Sometimes we make incisions back behind the hairline, as well, although in your case we avoided that, just in case your head gets shaved while you are in the field. We did your entire facial procedure through your mouth, and then the opthamologist did his thing while you were still under. He's given us a green light to take the cups off today, along with everything else."

"I'm ready."

"I'll bet you are. I have to break some of the thin plasters we had over setting bone. You'll hear some cracking."

The surgeon was close. His breath was in Blake's face, and it smelled like citrus Listerine. Blake liked people who attended to the details.

"So what is this place, anyhow?" Something cold and metalic was slid against his face, and he heard a sound like wallboard buckling, only smaller. "Some kind of black-ops clinic?"

"Gray-ops is more like it," the surgeon said. "Committees in Congress, the VA, DLA all know about it. Know about it and fund it. Officially it's a hospice for people from the intelligence community . . . folks with certain types of conditions. Some cancers can get pretty painful, and some neurological conditions can make you think dinnertime is a debrief at Langley. So if you've got information we can't let out and you're in your last days, we bring you here and let you die with all the dignity a grateful nation can muster. And to do that sometimes takes neurosurgery—disabling pain centers and so forth. So we also happen to have everything we need here to do side jobs like this. You bring a fella in here and nobody sees him leave, it doesn't raise any questions."

"And I guess it would be kind of convenient if I'd done something awkward, like die on the table."

Nobody said anything.

"That was a joke," Blake added.

"Hey," the Navy man said, "every surgery has its risks."

There was the cool sensation of air hitting his face.

"Okay," the surgeon told him, "this is just a little saline, cleaning off the plaster residue."

The wet swab felt good; Blake hadn't washed his face in weeks.

There was a creak as the surgeon sat back on his stool. "Miss, can you catch the rheostat by the door over there? Dim the room lights as far as they'll go without going dark completely."

"Of course." Was that a touch of nerves in Alia's voice? Maybe she was as apprehensive about this unveiling as he was.

"Okay. Keep your eyes closed, Army."

Blake did as he was told. Even with the lighting lowered, a pattern, dark red with yellow speckles, appeared on the inside of his eyelids. The surgeon swabbed off the area around his eyes, as well. Blake felt something being placed over them, elastic around the back of his head.

"Let me guess. I'm Zorro."

"Zorro had eyeholes. Keep this on until Colsun and I are out of the room. Young lady, you can bring the room light up by degrees once we'd stepped out?"

"I'd be happy to."

"Okay, then. See you in a bit."

The door hissed opened. Shut.

"All right." It was Alia, standing by the door. "You can take it off."

He did. Alia had turned the room lights all the way off; the only illumination came from a night-light burning in the bathroom, washing out through the half-open door.

"I'm good," Blake told her. "You can take it up a notch."

"Close your eyes—just in case I take it up too high."

"Sure thing." Blake closed his eyes.

"Okay. Try it now."

Blake opened his eyes, blinked, squinted, blinked again.

Then he laughed.

"What's funny?" Alia asked.

"Well, I can't see much of you. But I can tell that you're not a four-hundred-pound woman with man-hands."

The shadow that was Alia crossed her arms. "And if I had been?"

"I would have been ready for that." Blake motioned toward the light switch. "You can take it up another notch if you want."

She did. This time Blake didn't just blink his eyes; he shut them.

"Okay." He squinted. "That'll be good for a while."

The room, washed out at first, assumed color as the after-images faded away. Blake looked at Alia, found himself staring, and glanced away.

"It is all right," Alia said. "I have been wondering what was under your mask for these past few weeks. I understand your curiosity."

Blake walked over to her, put his own hand on the dimmer for the room lights, and brought it up one level, then another.

"Be careful." Alia's voice was barely a whisper. "Not too quickly."

"You," Blake's voice was also low, "have blue eyes."

"Well, there is nothing wrong with your vision." She smiled. Blinked. Looked down. "They are rare in Indonesia but by no means unknown. Many Europeans, mostly French, settled there in the last two centuries."

Alia looked up at him again. "Haven't you the slightest bit of curiosity about your own appearance?"

Blake shrugged. "It is what it is."

Alia crossed her arms again. Her features were not sharp enough to land her a job as a runway model, but she was undeniably exotic. Her hair, while cut short in a style slanted across the end of one eyebrow, was full and so black it nearly looked blue. Her face was oval, her cheekbones rounded, her eyes had only the slightest hint of an almond shape, and she looked slightly tanned but evenly so. She was a full head shorter than he, just as he'd thought she would be. Full lips. Even, white teeth. And she was slightly built, matching her footfalls.

"You are staring into my eyes," Alia told him.

"Okay, so it is what it is, but I'm trying to gauge your reaction."

She smiled. "I think they had a good canvas to work with."

She crossed to the bedside table, picked up a hand mirror, and held it out to him.

Blake tried to look nonchalant as he accepted it. He had a look.

It wasn't him. Or rather, it was vaguely him, but the eyebrows were slightly more prominent, the nose a little straighter, the cheekbones broader. The chin was more pronounced and . . .

"I've got a chin butt," he said dully.

"It is called a 'cleft chin,' and I think it quite handsome," Alia told him.

"It makes me look like a jarhead . . . a Marine," he said, shaking his head, still looking in the mirror. He looked up at her. "I guess we may as well call them in."

Alia opened the door, and Atwater and the Navy surgeon came in. Blake was still looking in the mirror.

"You gave me brown eyes," he told the surgeon. "How'd you pull that off?"

"They were hazel to begin with," the surgeon told him. "Our eye guy did a light micro-abrasion to the iris to make it receptive and then dyed it. Same principle as a tattoo, just not as permanent. You'll get the natural color back in a year or two. But for the next seven or eight months, that color is as good as permanent."

"Look this way." Blake looked at Atwater, and the CIA man backed up a step and took a photo with a digital camera. The camera had a flash.

"That hurt," Blake said, blinking. "Just in case you were interested."

"Then it won't hurt to do a couple more." Atwater took another picture, straight on, and then stepped to the side and shot Blake in profile.

"The doctor's got some measurements to take." Atwater nodded to Alia. "Want to give me a hand pulling something off the servers in Langley?"

"Certainly."

"Pretty girl," the surgeon said after they'd left the room.

"What?" Blake asked him. "You couldn't have told me that while I had the cups over my eyes?"

"Behind on your game, Army?" The surgeon held a small plastic ruler just beneath Blake's eyes, took it away, and jotted a note. He did the same with eyebrows, lips, measured the depth of his upper lip, his chin. He took out plastic calipers and did more measurements. A lot more of them. In detail. It reminded Blake of a documentary he once saw on cable: Nazi scientists measuring the features of Jews in concentration camps.

"She around here a lot?" Blake asked.

"Who?"

"Very funny."

"Well, if you mean before you got here, no. It's not like I'm in residency here—Bethesda is my usual beat—but no; I never saw her before we worked on you. Atwater either: I've heard of him, but this is the first time he's put in an appearance. I don't know what your op is, but it's getting some extremely special attention. Don't move; keep your chin up where it was."

The surgeon continued measuring, making notes. He got out larger calipers and did some further measurements. Ten minutes passed before the room door opened again.

"We've got an issue," Atwater said as he entered. Alia was behind him, a file folder in her hand.

"I know," the surgeon said. "The zygomatic process; it's a good two millimeters too pronounced."

"That means his cheekbones don't match the subject's?" Atwater turned to Alia and accepted the file folder. He opened the folder and showed Blake and the surgeon an outline of a human head with a series of triangles superimposed over it. One, using the cheekbones and chin as its apexes, was in red.

"The criminal justice system doesn't use retinagraphy as a means of identification, so all we had to do was rearrange yours a little so it no longer matches DOD records," Atwater told Blake. "Fingerprints were easy; we just swapped yours for his on the FBI database and the hard copies at Marion. As for DNA, not even bin Laden's money can buy al-Qaeda the resources they need to do identity matches on all their people in transit."

Blake nodded. They talked about most of this before bringing him to the hospice.

"But facial recognition software is another story," Atwater continued. "The sophisticated stuff, what we use at borders, is fairly exorbitant. But garden-variety facial recognition is becoming fairly common. Apple even loads it onto their newer computers; you can teach your iMac to recognize Aunt Maude and group all of her photos into a single album. So we have to assume just about anybody will have the software to do the basic comparisons. And your cheekbones are a bit too pronounced for you to pass as the guy we need you to pass as."

"That part of the face, it's not an exact art," the surgeon added. "We have to take an educated guess at how much the maxilla will regress as it heals. I may be educated, but obviously I guessed wrong."

Blake's considerable respect for the surgeon went up even more.

"Can you fix it?" Atwater asked.

"Shave it back a bit? Sure. How long before he goes into the field?"

Atwater glanced at the date on his BlackBerry. "Twenty days."

The surgeon shook his head. "Procedure we're talking about, it'll cause a considerable hematoma. A bruise. Not the kind that's gone in a week. We could reduce that with anticoagulants, but I don't want to introduce those into a man heading out to the field. Mother Nature makes us clot for a reason."

Atwater looked at Blake, then at the surgeon. "What will these bruises look like?"

"They'll follow the voids around the orbits of the eyes," the surgeon answered. Then, when Atwater shrugged, he explained, "It'll look like he's getting over a couple of shiners."

"Two shiners? Then that's not a problem." Atwater closed the file and handed it back to Alia. He nodded at the surgeon. "Do the procedure."

CHAPTER THIRTEEN

❑ ❑ ❑

United States Penitentiary, Marion, Illinois

Grant Reinbolt wore a grin all the way back from the deputy warden's office. Ibrahim assured him it would go this way. And when Ibrahim asked Grant if he believed this, Grant said, "Yes." Still, when the deputy warden told him, you could have knocked Grant over with a feather.

The week before his parole hearing, five times a day—right after prayer—Ibrahim and a few others coached Grant: do not deny your crime; admit your guilt; show remorse; say you found strength in your faith, but do not identify that faith as Islam unless they ask, which is highly unlikely; when answering a question, look in the eyes of the board member who asked, but do so respectfully; do not glance away while speaking; say "ma'am" and "sir;" stress that you have a job and a supportive "church" community waiting for you when you get out; and above all, present a peaceful demeanor and do not become angry or impatient.

"These things will impress all the members of the board," Ibrahim said. "And one of the members of the board, an important one . . . well, let us just say he has been provided with an incentive to lobby aggressively for your freedom."

Still, even though the fix was in, hearing about it in theory and actually getting the news were two different things. Grant wept in the deputy warden's office when the man told him he would be out on parole in less than two weeks' time, the time it took to get him in the system and set him up with a parole officer. And while federal policy was to release a parolee back to his last city of residence, Grant asked to be released to Washington, where he had proof of a job offer, and the board agreed.

He stopped at the entrance to C Block, his building, still grinning while the correction officers frisked him and passed him through the metal detector. One of them scowled at him, gave him a what-are-you-so-happy-about sort of look. He didn't care. In ten days he would be out, and he could *sleep* through ten days if he had to.

Down the base of the gallery, up two sets of metal stairs. He stepped into his cell. . . .

Strong hands gripped his arms from behind, pulled them up behind him.

"Say a word, and we cut your throat right now, cracker." The whispering voice was vaguely southern, vaguely Hispanic.

A second man stepped in front of him—the distinctive V-shaped build of someone who spent every open minute on the weight benches in the prison exercise yard, black tattoos on brown skin. He had on a black head wrap, worn down over his nose so it made a mask, slits cut in it for eyes, like whatshisname, that guy in the movies. Zorro.

He looked at Grant like an artist assessing a canvas.

"Hold him still," he said. This one didn't sound Hispanic. He didn't sound like anything.

BAM! Stars erupted in Grant's head, and he was instantly sick to his stomach. Now the guy behind was holding both his forearms with just one hand. With the other hand, he had a fistful of Grant's hair, pulling his head back.

Grant's left eye was blurry, vaguely red, and as he squinted at him, the masked man in front of him cocked his head. Grant barely saw his fist begin to move a second time.

BAM! The other eye this time, and now Grant was definitely sick to his stomach. The man behind released him, and Grant fell immediately to his knees and curled instinctively into a fetal position, waiting for the rest of it.

Footsteps. Going away. A minute passed. Two.

Nothing.

Both of his eyes were already swollen shut. He forced the eyelids on his right open with his fingers and peered around. The cell was fuzzy looking. And empty.

Two black eyes. That was all they had given him.

"Is that it?" His voice was that of a man in pain—and astonishment.

CHAPTER FOURTEEN

❑ ❑ ❑

Georgetown, Washington, DC

The Sea Catch Restaurant and Raw Bar is one of those places you pretty much have to know is there to find it. The entrance is through a plaza—Canal Square—off 31st Street, Northwest, not far from M Street, Northwest. Originally a nineteenth-century warehouse for barge traffic on the adjacent C&O Canal—now a quaint, picturesque, and mostly empty waterway, its towpath used by strolling couples—the brick-and-stone building combined the historical flavor of old Washington with the contemporary trendiness of modern Georgetown.

Today the Sea Catch is popular with professionals: attorneys, Georgetown University faculty, office workers from nearby accounting firms . . . and people in the intelligence industry. In fact, the latter group is there so often rumor has it both CIA and DIA regularly sweep the building for listening devices, and any new waiter hired by the Sea Catch gets a background check neither he nor his employers will ever know about.

Colsun Atwater, Blake, and Alia could have passed for three of the university crowd: a graduate-student couple having lunch with a parent. The May weather was fickle, cool with a sprinkle of rain, so the maître d' hadn't even suggested a table out on the terrace overlooking the canal; the three of them sat at a table back a little from the windows.

"If you're like me when I was your age, you're probably thinking 'steak,'" Atwater told Blake. "But it would be a shame to get anything but seafood here."

Blake was wearing light-colored, wraparound sunglasses—what he thought of as his rock-star look—to disguise the bruising left by the second surgery. Just as the Navy doctor had predicted, the second surgery had left him looking as if he was wearing the remnants of a couple of shiners.

Behind the glasses Blake's eyes left the filet mignon on the menu and settled on the Atlantic salmon. Atwater ordered jumbo lump crab cakes, and Alia asked for the littleneck clams with wild mushrooms over linguini.

"We're on schedule," Atwater said after the waiter left. He spoke in a normal conversational voice, no whispers.

"That's why we're out, then." Blake laughed. "My last meal." Alia gave him a glance when he said it, and he saw hurt in her eyes and regretted the joke.

"Well, the house is nice," Atwater said. "But I figured you needed some air."

A week earlier Blake had been moved from the rural hospice to a CIA safe house in Georgetown, a brownstone townhouse adjacent to the university.

And Atwater was right; it was good to get out. It felt weird to be wearing the sunglasses indoors, but if the restaurant staff noticed, they didn't show it. Maybe they were accustomed to weird.

"You'll be coming here, to DC," Atwater said. "They take the parolees from Marion by bus to Carbondale, put them on a train there. You'll take train number 390, the Saluki, from Carbondale to Chicago and then switch over there to the Capitol Limited. Grant's friends here have paid for an upgrade, bought him a Superliner

Roomette, so he can pray. Makes it convenient for us; we'll do the switch on the train. You get to Union Station here in Washington, there'll be a driver waiting for you with Grant's name on a placard. He'll take you to a Starbucks at a shopping center out in Bailey's Crossroads, out by Arlington. You'll meet a man named Raheesh. Raheesh is the one who will fix you up with your room and get you your job driving a taxi. He's the brains. Their plan is to keep Grant here long enough for him—you—to do a couple of parole-office visits."

"Parolees can drive a cab in DC?"

"They can. And if they couldn't, these people probably have the grease to make it happen anyhow."

"The cab waiting for me, my meet with Raheesh—how good is our intel on all of this?"

"Impeccable. I've seen the video myself: shot in Raheesh's study."

Blake sat up. "You bugged his house?"

Atwater shook his head. "Didn't have to. Raheesh and his organization have the latest-greatest in technology: computers with built-in microphones, high-resolution Webcams. As long as you have the MAC address of his machine and surveillance software that'll turn it into a narrowcast station, anything it sees and hears, we see and hear. Even works when the computer's hibernating. I'm using *we* euphemistically, of course. CIA is prohibited by law from collecting domestic intelligence. But the Mossad is not, and their DC station chief and I go way back."

Blake glanced at Alia. "He always this sneaky?"

"I'm sorry. I can't answer that; it would be a felony." She smiled and took a bite from the celery in her Virgin Mary.

A faint buzz sent Atwater reaching for a small holster on his belt. He pulled out his BlackBerry, peered at it, and looked up. "You two excuse me? I've got to make a call on a landline."

"Sure." Blake watched the older man get up and head for the pay phone outside the restrooms. He looked back at Alia, whose head was bowed, stirring her drink. Were the hour later, it could have seemed the two of them were out on a date—two young people on the town in Washington without a care in the world.

He found himself wishing it were so.

She looked up, and he felt his face flush warm as their eyes met.

"Nice place," he said, covering for his embarrassment.

"It is."

"Have you been here before?"

Alia nodded. "Colsun brought me for lunch . . . on Administrative Professionals Day."

"On what?"

She laughed. "I think it's a holiday the dining and greeting-card industries dreamed up to drum up business. It was this past April. Quite a few people from the . . . the company come here."

She fell silent but did not look away. This time it was she who seemed flustered by the eye contact.

"IBM was started here," she said. "Did you know that?"

"At this table?"

"There was some tabulating-machine company that merged with two others in 1924," she said, ignoring his attempt at humor. "And they became International Business Machines—IBM. The world's first modern computer was built right here in this building decades ago. They have a display on the wall over there with some of the original punch cards."

"Well, that's really something." *Brilliant conversation.* It sounded stupid to Blake just as soon as he said it. He shifted in his seat, and the light leather jacket he was wearing moved as well, an envelope in its pocket brushing against him. It gave him a thought.

"Listen," he said. "Can I ask you a favor?"

Alia studied his eyes for a moment. "Of course you can."

He reached into his jacket and took the envelope out.

"I was going to give this to your boss," he said. "I have a savings account and the Army has a will on record for me. If anything happens to me, the savings go to my mother. But I also just sold a motorcycle, a car, a weight machine, some gold I'd bought back when the price was low, and, really, everything in my apartment. It came to enough that I didn't want to deposit it in savings; that much going in all at once might have attracted some attention. So I bought a bearer bond with it."

"A bearer bond?" Alia asked. "There is no name associated with it. Is that right?"

"That's right. If you have it, you can cash it. And I was wondering if you could hold onto it for me, put it in a safe back at the office or something. And if anything happens and I don't come back . . ."

"Don't say that."

They both stopped talking as the waiter brought the salad course, offered ground pepper, and then vanished toward the back of the restaurant.

"It's a possibility, Alia," Blake told her. "And if it happens, I would like you to take this envelope to a man named Sam Wilson. He's a retired general, and he has an office at Hampden-Sydney College in Virginia. Can you remember that?"

"General Sam Wilson at Hampden-Sydney." Alia closed her blue eyes for a moment and then opened them and nodded once. "Yes. Of course. I can remember that."

"Good. Tell him the man he told Colsun Atwater about is not coming back, and ask him to take this envelope to my mother. That way it goes to her, and you never have to know who I am."

"Grant . . ."

Blake shook his head slowly. "You don't need to call me that; I'm not Grant. But if you can do this for me, I can go into the field knowing things have been taken care of. I don't want to ask you to do something that violates any policies, though. Is this something you'd be able to do? That you'd want to do?"

"Yes, Gra—" Alia stopped herself before saying the name a second time. "Yes. Of course. I can do this for you."

She accepted the envelope and gave him another glance before she slipped it into her purse. She looked as if she was about to say something further but then she stopped herself, and Blake knew without turning around that Atwater was coming back to the table.

The CIA man thumbed something into his BlackBerry, slipped it back into the belt holster under his jacket, and sat down. He nodded to Alia, then turned to Blake.

"Your . . . removal . . . it happens tonight. All we'll release to the media is that a Green Beret died while training for a clandestine mission. Special Forces command will get all the details behind the legend we've created for the accident, and they'll mark you as deceased. Nobody there will be aware you're actually still alive. I know those boys can keep secrets, but this has to be highly compartmented. Your . . . family—she'll be notified. But she'll be asked not to speak to media for national security reasons. And we won't be releasing any names to the media. Although it will get leaked, of course. That's the whole point."

Blake said nothing. He'd just been told that, as of the morning, he'd be officially dead, that his mother would be grieving in less than twenty-four hours' time; what could he say? He forced himself to nod, to show he heard what Atwater had just said.

The CIA man leaned forward.

"Son . . ." It was only the second time Atwater had used that term in reference to Blake. "You just say the word, and I can pick up the phone right now and call this whole thing off. No questions asked, no hard feelings, your mother doesn't have to go through this heartache, and you keep your commission, have a nice, straightforward, Army career."

Blake waved at his face. "Nobody in the Army would recognize me."

"We can undo most of that."

"Then you'll have made a whole bunch of effort for nothing."

Atwater smiled. "Seriously, if this is taking you, taking your family, someplace you don't want to go, it's not too late to pull the plug on it all. I know we're asking a lot. As for the time and the dough, we're the government. Wasting time and money is what we do best."

Blake chuckled. He needed the laugh.

"No, sir. I'm good to go."

"Well, all right, then." Atwater looked up. "Here's lunch."

The food looked perfect, the table immediately emanated a bouquet of aromas.

Blake looked down at his plate, closed his eyes, and silently said grace. It was a lifelong habit, but when he opened his eyes and looked at the expertly seared salmon, all he could think of was a government Ford pulling up into the drive at the old farmhouse in Virginia, the Special Forces officer, and the chaplain getting out of the car, and knocking on his mother's door.

He picked up his fork and just sat there, his appetite absolutely gone.

CHAPTER FIFTEEN

❑ ❑ ❑

Fort Bragg Military Reservation, Cumberland, North Carolina

The sound of a helicopter, even a dual-rotor, heavy-lift helicopter like the CH-47F Chinook, is not unusual at Fort Bragg, one of the busiest military bases on the Eastern Seaboard. Nor was it unusual to hear such sounds at two in the morning. In fact, Rangers and Special Forces teams often train at night, making the heavy chop of rotor blades most prevalent after dark.

Still, since taking off from a remote region of Pope Air Force Base, the huge helicopter flew low, as close to nap-of-the-earth as it could with its cargo—a two-and-a-half-ton OH-58D Kiowa Warrior reconnaissance helicopter—suspended beneath its belly on seventy-foot nylon lifting straps. Under its MMS—its Mast-Mounted Sight system, a gyro-stabilized electronic imaging array striking up from the hub of the rotor blades like a large alien head on an overlong neck—the smaller helicopter had its rotors deployed: not a standard configuration for transportation. So even though the Kiowa was laughably light compared to the Chinook's maximum lifting capacity, the smaller four-place helicopter caught the air as it was carried along, making it cumbersome. The Chinook lumbered along at seventy knots, one hundred under its maximum cruise, its pilots giving a wide berth to the taller trees and hilltops below.

The big helicopter homed in on the rugged terrain in the northern part of the military reservation, the only part of the extensive piece of property not easily accessed by roads or trails. The pitch of its turbines increased as the big machine gained altitude.

In the huge, empty cargo bay, two men—wearing safety harnesses and secured to floor-mounted D-rings by nylon tethers—leaned from the open side hatch, night-vision gear on their helmets, and watched the captive Kiowa swaying beneath them.

A third man approached from the flight deck. Like the two in the cargo bay, he was dressed in military fatigues but wore no unit insignia, no patches or identification of any kind. He keyed his helmet headset and spoke to them over the aircraft intercom.

"Thirty seconds."

One of the men at the door flashed him an "okay" sign.

The Chinook continued to climb.

After half a minute the flight engineer held his hand to the side of his flight helmet, listened for a moment, and keyed his mike again. "We're circling in position, ground speed about sixty knots. Your bird is two-five-zero feet above terrain; that's high enough to start her in autogiro but too low to slow her up more than a touch. Ready when you are."

Another "okay" sign.

"How much is Washington paying for these things these days?" The first man in the cargo hold shouted the question to his colleague, not bothering to use the intercom.

"An OH-58D?" Leaning close to the man who asked the question, the second man didn't bother with the intercom either. "About five million. Quite a bit less if it's one of the old ones: the 58A with the upgrade."

"Doesn't matter; this is going to be, by far, the most expensive thing I've ever done. Lift your NVG for a sec, pard; otherwise the charges will flare out the display when they go."

"Gotcha."

Both men folded their night-vision gear up against their helmets, and the second man flipped up the cover protecting the button on a hand control. Next to it a small LED glowed green. He pressed the button, and the LED changed to red. Half a second later four blossoms of white light erupted below, and an audible WHUMP sounded over the noise of the rotors. The Chinook leapt skyward as the cargo straps parted, and the smaller helicopter fell away.

Without saying a word, both men in the cargo bay flipped their night-vision goggles back over their eyes and watched it drop. It was facing in the same direction as their flight path, and its rotors, set to autogiro, began to spin rapidly. Had they dropped it from five hundred feet higher, the Kiowa might have built up enough rotor speed, just from the wind rushing up past the blades, to cushion its landing and prevent serious damage. But from 250 feet, with the rotors starting from full stop, the little helicopter was too low for an autogiro landing. It crashed into pine trees and scrub, pitched tail high, and then tumbled down the hillside, shredding its empennage, MMS, and rotors as it rolled. It came to rest on its side in a ravine, the cabin still intact.

The first man clapped the second on his back.

"There you are," he said, grinning. "Your tax dollars at work."

Three hundred miles away, at the CIA safe house in Georgetown, Blake, Alia, and Atwater were gathered around one end of the kitchen counter as Blake watched images progress on a laptop screen.

"That's D Block at Marion; I was housed there by myself on the second tier. This is Ibrahim, the unofficial mullah to the group of Muslims with whom I associated. His last name is Pahlavi, same as the last shah of Iran, although he is quick to point out that they are not related. He never told me what he was in for, although I was told it was racketeering, gun-running, and counterfeiting: several dozen charges of each. These are the five men who usually associated with him. First names Samir, Abbas, Majd, Sharif, and Waahid. Their last names . . ."

"We're good," Atwater said. "Let's go over the contingencies again."

"We've kept them simple and related," Alia said. "If you need to contact us, you will have to get to the nearest embassy—American preferred, but a cobelligerent nation will do. Ask the desk to give the chief of intelligence a two-word message: 'yellow butterfly.' If they contact CIA with that, it will give a flash-priority message to Colsun and to me, and we will handle you from there."

Her fingers danced on the laptop keyboard, and a page came up, full of Arabic.

"This is the Abdul-Rassul.com Web site. The name means 'servant of the prophet,' and we know its blog is monitored by every al-Qaeda clique and training camp. Even those places that do not allow computer access will print out the main blog and post it on a daily basis. Access to post to the blog is moderated and strictly controlled, but we have hacked several identities. If you are in jeopardy and we need you to get out of wherever you are immediately, we will post a blog entry with a nearly nonsensical Arabic subject heading that would not normally appear in Abdul-Rassul. The heading is *'Farasa asfar,'* which means . . ."

"'Yellow butterfly,'" Blake said.

Alia smiled. "Exactly. If you see that, leave. Covertly if you can, overtly if you must, but leave. A blog entry with that heading is the signal that you are in imminent danger and must remove yourself from whatever situation you are in at the time. Don't try to respond; it is unlikely they will give someone as new as you the access to post to the blog. Just leave."

"Got it," Blake said. "Let's do one more pass-through on what we know about my situation once I get to Bailey's Crossroads. . . ."

Back on the Fort Bragg Military Reservation, the two men in the cargo bay of the Chinook rigged mountaineering lines from the deck-mounted D-rings and unclipped from their tethers. Both passed bights of the dark kernmantle rope through and around rappel rings, which they clipped to the waist belts of their harnesses with locking carabiners.

The rear ramp was down, and the first man backed to the edge of it, took up tension in his rope, and leaned back, looking down through his night-vision goggles. When the last twenty feet of rope was lying in coils on the ground in a small clearing below, he nodded to the flight engineer. Neither of the harnessed men was hooked in to the intercom any longer, and the mission precluded the use of radios.

"Go!" he shouted as he pushed back, letting the line run through his gloved hand. His companion did the same, and by the time they applied tension to the rope with the descending rings, they were forty feet down, swinging directly under the belly of the big helicopter. They let the lines run enough for a fast rappel, braking to a full stop only when they landed, their knees bent, on the ground. Leaving the eight-rings on the ropes, they undid their locking carabiners, removed them, and—hunkered down under the rotorwash—stepped back from the ropes, lifting their hands over their heads in an "O" shape once they were well clear.

Immediately the Chinook lifted away, taking the ropes with it. The double *whump-whump-whump* of its six rotor blades faded as it became a smaller black shape against the starlit sky. A minute later the only sounds were the returning buzz of insects and the sounds of nocturnal birds.

"Okay," the first man said. "The chopper's emergency beacon would have activated on impact. It's been transferred by satellite to FAA by now. When they see it's military, they'll be on the horn to Air Force ATC for the eastern seaboard. We've got about twenty minutes before people begin scrambling search parties for this bird."

His companion nodded, and they made their way downslope to the wrecked Kiowa.

The helicopter's side door was missing, lost on impact, so they clambered up and dropped in that way. The small cabin was thick with the reek of kerosene.

"Jet fuel," the first man said.

"We weakened all the lines so they would rupture on impact. Make sure everything's good and soaked. If it isn't, there's a spare fuel bladder strapped down where the port observer's seat is supposed to be. We can use that to saturate things."

The first man clambered forward to the flight deck. Two dead men were strapped into the pilot's and copilot's seats.

"These guys look like Arabs."

"Close. They're Iraqis. Prisoners from Gitmo. Suicides from the summer of 2008: no next-of-kin. Langley has had them on ice in a secure morgue since then."

"They don't even look like Americans."

"Don't have to. They're going to be burned beyond recognition. Or they should be soon. They wet with fuel?"

"Soaked."

The two men bent over the third body, strapped into the starboard observer's position. It was that of a young man in fatigues.

"'Kershaw,'" the first man said, reading the name on the breast tag through his night-vision gear. "At least *he* looks American. Where'd he come from?"

"Don't know. Looks too buffed to be homeless. Probably a John-Doe car-strike on some highway. That or he had a car wreck and left his body to science; the Company buys some of those when it needs them. Whew, he's got enough jet fuel on him to fly to Phoenix. Let's place it."

The first man reached into the billows pocket on his fatigues and took out a strip of putty-like material wrapped in a cellophane-like wrapper. He used duct tape to secure it to the vertical decking, just above the pooling aviation fuel.

"We're gonna have to toss these boots," the second man said.

"We're going to have to toss everything once we get back. Toss it and incinerate it."

"This charge is going to leave fragments," the second man observed. "Fragments, distinct point of ignition . . ."

"Doesn't matter," the first one replied. He pressed a small device with an antenna into the putty-like block. "When they pull the flight plan on this bird, it will show its mission as classified. NTSB will get photography—some of it—and a military report, edited. But they'll never touch the wreckage, never actually see it. The Army'll keep a lid on it. Kiowa here crashed and burned, end of story."

He pressed a button on the side of the device. A small diode pulsed yellow three times and then glowed red.

"We're armed," he said. "Time to roll."

The two men clambered out of the helicopter and, moving with the ease of people long accustomed to rugged country, climbed back up the slope to the clearing where the Chinook dropped them.

The first man opened a breast pocket and took out a small marine radio. When he turned it on, a dim green screen lit up, showing a full battery. Using a numerical keypad on the radio's front, he keyed in a frequency of 156.050 megahertz.

"You don't think that'll get detected when we key it?" The second man was a little too nervous for his line of work.

"FCC assigns this frequency for port and traffic control in the New Orleans area. It's not military, it's not used by civilians, and it's not employed in this area; no reason for anybody to be listening for it within a thousand miles of here. So . . ."

He stopped talking. The steady double thrum of the Chinook's rotors was returning.

The second man clipped a locking carabiner onto his harness. He looked over at his partner.

"Not that I think you'd tell me if you knew, but why are we doing all this?"

The first man smiled. "If you want to understand the rationale behind everything you do, you *so* made the wrong career choice by signing on with CIA."

He laughed. "And if it makes you feel any better, I haven't the slightest idea why we're doing this."

A minute later the big Chinook, all of its running lights extinguished, was hovering over them, a darker place in the sky, its rotor wash thundering down on them like an extremely localized hurricane.

Two lines were dangling from the helicopter, and the men let them touch the ground to dissipate the static electricity. Then they jogged forward, stepped into foot-loops tied into the bottoms of the lines and clipped the carabiners on their harnesses into a second loop tied at waist level.

The first man windmilled the radio over his head, and the Chinook rose, lifting them from the ground. When they were above the treetops, the first man brushed his night-vision goggles up, away from his eyes, using the back of his arm. Staring down into the pitch-black ravine, he keyed the radio: one time, two times, three. . . .

Yellow flame mushroomed from the wrecked Kiowa, the heat of the fire reaching the two men as they dangled from their lines a quarter-mile away. The first man shielded his face with his arm for a moment and then took a second look: the flames were curling nearly two hundred feet high.

He windmilled his arm again, and the big heavy-lift helicopter rose and banked, carrying them away from the scene of the crash.

CHAPTER SIXTEEN

Amtrak's Capitol Limited
Chicago Union Station

Grant Reinbolt slid the door closed on the Superliner Roomette and threw his duffel bag on the forward seat. The room was small, no larger than a walk-in closet, but it had a window, and a door he could lock and unlock, and those were amenities he had not seen in nearly four years.

The floor space was miniscule, not large enough to pray on, but if he folded the seats down to make the lower bunk, he could pray on that. Not that he needed to do it right away; he'd already missed the time for late afternoon prayer, just as he missed the late morning prayer time.

Grant opened the duffel and took out the rug, his Qur'an, a pen, and a notebook in which he had been keeping track of his ideas and questions concerning Islam. He sat down on the empty seat, the Qur'an in his hands.

The last time he knelt before Allah was morning prayer, back at the joint, after which Ibrahim and the rest of the men embraced him and blessed him and wished him a safe journey. But the train up from Carbondale was seats only, no sleeping cars, and Grant wasn't quite gutsy enough to go back to the open space they had for luggage, take his prayer rug out of his duffel, and kneel and face east, not in front of the southern Illinois good old boys in the railcar with him.

The name of that train was the Saluki, which the conductor had told him was a kind of dog and that figured. Ibrahim taught him that a dog was a filthy animal because it eats its own vomit. Grant had sort of liked dogs before, but he'd never thought about the vomit-eating thing, and he knew that was true.

His layover in Chicago lasted almost seven hours, and at first he just wandered around the big train station, but that got old after about ten minutes. He spent fifty cents to put his duffel bag in a locker, and he stepped out onto Adams Street. He saw that Sears Tower, the tallest skyscraper in Chicago, was right across the street, but they wanted almost eighteen bucks for an elevator ride up to the observation deck, and that was just nuts. So he walked down Adams Street toward the lake, craning his head back and looking at the skyscrapers as he went.

What he'd really wanted was a woman because he had not been with one since his arrest. But Ibrahim taught him that if he wanted such a thing he should take a wife because the Prophet taught that fornication was an abomination in the eyes of Allah.

If there was anything Grant didn't like about Ibrahim, that was it right there: the fornication/abomination thing. It reminded Grant of his father, whose every other sentence had seemed to end in some kind of "shun:" fornication, abomination, salvation. The old man fixed cars for a living, but he fancied himself a lay evangelist, even though most churches never had him in but the one time; and once word got around that he was crazy as a sprayed roach, most churches never extended even the first invitation.

So his father decided to make Grant his reluctant congregation of one. And he told the six-year-old Grant that all children were full of the devil and that he was going to preach it out or beat it out, whatever it took, and the beatings were what the old lunatic resorted to most of the time. He was old—sixty-eight years old the year Grant was six, which seemed ancient to Grant at the time, especially as his mother had only been a shy and deferential twenty-two. The old man beat her as much as he beat Grant, and when a Ford F-150 fell off a lift down at the garage and crushed the raving fruitcake, neither one of them was that sorry, although for quite a while there his mother sorely missed the regular paychecks.

So the fornication argument didn't go that far with Grant, but downtown Chicago seemed pretty high-class and an unlikely place to find a hooker, and even if he had, how was he to know whether it was a real working girl or some woman cop out working under cover? That would never do: to get busted in the first twelve hours of his parole and have to go back to Marion and tell Ibrahim he could not do what he promised to do, could not serve the faithful, because he offered an undercover cop money for sex.

And money was the other thing. He had over nine hundred dollars he saved from doing laundry in the joint, but eight hundred of that was in a government check, and he supposed he needed pretty much every penny for a place to live when he got to DC. It didn't make sense, blowing any of that just to scratch an itch.

So Grant just wandered around downtown Chicago all day. He went to that art museum, the Art Institute, and tried to go in when he saw some cute college girls flouncing up the steps between the two bronze lions. But there was an admission there as well; what was with Chicago that you had to pay eighteen bucks just to go in anyplace? And besides, Grant still had the remnants of the two shiners he got in the attack in the joint. He still wondered about that—all that trouble, just to give him a couple of black eyes. Talk about random . . .

So to kill some time, he'd walked through some stores in a downtown area called "The Loop," but he got security people following him because those guys have radar for somebody fresh out of the joint. So mostly he walked around outside and got hot, footsore, and hungry; and he paid twice as much as what he'd thought was reasonable for a hamburger, fries, and a chocolate shake. Then he went back to the station, and as soon as they'd let him, he boarded the train.

Through the window he could look out onto the platform and see people milling back and forth. He was just about to drop the blinds when he saw two EMTs—big guys in Chicago firefighter uniforms—pushing a gurney and a crash cart, walking quickly. Looked like somebody had boarded the train early and then had a heart attack. That'd suck.

There was a knock at the door.

Grant flinched. "Who is it?"

"Conductor, sir. Need to check your ticket."

"The other dude already checked my ticket."

"I'm sorry, sir. One of our attendants called in, and we had to change car assignments. I apologize for the inconvenience. This won't take but a minute, and then I promise you we won't disturb you again."

Grumbling, Grant stood, unlocked the door, and slid it open. Then he froze.

The man standing in the corridor was dressed exactly the same as Grant: same Wrangler blue jeans, same gray hoodie, even the same blue Adidas running shoes Grant bought because he refused to walk around outside in the real world wearing cheap black prison-issue broughams.

And here was the weirdest part: the face on this dude was exactly the same face Grant saw in the mirror every single morning. He even had the lingering yellow remnants of two black eyes, just like Grant's.

"Wha . . ." Grant blinked. "Who are you?"

"You." The other guy reached out, and Grant felt a sharp pain, a needle-poke at the base of his neck. It went hot there for just a fraction of a second. Then the world swirled, tilted, faded, and went black.

CHAPTER SEVENTEEN

❏ ❏ ❏

Blake caught the other man as he staggered, walking him back into the little two-seat room and settling him heavily onto the rear seat. He recapped the morphine syrette and shot him with a second hypodermic: atropine, to keep him breathing. Then Blake backed out into the corridor, motioning to the two men dressed as emergency medical technicians.

They squeezed into the room with him and lifted the unconscious man to his feet, holding him there while Blake emptied Grant's pockets, taking out a wallet, a pocket comb, forty-two dollars in bills, two quarters, and a wrinkled government check in the amount of $800. He checked his hands and was thankful there was no ring—the chances of them sharing the same ring sizes were extremely slim.

Blake checked the other man for a necklace or choker and found none.

"Take off his sweatshirt," he said. The two men did as they were told, and Blake examined Grant Reinbolt's arms and then lifted his T-shirt and examined his chest and back.

It looked as if the Muslims befriended Grant Reinbolt early on; the man had acquired no prison tattoos while he was inside at Marion.

"Okay." Blake nodded. "Let's get him out of here."

The other two men lifted Grant and carried him to the gurney waiting in the corridor. Blake followed them and looked around. They were early—the other passengers had not yet begun to board—and less than a minute passed since he knocked Grant out with the drugs. No gawkers had their heads poked out of the other compartments, and he wanted to keep it that way. He put the sweatshirt and the syrette on top of the unconscious man and covered him with a blanket while the other two men fitted an oxygen mask, obscuring Grant's face. Thirty seconds later the straps were tightened, and the two men dressed as EMTs were lifting the gurney to negotiate the turn out of the railcar. Perhaps three minutes had passed since Blake first knocked on the compartment door.

As soon as they were out, Alia came into the car, clutching a shopping bag by its handles. Without a word she entered the compartment, and the two of them methodically set about removing the contents of Grant's duffel—a pair of no-brand jeans, some khaki Dockers Reinbolt wore to his court appearance, three white T-shirts, five pairs of briefs, four sets of plain white socks, a blue denim shirt, and a blue Sears St. John's Bay dress shirt (also left over from the court appearance), and a small canvas toilet kit containing a toothbrush in a once-transparent plastic tube case, Colgate toothpaste, two disposable razors, a can of shaving cream, and a tube of Speed Stick Extra Dry Pro deodorant—and replacing them with identical items from the shopping bag, all purchased in Blake's size, using Reinbolt's exit manifest from United States Penitentiary Marion as a shopping list.

"We washed all the clothes five times, using the same type of laundry detergent they use at the prison," Alia said. "And I ran the toothbrush and its tube in a dishwasher to age them."

Blake nodded. He knew that and knew, too, that Alia was speaking because she had to—talking away her nervous energy. He felt the same urge but restrained it; years of training and missions had taught him to swallow his nerves.

Or maybe not completely swallow them. He found himself packing as he had packed since boot camp—rolling the clothing into snug bundles that would travel well, resist wrinkling, and take up little room. He stopped himself and loaded the duffel the way a civilian would load it: folding each item individually.

There was a manila envelope on the sleeping-compartment seat, and Blake pulled out the contents: Reinbolt's release papers from Marion, his health records, his parole instructions, and a notebook, the kind with the marble-like pattern on the cover. Blake opened the notebook and thumbed through it.

"I can take that, if you want," Alia said. "It's in his handwriting. Yours won't match."

Blake shook his head.

"I can read this to get a better handle on how he thinks," he said. Then, patting the hand-warmer pocket on the hoodie, he added, "And I've got another notebook here I can use until I toss it in DC. I'll practice with his, learn to write like him."

Alia's jaw dropped, ever so slightly. "You can do that?"

Blake lifted both eyebrows and grinned a little in reply.

Alia removed a small paper sack from the shopping bag.

"Turkey sandwiches, some carrots and celery, a couple of bottles of water," she explained. "Nothing that will keep you awake. You'll need your sleep."

"Thanks; I appreciate that." Blake put the sack on the seat and double-checked the compartment to make sure nothing was left from Grant Reinbolt's duffel.

"Okay," he told Alia. "You'd better go. Conductor finds you in here, he's gonna make you buy a ticket."

His attempt at humor wasn't working. He could see tears welling in her eyes.

"Hey," he said. "I'm taking a train ride. That's all. Then I get to DC, and Atwater and I have worked out ways to make contact."

"And after DC?"

There was no truthful answer for that, and Blake knew it. So he made the same empty promise soldiers have been making to their loved ones since the Spartans first packed to go to Thermopylae.

"Don't worry," he told Alia. "I'll be fine."

She just stood there, eyes about to brim, and he put his fingertips under her chin, softly tilting her head up so she was looking him in the eyes.

"Alia, you, Atwater, the Army . . . I'm as well prepared for this as a person can be. I know I'm a better warrior than anybody I'll meet along the way. I'm ready. Absolutely. Can you see that?"

She nodded, and he wiped away her brimming tears with the back of his hand.

"It's time to go," he told her.

She nodded a second time, picked up the shopping bag, and he slid the compartment door open. She was just turning to leave when he said her name again. She looked up at him.

"There's something I want you to know," he said, his voice low, so it would not carry. "My name. It's Blake. *Blake*."

She took in a breath through her nose, held it, and put her free hand behind his neck, guiding his face down to her level.

"Then may the Lord Jesus Christ guard and protect you, Blake." She whispered in his ear, kissed him on the cheek, and added, "Come back to me, you hear?"

She turned, walked down the corridor and, with a single, fleeting glance back, disappeared down onto the platform.

CHAPTER EIGHTEEN

❑ ❑ ❑

Union Station, Washington, DC

South Bend, Elkhart, Waterloo, Toledo, Sandusky—Blake stayed awake for all of those as he sat in his little compartment and read Grant Reinbolt's notebook and practiced writing in the other man's awkward hand. There was nothing in Reinbolt's file to indicate he had learning issues, only a set of high-school grades that showed frequent Cs and the occasional D. But Blake noticed he frequently transposed letters—the "g" and the "h" in "night" were switched almost every time, as were the "a" and the "y" in "prayer"—and, thinking back to his college psychology classes, Blake wondered if Grant Reinbolt was disgraphic. He saw that spelling error, and several like it, and he wondered what the ex-con's life might have been like had someone spotted that issue when he was young, maybe six or seven.

He'd also wondered what Reinbolt's life would be like for the next year or so. In years past someone grabbed for a snatch-and-switch—and particularly someone known to be associated with terrorist activity—would have gone to Guantanamo. But that was no longer an option.

So he was probably on his way to a cobelligerent nation, and not one of the first-tier countries. Not Britain, Australia, New Zealand, or Germany. No, Grant Reinbolt was on his way someplace a little closer to the back of beyond. Israel was the leading contender.

Closing his eyes, Blake tried to imagine what it would be like for a recent convert to Islam to spend the next year or so in the hidden holding cells of the Mossad. A recent convert who was also a known associate of terrorists.

Blake took a deep breath. He banished the thought from his mind and left the compartment so the coach attendant could make up the bed.

About the time the train was passing between Connellsville, Pennsylvania, and Cumberland, Maryland, Blake rose and went to the car's restroom compartment to wash up and shave before the rest of the railcar's occupants got up and began tying it up. He put on jeans and a T-shirt and wore those while he traveled through the morning, changing into the dress shirt and Dockers only after the train pulled out of the Rockville station, in Maryland, so his clothing would be both clean and unrumpled: a good first impression for the meeting he knew would be coming.

His dossier showed that Grant Reinbolt barely made it through basic training before the Marines determined he was psychologically unfit for duty and washed him out. Putting himself in Reinbolt's place—as, indeed, he was—Blake assumed the other man would try to look as soldierly as possible before he went to meet his Washington contacts. So Blake brushed his teeth, used the razor to level and straight-edge his military-length sideburns, and even cleaned the edges of his running shoes. By the time he was packed and the train was pulling into Washington's Union Station, he was as parade-ready as a person could be and still look as if he had spent fewer than 110 days in the service.

Now, duffel over his shoulder, he walked down the shopping concourse, its marble floors sounding with the footsteps of a thousand other travelers, and stepped out into the sunlight on Massachusetts Avenue.

That he was being observed, and observed closely, went without saying. Atwater would have people here, watching his arrival. And Raheesh would have at least one person looking for him, to pick him up.

His training told him to look for the watchers. But his common sense told him he could not. He was playing a role—that of a kid from the sticks, not an operative—so he did what came naturally. He gazed past the replica of the Liberty Bell in the plaza in front of the station, down Delaware Avenue, where the facade of the Rayburn Senate Office Building faced the street like a Roman temple, and looked past that, over late spring treetops, at the dome of the United States Capitol, white as a glacier in the sunlight.

Then he glanced at the taxis at the taxi stand. Outside one, a man with dark hair, a beard, a plain short-sleeve shirt, too-tight belt, and work pants of taxi drivers everywhere was holding a hand-lettered sign. Blake came a little closer and made out MR. REINBOLT. He walked up to the cabbie and held out his hand.

"I'm Grant Reinbolt."

The cabbie said something in rapid-fire Arabic and, when Blake pretended not to understand it, the other man smiled and explained, "I just said, 'Praise the name of Allah, the all-knowing and the merciful, who has seen you safely here after your long journey.'"

Blake shook his hand. "I'm sorry. My Arabic is still very poor."

"You are to be commended for learning it at all. My name is Qasid. Tell me, Mr. Grant: have you taken your lunch?"

"I haven't; the food on the train . . . well let's just say I doubt it was halal. Wrapped things they stick in the microwave . . . that doesn't really qualify as food."

Qasid smiled. "Then let me take you to a good place not far from here."

"The person I am to meet—will he be there?"

Qasid kept smiling. "And what might that person's name be?"

Raheesh ran through Blake's head. But he only knew that from the surveillance of Raheesh's study. As far as he knew, Grant Reinbolt was never told Raheesh's name. It was easy for Blake to look a little flustered as he replied, "I'm sorry. I don't know his name. All I know is that, when I meet him, I am to tell him that Ibrahim sends his greetings and his blessing."

Qasid smiled more broadly. "But of course. And no, the person you are to meet will not be at the restaurant. At this time of day, he will be at the coffeehouse."

"Could we go there then?"

"But of course."

Qasid's cab was a ten-year-old white Lincoln Continental with a small number in the back window, a license in the passenger's side of the front window, and "Baker Car Service" written in script on the front doors. The driver took Blake's duffel and put it in the trunk and seemed pleased when Blake took a seat not in the back but on the passenger's side, up front. Inside, like out, the car was immaculately kept, not new but extremely well cared for.

"It is your first time in Washington, Mr. Grant?"

"Actually in the city? I've been here before, but on school trips years ago." It was an answer, Blake knew, that would match whatever file they might have on Grant Reinbolt.

"There is much beauty here. Also much crime. But do not worry. We will keep you safe."

They drove for twenty minutes, and Blake evaded further casual interrogation with the oldest trick in the book: he pretended to doze off. He then feigned coming awake as they passed a tall office tower which he remembered Atwater told him was the vantage point from which the September 11 terrorists planned their flight path into the Pentagon, just across the river.

The cabbie turned into Bailey's Crossroads, an older shopping center, parking at the near corner, outside a Starbucks.

"We are here," he said with his fixed smile. "You may leave your bag in the trunk. It is quite safe."

Together the two men approached a group of men sitting around small patio tables on the sidewalk. The three older men wore the *taqiyah*—the short, rounded cap traditional in Islam—and long shirts, while the younger men looked much more metrosexual, right down to gold wristwatches and neck chains. Qasid said something to the older man, who nodded and stood.

"Grant Reinbolt?"

"Yes, sir."

The older man's face was impassive, his eyes deep and dark.

"We have much to speak of, young man. And I will begin with what is on my heart; you do not appear to be who you say you are."

CHAPTER NINETEEN

❑ ❑ ❑

Special Forces snipers possess an extraordinary ability to repress, by simple force of will, a racing heart or an attack of nerves. Even in the heat of battle, a trained sniper can lower his blood pressure and reduce his heart rate to that of a resting athlete, providing a stable platform from which to take a shot.

Without taking his eyes from those of the older man, Blake Kershaw called upon those skills right there, outside the Starbucks, calming himself. And after the few seconds it took him to do that, he cocked his head and asked, "Sir?"

The older man pointed with an open hand, indicating an empty wire patio chair. "Sit, young man."

Blake did as he was told, and the older man sat as well.

"My name is Raheesh," he said. "Did you hear of me . . . where you were kept?"

Blake shook his head. "Ibrahim told me he had brothers in the faith here in Washington. But he did not tell me your names, only that you were good men and closer to him than family."

"As he is to us, may Allah bless him." Raheesh turned to one of his compatriots. "Bring our young friend coffee."

The man whom Raheesh addressed looked at Blake, eyebrows up, and Blake said, "Black, please."

Raheesh laughed. "You drink it like a man. So many of these here take their coffee with a sugar cube in their teeth. They say it improves the flavor, but I think they never lost their childish love of sweets."

Blake didn't react.

"Then again, that is our culture—we were born to it," Raheesh said. He looked Blake in the eyes again. "But you were not. You were born Christian?"

Blake nodded. "Yes, sir."

Raheesh glanced at one of his colleagues. "This is how the young men of the southern states are raised. They learn to call their elders 'sir.'"

He turned back to Blake. "But not all who are born Christian were raised Christian. Were you?"

"My father," Blake said, going from the legend he'd memorized, "thought of himself as a preacher."

"But not a very good one, I take it." Raheesh sipped his coffee; Blake noticed he, too, drank his coffee black. "Yet if that was the faith in which you were raised, then your embrace of the one true faith—it is apostasy, is it not?"

It was a word Blake figured Grant Reinbolt would not know, so he simply asked, "Sir?"

Raheesh sat back. The sounds of the world at large came flooding back in: the traffic out on the main road, Jefferson Street; the sound of car doors as cabbies came in for their coffee break, the distant roar and whine of a jet on final approach to Reagan National Airport

"To turn one's back on one's faith: in Islam such a thing is unthinkable," Raheesh said.

"But if that faith is false, then you've turned your back on nothing. Isn't that right, sir?"

Raheesh smiled. "Jesus was a great prophet, beloved by Muhammad, may Allah bless his holy name. It was the followers of Jesus who suggested he was an abomination, that God would enter the filthy, unholy body of a man. It is their error that millions follow today. And it is essential to Islam that they recognize that error, that they embrace the true faith. Yet when I meet a young man such as yourself, one who claims he has—a young man who looks like so many others of those who live here, in the land of the great Satan, I am given to wonder why."

"You saved me."

"And Jesus did not?" Raheesh studied Blake's eyes. "It is not enough that you give Islam your gratitude, Grant Reinbolt. Islam is not part of your life; it *is* your life. We ask that you give it your heart, your spirit . . . your self. My young friend, can you do that?"

"I already have, sir."

"And if you have, what would you do for this faith?"

"Anything, sir. Anything at all."

Raheesh leaned forward a bit, his eyes fixed on Blake's. He turned to Qasid. "You remember where our young friend is to live while he is here with us?"

"With your nephew Tareef. At the Carousel Apartments, just across the way."

"Very good. Then take him there, my friend. But by all means feed him first. He has traveled far to join us."

Qasid did as he was told, taking Blake to one of a number of plain, small, Middle Eastern restaurants in a small, older strip mall, their plate glass front windows trimmed with gilt fringe and small Persian rugs. Qasid introduced the restaurant owner, an elderly man who bowed a lot, and made several suggestions from the menu. But then, oddly enough, Qasid left, so Blake ordered in deliberately halting Arabic that, even fractured as it was, visibly impressed the old restauranteur.

As plain as the restaurant was, the food was outstanding, just spicy enough to please a Green Beret who took most meals since boot camp with a bottle of Tabasco sauce within reach. And at the end of the meal, the owner brought, unbidden, a cube of vanilla cake—like a vanilla pound cake—with pomegranate sauce and a small cup of espresso-like coffee.

The cake was richer than Blake's usual fare, but he reasoned that a man one day out of prison would have a bottomless appetite for sweets, so he finished it, plus the cup of coffee and then another cup.

He was just setting the empty cup down when Qasid came back, a large plastic shopping bag hanging from either hand.

"How was your dinner, my brother?"

Blake smiled. "Best of the last few years. That's for sure."

"I have no doubt." Qasid held up the bags. "Some gifts, my brother. From Raheesh."

Blake looked in the first bag. It was three pairs of dress slacks, a couple of polo shirts, dress socks, and a black leather dress belt. The other bag held some collared shirts—short-sleeve and casual yet very presentable—two packages of underwear, and a Windbreaker-like jacket.

"Wow." He looked up. "How did you know my sizes?"

"Simple, my brother; I looked in your luggage." And then, when he saw Blake's expression, Qasid quickly added, "Do not be concerned, my brother. We are not thieves here; you are among friends."

Blake took out one of the collared shirts and looked at it. "Shouldn't I be wearing something more . . . traditional?"

Qasid offered a half-smile. "You mean the way Raheesh dresses?"

"Well . . . yeah."

Qasid laughed. "My brother, you are not married. And no woman is going to give you a second glance if you look like her father. The single man needs a little fashion, a little style, you know?"

Blake nodded. "Okay."

Qasid smiled broadly. "I did not buy shoes. They are best tried on, yes? But we can do that later: tomorrow, after you are rested. You would like to see the apartment now?"

"Sure." Blake reached into his pocket. "As soon as they bring me the check."

Qasid laughed. "There will be no check here today, my brother. The man who owns this restaurant—he is honored that you are taking your first meal here after your long journey. The meal is his way of welcoming you to the community."

Blake stood and turned to face the proprietor, who was standing a few feet away.

"Shukran jazilan," Blake told him, palms together, with a bow of his head.

The old man smiled, put a hand over his heart, and bowed in return.

"Okay," Blake told Qasid as he picked up the shopping bags. "Let's go look at the digs."

CHAPTER TWENTY

❑ ❑ ❑

Blake Kershaw had always been able to wake without an alarm clock. Even in the field in Afghanistan, he was able to look at his wristwatch in the dark before going to sleep, concentrate on the luminous dot representing the hour at which he needed to wake, and without fail he would come awake and alert within five minutes of that time.

He didn't have a wristwatch now; Grant Reinbolt had not been wearing one when they made the switch, nor had they found one in his duffel bag. Apparently, watching time had not been much of a priority while Reinbolt was *doing* time.

It didn't matter. Blake had been doing the same thing long enough that he had long since learned to manage the same trick without a watch.

It was just before five in the morning. It *felt* like just before five in the morning, and he sat up in bed and listened to the sounds of the two-bedroom apartment: the distant humming whirr of the refrigerator, the low and nearly inaudible buzz of some other appliance—the TV cable control box, probably. And yes, there was another sound, coming from the next room—low snoring.

The window in the bedroom was gray with predawn light. Alia taught him that Islamic groups differed over the exact times for prayer: many generated tables that listed times accurate down to the minute, and during the summer, the Islamic Center on Washington's Embassy Row often had taxi cabs lining adjacent streets at three in the morning as cabbies whose schedules prevented them from taking part in late-night prayers came in for *Fajr*, the predawn prayer time allowing them to get in their alloted five a day.

The reports from Marion told him Ibrahim's group tended toward regular prayer times rather than a to-the-minute schedule. But they always prayed, as did most Muslims around the world, at local sunrise.

Blake swung his feet to the floor. His apartment mate, in the next room, had not gotten up for Fajr. Blake was certain of that; the sound of any movement, however subtle, would have awakened him. And from the way Raheesh's nephew was sawing wood, it didn't sound as if he was planning to pray at dawn, either. Then again, the man appeared slightly drunk—slightly drunk and a little irritated at having company—when Qasid and Blake showed up the previous afternoon.

The nephew had mumbled something and then left, coming back long after Blake had turned in for the night. Qasid explained that the leader kept the apartment for the young man because he was the son of Raheesh's dead brother, but he was "about through with him" because he could not keep a job.

Which may have been true or may have been a story just to see how Blake reacted when there were no devout Muslims around. And as the apartment was leased in Raheesh's name, the cell leader would have had plenty of time to place surveillance in it, for two reasons—his ne'er-do-well nephew and the relatively unknown apartment's newest resident.

Blake was not about to give the cell leader a reason to doubt the new resident. He got out of bed, washed his hands, arms, face, head, and feet, and fetched Grant Reinbolt's *sajada*—his prayer rug.

An hour and a half later, Blake was showered and changed into a set of his new clothes. Raheesh's nephew was still snoring behind his bedroom door. The apartment, while clean—given the shiftlessness of the nephew, Blake assumed this was the doing of a cleaning lady—was cramped; a big-screen TV and a recliner only served to make the living room seem even smaller. It wasn't the sort of place that made you want to hang around. Gathering up Grant Reinbolt's Qur'an, notebook, and release papers, Blake put on his shoes and left the small apartment.

It was a beautiful morning: blue skies and none of the oppressive humidity that would characterize the Washington area in just a month or two. Blake stretched and looked at the sky, remembering that news reports said it also was a beautiful morning with blue skies the day the September 11 skyjackers flew a Boeing 757 into the Pentagon. The flight path would have passed almost directly over the spot on which he stood. He wondered if Raheesh and his cohort had been watching it from their tables outside the Starbucks.

As Blake stretched, he glanced both ways up and down the street. To the right—east—there was a gray Ford Focus with a single occupant, a man in the driver's seat. From where he was parked, the driver had a clear view of Blake, the sun mostly behind the car: a nearly perfect setup for photographing anyone coming out of the apartment.

It wasn't the direction he intended to travel, but Blake walked toward the car, Reinbolt's Qur'an open in his hands, his head down so anyone taking his picture would not get a clear shot of his face. As he got nearer, the driver busied himself with a BlackBerry, his head down as well.

Blake walked past. The car had District plates, the ones with the "www.dc.gov" tagline and not the "Taxation Without Representation" slogan that always got a rise from the tourists. Blake remembered reading in the *Washington Post* that fewer than four thousand vehicles in Washington used plates with the Web site address—almost all of them government vehicles whose agencies, for one reason or another, did not wish to display federal plates.

So the car was almost certainly tagged to a federal agency and, yes, the driver was sneaking a peek at Blake in the rearview mirror; when he saw Blake turn and look at the car, he bowed over his BlackBerry again.

Blake went to the end of the block, turned left, walked a block, waited for a break in traffic on Columbia Pike, and crossed it. He crossed the even busier Leesburg Pike at the shopping-center entrance and cut across the parking lot. From a hundred yards away, he could see Raheesh was already holding court at his outdoor table.

At twenty-five yards Raheesh noticed him, raised a hand in greeting, and said something to one of the men standing nearby. The man disappeared into the coffee shop as Blake was waving back.

"Good morning, my brother!" Raheesh pushed a chair back and offered it to Blake. "Did you sleep well?"

Blake offered a smile. "Very well, thank you, sir. I appreciate your hospitality."

Raheesh shook his head. "It is you who do us the honor with your presence. Ah, and here is Naib; one cannot do a proper breakfast at a coffeehouse, but perhaps this will slack your hunger until you can take a meal."

The second-in-command presented Blake with a steaming cup of black coffee and a cinnamon roll. Blake bowed and said, *"Shukran jazilan,"* bringing a smile from all the men.

Bowing over his food, Blake said, *"Bismillahi."* It was the traditional Muslim blessing, and its literal meaning was, "In the name of God." Alia had assured him Middle Eastern Christians often used it as their prayer before meals, as well. When he looked up, the men were smiling again.

"This is why I am pleased our new brother is sharing a roof with my worthless nephew," Raheesh told his companions. "I am sheltering him to honor my sister's name, but there are days when only the words of the Prophet—may Allah bless his name—keep me from turning the ingrate onto the street. But perhaps living in the company of a pious man will get Tareef off his recliner and into a mosque."

Blake didn't look up, much as he wanted to. For a Middle Eastern Muslim to speak so frankly about the shortcomings of his family was, from what Blake understood, virtually unheard of. Raheesh was much more complicated than Blake originally assumed. That meant he was intelligent, discerning; there was cunning behind his maxims and his rote references to Muhammad.

And that meant Raheesh was more dangerous than Blake first assumed. He would have to be careful.

So he did the only thing he could. He sipped his coffee, finished his cinnamon roll, and then he bowed his head and said, *"Al humdu lillah."* It meant, "All praise is due to God." Alia had assured him, in the Middle East, Christians oftentimes said that small prayer as well.

Blake looked up.

"What do you have planned for your day, my brother?" Raheesh smiled as he asked it.

Blake tapped the papers sticking out of his notebook. "I have to go to the federal courthouse in Alexandria and report to my probation officer."

"Yes." Raheesh nodded. "They keep you on a leash, yes? But we will make certain it is not a tight one. Then when you are finished, we will set you up with the job driving the taxi—a tidbit to convince the authorities that you are settling in."

"I appreciate that." Blake pursed his lips. "But I don't have a chauffeur's license. Matter of fact, I don't even have a license. Mine expired while I was inside."

"That is not a problem." Raheesh turned to Qasid. "Make sure to take our brother to the Walmart, the photo department, and get some passport-style photos. Get something that can be e-mailed."

"Of course."

An airliner, flaps extended and screaming, roared overhead on its way to Reagan National. All talk stopped, and some of the men looked up at the plane. Blake wondered what they were remembering.

Raheesh put his hand on Blake's shoulder.

"Qasid will take you wherever you need today, my brother. And before you go to the courthouse to see your officer, let our brother here buy you a better pair of shoes. Good ones, but not too . . . stylish, you know? People are impressed by shoes."

"Thank you, sir. But I can buy my own shoes. I have money."

"Of course you do." Raheesh patted his shoulder. The older man's fingers were long and thin, like those of a concert pianist. "But you do us a great honor if you allow us to buy them for you. Please."

Qasid's idea of a fashionable shoe was a Florsheim, which amused Blake, who let his guard down enough to say, "My father used to wear Florsheims. Called them his 'Sunday-go-to-meeting shoes.'"

"Your father," Qasid asked as Blake tried on a pair of oxfords, "he is still alive?"

"No." Blake kept his head down, avoiding eye contact as he laced the shoes. "He died."

"I am sorry, my brother."

"Don't be," Blake told him. "I'm not."

That's a lie. The thought registered with him with a jolt that would have sent a polygraph crashing off the table. Blake was certain he did nothing that sent a signal to Qasid, but still, somehow, what he just said felt as if it fell outside all the other untruths he had told Raheesh and the members of his group. Those were misinformation; this was a lie. And the fact it was exactly what Grant Reinboldt would have said did nothing to make it feel less a lie.

He stood, walked in the shoes a bit.

"These are great."

Qasid smiled. "Then wear them, brother. I'll go pay."

As they stepped out of the leathery air of the shoe store and into the still-fresh morning air outside, Blake paused, letting his eyes adjust to the sun. The shoe store was in a strip mall, and none of the cars parked there looked suspicious. But just across the street sat a Chevy Equinox he was pretty sure he saw back at the Starbucks, parked well out in the lot.

Smart. Whoever was watching him at the apartment realized he may have been made, so they changed cars. Either that, or whoever was following him was using a "moving tail," handing off the hunt from one vehicle to another. Equip the drivers with cell phones and ear buds, and that would be simple enough to do; no telltales like the lifting of a microphone or an unusual antenna on the vehicle.

He nearly checked his wrist, then remembered Reinboldt didn't wear a watch.

"What time is it?"

Qasid checked the face of his cellphone. "Nine-thirty, brother."

"We'd better go; I'm due at the courthouse in half an hour."

They got into Qasid's Continental, and Blake watched the Chevy with his peripheral vision as they pulled out onto the road. It waited until they were half a block away and then pulled out after them. It followed, usually with two or three cars between it and the cab.

"Qasid," Blake asked. "How are you going to make any money today if you never turn on the meter?"

"That thing?" Qasid waved a hand at the digital box mounted next to his GPS. "I hate it. Before 2007, all the driving around Washington was zone to zone. You got in my cab, you told me where you are going, and I could tell you right then how much it would cost. But these politicians say it encourages gypsy cabs; eight years I have been driving a cab here, practically since I got here, and not once have I seen a gypsy cab. But now anybody can turn on a meter and take the long way to the airport or drive the busiest way and charge double what we charged driving zones. These politicians let the crooks in."

"No kidding?" Blake was glad he'd hit a hot button with the cabbie. It kept him from checking his mirror and picking up on the tail following them. They pulled onto a divided highway, three lanes each way, and this time the Chevy stayed a lane over and several cars back.

It exited at the next ramp.

Handoff, Blake thought. He glanced back, trying to see if he could, in a single look, pick up on whoever took over the tail. It was hard to say; several of the cars behind them held only the driver and were new enough to be federal fleet vehicles.

"But today I'm hired by the day," Qasid continued. "So no meter."

"Who's paying you? Raheesh?"

Qasid grinned. "You've got more friends here than just Raheesh, my brother. Don't worry. We will take care of you."

And that's all he would say. Five minutes later they exited and pulled into the parking lot at the courthouse, a blocky glass-and-steel building, the sort of thing that looked modern back in the fifties. No car followed them in.

"You want to come in?"

Qasid's grin looked sheepish this time. "I'll stay out here, my brother. I do not care for these places."

"Don't blame you."

Blake had a picture in his head of what the probation offices would look like, and the reality matched almost perfectly. He checked in with a middle-age woman in something that looked like a bank-teller's cage. She looked at his papers, never looked up at him, and directed him to a waiting area furnished with scuffed vinyl chairs and the faint aroma of old, burnt coffee. There were two other men in the waiting area, and both gave him the same wary glance he gave them. He settled down with an issue of *Sports Illustrated* that promised a preview of the college football season that ended nearly five months earlier.

The other two men answered pages and left the waiting area. He was on his second magazine when the ceiling speaker asked, "Grant Reinbolt?"

This time, the woman behind the glass did look at him.

"Go to the door behind you and wait," she said. "I'll have to buzz you through. Your case officer is Mr. Jensen, third office on the right. Close the door behind you after you enter, please."

She looked back to her computer screen: *conversation over.*

The door buzzed. Blake opened it, stepped through, and closed it. He went to the third door on the right. A man in shirtsleeves was at a computer, his back mostly to Blake.

"Come in, young man. Shut the door."

The voice was familiar. And when "Mr. Jensen" turned around, it was Colsun Atwater.

Blake closed the door, went to the desk, got a piece of paper, and a pen and wrote: EVERYTHING I AM WEARING WAS GIVEN TO ME BY OUR SUBJECTS.

Atwater nodded, opened a briefcase, took out a small box with a digital readout and turned it on. He unplugged the computer on the desk, took the battery out of his BlackBerry, and checked the meter again.

"You're clean." He returned the radio-frequency meter to his briefcase. "That's what I'd expect. The individual cells that make up al-Qaeda aren't very sophisticated. Strictly off-the-shelf technology for the most part, although I'd watch myself indoors and in vehicles, if I were you. Places like that are pretty easy to keep an eye on. Cell phones and baby monitors will do the trick."

"Unlike you. What did you do with Mr. Jensen? Stuff him in a closet?"

Atwater laughed.

"He doesn't exist," he said. "Several of the intelligence agencies have an informal arrangement with Probation and Pretrial Services. You'd be surprised what you can learn from somebody who just spent a few years associating with criminals in a federal prison."

"Actually, that doesn't surprise me. But whatever happened to 'CIA is prohibited by law from collecting domestic intelligence'?"

"We get a little latitude when we're watching somebody with known ties to an overseas organization." Atwater gave a little half-shrug. "So what have you heard from your end?"

"They've set me up with an apartment; Raheesh is hoping his nephew will adopt some of my ways."

"If only he knew."

"If only." Blake sat in a blocky, vinyl-upholstered chair obviously provided by the lowest bidder. "They bought me clothes, fed me; they're setting me up with a job driving a taxi."

"Preventative maintenance," Atwater said. "I wouldn't start decorating that apartment if I were you. We picked up fresh intel from Raheesh's end. They're getting ready to ship you out just as soon as they can arrange transport. Within the month for sure. Probably sooner."

Blake sat forward. "Where?"

"London, to start with." Atwater rubbed his forehead. "After that, we don't know. Most of the long-term training these days is happening in Yemen; they've got a friendly government there. But some of the short-term stuff still goes down in Afghanistan, Pakistan, even though the Taliban and al-Qaeda are starting to lose the popularity contest in that neck of the woods. Still, mountainous borders are hard to protect, so both countries are a distinct possibility. If I had to take a guess where they're sending you . . . quite frankly, I wouldn't. These guys are being careful what they say when they're on the phone."

Blake heard the muffled sound of the door-lock buzzing in the hallway behind him. Some other parolee was heading to some other office for a reminder that, although he was walking around, he was not free.

"So the only thing we're sure of is that I'm headed to the Middle East."

"Ninety percent sure," Atwater agreed. "And I know; that's a needle in a haystack. But better a haystack than a hay field."

He pulled a map of Washington out of his briefcase. "You driving a cab jives with the intel we got out of Marion. Let's go through some drop points we'll be watching regularly."

Blake leaned over the map, and the two men compiled a short list of public places they were both familiar with.

When they were done, Blake stood.

"That's how I get information to you," he said. "What if you have something to get to me? How do we do that?"

"Like this," Atwater waved a hand at the room. "We'll find out where you're going to be, and I'll be there ahead of you."

"Only you?"

"Has to be. I'm the only one who's privy to 100 percent of the data on this. There are assets within CIA feeding me information, but they don't know the game plan."

"Okay." Blake stood. "But as for your assets, have them be a little more careful."

Atwater looked up. "Why's that?"

"The people tailing me. They're not covert enough. I picked the first one up just as soon as I left the apartment."

Atwater scowled.

"Blake, we knew where you were going yesterday and knew where you were coming this morning."

"I know that." Blake put his hand on the doorknob.

"So there's no need, Blake. CIA doesn't have anybody tailing you."

Blake let go of the doorknob. "But I saw them. Two different vehicles."

"And absolutely, I believe that," Atwater said. "You say somebody's following you? Then somebody's following you. But, son, I'm certain it's not one of us."

CHAPTER TWENTY-ONE

❑ ❑ ❑

The door was ajar so Blake knocked on it once and then pushed it open an inch or so.

"Good morning, Tareef. It's time for prayer."

A groan emanated from the darkness within, which smelled like pizza, stale whiskey, and old socks. "Wha—?"

"Time for prayer."

"Oh." There was the clunk of a bottle falling from a nightstand, a muffled curse. "I cannot pray, my friend. I am sick."

Blake grinned. At least Raheesh's nephew knew Islamic convention; illness was the one valid excuse a Muslim could offer for not rising to pray.

"Are you sure?" Blake asked.

"Quite sure, my friend. I am quite ill."

Blake grinned again. "Maybe if you did not stay out late and drink so much, you would feel better."

"You are joking, of course, my friend. You know that I do not drink."

"Then we'd better change the locks, Tareef. Someone has been getting loaded and sweating in your bed."

Silence.

Blake pushed the door open another inch. It caught on a shoe, clothing—something. "Come on, Tareef. You'll feel better if you pray."

"Please. I beg you, my friend. Let me sleep." Raheesh's nephew coughed. The symptom sounded as fake as the illness.

"All right, my brother," Blake said. "Be well."

He closed the door.

If anything, Blake supposed, it was he who needed to pray because he was having this predawn exchange every morning for two-and-a-half weeks, and he had to admit he took a secret delight in tormenting Raheesh's thirty-something slacker of a nephew. Truth be told, the shiftless drunk posed the least danger of anyone Blake had met in this community so far; he was too lazy to be a threat.

Then again, if the apartment was being watched, Blake was playing the part of the pious, recently converted Grant Reinbolt to the hilt. And staying on Raheesh's good side at the same time.

Still, deep inside, Blake knew if he'd ever encountered the likes of Tareef in the army, he would have dragged him out of bed and forced him to run ten kilometers before sunrise. And if he was feeling charitable, he would have let him wear shoes.

So a healthy measure of humility was in order. He aligned his *sajada* toward Mecca and began doing Muslim morning calisthenics. But inside he was asking his heavenly Father to make him more like Jesus.

Rasheesh was not kidding about the driver's license not being a problem. Two weeks earlier Qasid delivered a Virginia chauffeur's license and a District of Columbia taxicab certificate, both bearing Grant Reinbolt's name and the photo they shot at Wal-Mart. And while Blake had yet to meet the "McNamara" whose name was on the side of the yellow Ford taxi, the car and a fleet gas card were delivered to him the day he received the license, with instructions to wait in the taxi queue at Union Station when not actively engaged and to give his fares at the end of the day to Raheesh, retaining a hundred dollars in twenties, tens, fives, and ones so he could make change the next day. At the end of his shift, he was to drive the taxi home. He was even allowed to take it out at night if he so wished, although he never did. The Grant Reinbolt he was presenting was dedicated to the faith and would never do anything so frivolous as head out to a night club.

Then again, Blake was never much of a clubber himself. He liked girls; he just didn't care to go out with the kind that enjoyed hanging out in meat markets.

He finished dressing, pocketed the wallet containing his license and his gas card, picked up the zippered pencil case containing his till for making change, and stepped out into the light of a summer dawn. Unlocking the taxi and popping the hood, he made a show of checking the oil while he glanced up and down the street. It was the Chevy Equinox pulling the early watch this morning.

Blake was 95 percent certain they were federal. They could have been Virginia state police working undercover as well, but feds seemed the better bet.

The question was, which feds? Immigration probably had their reasons to keep an eye on Raheesh's cell. So did Internal Revenue, seeing as a lot of the income flowing into the group probably went unreported. And many Muslim cells funded their operations through heroin trafficking and counterfeiting; that alone could attract the attention of DEA, U.S. Customs, Secret Service, ATF, or the FBI.

Then there was always the possibility the tail was actually Raheesh's people or people he hired. The drivers of the cars did not look Middle Eastern; one was African American, and the other two appeared Anglo.

Then again, Grant Reinbolt didn't look Middle Eastern either.

Blake slid the dipstick back into its tube, closed his hood, started his taxi, and headed downtown.

"Airport, please," the man said as he got into the cab.

Blake looked up. "Dulles?"

"No. Reagan."

An out-of-towner: most Washingtonians still referred to it as "National."

Blake started the cab. "What airline?"

The man, bent over a PDA, didn't say anything.

"Sir?"

The guy looked up. Blake had the quickest glimpse of gray eyes. "Sorry. Delta."

"You got it."

Blake pulled out into the flow of traffic headed to and from the Hill, passed through the Greco-Roman marble of downtown Washington, and headed across the river. He was just pulling into National when his fare cleared his throat.

"Excuse me. Cabbie?"

"Sir?"

"I'm earlier than I thought. You know where the Crystal City Hilton is?"

"Sure. Although I'm pretty sure they have a shuttle, if you want to save the extra fare."

"I'll take the shuttle back. Drive me over there. I have a colleague I can meet with while I'm killing time."

"No problem." Blake turned on his blinker, weaved out through a thicket of cars doing kiss-and-fly dropoffs, inched past a cop who gave him a scowl, and made the two-block run over to the hotel.

"That's twenty-one," he said as he stopped the meter.

The man passed a twenty and a five forward. "Keep the change."

He was already out of the cab when Blake noticed the slip of paper between the bills.

OUT OF PORTICO AND HANG A RIGHT, the block letters read. PICK UP FARE WAITING ON SIDEWALK.

Blake left the hotel, turned right. On a deserted stretch of sidewalk near the hotel's loading dock, a man in a suit coat stepped to the curb.

Atwater.

He was carrying a leather attaché, the kind in which you'd put a laptop. He opened it as soon as he got in the cab, fiddling with something that looked to be about notebook-computer size but wasn't a notebook computer. There was a click, and the dispatch screen on Blake's dash flickered and then read: NO SIGNAL.

"There we go," Atwater said. "Might have just been your two-way there, but Mike—that was Mike you just dropped off—was getting a reading in here. So he sent me a text, advised an R-F block, just in case. How you been?"

"Good. What's up? I thought I wasn't supposed to see you again until the next probation report."

"That's a week away, and our latest intel from Raheesh Central is that they will probably be moving you by then. Maybe long before then. Like the next couple of days."

Blake pulled away from the curb. "Where?"

"Pakistan. Just head back to the airport; we'd better not keep you off-air too long; they might wonder what's up."

Blake cut up a side street and got back onto Jefferson Davis Highway. "Where in Pakistan?"

In the mirror he could see Atwater scowl. "That's just it. We don't know."

Blake shrugged. "Then I play it by ear."

"I don't know about that."

Blake glanced to the mirror again. "How's that?"

Atwater was looking right back at him in the mirror. "I need to know where you are, guy. In case I have to get you out. In case I have to intervene to prevent a strike while you're still in-country: taking out a camp while you're still in it. This is risky enough. We don't want to make it a one-way trip."

"You need the information."

"And for that we need to get you back."

Blake pulled into the airport. He'd been driving slowly, below the limit, but it was so close it was hard to keep the ride anything more than a short dash.

"Colsun . . ." He looked up, at the mirror again. "I didn't come this far to stop now."

"And I didn't bring you this far to kill you for no good reason. If we can't come up with a definite twenty on wherever they're sending you, I'm bringing you in. And that's not negotiable." The CIA man handed Blake a ten. "Keep the change."

CHAPTER TWENTY-TWO

❑ ❑ ❑

Blake got the message on his dispatch display at lunchtime: BAILEY'S CROSSROADS. STARBUCKS. WAITING OUTSIDE. ONE PSGR TO MASS AVE / EMBASSY ROW.

Intrigued, Blake drove across town to the Starbucks and, sure enough, his fare was a tall, bearded man wearing a pajama-like *salwar kameez* suit in a light tan fabric, a long brown vest over it, a traditional cotton kufi on his head, and a pair of plain brown sandals on his skinny, tanned feet.

Raheesh.

Or at least Blake's ostensible fare was Raheesh because, seeing as the man was Grant Reinbolt's benefactor, Blake did not start the meter.

Raheesh got in back, apologizing as he did so, "We are watched sometimes, you know, my brother? And it is best if I look like any other customer. Tell me, my brother, have you ever been to the Massachusetts Avenue mosque? No? Then you will come to prayer with me this day. It is the most beautiful mosque in Washington, perhaps on all the East Coast."

Blake headed down the aging suburban sprawl of Leesburg Pike and got onto Interstate 395, heading northwest, into the capitol. Washington's icons—the tall obelisk of the Washington Monument, the white egg of the Capitol, the columned dome of the Jefferson Memorial—were visible off and on, but mostly the city looked to Blake like a city, overcrowded, and anathema to a country-bred man like him.

They were exiting the interstate when Raheesh's cell phone rang.

"A thousand pardons, my brother," the older man said to Blake. Then he opened his phone and, in English, asked, "Hello?"

In the rearview mirror Blake saw him smile.

"Aap barkat dena, bahai; aap kesay hein?"

Bless you my brother; how are you? Blake translated it silently, without even thinking: Raheesh was speaking Urdu.

Blake kept translating: *"Yes, all is ready, and the Westerner we were waiting for is here. He is a brother; he will do as we ask. The camp is in the same place? The Garj Valley, south, near the Afghanistan border? Good, good. And there is no trouble? Excellent. We need to transport right away."*

Raheesh listened without speaking for a good minute. Then he started speaking again.

"No, of course you are right. Dulles will be watched, and the New York airports are no better. Boston is perfect. Yes, an e-ticket on the Northwest flight from Logan, and then have him stay at the usual place; there is good train access. How soon can we do this? Tomorrow? That is perfect. Make the arrangements, and we will get him to Boston by six tomorrow."

Blake flicked the turn signal, changed lanes, and pretended to be absorbed in the chore of driving. When Raheesh closed his phone, Blake looked up at the mirror.

"My Arabic is worse than I thought; I didn't understand a word of that."

Raheesh laughed. "It was not Arabic, my brother. It is a simple hillsman's tongue, one I learned as a child. Some of our brothers, they can sound out the Arabic script and make the noise of the holy Qur'an but have no idea what the words mean. It is a shame, and in my estimation it is not what the Prophet meant when he said that Allah's voice can only be heard in the language of the Prophet. After all, you are learning the language of our faith; you are quite proficient in it, in fact. Why is it we cannot say the same of those who were born into Muslim families?"

They talked casually about this for the remaining five minutes of the drive, Blake feigning ignorance about some of the finer points of Arabic, Raheesh answering his questions, and Blake thinking *Garj Valley, Garj Valley, Garj Valley* the whole way.

It wasn't really as if he was likely to forget it, though.

Garj was the Urdu word for "thunder."

Embassy Row on Massachusetts Avenue looked like a scene straight out of Mary Poppins: stately Victorian mansions, many with fences and gates, the flags and brass plaques the only indication these were homes to ambassadors and their assistants rather than the children of old money.

There was no parking available in front of the mosque, a white stone building with archways leading into a courtyard and a single minaret, so Blake drove down a side street and parked his taxi at the end of a row of several others, along the side wall of some embassy.

Raheesh smiled as Blake opened his door. "Ah, Grant, my brother, you are in for a treat. This mosque was dedicated in 1957 by your President Eisenhower, and while it is made of marble quarried from the hills of Alabama, it is furnished with items from the nations that helped build it. The chandelier and the minbar are from Egypt, the tiles from Turkey; the carpet was a gift from the shah of Iran."

It was near prayer time, and men, most of them bearded, were walking toward the mosque. Some of them recognized Raheesh and greeted him, and Raheesh introduced Blake: the Muslims shook his hand and looked at Blake with ill-disguised curiosity.

The entrance to the mosque was at the far end of the courtyard, but rather than going in there, Raheesh and Blake went through a side door and downstairs to a large, carpeted room where they removed their shoes and socks before entering a large, green-tiled room with a troughlike basin running the length of its wall. Following Raheesh's example, Blake knelt there and washed his feet, his head, his arms, and his hands. Then they went upstairs.

The mosque was like a little piece of the Middle East transported to metropolitan Washington. The tile work was intricate and covered the columns and walls. The hand-woven rug was huge, covering the entire floor. And while the space was impressive, it was nothing compared to the vastness of a Western cathedral. About a hundred men were in the mosque, and even with that number it was crowded.

"On Fridays, the Muslim Sunday," Rahessh whispered to Blake, "people bring their own rugs and fill the courtyard, sometimes even the sidewalks down the block."

Then the mullah arrived and called them to prayer.

Blake recited the Arabic with the rest of the men in the mosque. But inside he was saying his own prayer: *Lord Jesus, I leave tomorrow. Please bless me and help me fulfill my mission. Please help me get this information to Atwater.*

In unison with the rest, he knelt and lowered his head to the floor. *And please, heavenly Father, in Jesus Christ's name, I ask that you guard and protect Alia while I am gone.*

The last part surprised him; he hadn't seen it coming. But he was pleased at the thought of her under heavenly protection.

At the conclusion of prayer, as they went downstairs to retrieve their footwear, Raheesh took Blake by the elbow.

"Grant, my brother, there are some men here I need to meet with. They will drive me back to the coffee shop when we are finished. Will you forgive me for leaving you like this?"

"Of course, sir. I need to get back to work anyhow." That was what Blake said, but inside he was thinking, *Thank you, Jesus.*

With the rest of the men, he walked out the front of the courtyard and spotted the car parked half a block down the street: a gray

Ford Focus, one person in the driver's seat—the same car he spotted in front of the apartment the first day.

He couldn't have a tail. Not for what he had to do. Blake thought about this as he walked back to the cab, unlocked it, and got in.

The Focus was parked on the far side of Massachusetts Avenue, pointed southeast, back in the direction from which Blake came when he arrived at the mosque.

Blake started the cab, backed into a driveway, and turned around, coming out to the avenue as a crowd of men emerged from the mosque. Timing his departure with a gap in the crowd of pedestrians, he turned right onto Massachusetts, the opposite direction to the Focus.

In his rearview mirror, he could see the Ford pull out and then stop; cars were leaving up and down the street, and there was no gap in the traffic. The next right was Waterside Drive, and Blake took it, driving as fast as the narrow street would allow and emerging at a narrow angle onto Rock Creek Parkway.

There would be a second tail. If whoever was following him was competent at all, there would have to be a second tail. But he was pretty sure they didn't have eyes on him yet. Passing two cars, he drove nearly twenty miles over the speed limit, prayed no DC police were on this particular stretch of road, and got off at the first exit: Beach Drive Northwest. This put him near the National Zoo, and he went up to Harvard Drive, made a hard left, and entered the zoo's parking area.

Banners hung from lightposts, extolling the charms of Chinese pandas. Children crowded on the sidewalk. Blake drove through the parking area until he found three taxis parked along a curb in a waiting area. He pulled in behind them and killed the engine.

He waited. Three minutes passed. Five. No government sedan prowled the parking lot. Blake restarted the engine, left the zoo, and went back down the parkway, exiting onto US-29 and following it across the Potomac. In a matter of minutes, he was pulling into the parking area of one of the five drop points that he and Atwater agreed upon after his arrival in Washington.

CHAPTER TWENTY-THREE

❑ ❑ ❑

Like most people in America, Blake was familiar with the image of the bronze-and-marble sculpture standing on Arlington Boulevard, just outside the National Cemetery. Seventy-eight feet tall, it depicted five Marines and a Navy hospital corpsman raising the flag over Mount Suribachi on the island of Iwo Jima—an image so well-known most people referred to the sculpture as the "Iwo Jima Memorial," even though its actual designation is "Marine Corps War Memorial."

It was based on what is perhaps the most famous combat photograph of all time, even though Blake, like most Green Berets, was known to remind Marines that the image was not technically a combat photo at all. The six-man detail was sent to the summit of Suribachi not to hoist the flag but to replace it. The actual flag-raising over Iwo Jima took place earlier in the day; and, as it was the first time a hostile force planted a foreign flag on Japanese soil, the original flag was requisitioned by James Forrstal, the secretary of the Navy. So the six men were sent to the summit to replace it with a larger flag and, according to one of the survivors' accounts, went swimming afterward. That being the case, it became a Green Beret tradition to remind Marines that the image of their most famous combat moment was actually the conclusion of an officer's souvenir hunt; the remark was almost always a guaranteed fight-starter.

Souvenir hunt or not, Blake knew that three of the six men depicted in the sculpture did not live to leave the island of Iwo Jima. The image may have been recorded in an interlude, but it was one of the bloodiest battles of World War II, and in his mind that made them heroes, souvenir hunt or not.

He saw the film Clint Eastwood had made about the survivors of the flag-raising. The movie was about the exploitation of heroes, but what Blake recalled most vividly about it was the men atop the mountain, hearing muffled, subterranean explosions—the sounds of Japanese troops, burrowed deep within the mountain, taking their own lives with hand grenades.

Spetznaz GRU—Russia's counterpart to the American Special Forces—supposedly had a similar tradition, always reserving one hand grenade to ensure an operative would not be captured alive. And while Blake understood the tactical importance of not allowing intelligence to fall into the hands of the enemy, and understood as well that death in combat was an integral part of war, ending it all by hugging a hand grenade struck him as stupid and little more. Killing yourself was just doing the enemy's job for him; if Blake was going to go out in combat, it was going to be *in* combat, taking as many of the opposition with him as possible.

He pulled into a space in the memorial's parking lot, killed the taxi's engine, and sat there for a moment forcing back the adrenaline-induced stream of consciousness and concentrating on the task at hand.

In the door pocket of the taxi was a stack of Post-it notes and a felt-tip pen. Uncapping the pen, Blake wrote:

Pakistan—Garj Valley,
south, near border w/A.
Depart tomorrow via Boston,
stopping London.
20 in London near
major rail junction.

Then he opened the glove compartment door and took out an individually wrapped Huggies infant diaper he purchased just for this contingency.

Locking the cab, Blake walked down a small berm and onto the sidewalk encircling the memorial and the broad lawn surrounding it. It was early afternoon and getting muggy. Only a couple of other cars were in the lot, and a total of five other people were visible on the memorial grounds, all of them focused on the monument.

He followed the sidewalk to his right, coming to an installation of three green Porta Potties, the worn ground around them mute testimony to the fact that, while designed to be temporary fixtures, the three portable toilets had been in place for years.

Stepping into the one nearest the parking lot, Blake closed the door and locked it, the heat of the day making the scent of antiseptic and urine even more intense in the closed, warm space. He pulled the Post-it note off its stack and slipped it up, inside the plastic toilet-paper dispenser, double-checking to make sure it could not be knocked loose when someone pulled on the roll.

Next he opened the disposable diaper completely, and then balled it up upon itself so it appeared used. Stepping outside the portable toilet, glad for the fresh air, he checked to make certain he was not under surveillance and then stooped, set the diaper on the ground at the side of the Porta-Pottie, and walked back to his cab.

From the driver's seat he examined his handiwork. The disposable diaper was clearly visible, a dot of white at the base of the distant green portable toilet. And because it appeared to be a used diaper, it would stay there. Do-gooder citizens might pick up a Coke can or a scrap of newspaper and carry it to the nearest trash can, but a used diaper crossed the line. It wouldn't be removed until the Park Service sent their clean-up detail through at dawn. So when Atwater drove through later in the day, checking their agreed-upon drop points, the marker would be there, signaling a drop had been made.

Game on. There was nothing more to do here.

Blake started the cab and drove away.

CHAPTER TWENTY-FOUR

The door to the apartment was unlocked when Blake got home, and he opened it cautiously. The living room was dark.

"Tareef?"

"He is not here."

A table lamp came on.

It was Raheesh. "I hope I did not startle you, my brother."

Blake slipped off his shoes at the door. "Not at all. To what do I owe the pleasure?"

Raheesh stood and shook his hand. "The time has come, my brother. Qasid will be here to pick you up tomorrow."

Blake lifted his eyebrows, hoping it came across as surprise. "To pick me up?"

Raheesh clapped him on the shoulder. "Sit, my brother."

Blake sat on Tareef's worn recliner, facing Raheesh, who took the sofa.

"I cannot tell you where we are sending you, my brother. It is best for all if I do not. Should you be questioned, you cannot tell what you do not know."

Blake nodded. "That makes sense. What do I bring?"

"Dress comfortably, as if you are leaving for a day of work. Blue jeans are entirely acceptable. Bring your wallet: what you would normally carry. Nothing else."

"Not my Qur'an? My prayer rug?"

Raheesh shook his head emphatically. He leaned forward on the couch.

"My brother, you are now a soldier in a war. And Islam understands that sometimes a soldier cannot stop to pray, so then the battle becomes his prayer. And in your case one of your great weapons is that you do not look like this, yes?"

Raheesh moved his hand from his chin to his knees, taking in his features, his beard, his mode of dress. "So we must preserve that weapon, my brother. As you travel, whenever you are where infidels might see you, you cannot pray; you cannot read the holy Qur'an. This is essential to our cause, my brother. I know it sounds contrary to logic, but you will honor us most by not appearing to be observant at all. We need you to be invisible."

Blake nodded slowly, trying to convey the impression that this was all dawning on him for the first time. It was what Raheesh would expect from Grant Reinbolt, who was not the sharpest knife in the drawer.

Which made what Blake had to say next quite risky.

"Raheesh," he said. It was the first time he had addressed the older man by name. "There could be a problem."

The other man's face grew solemn.

"Ever since the first morning I left the apartment," Blake said. "I have seen cars—cars parked where I could be watched. I think . . . no, I'm *certain* I am being followed. And I am worried that, if they see me leave, they may intervene, may stop what we are about to do."

It was the first absolutely truthful statement he had made to the older man.

Raheesh nodded slowly. "And this is further proof that we chose well when we chose you, my brother. Your FBI follows us. Sometimes I believe they are trying to frighten us. But do not be concerned. Qasid will be here at six in the morning to pick you up."

Blake cocked his head. "And the FBI?"

"Do not worry." Raheesh smiled. "We shall take care of them."

CHAPTER TWENTY-FIVE

❏ ❏ ❏

Blake opened his eyes at 4:25, and the alarm went off five minutes later. This last morning, he decided to let Tareef sleep off the night before in peace, and Blake went through the motions of Muslim morning prayer more slowly, lingering as he bowed prostrate, picturing in his mind how a devout follower of Islam would linger over his prayers if he thought they were the last he would be able to say for the immediate future.

Raheesh had said to bring his wallet, and because Raheesh and his colleagues funded everything, Blake had all the money Grant Reinbolt left Marion with, plus what he earned in two weeks of driving the cab. And because it was in cash, with no taxes reported or paid, Blake's total cash on hand came to a little over twenty-five hundred dollars, all of it in large bills. He folded the wad up and stuck it in his jeans pocket.

He had just put on his shoes—the Florsheims, which looked a little odd with the jeans but, old-man shoes or not, were comfortable—when a knock came at the door. Blake opened it, left his apartment keys on the entry table, and stepped out to shake hands with the ever-grinning Qasid.

"Good morning, my brother," the taxi driver said. "Did you sleep well?"

"Hardly at all," Blake said, although that was a lie. For reasons unfathomable to him, he always slept like a baby the night before a mission.

"Ha! You are an honest man."

They walked toward a small, dark Toyota Yaris.

"Continental in the shop?" Blake asked.

Qasid grinned. "This is my brother's car. This morning I thought we would just use this."

Blake quickly scanned the street. The Ford Focus was holding position in its usual spot. He debated saying something. But Raheesh said not to worry; to bring it up again might be construed as an insult. That, or a lack of confidence. He held his peace.

But he kept his eye on the Ford in the mirror as they pulled out and headed down the street in the opposite direction. The FBI car's headlamps came on, and it left its parking spot, following them.

They passed more parked cars, a bread truck idling in a restaurant driveway. The Ford closed some distance. And then, just as the FBI car came even with the restaurant, the bread truck backed out rapidly, T-boning the Focus.

"Hold on, my brother," Qasid said. The little Toyota picked up speed and tilted as they careened around a corner. Blake could just see men standing in the street, gesturing at one another, at the accident scene. Qasid drove a hundred yards further and darted into a convenience-store parking lot. His white Continental was sitting there, two men standing next to it.

"Quickly, my brother!" Qasid yanked on the parking brake, threw the transmission into neutral, and jumped out almost before the little car came to a halt. Blake jumped out his side, and the two waiting men leapt into the Toyota and drove away.

"Into my car before the other tail comes," Qasid said.

They got in, Qasid taking the driver's side, but not starting the engine. Thirty seconds later the silver Chevy Equinox flashed by, going well above the speed limit.

Qasid waited until the FBI car was out of sight. Then he started the Lincoln, the headlamps coming on automatically.

"Okay," he said. "Now we can go."

He took the shortest route to the interstate, and they headed for downtown Washington.

"Look in the back, my brother," he told Blake.

Blake looked. There was a green canvas duffel, and when he opened it, he found another pair of jeans, some Dockers, two polo shirts, a long-sleeve shirt, underwear, a shaving kit, and a pair of Ray-Ban Aviators.

"Not much, but enough to get you where you are going, yes?"

"I appreciate it."

Qasid grinned. "It is our people who thank you, Grant Reinbolt."

They took an exit for downtown. Grant looked around.

"We're headed for the train station?"

Qasid nodded. "The Acela. You ever ride it before? It feels like you are on an airplane, my brother. It will have you in Boston before sunset."

He handed Blake a train ticket and a manila envelope. "When you get to Boston, take a cab to Logan airport. It is only ten minutes from the South Station, and you will have plenty of time to have dinner before your flight. You are booked on the Northwest Flight to Gatwick, an e-ticket, and when you get to Gatwick, you should take another cab to the Grosvenor Hotel, near Hyde Park. Just leave the room on the credit card it was reserved under. You can remember that?"

Blake nodded.

"You will be contacted the next morning," Qasid said. "So relax the first day. Sightsee. The London Eye, you know? But stay around the hotel the second day. Do not worry about finding us; we will find you. This, too, is clear?"

Blake nodded.

"Then Allah bless you, my brother."

"And you." They shook hands.

Blake got out of the cab, and with a single wave Qasid pulled away.

Walking inside, Blake paused just beyond the station entrance to check the envelope. It held an Irish passport, slightly dog-eared and with several entry and exit stamps, his picture, Grant Reinbolt's name, and a Dublin address. And stuffed next to the passport were two bundles of bills: a thousand dollars and a thousand euros in cash.

All that money to pay for two cab rides and a dinner.

Yep. That would cover it.

He found the gate number and headed for his train.

CHAPTER TWENTY-SIX

❑ ❑ ❑

Defense Intelligence Analysis Center
Bolling Air Force Base, Washington, DC

The director of the Defense Intelligence Agency was, like all his predecessors back to 1961, a three-star military officer. He was a lieutenant general in the Army, a West Point graduate who saw combat experience as both an armored and an infantry officer until moving into intelligence. That field proved to be his heart's calling, and he was still occasionally surprised when he looked at a calendar and realized he had worked in that netherworld now for more than two decades.

A slender five-foot-eight, the director was small of stature for a general officer, and he was slightly built as well, despite the fact he ran three miles every morning and put in regular time at the gym. At fifty-nine, his face was still boyish despite his receding gray hair, and he wore steel-framed glasses for his near-sightedness. He also had a naturally kind face, and at the Baptist church where he worshipped, visitors often mistook him for the pastor. Physically, he did not look like a man accustomed to command. The fact he commanded the military's senior intelligence organization spoke volumes about the power of his mind and the force of his personality.

The office door opened, and a young woman looked in.

"General? Colonel Musashi and two gentlemen from the British embassy are here. I didn't see anything on your Outlook . . ."

"That's fine, Vicki. It's something I set up. Go ahead and send them in."

The assistant disappeared. Ten seconds later two suited men and an Army officer—an Asian-American woman—entered the office.

"Reggie." The director shook hands with the older of the two men; then he turned to the colonel. "Angela Musashi, this is Reginald Culpepper. Officially, he is cultural attache with the UK embassy. Reg, Angie is our chief in the Directorate of Human Intelligence."

They shook hands, and if Musashi suspected that "cultural attache" was a cover—as the director well knew she would—she did not show it.

"And may I have the honor of presenting . . ." Culpepper indicated the man next to him. ". . . my colleague, John Chambers."

"Officially, I am nothing over here," Chambers said with a smile as he shook hands with the two Americans. "But back home I run the Pakistan desk—MI6."

"Ah, candor." The director laughed. "I'm afraid that's a quality you'll have to lose if you hope to get far in the intelligence business, John. Can I get you gentlemen anything? Soft drinks? Coffee? Tea?"

"Thank you, Ron," Culpepper said, "but we're fresh from breakfast, and we shan't be long."

"All right then." The director held a hand out to the conference table. Then he shut the office door and joined them.

"Reggie," he said, "I kept this to a short complement, as you requested: just Angie and me. Although I must admit, I'm curious as to why you asked."

"We have some information we have to keep tightly compartmented," Culpepper said.

"Information?" The colonel put her hand to her chin. "Protocol calls for you to share any intelligence with your counterparts at CIA, sir. They disseminate it through the National Clandestine Service; and if the Director of National Intelligence decides it's pertinent to us, NCS hands it on."

"Yes," Culpepper agreed with a single nod. "That is the usual protocol. But we have had . . . certain misadventure with intelligence shared with CIA in the past, and I'm afraid I only know its director casually, whereas Ron and I have known each other since his London posting. Quite frankly we trust you more, and this is information we can only share with someone whom we trust implicitly. Prudence demands we share it as soon as possible with someone on your side of the pond."

"Well, I appreciate that, Reggie." The director willed himself to sit back in his chair, to avoid looking as interested as he felt. "And to save you from asking, I will assure you that neither Colonel Musashi nor I will pass along a word of what you are about to tell us—not within our agency or outside it—unless we have informed you first."

He glanced at the colonel, who nodded her agreement.

"Thank you, General," Culpepper said. "Then in that case I shall yield the floor to Mr. Chambers."

"Right, then." Chambers leaned forward, his hands folded and on the table. He looked so British he could have come from Central Casting—Harris tweed sport coat, an oxford-cloth shirt a bit heavy for the season, and a thick woolen tie. "As you know, al-Qaeda and the Taliban have been fairly tight ever since Osama bin Laden arranged the assassination of Amad Shah Massoud, which pretty much cut the legs out from under the Northern Alliance. And while the official posture of Pakistan is that the Taliban is an insurgent organization, Asif Ali Zardari has made some major concessions to them, such as imposing sharia law in some provinces and preventing the education of girls. The Pakistani Army still raids Taliban camps—they have to, or the international pressure would grow too great—but eradicating the Taliban is far too tall an order for them, as it has been for everyone to date, so the camps persist. Even the recent slight turn of Pakistani public opinion against the Taliban hasn't diminished the presence of these camps significantly."

He looked up at the two Americans, who had settled back in their chairs. "Then again, you already know all this. My apologies, General, Colonel . . . I'm accustomed to briefing politicians who refuse to read newspapers."

The director chuckled and motioned for Chambers to go on.

"Anyhow," Chambers continued, "as you know, this climate has encouraged al-Qaeda to keep much of their higher-level training in Pakistan, particularly training for those units with targets within Western nations. And we have human intelligence on one of those camps that was urgent enough to request this meeting with you."

"And," the colonel asked, "that information is . . . ?"

"That al-Qaeda is preparing a team to insert a weapon or weapons of mass destruction into your Eastern Seaboard—and that team is approaching the final stages of its preparation in Pakistan."

For several seconds the room was silent. The director looked down at the dark oak of the conference table, framing his thoughts. Then the colonel spoke up, saving him the trouble.

"What sort of weapons, sir? Chemical? Biological?"

The MI6 man folded his hands. "We have not ruled those out, Colonel. But early indications would seem to suggest nuclear."

The room fell silent again. The air conditioning started up, filling the background with a blanket of soft white noise.

"So," the director said, surprised his voice sounded so even, "you have information suggesting a nuclear strike against the eastern United States by a nongovernment organization is a viable possibility."

Both the British officials nodded.

"And the delivery method?"

Culpepper looked at Chambers, who shook his head and said, "I'm afraid we've yet to develop that information."

Another silence followed. Then the colonel spoke up.

"Mr. Chambers . . ." She closed her eyes, took a breath, opened her eyes. "The people on the Hill and in the White House tend to be extraordinarily skeptical when we come to them with reports of WMDs these days. The intelligence would have to be . . . quite compelling: a lot more than someone looking at satellite imagery."

"The intelligence is impeccable," Culpepper said. "We are absolutely certain of what we are telling you today. True, we don't know the nature of the weapon with absolute certainty, but we do know there is a weapon and it is definitely coming your way."

The two Americans looked at each other.

"Reg," the director asked, "what's your source?"

Now it was the Brits' turn to look at one another.

"I'm afraid we can't tell you that specifically," Chambers said. "Only that we have an asset who is close to the organization, and the credibility of this asset is absolutely unimpeachable."

The colonel leaned forward. "How close to the organization is this . . . asset?"

"Quite close," Chambers said. "But that's all I can say, General. I trust you'll understand. I must protect my people."

"I've been there," the director said. "And I understand. We'll put some eyes on this team, using full discretion of course, and develop our own intelligence, independently of yours."

"That was our hope," Culpepper said, visibly relieved.

"Okay." The colonel took out a small notebook and a pen. "We can do that. Where in Pakistan is this camp?"

"Quite near the Afghanistan border," Chambers told her. "A place called the Garj Valley."

Then the Lord said to me,
"The prophets are prophesying lies in my name.
I have not sent them or appointed them or spoken to them.
They are prophesying to you false visions, divinations,
idolatries and the delusions of their own minds."

Jeremiah 14:14

CHAPTER TWENTY-SEVEN

❑ ❑ ❑

Grosvenor House Hotel, London

Blake washed his hands, left his bathroom, and wondered why London, where the modern flush toilet was invented, seemed to have the most anaemic plumbing of any Western city.

Several of the guys in his Special Forces team claimed that the guy who invented it was named "Thomas Crapper." But Blake knew that, while there actually was a London plumber called "Crapper"—the manhole covers outside Westminster Abbey with his firm's name on it were something of a minor tourist attraction—he only sold toilets; he didn't invent them.

The actual inventor was Sir John Harington, a godson of Queen Elizabeth I. He was also a poet, which in Blake's mind was a profession not all that far removed from flush toilets, and it was also the reason Blake knew about him. Miss Coulter, his English teacher from high school, encouraged him to read and study literature, telling him he had "a natural gift for language."

Looking out his window at the distant green progression of Hyde Park, Blake wondered what Miss Coulter would think if she knew he was using that natural gift for language to converse in Arabic and

Urdu with anti-American zealots who would like nothing better than to obliterate her and as many of her countrymen as humanly possible. Because, beyond the "brother" talk and the courtesies, he knew that was the aim of Ibrahim and Raheesh and their colleagues.

Blake's Northwestern flight from Boston landed at Gatwick at 9:00 in the morning, and while he carried on his single bag and used the EU Resident line at Customs and Immigration—where his doubly fictitious passport was accepted by the swipe system without so much as a hiccup—it had still been after noon by the time his cab got him to the hotel.

The cab was a silver Volvo wagon, not the black, old-world London taxi they always use in films, its driver was an Afghani in a kufi who had a cousin in Dublin and wanted to talk about it. So Blake, who had never been to Dublin and knew only that James Joyce once lived there—Miss Coulter's work again—had broken out the old trick again and pretended to fall asleep in the back seat. Then pretense led to reality; he nodded off and did not awaken until the cab arrived at the hotel.

As he checked in, he'd still been groggy enough to search in his wallet for a credit card before telling the clerk to leave the room on the card with which the reservation had been made. Any credit card in Grant Reinbolt's name expired while the man was in prison. But this got him only a cursory glance from the clerk, who asked, "Been away from Dublin for a while?"

"Prep school and college in the States," Blake told him. "Haven't been home for years, except for holidays." Which he hoped would explain his accent, because while he was trying to sound Irish, he knew that, to a native ear, his attempt would ring false. It was something they never would have done in Special Forces: give him a legend for which he had not been thoroughly prepared. He secretly hoped Ibrahim's and Raheesh's organization would be similarly sloppy with other details.

And now, having checked in, he put his shaving kit in the bathroom and left the rest of his duffel unpacked on the shelf in the closet.

Qasid mentioned sightseeing—the London Eye—for his first day in London, but Blake thought of the London Eye as a Ferris wheel. It was larger than what you found at a carnival, and more permanent, but it was a blight on an ancient and historical city, and it held no draw for him.

Lunch was a different matter.

Northwest offered to sell him a breakfast on the airplane, but Blake refused on principle to pay for airplane food, especially airplane food that sat in a holding tray for a minimum of seven hours. Now it was lunchtime, or a little past, but his body was telling him to find breakfast. So even though he gave a moment of thought to getting in the shower and washing the staleness of the airplane off him, hunger won out. He locked his passport in the room safe, put all of his cash—what he brought from the apartment and what Qasid gave him—into his front pockets, and headed out.

Indian food was, Blake knew, the Mexican or Chinese food of major British cities: widely available, relatively cheap and satisfying. And as his hotel was just across the street from Hyde Park, he had only to walk south along Park Lane, the street facing the park, to find several Indian restaurants offering an only slightly overpriced lunch to the businesspeople of the Mayfair district.

He chose the one that looked busiest, ordered butter chicken without looking at the menu, and enjoyed a lunch that completely fulfilled his expectations. When he called for the check, it came in pounds sterling, but the waiter said nothing as he paid in Euros and tipped 20 percent, rounding to the nearest ten cents. Then he stepped back out into the sort of bright early summer day tourism bureaus dream about.

If anyone had him under surveillance, they were doing a far better job of it than the FBI back in Bailey's Crossroads. There were plenty of people on the street, but nobody was sitting on a bench and reading a newspaper, or window-shopping, or tying a shoe, or otherwise drawing attention to themselves with a hey-I'm-watching-you activity.

Then again, a good team would be practically invisible, and the fact that just about everyone on the street probably had a cell phone made passing information a snap. Someone could be watching him from a block away and just phone or text ahead when he turned a corner.

Of course, that would require quite a few folks. And while a government surveillance team would be able to have the manpower, it wasn't a government surveillance team he was concerned with at the moment. He just wanted to be out of sight from the people who were shipping him to Pakistan, but he didn't want to make it obvious he was trying to stay out of their sight.

So he walked away from Hyde Park, found a druggist with an entry about twenty feet from the corner, walked past it, and turned the corner.

He was in luck. The same druggist had an entry facing the street he'd just turned on, and Blake opened the door and stepped inside.

The shop had the foreign feel most Americans sense in the smaller stores abroad: the aisles narrower than he was used to back home, the shelves at slightly different heights, the packaging unfamiliar.

And Blake noticed something else. Of the nine women he spotted perusing the shelves, four wore veils. That reminded him of something he'd read in his sociology studies at Hampden-Sydney: that some experts expected mosque attendance to pass church attendance in the United Kingdom by 2020, making Islam the dominant British religion.

As one Fort Bragg language specialist, a master sergeant from Iran, told him, "People say everybody ought to be tolerant, but they don't understand. When a Christian witnesses, he's interested in saving the other person's soul, but in Islam, the purpose is to get you either in the fold or out of the way. They have a saying: 'Use reason or use the rifle.' And they don't really care which one it takes. Don't get me wrong; there are good Muslims, and there are peaceful Muslims, and they are even the vast majority, but there is no good and peaceful Islam. The Qur'an says, 'O ye who believe! Fight those of the disbelievers who are near to you and let them find harshness in you.' It gives the ammunition to those who want to use it. And to think Islam is going to make nice with Christianity forever is like Chamberlain before World War II, believing the Nazis were going to make nice with the British. You trust me, bro, that kind of thinking is going to come around and bite us big in the backside."

Now Blake was thirty-six hundred miles and five time zones from home, masquerading as the man who signed up to help facilitate that big bite.

He did a quick, scanning glance to see if any of the other customers were keeping an eye on him. They were not, but the Muslim women in the store brought Alia into his mind.

Not the time. Not the place.

"Come back to me," was the last request Alia made of him, and if he was to honor it, he had to concentrate on the work at hand. He crossed the store and left by the first exit, the one he passed just a few minutes earlier. Stepping out onto the sidewalk, he turned right and began walking rapidly back toward the park, moving as quickly as he could without drawing attention.

Blake read a London guidebook on his first Middle East deployment, when he learned his team was going to be in the British capitol for three days while they waited for transportation to Germany. He knew Hyde Park was once church ground and that King Henry VIII originally purchased the park from the monks of Westminster Abbey as a hunting ground.

The place was manicured now, but it gave the southern Virginia boy a feeling of home to know that, at one time however long ago, men went out in the morning to hunt deer here, to take a wild boar and bring it back to share with family and friends.

He walked briskly along the north side of the Serpentine Road, with the water and the boaters of the Serpentine on his left and bandstands, statues, and the green expanse of the royal parade grounds on his right. They fired artillery here to celebrate royal holidays, and in the back of his mind, Blake wished today was a royal holiday because artillery reminded him of God; it was support from afar, support from a source he could not touch and he could not see but was tangible nonetheless.

Across the Serpentine he could see a small crowd of tourists—a busload, very probably—gathered at the Princess Diana Memorial Fountain. Blake saw it on that first London trip, and thought it looked like a circular bobsled run, the sort of fountain that was more a memorial to the artist than it was to its subject.

He left the road for the smaller Peacock Walk, on his left a sculling team lifted its oars and coasted on the Long Water. The trees became thicker along this section, and he stopped for a few minutes, just to take a long, careful look at his surroundings. If anyone was keeping an eye on him, they looked like a park bench, like a tree. He hurried up the walk, past the fountains and Queen Anne's Alcove, and out the Marlborough Gate.

Passing the Royal Lancaster Hotel, Blake started walking in the direction of Paddington Station, reading the lettering on the brass plaques next to the small shops until he found what he was looking for.

The sign next to the door read "LANCASTER COIN." He had to buzz to be let in and was greeted by a clerk in a dark suit appropriate for a funeral.

"How may I serve you, sir?"

"Do you carry Krugerrands?"

The clerk worked his lips. "If you are looking for collectible gold, sir, you may be better served with a George the Fifth Indian gold sovereign. We have several in brilliant and uncirculated condition, and as you probably know, they were struck for one year only, at the end of the Great War."

"Thank you. I'm looking for Krugerrands. Quarter-ounce."

The clerk nodded. "The gentleman knows what he is seeking. Is there a particular year you had in mind, sir?"

"The most plentiful. I'm purchasing purely for the gold value."

The nod was more curt this time.

"But of course." The man pointed, all five fingers, at a wingback chair facing a small mahogany Chesterfield table. "Please take your ease, sir. I will find you a selection. Would you care for tea?"

"Thank you. I'm fine."

Blake had never done his shopping sitting down before. But this was only a stone's throw from Mayfair, London's most fashionable shopping district.

Then again, there could have been a utilitarian purpose to the courtesy. He imagined a thief would also find it more difficult to bolt with the goods if he had to start from a seated position in an easy chair.

The clerk returned with a small plastic case and a dark velvet cloth, which he spread on the table. He selected one coin from the case and presented it in a clear plastic holder, along with a small magnifying glass.

"This is the 1984 minting, which trades with the least premium," he said. "We ask seven pounds, fifty, over spot value on the quarter ounce."

"And spot value today is . . . ?"

The clerk extracted an iPhone from his inside jacket pocket and consulted it. "That would be 596 pounds sterling to the troy ounce, sir. So 149 for the quarter, plus the seven-fifty."

Blake did the conversion in his head.

"Seven-fifty seems a bit steep. Would you consider five pounds over spot?"

The clerk pursed his lips. "Sir, this is not the Meena bazaar. We generally discourage haggling here."

"I'd be buying eight coins."

The clerk smiled. "Then I would believe we can make that concession, sir. Are these a gift?"

Blake smiled back. "An investment. I'll just take them as they are."

Given the clerk's serious demeanor, the velvet cloth, and the magnifying glass, Blake went along with the program and left the coin shop with his purchase in a small canvas bag. He waited until he came to a curbside trash bin before he broke the coins out of their plastic holders and tossed the holders, the bag and his receipt into the bin. Then he dumped the Krugerrands into his pants pocket like so much loose change.

Now he had the equivalent of about two thousand American dollars in a commodity understood and accepted in any country on earth. And because the quarter-ounce Krugerrands were small coins, only slightly larger than an American nickel, he could mix them in with his spare change and dump them in the hand-bin at airport security checkpoints without drawing too much attention to himself.

Strolling along the sidewalk, not minding if he picked up a tail now that he had this business concluded, Blake made his way back to his hotel.

CHAPTER TWENTY-EIGHT

❏ ❏ ❏

The breakfast buffet at Grosvenor House differed from what Blake would have expected at an American Marriott in a couple of respects.

First, there was kippered herring in a steam tray next to the bacon and the sausages, the tail and skins still on the split, salted, oily fish. And second, the sausage was Irish bangers, much larger and lighter in color than American breakfast sausage.

But just as tempting. Maybe even more so, which was a shame, because Grant Reinbolt was a practicing Muslim, making both the bangers and the bacon absolutely out of the question for Blake.

A kipper was permissible if not fried in lard, but that didn't matter because, except for the occasional smoked salmon at brunches, Blake had never eaten, and never intended to eat, a herring, be it for breakfast, lunch, or dinner. This was a bone of contention many years before with his mother, who considered pickled herring to be a necessary and traditional part of New Year's celebrations, but Blake held fast.

His mother. She was now in her second month of solitude: long since widowed and her only child dead and gone. At least as far as she knew he was.

"You shalt not bear false witness." . . . Blake learned that commandment when he was what? Five? Or six? Now his mother was grieving. For a lie.

His mother. "Honor thy father and thy mother. . . . " *By tearing her heart out?* He pretty much trampled that one as well.

And then there was "neither shall you steal." Yet he took Grant Reinbolt's name and his freedom. Half the Krugerrands in his pocket were purchased with Grant Reinbolt's prison earnings.

And yes, it was all for the greater good. But still . . .

He wondered how many more commandments he would trample before this thing was over.

For Blake Kershaw, former cochair of the Hampden-Sydney Student Court and enforcer of its honor code, and a Green Beret who had gone through all his battles in uniform, it was a filthy way to do business.

But for Grant Reinbolt, whose identity he assumed, it was time for breakfast.

So, skipping the bacon and the bangers and the kippers, Blake asked the chef to make him a cheese-and-pepper omelet and got some roast beef, done medium-well, from the carving station.

One of the sergeants back at Bragg told Blake the most positive postwar American influence on Britain came, not from Apple or IBM or the auto industry, but from Starbucks. Now it was actually possible to get a great cup of coffee in London, and Blake took a traveler with him as he left the restaurant.

He stepped into the elevator, and the door was just closing when a man—about his age, slender, swarthy, black hair and beard clipped close, thin-framed sunglasses, and a suit that said *I didn't buy this off the rack*—stopped it with a Gucci loafer and stepped inside.

Blake stepped aside. "What floor would you like?"

"What you have there is just fine." The stranger's voice sounded like expensive English prep schools.

Blake pointed at the buttons with his coffee cup. "I haven't pressed anything yet."

"Right you are." The stranger pressed the button for the top floor, the doors closed again, and the elevator began to rise with a mechanical hum. "Are you enjoying the capitol, Mr. Reinbolt?"

Blake pressed another button. "I believe you've mistaken me for someone else."

The stranger pressed a third floor. "And I believe you have selected the floor above your own, Grant."

Blake looked him in the Maui Jims. "And you are?"

The stranger shook his head. "Better you don't know, my brother."

He handed Blake an envelope. "This is a pass for the tube to Paddington station and a National Rail ticket for Victoria to Liverpool. When you get to Liverpool, leave the station by the main entrance. There will be an Internet cafe across the street and half a block to your right. Don't worry about remembering this; there are written instructions in the envelope.

"At the Internet cafe, go to the Port of Liverpool Web site. That's merseydocks-dot-co-dot-uk. Click the departures tab and look for a container ship of Albanian registry called the *Balthazar*. When it leaves port is, unfortunately, up to the work ethic of the British dockworker, but it won't be before midnight and may be as late as tomorrow noon. Whatever time it departs, go to Mariner's Wharf car park near the main entrance to the marina building and be there a quarter-hour later.

"You have two hundred pounds sterling in four fifties and two thousand dollars American in hundreds in that envelope and, yes, I realize you probably still have most of what Raheesh gave you . . ."

"No names," Blake said.

"You watch too much television. Save the money you brought from the States for your out-of-pockets; you may need to get a room if the ship has a late-morning departure, and you'll probably want some clothes; you have a lot of travel after this. Give two of the fifties to the man who meets you in the car park, and don't give him the other two fifties until he has run you out to the ship. Once aboard, the captain will meet you personally. Give him one thousand up front and do not give him the second thousand until he has you safely ashore."

The elevator reached the top floor, and the doors opened, closed.

"Ashore where?" Blake asked. The buttons all went dark, and he repushed the one for his floor. His real floor.

"Ashore where he takes you. You'll know you are in the right place because of who meets you. That's it. Tear your instructions up and discard them when you get to Mariner's Wharf. Do not burn them, or some idiot might call the fire brigade. You won't see me again. Any questions?"

"What sort of clothes?"

"Boots." The man peered over his sunglasses at Blake's Florsheims. "Hiking, not fashionable. And get stuff for cooler weather. And for hot."

It was as much a confirmation as Blake needed that he was headed to Pakistan. Or Afghanistan. Neither one had what you would call a chamber-of-commerce climate.

"Anything else?" The stranger's hand hovered over the elevator buttons.

"Yes," Blake said. The doors opened for his floor. "When do I leave?"

The stranger nodded at the open door. "Go to your room and grab your kit. Your train to Liverpool leaves in one hour."

CHAPTER TWENTY-NINE

Liverpool, Merseyside, United Kingdom

The Internet cafe was right where the man in London said it would be: out the station, across the street, half a block to the right.

Liverpool was . . . well, a British city. Not as ancient and cosmopolitan as London. Plainer. More working class. A few ten-year-old Ford Cortinas were parked parallel on the street, mixed in with Volkswagens, Toyotas, Nissans, and delivery trucks. That was about the spectrum for vehicles. If anyone in town owned a Jaguar, they weren't driving it today.

Blake checked the street as he walked and absolutely nobody appeared to be giving him more than a passing glance, surreptitious or otherwise.

He pushed open the glass-paned door to the coffeehouse.

Inside, most patrons were on their own laptops, nursing on the shop's Wifi signal. The only shop computers for patron use were toward the back, and the monitors were from that brief time when flat-screen didn't necessarily mean thin. Both of the blocky monitors were running the same screen saver, which showed the time—1:12 p.m.—and the date bouncing from corner to corner.

"They aren't here," the guy behind the counter said when Blake ordered a black coffee.

"Who's that?" Blake looked up from the euro coins he'd just fished from his pocket.

"The Beatles. They aren't here."

"Aren't they dead?"

The shopkeeper huffed. "Not all of them. But even if they were, that wouldn't stop Yanks from looking for them all over Liverpool."

"What makes you think I'm a Yank?"

"Dress like one."

Blake shrugged. "You dress like you're homeless, but you're obviously employed."

The man stopped in middraw on Blake's coffee, stared at him, and then broke out laughing.

"That's the thing, mate," he said, offering his hand. "Don't take lip off the riffraff. Fancy anything with this?"

Blake shook his hand. "Do I get a lecture on dead rock stars if I ask if you have anything like a turkey sandwich?"

"Coming up." The man handed him his coffee in a thick ceramic mug. "Have a seat, and I'll bring it to you. Help yourself to one of the Dells if you need to check e-mail or the like. Password's 'Ringo.'"

"Ringo?"

The shopkeeper grinned. "One 'a the ones that's not dead, what?"

Five minutes on the old computer was all it took for Blake to find the port's departure schedule and see that the *Balthazar* was due to finish loading and depart at three in the morning. He had fourteen hours to kill.

The sandwich turned out to be something like a sandwich: a wrap, made with cheddar cheese and mayonnaise and lettuce, and actually quite good. It came while he was checking the news on one of the American TV news Web sites. He looked at baseball scores while he ate and then, once the wrap was gone, glanced around casually to make sure no one was watching his screen, and tapped in the address for the Abdul-Rassul.com Web site.

He didn't stay on long. He just scanned the blog headings looking for the Arabic script that would translate as "Yellow Butterfly." Not finding it, he left the site, going up into the menu bar to clear the history on the computer so no one could see where he'd been. Then he sat back in his chair, wondering if Alia was on the terrorist Web site right now, monitoring the blogs. It would be about 8:30 in the morning in Washington; it was entirely likely she had been at work for close to an hour by now.

Blake checked the computer menu for a copy of Google Earth. There was nothing installed. And when he went to the Web site he found, as he'd thought he would, that he needed administrator rights to put a copy on the machine.

It was all right. It was probably pushing things to try to pinpoint the Garj Valley on his own, and besides, he doubted the valley was in Google Earth's list of place names.

He wiped his mouth with a napkin and finished the rest of his coffee.

Clothes for warm weather. Clothes for cold weather. A good pair of boots. Blake had a good four hours at least before any of the shops would be closing. He Googled "outdoor clothing" and "Liverpool," found a company called "Trespass," and wrote down the street address.

Mariners Wharf looked like a place no one with a merchant seaman's card ever visited. It was not a yacht club by any means, but it had the gabled-wall architecture and parking-lot landscaping of a pleasure-boater's marina.

A stranger carrying a duffel bag in the wee hours of the morning can attract attention, particularly around unattended parked cars, so Blake found a hotel room within walking distance of the marina.

He stretched out on the bed at five in the afternoon, woke just before midnight, and stayed up, hesitant to go back to sleep. The room had an electric alarm clock, but he knew enough guys who came back late from leave after the alarms in hotel rooms failed to go off, and he wasn't about to ask the front desk to call him at three. He was, after all, standing in for Grant Reinbolt, and Grant Reinbolt didn't want to be memorable.

So Blake showered, redonned the clothes he'd been wearing—he had a pretty good suspicion they would be wet with salt-spray shortly—sat on the edge of the bed, and checked the drawer of the nightstand.

Yep. The Gideons had been there.

Blake took the Bible out of the drawer and opened it. In Afghanistan, all through the time he billeted at Bagram, during his hospitalization, and throughout his four years at Hampden-Sydney, his Bible was a morning companion. Every day he found time to read at least a chapter of the Old Testament and a chapter of the New—at least a chapter with no upper limit. If his schedule allowed, sometimes he'd read for an hour.

Yet, sitting in the hotel room in Liverpool, he was unable to remember where he last left off in his morning Bible study. It had been too long, so he just started over at Genesis 1:1 and Matthew 1:1, and when the clock in the room approached three, he reluctantly put the book back in the drawer.

Leaving at three in the morning put him at the door of the marina chandlery at 3:12. A minute later a man in jeans and a faded pullover Windbreaker showed up. He was solidly built and had, Blake could see in the carpark's sodium-vapor lighting, a tear tattooed on his right cheek.

A footballer who's done time. That was Blake's five-second assessment.

"You ready?" That was all the man asked.

Blake nodded.

"Follow me." The man turned on his heels and started walking.

Blake tore his instructions into bits, deposited them in the rubbish-bin next to the door, and followed his contact around the building. The basin was separated from the Mersey by a seawall and crowded with several dozen small vessels. Most looked like the sort of thing a family man would use to go fishing with his buddies on the weekend.

They followed a concrete dock out to a rigid-hull inflatable with a center steering console. It looked as if it had seen some wear; the Plexiglass windscreen in front of the console had a crack visible in the moonlight, and one section of inflatable tube looked darker than the others, as if recently replaced. Water sloshed on the deck near the stern where a second man was topping off a fuel tank from a plastic can, not bothering to remove his cigarette.

Blake set his duffel on the seat forward of the console while the man who met him squeezed a rubber bulb in the stern, charging the fuel lines, and the other one cast off the lines. It took the first man three tries to get the motor started, but once he did, he backed out into the basin with the ease of someone who had done it hundreds of times. Moments later they were passing the navigation lights at the inlet in the seawall. Then they were out in the Mersey and headed west, the lights of sleeping Liverpool on either side. The second man, who had yet to say a word, stood next to the console while the first man drove, so Blake stood on the opposite side, trimming the boat, bending his knees slightly to cushion the bump as they crossed over the frothy, gray wake of a passing barge.

No GPS or LORAN screen glowed above the wheel. Blake saw only a compass in a swivel, its lubber-line faint, having lost whatever luminous qualities it once had. The man driving the boat aimed it dead center up the Mersey, reduced the throttle a couple of notches, and let go of the wheel to face Blake.

"Right, then," he said. "Down to business. There's the matter of two hundred quid."

Blake unbuttoned his shirt pocket, reached in, and took out two bills. "Here you go."

The boat driver scowled at the money in his hand. "I only see a hundred here, Sunshine. Let's have the rest."

"You get the rest when we get out to the ship."

"I think not." The boat driver reached for Blake's shirt pocket with his left hand.

Blake stepped right, sweeping the driver's outstretched hand with the back of his right wrist, and cupping the back of the man's head with his left hand. With two quick, opposing movements, he wrenched the driver's arm up between his shoulder blades and drove his head into the edge of the windscreen, where it connected with a satisfying thunk.

There was a click as the second man flicked open a knife.

"Set it down," Blake ordered. He wrenched the driver's arm upward, eliciting a sharp groan. "Set it down there, on the seat, or I break his arm."

"Do it," the driver groaned, and the second man set the knife, a folding tanto, onto the bench seat behind the driver. Blake switched hands on the driver's wrist, picked up the knife, and then let the driver go.

"Bloody wanker . . ." The driver reached for Blake again but got the point of the knife under his chin for his efforts, Blake putting just enough pressure on the blade to lift the man's head without breaking the skin. It took the fight out of the other man immediately.

"What the devil's gotten into you?" The driver backed away, rubbed his wrist, and then touched his eyebrow, which was bleeding from a small split. "Like to blinded me, you twit."

"You'll keep your hands to yourself and drive the boat," Blake said. "Junior, over there, will stay quiet, and nobody gets hurt any worse. You get the other hundred when I'm on the ladder, climbing onto the ship, and not a second sooner. You got that?"

"Who do you think you are, giving us orders on our own boat?" The driver was dabbing at his eyebrow with a dirty handkerchief, huffing as he looked at the blood.

"I'm the man who is going to throw you both overboard unless you get with the program. There can't be that many freighters leaving Liverpool at this hour; I'm sure I can find mine. Now do you want your other hundred when we get there, or do you want to swim and lose the boat?"

The driver sized Blake up and then shook his head.

"Calm down, mate." The driver went back to his wheel, pushed the throttle forward holding the handkerchief to his head. All three men leaned forward as the boat went up on plane. "Just trying to make sure we get what's ours."

"You will. Out there."

It made for a tense thirty-minute ride. They passed the downtown waterfront and canted left as the Mersey grew wider. By the time they were abreast of the channel lights, small ocean rollers, barely visible in the light of a setting moon, were lifting the little boat and then dropping it again as it crossed from crest to trough. As the channel lights dropped astern, they entered the ocean proper, and the size of the swells picked up. Constellations—the Big Dipper and its companions—wheeled above them as the driver leaned the boat into a turn and aimed them south. Far to their left, the lights of rural Merseyside blinked in the distance, but to the right was nothing but the black of empty ocean. Ahead, though, Blake could make out the lights of a freighter under way, and the lights drew nearer as the little boat sped through the night. They bumped over the freighter's wake, and a few moments later they drew alongside, the freighter's hull a huge steel wall to their left.

"Heads up," called a deep African voice above them, and a slender rope ladder with wooden rungs came clattering down. The RIB driver matched the freighter's speed perfectly and brought the small boat's inflatable port tube right up against the steel hull of the freighter while Blake slung the shoulder-strap of his duffel across his chest.

"I'll have my hundred," the driver said, shouting to be heard above the rattle of the freighter's engines.

Blake stepped up onto the tube, reached high, and grabbed the rope ladder with his right hand, stepping up onto a rung at the same time. The ladder swung so he was facing stern, and he reached into his breast pocket, found the two bills, and held them out. The second man came around to take them and spoke for the first time: "Here, now. What 'bout my knife?"

Blake fished it out of his pants pocket and dropped it onto the small boat's bouncing deck.

"Wanker . . ." The Liverpool man's voice receded in the darkness as the inflatable swung away, leaving Blake on the rope ladder just three feet above dimly phosphorescent waves. Tightening his grip on the wet wooden rungs, Blake looked up and began to climb.

A minute later strong dark hands gripped him under the arms as he swung a leg over the freighter's steel rail. Blake was face-to-face with the blackest man he had ever seen in his life, a man so dark his features seemed a shiny dark blue in the starlight.

"Welcome." The black man's voice was the mellow, melodic bass of East Africa. "I am Captain André Chocteau."

"Grant Reinbolt, Captain." Blake shook the officer's hand. It was like taking hold of a knot of thick, hard hemp rope. Blake unbuttoned his breast pocket. "I have some money here for you, sir . . ."

"No, no, no . . ." Chocteau shook his head. "Do not trouble yourself over such things, my friend. Please. I trust you. When we get to your destination, if you feel you have been well served, then you can pay me your money, yes? But right now, let us get your things into your cabin, and then Cookie has saved you a bowl or two of mutton stew from last night. His specialty." He pronounced it in the old British fashion: *speciálity*. "A little something warm after your long ride out here in the dark, yes?"

"Okay." Blake smiled. It was impossible not to; the freighter's master was instantly likable.

"It is good to have you aboard," the captain said, handing Blake's duffel to a crewman as they ducked through a hatch. The companionway inside was illuminated by caged bulbs, and Blake squinted in the bright, white light. After a few moments his eyes adjusted, and he could see that the captain looked to be in his midfifties, his kinked hair trending gray at the temples, his features hard and sallow. His skin, widely pored, was indeed the blackest Blake ever saw on another human being.

"My crew is almost all Filipino," the captain said as they walked. "They are good men and hard workers, but they like to keep to themselves. I shall welcome your company. Tell me, Mr. Reinbolt, do you play chess?"

"It's 'Grant,' sir. And no. I'm afraid I never learned."

The captain put his hand on Blake's shoulder. "No worries, Grant Reinbolt. We have nearly a week's voyage ahead of us. It shall be my very great pleasure to teach you."

CHAPTER THIRTY

❑ ❑ ❑

The Arabian Sea

Squinting in the muted light of the pilot house, Blake moved his rook the length of the printed canvas "board," all the way to André's end row. The captain's king was in the corner, prevented from moving forward by his own bishop and pawn. The African grinned broadly and moved aside his king—it was actually a wooden disk with a crown printed on it, a magnet on its base holding it to metal squares sewn within the canvas. He reached across the chart table and offered his hand.

"Congratulations, my friend."

Blake cocked his head and looked at the wooden board. "You mean I finally actually won one?"

"Won one in classic fashion." The captain pumped Blake's hand as if he had just taken the lottery. "You have a fine strategic mind, Mr. Grant Reinbolt."

"I would say that, if anything, I have a good teacher."

The black man grinned and dismissed the compliment with a wave of his hand.

"Captain . . ." The Filipino helmsman's voice was so high it nearly squeaked; it didn't seem to go at all with the man's fireplug build. "We've reached Astola, sir. She is passing half a mile to our east."

The captain peered into the blackness beyond the pilothouse windows and then checked the night-dimmed screen of the radar. A narrow island sat at the end of the half-mile ring. He came back to the chart table, moved the chess set, and looked at the chart of the Arabian Sea.

"Come to heading two-nine-five true," he told the man at the wheel.

"Making heading two-nine-five true. Aye, sir." The stocky man turned the wheel.

The black man patted Blake's shoulder. "I shall miss our games, Grant Reinbolt. Now you had best gather your things and pack your kit. We shall be putting a boat in the water just a little over an hour from now."

Sixty-five minutes later, Blake stood, his duffel packed, ready and waiting at his feet, as he and the African captain watched the freighter's launch being winched off its mount aft of the pilothouse. Work lights illuminated the operation, but except for a cluster of lights on the horizon, the night was moonless and dark.

Blake handed the captain an envelope.

"What is this, my friend?"

"The passage, Captain. My fare. Two thousand dollars."

The black man accepted the envelope and put it in his pocket without bothering to open it. "You are not yet ashore, Grant Reinbolt."

"I am not, but I trust you, sir."

Both men laughed.

"There is a good pair of Florsheim shoes in my cabin, Captain," Blake said. "I have not worn them that long. I hope they'll fit you. And if not, perhaps one of your crew. I won't need them where I'm going."

The captain smiled. "Then I shall wear them on the town when *Balthazar* goes in for refit. And I also have something for you."

The captain handed Blake what looked like a rolled piece of oilcloth, tied with a canvas ribbon. Blake turned it in his hand.

"What's this?"

The captain grinned. "Open it."

Blake undid the knot. Sixty-four squares, half black and half tan, made up the canvas board. Thirty-two wooden circles were arranged on it, each one imprinted with the symbol of a chess piece. It was the older man's chess set.

"I can't accept this, Captain."

The black man barked a laugh. "Grant Reinbolt, I would say that, with a pair of Florsheims, I am the one who is far the better for this exchange. That is nothing but a game. And none of my crew knows how to play. But perhaps you can use it to practice as you travel."

"I will." Blake rolled the game up, tied it, and zipped it into his duffel.

The launch was lowered. Soon it was rising and dropping on the dark, rolling waves alongside the *Balthazar*.

"I must tell you, Grant Reinbolt," the captain said, "I have done passages such as this before. If I do not do it, someone else will, and I send the money home to help my daughter. Her husband was injured—hurt badly last year—and cannot work. But I know that when a person travels by such . . . unofficial means, the chances are either he is a journalist who wishes to go places the government does not allow, or he is up to mischief. I did not ask when this passage was arranged because such questions are not to be asked. And I will not ask you because I respect your privacy." He said it *priv*-acy.

"But when you are gone ashore, Grant Reinbolt," he continued, "if it is all the same to you, I shall think of you as a journalist. I would like that."

"So would I, Captain," Blake told him. "So would I."

CHAPTER THIRTY-ONE

Pasni, Pakistan

"The docks at Pasni were built during a time of great optimism," Captain Chocteau said, raising his voice to be heard over the launch's four-cylinder diesel motor. "Good docks, concrete, what was a good basin before the typhoons began refilling it with sand. But the commercial vessels, the yachts, they never came, you know. So now we have this."

The launch came to the end of a seawall and turned through the inlet, past red and green navigational beacons. Chocteau turned on the launch's search lamp and played it over the benighted harbor. There were no vessels resting in orderly slips. Rafts of traditional Pakistani fishing boats, their bows and sterns high and pointed, were roped together and extended from every pier, like bacteria multiplying on a blighted organism. As the light played over them, Blake could see that some of the boats were painted in brilliant reds and oranges and blues, but on most the paint was faded, and some appeared simply to be weathered and unprotected wood.

Blake wondered how they would find a way through the clutter of vessels. There didn't seem to be a single foot of dock without fishing boats moored to it six and seven deep.

He got his answer when the captain cut the engine and turned the rudder hard. Two crewmen threw rubber fenders over the side, and the launch came to rest lengthwise against one of the larger fishing craft. The crewmen made bow, stern, and spring lines fast, and Chocteau stepped onto the sponson nearest the fishing boat.

"Just follow me," he said. "No one will mind. It is how one comes ashore here when the fishing fleet is in. And these days the fishing fleet is in quite often."

Blake followed the captain, stepping across the thwart of the fishing boat and into the next vessel over. The two Filipino crewmen stayed on the launch, hands on the lines, obviously ready to depart at a moment's notice.

Three boats over, Blake's new boots slipped as he stepped aboard, and he slid an inch or two, waking a man sleeping on some folded fishing nets. The man made a shushing sound, pointing to a small child curled up and asleep in the bow. Blake nodded and moved on to the next boat.

When they got to the concrete pier, Blake mantled easily up onto it, then extended a hand and helped the older captain up to join him.

"Welcome to Pakistan," the African said. He looked around and then nodded toward a distant, trucklike vehicle, parked in the open area at the end of the pier. Two men were standing next to it. "Come, let me see you off."

"That's all right," Blake said. "Neither one of us has gone through customs and immigration, and you had best get back to your ship. But here; I want you to have this."

He reached into his pocket and took out two hundred-dollar bills.

The captain held a hand up, palm out. "No, no, my friend. You are an honorable man; you have paid me in full already."

"But this is not for you, Captain. This is for your daughter: to help her and her husband."

The black man hung his head and shook it. "Then in that case I cannot refuse. And my daughter thanks you. Travel safe, my friend."

"And you." The two men shook hands.

"You . . . are a journalist," the captain said. And then he was gone, walking back across the boats.

Blake walked landward on the concrete pier. The vehicle was backlit by a lamp hung from a post near the street, but he could make out enough of the shape of it to see it was a Land Rover—not the gentrified version one saw around suburban Washington but an old Defender 110, the Land Rover utility vehicle still sometimes used by British military units and by utilities and other businesses that needed to travel off-road. It had a roof rack, a brush guard out front, and generally looked like a vehicle accustomed to rough country.

Behind him, he could hear the diesel engine of *Balthazar*'s launch start up, lift in tempo, and then recede as it headed out of the small, man-made harbor and back to sea.

No turning back now.

The two men were less than a hundred feet away now, still silhouettes, the one weak lamp behind them.

"*Assalamu alaikum*," Blake called out to them.

"*Assalamu alaikum*." The taller of the two walked to meet him, and when the light hit his features, Blake stopped walking for a split second.

The other man laughed.

"No, my brother, I am not who you think I am," he said in unaccented Arabic. "I am not Raheesh."

They met and bowed as they shook hands.

"Welcome, my brother Grant Reinbolt. Welcome to Pakistan, and welcome to our cause. I am Saif, and to answer the question in your head at this very moment, no—Raheesh and I are not twins. But we are, as you must have assumed, sons of the same father, the same mother, born one year apart, and he is the eldest, although we both now have gray in our beards."

"You are right," Blake admitted. "I see Raheesh in you. The resemblance is . . . really something."

"Yes. And always it has been this way. We had fun with our teachers when we were in school. Tell me, my brother, are you hungry?"

"Thank you. The ship's cook made me a meal just before I departed. I am fine."

"Then let us begin our journey. Please, take the backseat. Mahmoud will need the front for his rifle."

Mahmoud grinned. He was missing a front tooth. But his weapon looked extremely well cared for: an AKS-74U with its folding stock removed. Blake knew it as a weapon that could take tremendous abuse and still function with reasonable accuracy.

Blake opened the door and got in back.

"Have we far to go?"

"Quite far, I am afraid." Saif got in behind the wheel, on the right. "Our destination is nearly a thousand kilometers distant as the eagle flies and half again that by road. And we must travel by road because your country's AWACS planes would pick us up in an instant if we attempted to use aircraft. So we drive; it will take us four days. Make yourself comfortable back there, my brother. Sleep; we shall have plenty of time to talk later on our journey."

CHAPTER THIRTY-TWO

❑ ❑ ❑

Blake came awake—wide awake—to the sound of small-arms fire.

"What is it?" The words came out before he realized he'd asked the question in English.

"Just a local wedding," Saif said over his shoulder, also in English. "We are passing through a town. The wedding party is celebrating."

Mahmoud turned and smiled his gap-toothed smile. It was clear the man did not speak English. But he was also clearly amused by the way Blake startled awake.

"We're lucky I did not soil my trousers," Blake told him in Arabic, and the man laughed, a loud, high, cackling laugh.

Blake sat up. He supposed Qasid would have been horrified to learn he was now dressed the same as the other two men in the Land Rover. This was their second day of travel, and at the end of the first, Saif stopped in a town and bought him two sets of long, light, pajama-like trousers and shirts, an equally overlong vest, a pair of sandals and a *purgee*, or turban, which he wore with a bandanna-like triangle of cloth covering his chin because, as Saif pointed out, "A shaved chin is the sign of an infidel in Pakistan; every man here, young or old, wears a beard to honor the Prophet." And while Blake had not shaved since he was on the freighter, all he had on his chin at the moment was a thickening stubble. So he covered it like a tribesman.

The three men had every window rolled down on the old Land Rover, the faint breeze bringing with it a light coating of dust as it wafted through the vehicle. Saif led the men through hurried prayers both the night before, when they stopped, and that morning, when they rose from borrowed pallets to resume their drive. They took both dinner and breakfast at the home of the goatherd where they stopped for the night; the customs of Islam left no doubt of his hospitality. And he also gave them flatbread for their journey.

But they did not stop to pray during their drive. They only stopped for fuel, and when they purchased gasoline—hand-pumped from fifty-five-gallon drums and filtered through muslin in the bottom of a funnel—they filled not only the fuel tank but a large jerry can strapped to a holder above the rear bumper and four metal cans tied with rope to the roof rack. In the back of the Land Rover, Saif had half a dozen old Soviet canteens, and they also filled those with potable water at every stop.

Blake looked out the open window at low, flat, mud-walled houses with small plots of property surrounded by low, flat, mud walls.

"How many more towns will we pass through?" Blake asked.

"It depends on what you consider a town, my brother," Saif said over his shoulder. "Half these places have no names, and half the names have no places. Have you ever heard of a village called 'Chagai'?"

"No."

"No reason you should have. But when we get to it, midmorning tomorrow, we will turn off onto a road that makes the goat path we are on right now look like one of your American interstates. And by sundown tomorrow, we shall have reached our camp."

CHAPTER THIRTY-THREE

❏ ❏ ❏

The last thirty kilometers were done so slowly, Blake was reasonably certain he could have walked it faster. The Land Rover crawled up and over ledges and boulders, along a ridge trail with precipitous drops to either side, and up a mountain stream that looked more appropriate for a kayak than four-wheel-drive. The utility vehicle, which Saif and his lieutenant loaded with canned goods and powdered foods at the last town, canted nearly to forty-five degrees left, right, up, and down—and sometimes in all four directions within the space of a minute. As they drove, the vegetation grew gradually more sparse, and the country became rougher.

From time to time, as they crested a rise, Blake could see jagged strips and pyramids of brilliant white through the passes to the north: the snow-crested peaks of the Hindu Kush. Pakistan had, he knew, some of the roughest mountain ranges in the world: K2, in the Karakoram Range in the country's northeast quadrant, was considered the most formidable high-altitude climb in the world, despite being second to Everest in height. Over the years it killed one out of every four attempting to climb it.

"Last fall, the Pakistani Army tried sending a squad in a truck up here," Saif said as the Land Rover crawled up yet another ridge. "We don't think they knew about the camp; it was just ground surveillance, following tire tracks. And there it is."

Blake peered out the right side of the Land Rover. The earth dropped away for a good five hundred feet. And there, upended at the bottom of the steep ravine, were the tandem wheels and undercarriage of a 1950s-era deuce-and-a-quarter. Mahmoud made a rolling motion with his hands, and then parodied the noise of a crash.

"We heard the helicopters for nearly a week afterward," Saif said. "The Pakistanis use their helicopters quite sparingly, particularly up here, where the air is thin for the older Hueys they still fly. Still, it took them four days to get all the bodies out. They have not tried to come back since. But us? We run this route two, three times a week. It is how we get our supplies. And then there are the foot-trails. Those, only we know."

Blake looked again at the old wreck as they crested the ridge and then moved onto more level ground. Saif shifted into the next gear up, and the growl of the Land Rover's engine dropped in response.

They traveled for nearly another hour before entering the southern end of a long valley. Too high for vegetation, the landscape was all rocks and hard-packed soil, the ground sloping, with occasional level spots. They lumbered through the glassy sparkle of a small mountain stream, snowmelt from the distant Kush.

They reached the top of the rise. A man carrying an AK-47 stepped out from a cleft in the rocks and raised a hand in greeting; Saif waved back.

The valley beyond opened up, more than three hundred meters wide, and in its center sat a rudimentary compound. There was a long, rectangular, two-story building: flat roofed, with a long side porch supported by rough logs. It had a wall running from it, enclosing a space about an acre in size. A second building, about fifty meters distant, was single-story, and, like the first, its walls appeared to have been plastered with mud. On its flat roof, two men were hanging laundry over wooden frames.

Beyond that, four large dome tents, olive in color, were spaced under tan camouflage netting covering an area about sixty meters square. Blake assumed the netting was there as much to provide additional shade as it was to disguise the tents. There was what appeared to be an old two-ton flatbed truck of British military origin, and parked next to it was a desert-camouflage Russian Ural motorcycle with a sidecar.

Blake had read about the Urals. They were Russian-built copies of German military BMWs from the late 1930s. With powered wheels on the sidecars, they were formidable machines, capable of taking sand, loose gravel, and even steep terrain in stride—the Germans used them as a fast and mobile machine-gun platform in World War II.

The only other vehicle was an old Jeep lifted off the ground on jack stands, its wheels and tires removed. Anemic-looking weeds were growing in the partial shade next to the jack stands. If that Jeep was being worked on, someone had stopped in midproject weeks or even months before.

Two men were walking back from a cleft that appeared to lead into an adjacent valley. One was carrying an empty rocket-propelled grenade launcher, and the other had a sporting rifle of some sort. Like the sentry, they lifted their hands in greeting. Apparently the Land Rover came and went with some regularity. The day was nearly cloudless, the sky that deep, startling blue one only sees at altitude; and despite the heat creeping in through the Land Rover's open windows, everyone was dressed in long, heavy, traditional clothing, their bearded faces and tanned hands the only parts of them visible.

They lumbered into the walled yard outside the larger building, and immediately a team of three men came outside, said, "*Assalamu alaikum*," and then, when Saif opened the back of the Land Rover, began unloading the supplies and carrying them inside.

"Tell me, my brother, are you accustomed to sleeping rough?"

Blake laughed. "I just spent four years in prison."

Saif clapped him on the back. "Then that was excellent preparation. While our men train here, they live, except for the officers, in tents. I hope you will not be offended."

"I will be honored," Blake said, "to be under canvas with my brother *jihadin*."

It was the right answer. Saif beamed.

Blake was shown to his tent by a man so young he seemed to be a boy. The tent was furnished with items both spartan and familiar: a footlocker into which he placed his clothing and toilet kit, a camp cot upon which a thin, ticked mattress sat folded, and a rough wooden shelf. Someone had left him a Qur'an on the shelf.

"I will draw a sleeping bag from stores and leave it here for you," the young man said. His Arabic was halting. Blake assumed his usual tongue was Urdu.

"Thank you, my brother." Blake offered his hand, and the young man shook it shyly.

It was a level of deference completely lacking in the next person he met, a Middle Easterner who appeared both taller and more solidly built than anyone Blake had met thus far in the camp. In fact, he also felt more solidly built because Blake walked right into him as he was ducking under the rain-fly of the tent.

"A thousand pardons, my brother," Blake said in Arabic.

The other man glared at him. "Who the devil are you?'

He asked it in English: English with a pronounced Iraqi accent.

"A servant of Allah and a fighter in his cause," Blake replied in better Arabic than he had used to date with anyone in this group. He held out his hand. "My name is Reinbolt: Grant Reinbolt."

"We'll see how much of a servant and a fighter you are," the other man grumbled. He said it, again, in English, as he pushed past Blake into the tent.

Blake dusted himself off and straightened up.

"Oh," the other man said from inside the tent, "and Reinbolt?"

English again.

"Yes, my brother?" Arabic again.

"Stay out of my way. And you are not my freaking brother, Yank."

Other than that, the welcome he received was entirely cordial. The same deferential young man who showed him to his tent took him on a tour around the camp, showing him a second small building that seemed to be both an arsenal and a quartermaster's hut and topping him out to a range where an older Arab was teaching a group of young men the fundamentals of riflery.

"And in the wadi beyond, there is another range with some old vehicles we use as targets," the young man said. "Just this morning, I was allowed to fire the rocket-propelled grenade."

"Did you hit your target?" Blake asked.

The young man grinned. "I came very, very close!"

The call to midday prayer came from a man who seemed too old to be soldiering, and Blake noticed that only about half of the people in camp answered it. But he did. The men clustered around galvanized metal tubs on the long porch and washed their arms, their hands, their feet, and their heads. They then went inside and unrolled a large woolen rug that covered every inch of a space that looked as if it doubled as a classroom. His feet bare, Blake joined them as they knelt for prayer.

After prayer a meal was taken in another large room, where the men sat on the floor around communal bowls. This time everyone showed up.

"We take our main meal here just after midday," Saif explained to Blake. "At night, it is mostly soups, for warmth."

He bent his head, said, "*Al humdu lillah . . .*"

All around him, men reached for the bowl, and Blake did as well, taking care to reach into the bowl with the thumb and first two fingers of his right hand.

It was lamb, a thick stew, and it was excellent. Baskets of torn bread were passed around; and once the meat was gone, Blake joined the others in sopping the rest of the stew with the thick bread. It was communal dining, and it served its purpose; the men, drawn from a number of backgrounds and countries, ate as a family. And when the meal was done, Blake felt ready for a nap.

So, by appearances, were the rest of the men—because the camp was composed entirely of men, although they ranged in age from sixteen to well over sixty. Perhaps eight wore pistols and seemed to be officers. The others, two dozen of them, were dressed simply, and the very youngest did not speak unless spoken to.

"My brothers," Saif announced in loud, clear Arabic, "I have very good news. A brother has joined us here from America, and he is here to help us defeat that great satan. Please greet our brother, Grant."

"*Assalamu alaikum*," rang out from every man in the room—every man except the tall one with the Iraqi accent. Blake noticed that. He couldn't help but notice it; he had to share a tent with the man.

And Saif noticed it, too.

"Kahlil," he asked, "how is it that you do not greet our new brother?"

"That is not the question," the big man replied in faultless Arabic. He got to his feet, the movement slow yet effortless. "The question, my leader, is this: how is it that you bring a spy among us?"

CHAPTER THIRTY-FOUR

❑ ❑ ❑

CIA Headquarters, Langley, Virginia

Alia was supposed to be culling the clip files. It was part of what she did every day; CIA had a clipping service that automatically pulled and sent her English- and Arabic-language wire stories from the twenty-two nations that resided on the Agency's terrorism watch list. She had already done the first part of the job, which was to perform a computer search on all the documents, using Agency software to look for and flag more than a thousand proper names and trigger words.

But the second part of the job, actually reading the flagged text to determined which documents should be set aside for Colsun Atwater's inspection, was giving her trouble. Every dateline she saw, every place name—Sana, Kirkuk, Masshad, Kabul, Lahore—triggered the same question: *Is he there?*

Alia pushed her desk chair back from the computer display and rubbed the bridge of her nose, her temples. She felt . . . "unprofessional" was the word that came to mind. It seemed unprofessional to get emotionally attached to anyone at CIA, let alone a field operative on a clandestine mission.

But during his orientation she had been with him every day, sometimes twelve hours a day, speaking with him, listening to him. She tried to keep it on a professional level, but even those conversations were enough to show her he had a good heart, he was pleasant to be around, he was someone with whom she would like very much to spend more time.

Maybe even a lifetime.

No. Alia clenched her left fist, unclenched it. *No. You are absolutely not supposed to fall in love with him.*

For all she knew, there was a woman in the field he was supposed to enter a relationship with. It was not beyond the realm of possibility. Many secrets were gained by using not just espionage and cunning but the heart as well.

So why hadn't he said anything? Why hadn't he cautioned her, told her it could not be so when she kissed his cheek and told him, "Come back to me?"

Where, why, who . . . all she had about this man was questions: questions and a first name—Blake.

Alia squeezed her eyes shut, opened them, took a breath, and rolled her desk chair nearer the screen. She willed herself back to work.

She was about halfway through the morning's news clippings when she heard the click of the card reader being activated on the office door. A second later the door swung open, and Atwater stepped in, carrying his briefcase and a travel mug. His morning smells came with him: aftershave, soap, coffee, and just the faintest hint of pipe tobacco.

"Good morning, Colsun."

"Alia. Anything new on that oil thing we were watching?" He nodded at her computer screen.

"Not so far. I've found a few stories, but they're all just recaps of what we saw on Friday."

"Figures." He juggled his travel mug over to the same hand holding his briefcase and checked his BlackBerry. "Say, can you make some calls this morning and free up the week after my Egypt trip?"

"Sure." Alia jotted a note. "You finally taking some time off?"

"Don't I wish. No, I've just got to make a run over to Pakistan, meet with our station chief there."

Alia looked checked her Outlook calendar. "Your assistant deputy is in Indonesia that week. Will that be an issue?"

Atwater thought a moment. "Is the director in town?"

"That week? Yes."

He nodded. "Then I should be fine."

"Want me to set up flights? Hotel?"

"Won't need it. Got stuck in traffic getting off the bridge, so I booked my flights on the BlackBerry while I was sitting there. And Barry's putting me up at his place outside Islamabad."

"Okay." Alia made another note.

"And Alia?"

She looked up at her boss.

"He's very well trained. He's as safe as a person can be in this situation. It's war, so there are no guarantees. But if anybody can make it back from this, he can."

Who? That was her first inclination, to fake ignorance. But Alia knew her boss was a person who saw through subterfuge every day. She felt her shoulders sag in surrender.

"Thank you, Colsun," she said. "I appreciate that."

CHAPTER THIRTY-FIVE

❑ ❑ ❑

"Keep your eye on the target." Blake's instructor, an older man with a Yemeni accent, thumped his walking stick for emphasis as he spoke.

No, Blake wanted to tell him. *You've got it wrong. When you're going for accuracy with a pistol, you don't focus on the target. You focus on the front sight.*

He did that, focused on the front sight and selected a spot a quarter-inch above the shoulder of the human outline drawn on a piece of poster board ten meters away. He squeezed the trigger on the Tokarev TT and produced precisely the near-miss he'd been trying for.

"Very good!" The old Yemeni thumped him on the shoulder. "You are getting close!"

It surprised Blake, as well. The Tokarev showed a lot of holster wear, probably an ex-Pakistani police pistol. Yet it shot like a tight, newer pistol. Blake assumed the Pakistani policeman who carried it previously rarely practiced with it.

"Very good? I wouldn't want to trust my life to his shooting."

Blake heard the comment clearly; like the rest of the people on the firing line, he was shooting without ear or eye protection.

It was Khalil, of course. The big Iraqi with the weight-trained body absolutely refused to cut Blake a break.

At dinner that first night, Saif was quick to rebuke Khalil. "Why do you say such things about our brother?"

"Look at him with his white skin and his bare chin. This man is no *jihadin*."

"It is as I told you, brother. He is an American who has rallied to our cause. Allah has blessed us. Our good fortune is unbelievable."

"'Unbelievable' is right. Why would someone like him side with us, take up arms against his own? I tell you, he is a spy."

The rash words had brought Saif to his feet. "My own brother, the flesh of my mother's flesh, has told us this man is a fighter in our cause. Are you calling my brother a liar?"

That was enough to get Khalil to drop the "spy" allegations. But it was not enough to get him to cease his criticisms of Blake. And for two weeks now, Blake had been weighing his options with this big man. To say nothing and take it would have been entirely within the cover he assumed. Grant Reinbolt had no reputation as a fighter.

Yet if he appeared too submissive, it could change the minds of Saif and his officers' cadre. At some point, if he was to be trusted with an important mission, Grant Reinbolt was going to have to grow a backbone.

Blake made his decision.

"Why don't you lighten up?" He said it to Khalil in English.

"Why should I?"

Dropping the magazine from his pistol, setting it on the crude shooter's bench in front of him, Blake switched to Arabic. "Maybe you're right. Maybe you can't change. Probably because of all that dog's milk you were raised on."

It was one of the most volatile insults imaginable; Blake had just called the man's mother a dog. And in Islam there is no animal more unclean, not even a pig.

It produced the desired result.

With a guttural roar Khalil took a step in Blake's direction, his right arm cocked back for the punch.

Blake swept his left foot behind the big man's heel and pulled. Khalil lost his balance, started to topple backward, and Blake jabbed with a single rapid punch to the big man's Adam's apple.

Khalil dropped, hands at his throat, gasping. His face turned red, then pale, as he tried to get air. He collapsed onto his back.

For nearly a minute he struggled like this, the men from the firing line gathering in a circle around him. One stooped next to him and glanced at his comrades, the worry etched on his face.

"Leave him," Blake told them in Arabic. "He'll be fine in a minute."

Finally, Khalil began to draw in short, ragged breaths. He sat up on the ground and ignored the hand Blake offered him.

"What did I say?" Khalil's voice was choked, barely audible, and he was speaking to the members of Saif's cadre, who walked over to the line after the scuffle. "You saw that? What he did? Where do you think he learned to fight like that?"

"In prison, you idiot." Blake said it in Arabic. Then he switched to English, "Now would you please just cut me a freaking break? We've got a job to do here. You're getting in my way; stay out of it."

Khalil's eyes flared at the last sentence, but he said nothing. He accepted a hand up from one of the other men and swaggered away as if he had not just been sent butt-first to the ground.

Behind him, Blake could hear the officers murmuring among themselves. He turned and looked at Saif. The elder nodded.

CHAPTER THIRTY-SIX

❑ ❑ ❑

Colsun Atwater was hunched over his desk, his computer keyboard set to the side, making handwritten notes on a plain white legal pad for better than an hour. And for better than an hour, Alia found things to do in her anteroom just outside his office.

She had worked for Atwater long enough to know he was more than computer-literate. He took notes on his BlackBerry, using an extensive library of self-devised macros to allow him to work in a sort of keyboard shorthand: letter strings such as "cvt" and "cln" were automatically translated into "covert" and "clandestine."

So if he was writing by hand, there could only be one reason for it: he did not wish to use the Agency's computers, not even his desktop machine, not even if he intended to delete the document after printing it. Whatever he was writing was eyes-only secret—far more sensitive than the thousands of top- secret documents passing through CIA's computer servers every single day. He even rejected Alia's suggestion that he use an old-fashioned typewriter, pointing out that the electronic models stored text in buffers, and even the most primitive manual typewriters left a trail of letter impressions on their ribbons. When working on something extremely sensitive, he wrote by hand, and he shredded the underlying pages in the tablet when he was done so no one could examine them later for pen impressions.

Once they were done, Atwater often trusted Alia to hand-deliver them to others in the Agency. The first time he did that, she'd been flustered, pointing out she didn't have the security clearances necessary to handle such materials. But he told her, "There are people with the proper credentials whom I wouldn't trust alone for five minutes with that envelope. If I didn't trust you, I never would have hired you. Now go ahead and deliver it."

So Alia became accustomed to handling such memoranda, and she never once so much as glanced at what they contained.

"Alia?"

She went into Atwater's office, where the shredder was digesting the remnants of a legal pad. He was sliding handwritten pages into a manila envelope, the kind that ties shut with a red string and a paper washer. As Alia waited, he wrote on the outside of it in block letters: DDO.

"Deputy Director of Operations" Alia read aloud. "So, you want me to deliver this . . . to you?" She didn't try to disguise the amusement in her voice.

Atwater looked at her over the tops of his glasses. "I want you to put it in the safe. If I don't come back from this trip—or any trip, for that matter—give that to my successor and have him open it immediately. And only he opens it. Not somebody from the director's office. Not some administrator. If anybody tries to clean the office out between appointments, take it and hide it."

Alia didn't accept the envelope.

"Colsun, are you going someplace dangerous?"

Atwater smiled. "Alia, do you know of any place on Earth that is not?"

Alia did not return the smile.

Atwater set the envelope down on his desk.

"Sweetheart, I am flying Western-flag carriers both way, using embassy ground transportation in both countries, and conducting my meetings in the embassies. In Cairo I'm staying on embassy grounds, with Marines outside the doors. In Islamabad I'm staying at Barry's, which is sort of like Fort Knox but without the tank noise. I am doing nothing covert, nothing clandestine. Not this trip."

He picked up the envelope. "And the only reason I am telling you about this is, if I have a heart attack while I'm waiting to change planes in Cologne, or if I choke on a shrimp on the airplane and nobody near me knows the Heimlich, I don't want this information to die with me."

Alia cocked her head.

"Your young man," Atwater explained. "It contains the information on his whereabouts."

Alia accepted the envelope and stared down at it as if it were a recently fired gun resting in her hands.

"We're just protecting him," Atwater told the young woman. "I'm being careful, that's all. Just in case we have a 'God-forbid' circumstance. Now go ahead and put it in the safe."

Feeling slightly numb, Alia walked to the closet behind her desk, keyed in a four-digit code, and then put her thumb on the biometric reader on the wall safe's face. It clicked, and she turned the handle to open it.

Atwater had several passports: his personal American passport, as well as one each from Canada, Turkey, South Africa, and Chile. The only one missing from the safe was his official one, the diplomatic passport he traveled on when he was working in the open, conducting official business.

That relieved her but only a little.

She turned the manila envelope over in her hand. No seal—the only thing holding it shut was the little red string.

She glanced at the door to Atwater's office. He was on the phone, turned with his back toward her.

There are people with the proper credentials whom I wouldn't trust alone for five minutes with that envelope. If I didn't trust you, I never would have hired you. Alia remembered Atwater's words as clearly as if he were standing beside her, repeating them.

Blushing, she slid the envelope unopened onto a shelf next to Atwater's passports, closed the safe, and locked it.

CHAPTER THIRTY-SEVEN

❑ ❑ ❑

Garj Valley, Pakistan

Blake looked down at the chessboard, knotted his fingers in his beard, and thought about hockey.

Actually, he was thinking about hockey playoffs—the NHL playoffs. He missed them this year. Or at least he thought he missed them. He was beginning to lose track of time. But his beard reminded him he had been in the camp for a while. It was long enough now to put any hockey player's "playoff beard" to shame.

He moved his rook on the board. He did it casually, masking his irritation. For weeks now all he did at this camp was go on hikes and take target practice with the rifle and the pistol. Other men cycled into and out of the camp, but he repeated the same routine. It was as if he was being trained for nothing.

Across the board, Saif reached for his king, touched the playing piece, and then folded his hands in his lap.

"This game," Saif said in Arabic. "This chess, it was invented in India in a more primitive form. But the chess we have today . . . did you know, my brother, that it was Muslim culture that introduced it to the world?"

"No; I didn't." Blake had become accustomed, almost without thinking about it any longer, to answering questions as he believed Grant Reinbolt would answer them.

"It is true," Saif said, nodding over the board. "In Persian, the word for 'king' is *shah*, from which 'chess' is a corruption. *Checkmate* comes from an ancient Persian phrase meaning 'the king is dead,' and Arabs carried this game with them throughout the Middle East, throughout Europe and Asia, as they traveled. There are tapestries showing the Christian Templar knights playing chess. Apparently, when they were not burning our towns, raping our women, and murdering our children, the Templars played games with us, just as you and I are playing this game right now."

He smiled as he said the last part.

Saif tapped a second time on his king, a wooden disk on Blake's cloth gameboard. "And I would say that we have reached stalemate again, my brother. Are you certain you only learned this game this year?"

Blake grinned.

Saif shook his head. "Then Ibrahim and my brother Raheesh chose well in you, Grant Reinbolt. You have a fine strategic mind."

That last sentence was exactly what the last man to play Blake on this chessboard said. Yet Blake felt he could remember that last man as a friend. He kept smiling but reminded himself that Saif and his brother were not men who would ever be his friends.

"I am going to turn in early, my brother," Saif said. "May I suggest you do the same? I would like you to take a walk with me tomorrow, and we must leave early. Mahmoud will come to wake you before dawn so we can break bread together before we set out. Will that be all right with you, my brother?"

"That would be my honor," Blake said.

But what he thought was, *Finally something different.*

CHAPTER THIRTY-EIGHT

❑ ❑ ❑

Blake blinked his eyes open at the sound of footsteps on the gravel outside the tent. A full moon was still up outside, and even through the tent and the rain-fly and the camouflage netting, some light penetrated, allowing him to see objects in the tent, if not details.

The tent flap was lifted, and even though the visitor carried a flashlight that prevented Blake from making out the details, Blake could tell from the slight build and the man's shuffling walk it was Mahmoud. Blake sat up on the cot.

"Ah, you are awake, my brother." Mahmoud spoke Arabic with an Afghan accent. "Good. Come to the command post. Bring your rifle, your pistol, and water. Dress to be out in the sun. We have a very long walk ahead of us."

Blake nodded and swung his feet from the cot, shuffling them on the ground; the camp seemed a little too high for scorpions, but one of his Special Forces team was stung once, and he didn't care to spend three days sweating and in agony, waiting for the swelling to go down. He reached down, knocked his boots together upside-down and then, after Mahmoud turned his back, removed the insoles.

Because he spent most of his training days in sandals, Blake took to using his boots as his bank. Muslims consider footwear to be as personal and as potentially unclean as underwear, so he put his Krugerrands in his boots, four in each one, under the insoles. The chances of anyone rooting around in his boots were about the same as anyone going through his skivvies.

For a moment he considered taking the gold with him. But this didn't feel as if they were leaving camp for good, and if they were traveling armed, he didn't need metal in his pockets where it could clink against a spare magazine. He put the eight coins in the bottom of his sleeping bag.

Mahmoud had not left. He was on the other side of the tent, waking Khalil.

"Both of us?" The big Iraqi was asking Mahmoud. "I thought it was just you, me, and Saif."

Makes two of us, man.

"Saif asked for you both. Come quickly. We have a long walk ahead of us, and we must be gone well before dawn."

The big man's response was more of a growl than words.

Blake pulled on socks, boots, and a jacket; put a water bottle, the pistol, and spare magazines into a rucksack; and shouldered the AK-47 he zeroed on the range just the day before. He left the tent while Khalil was still getting his things together and fell in with Mahmoud.

"It is a cool morning," Blake observed in Arabic. He knew better than to ask Saif's attache where they were going. Were Mahmoud authorized to share such news, he would certainly have done so already.

"No clouds," Mahmoud said, looking up at the spray of stars and the moon, a quarter of the way past its zenith. "Nothing to hold the heat. But stay covered, my brother. We shall have the sun beating down upon us soon enough."

They got to the headquarters building where the old man who served as quartermaster was now doubling as a cook, taking *naan* bread from the oven and handing it to Blake with a bowl of stew that smelled like curry and goat. Blake bowed his head silently over the meal for a moment and ate. Khalil came in five minutes later and ate as well, the two men saying nothing to each other despite the fact they were sitting next to each other on the floor, their knees practically touching.

"Good morning, my brothers." Saif said this from the steep steps leading up to the second level. Many of the officers' cadre slept on the rooftop when the weather was mild. "You have eaten? Good. Let me take a bit of bread, and then we shall start. We have far to go this morning: so far our footsteps shall have to be our prayers. But do not let this trouble you; Allah honors the warrior."

Khalil grunted his assent, which Blake considered a hoot: except for Fridays, when the entire camp turned out, Blake had yet to see the big man at prayer.

Saif ate standing, conferring in low tones with Mahmoud while Blake and Khalil took turns filling their water bottles from the big earthen jar next to the stove. Then Mahmoud did the same for himself and Saif.

The leader smiled.

"You are well, my brothers? Let us start walking before the heat of the day comes upon us."

Over the previous weeks, Blake had become familiar with several faint trails that, along with the two-track used by the vehicles, led away from the camp. There were trails leading to the ridgelines on either side of the valley, traveled daily by the sentries, and a trail leading past the weapons ranges and up into the mountains; one of the younger men told him this was a "smuggler's road" leading into Afghanistan, even though it was only five or six feet wide and did not at all fit the Western concept of a road.

The path they took to leave the camp led nearly due east, downslope, but at an angle from the dirt track used by the vehicles. It was narrow, less than a meter wide; they went single file, Mahmoud leading; and they changed elevation frequently. In some places, the climbs or descents were so steep all four men put hands on the rock to steady themselves. Blake assumed a goat could probably follow it, but it was out of the question for a horse, or even a burro.

The full moon, setting behind them, gave good light to travel by, and they moved quickly, the trail rising and falling before them but, for the most part, leading downhill. When the moon finally reached the horizon, its light was replaced by the graying horizon before them.

The gray sky gave way to slate blue, and the stars began to dim out. Through passes to the north of them, Blake could see the taller peaks of the Hindu Kush blushing a deep pink with the first light of dawn, the snow streaming from the summits like faint, thin, pastel veils.

Forty minutes later they crested a rise and were greeted by the sunrise itself, low and red on the eastern horizon. Wordlessly, all four men stopped, took water from their packs, and drank. Mahmoud sat although both Blake and Khalil stayed on their feet, wordlessly avoiding one another. Saif, the only one of the four who did not carry a rifle, had still not said a thing about where they were going or why, although he complimented the men on the time they made.

"We have three, maybe four hours to go at this pace," he said. "And then we will rest through the heat of the day."

Blake nodded, not asking questions, drank down a quarter of his water, and looked at the low, orange sunlight playing over the valleys and ridgelines at their feet. He rarely thought of Pakistan as beautiful, but in that moment it was a reminder that Earth's maker is an artist and that beauty was there, even in the stones.

The warmth of the day came on quickly, but all four men kept their heads and their arms covered, exercising the wisdom of people who have long lived with the desert, depending on their clothing to keep the heat of the sun at bay.

Two more hours of walking brought them to a more pronounced trail and they followed this down to a village composed of just three houses, each situated in the corner of a rectangle defined by a low mud wall. Women retreated into two of the houses as the four men approached, but the only male present was an elderly man who walked out into the sunlight beyond his yard and stood there, waiting for them.

"These people are goatherds," Saif explained. "Most of the men and all of the boys are out with their flocks. But the elder has waited behind for us."

He walked forward, and the two men faced each other at a distance of about a meter.

The old man spoke first, "*Pa khair raghley*." Blake recognized it as a greeting, the rough equivalent of "welcome" in Phalura, a language of which he only understood a few phrases.

Saif, on the other hand, seemed fluent in it, and the two men spoke for a few minutes. There was no handshake or embrace of any sort, just slight bows as they spoke, and then Saif turned to the three of them and said, "He says our meal will be ready shortly, and we should come inside where it is cooler."

The meal was lamb *tikka*, spicy and thick with curry, and filling. The old man served them, which did not surprise Blake; although the women undoubtedly prepared the food, they would not enter a room where there were strange men, particularly when their own men were away with their herds.

Their host was dressed differently from the way the men dressed in the camp. He wore a loose trouser-shirt combination and said little. But when the four men had eaten, he showed them pallets.

"We should rest now," Saif said. "This man will wake us when the sun has gone down."

"How do you know him?" Blake asked. "Is he family?"

"This one?" Saif shook his head. "I have never met him before. But he has been instructed to provide us with hospitality. He will do as he is asked."

Blake still did not know why they left the camp. It did not keep him from sleeping. He estimated they covered almost thirty kilometers over ten hours of walking, and he was ready to rest. When Mahmoud shook him awake, the sun was already set, and only the gloam of twilight was entering the open door of the hut.

The old man served them again. It was the same lamb tikka, but it had been kept warm near the fire and, if anything, grew spicier since lunch. Flat bread, like naan but thicker, accompanied the meal, and by the time they finished eating, full night had fallen. Saif spoke a word to their host, and the old man went outside, out of earshot.

"All right, my brothers," Saif said as they sat in a circle on the hut's earthen floor, "it is time for us to do our work. Two valleys over, there is a house, and the man who lives at that house will be arriving home late tonight. He was at meetings in the provincial capitol today, so he will be in his uniform. He will be unmistakable."

He paused, and Khalil asked the question: "What do we do with this man?"

"We kill him, of course." Saif opened his rucksack and took out a photograph, which he set on the ground between them.

It was a formal portrait, a picture of a man in the uniform of a Pakistani captain of police.

CHAPTER THIRTY-NINE

❑ ❑ ❑

If, in the process *of gaining the opposition's confidence, you must sacrifice one of our own, it raises a quandary that is positively Damocletian.*

When did Blake have that conversation with General Sam? Six months ago? Five?

Had it even been that long?

And now the old soldier was proving prophetic.

Blake remembered a story the sniper in another Special Forces team told him, how a Pakistani police officer took the initiative to cross into Afghanistan and warn American forces that units from the TTP—the Pakistani Taliban—were about to breach the notoriously porous border in an attempt to flank the Americans while the Afghan Taliban attacked from the other side.

He remembered being told the policeman was an officer . . . what sort of officer? Perhaps a captain of police? Possibly the very captain of police whose photograph he was just shown? Pakistan was the sixth most populous nation on Earth, but its federal police force could not number more than a few thousand, and of those, how many were police captains? A few hundred?

The odds were against it, but it was by no means impossible that the man they were heading off to kill was a man who risked his own life to save those of Americans.

He could very well be on his way to assassinate a hero.

There is the command imperative—the officer's imperative—to place the good of the many above the life of an individual. Yet if you exercise that imperative and take that life, you will be outside every law of this country.

Blake tried to remember Romans 8:28, the verse about how God can use all things to the good. But at the moment the only verse he could get into his head was Mark 14:36: *"And he said, Abba, Father, all things are possible unto thee; take away this cup from me."*

He thought for a moment. How did it end?

Oh, yes: "*. . . nevertheless not what I will, but what thou wilt.*"

CHAPTER FORTY

The policeman's house was in a hamlet of perhaps twenty houses, and it stood near the main road, which in this remote section of Pakistan was little more than an earthen track, deeply worn partly washed out in places. Had the house been in a larger town, it might have had a dog chained in the yard—many Pakistani Muslims hold the animal in contempt, but they know that dogs, ill-treated or not, are territorial and will bark at the approach of a stranger. Yet the small collection of houses and earthen yards was two kilometers or more from the next nearest village, and vehicles driving in the area were probably few, so nobody kept a dog. They probably figured anyone coming up the road would be heard long before they arrived.

The little village had hills to its east, and the moon was past full and had not yet risen. Stars speckled the sky, and oil lamps flickered from one or two windows. As they watched, there was the sound of a well-muffled small engine starting, and it growled like a lawn mower heard from a distance. Inside the policeman's house, lights came on, brighter than those of his neighbors.

"His woman started the generator," Saif whispered. "She expects him home soon."

His woman. So they were going to kill the man in front of his wife. On one level that disgusted Blake even further. But the warrior in him, the tactician, welcomed the sound of the generator. It would mask any noise of their approach.

Saif led them around the little hamlet to a place where the ground began to rise. They could still see the road, but they could also faintly see a narrow path leading back to the higher ground.

"This leads to pastures above the village," Saif told them, his voice low. "We will all wait here until we hear the policeman's truck approach. Then you . . ." he nodded at Blake and Khalil, "will go down there and do this business. Mahmoud and I will watch for other vehicles. As soon as we hear your shots, we will start up the trail and wait for you in the first pasture. Then we will cross the pasture and pick up another trail I know. It joins the one that brought us here, and we will take it back to our camp."

Blake nodded and Saif looked at Khalil. "Do you have your pistol?"

The big man nodded.

"Use it for this job," said Saif. "The whole village will hear no matter what you use, but the sound of a rifle carries farther than the sound of a pistol. And Grant Reinbolt, stay near the road and back him up with your rifle. Again, just as soon as you are done, come quickly up to the pasture."

Blake nodded and worked the action on his AK-47 slowly, chambering a round with as little noise as possible.

So I'm not doing the job.

It didn't matter. He would be standing by, backing up the shooter, making certain the job got done.

It was exactly the same thing.

"When your man is down, don't wait for me. Go to the trail, up to meet Saif and Mahmoud. I will cover you. Then I'll follow you." Blake said it all in a whisper as they watched the road.

"I do not need you to cover me." Khalil spoke softly, soft enough that Saif, standing ten feet away, would not hear.

"Just do it. The people in these houses will be confused at the sound of the shot. But it will not keep them inside for long."

If Khalil had a reply to that, Blake never heard it because a moment later Mahmoud looked down from his perch high on the trail and made a sound like the *ba-aah* of a goat.

"The car," Saif whispered. "He comes."

Blake and Khalil moved swiftly, crouched low and crossed the road, staying on the side away from the houses. Khalil squatted low, in a ditch across from the policeman's house, and Blake moved farther down the low mud wall to where he could use the light spilling from the open doorway to illuminate anyone who walked near it. He put the AK-47 to his shoulder, grounded his cheek to the stock, and kept watch over the sights.

Lord, turn that policeman back. Let him remember something he forgot at his last stop. Keep him away from here.

The truck approached and turned into the walled yard, Khalil waiting a moment and then trotting in after it, far enough back to avoid being illuminated by its taillights. He moved to the truck's left, squatting low.

The truck stopped. The driver's door opened, the cab light coming on.

Two men. There were two men in the cab: the captain of police in the driver's seat and another man on the passenger seat next to him, in traditional clothes.

Khalil can't see the passenger. He's too low. Blake watched, his stomach knotted with an it's-all-going-into-the-fan feeling.

Khalil stood, pointed, fired twice, the passenger's door opening as he fired the second round. There was movement to the rear.

The second man was moving behind, using the truck to conceal himself.

Khalil was standing over the fallen captain of police, his pistol trained on the man, prodding him with his boot.

The second man cleared the back of the truck and came around it. He had a rifle in his hands. He leveled it.

Blake squeezed the trigger, loosing a two-shot burst on center-of-mass that brought the second man completely upright. He raised the front sight so it occluded the man's head, and squeezed the trigger again. Ragged orange flame painted the night beyond the muzzle, and the second man dropped like a machine suddenly cut from its power.

Blake saw Khalil look straight at him and then turn and run, hurdling the low mud wall in stride and running swiftly yet nearly silently in the direction of the trail. Blake recrossed the road, sprinted along it crouched low, and then crossed back once he was well beyond the lighted houses. He heard the distant clack of a Kalashnikov being chambered and looked over his shoulder just in time to see a woman in a *bhurka* step out from the house and spray the darkness beyond with the rifle on full auto. She shot the chamber empty and then fell to her knees. The noise of the gunfire echoed away and was replaced with the keening of bereavement, a long, sobbing wail of grief.

Blake kept moving. There was no sign of Khalil ahead of him; the big man could really move. Then, off to his right, Blake detected movement in his peripheral vision, a man scurrying.

Blake stopped, aimed, and began moving the barrel across the area where he saw the movement: pointing, pausing, moving, pausing again. To the east the moon was just clearing the hilltops bringing with it a veil of blue light. He saw the movement again, aimed, and then lowered the barrel.

"Mahmoud?" He whispered it and the man stood up.

"Praise to Allah, it is you, Grant Reinbolt." He too was whispering.

Blake came nearer. "What are you doing here? We are supposed to meet you in the pasture."

The other man's face was twisted. "I was going there, my brother. I was leading the way. Saif was following me, but he stayed behind to watch the truck pull in. I was maybe three minutes ahead of him, and when he did not come up to meet me, I went back, and there were men facing him, surrounding him. I do not know where they came from. There are many paths leading into the pasture; perhaps they were coming down one as I was going up the other. But when they heard the shots, I saw one hit Saif with a rifle butt. Then they dragged him away."

The thin man's face looked tortured with grief. "Grant Reinbolt, they have taken Saif!"

CHAPTER FORTY-ONE

"Listen to me, Mahmoud. Khalil just passed here; he's up in the pasture by now. Go get him, come back, and wait here. If there are four men, we are probably going to need all of us. I'm going back to see if I can find where they took Saif. Can you repeat that back to me?"

The skinny man did as he was asked.

"Good," Blake said. "Then go."

Blake was well aware of what situation analysts referred to as the "cascade effect"; when one part of a plan slides into the fan, it tends to take other parts along with it. In other words, when things go badly, they tend to keep getting worse.

He wondered how much worse things would get before this evening ended. Saif seemed to be key to everything happening in the mountain camp. If he was captured or killed, Blake's usefulness here on site was about to come to a screeching halt.

There were shouts coming from the little collection of walled yards and huts. The policeman's wife was still wailing. Blake's training told him to drop and approach in a sniper's crawl, but his instincts told him every second counted. He approached the house the way he left it, using the roadside ditch to hide the lower half of his body. He could see a gaggle of people gathered around the left side of the pickup. At the far wall stood several neighbors, two carrying torches, the orange flames curling up into dark smoke. Blake moved farther for a better view.

Things were definitely getting worse. The men were shouting in Phalura and Urdu. You didn't need a translator to tell they were angry.

Saif was pleading with them in Urdu, and Blake translated as he listened: *Brothers, I beg you. I am a visitor here. I am staying in the next village over with my nephew. I was looking for a lost goat. I know nothing of these shots.*

The largest of the men around him, a stocky man in loose, tribal dress, hit Saif across the face with the back of his hand. *You are no goatherd. You are not from around here. You were with them, you lying dog.*

A second man punched Saif. The other two took him by the arms and dragged him out to the center of the courtyard.

Things are definitely getting worse.

One of the men slugged Saif in the gut with a rifle butt. The terrorist leader doubled over and sagged to his knees. The men backed away and chambered their rifles.

Normally snipers hate the moon. Night-vision scopes and darkness are the concealed shooter's friend. But armed with an AK-47 and open sights, Blake needed to be able to see his front sight, and the moonlight was providing just enough illumination to make that possible. He centered the sight on one rifleman's head and then moved to the other, practiced the movement twice and then fired two single shots in rapid succession. Both men went down.

Shoot, then move—Blake was not about to ignore that part of his training. He scuttled to his left, moving a good thirty meters before dropping to one knee, staying just high enough to see over the yard's mud wall. The two other men who had taken Saif prisoner jumped behind the truck and were returning fire to the area where Blake took his first two shots. Both of the men at the wall dropped their torches, one falling into the yard, and the villagers scattered back to their homes, the women screaming at the children.

Blake took advantage of the chaos to advance, staying well back from the wall, until he was perpendicular to the men behind the truck. They were no longer behind cover; now they were in profile to him. Two more shots dropped them both, and Blake ran, putting down one hand to pommel-jump the wall.

The policeman's wife was still in the doorway, screaming. She darted out and picked up one of the fallen riflemen's guns. Blake flicked the AK to full automatic and let loose with a hail of bullets, just over her head. Still screaming, she dropped the rifle and fled into the house.

Saif had risen back to his knees and was looking first at Blake and then at the house, dazed.

Need to keep everybody's head down until we're out of here.

Blake aimed his rifle at the back of the truck and shot two bursts into it low, just ahead of and just behind the rear wheel. The first burst produced the desired result; gasoline began raining onto the hard-packed earth of the yard.

Blake darted to where the villager dropped his torch, picked it up, and slung his AK over his shoulder. He grabbed Saif with his free hand, pulled the old man to his feet, and began half-walking, half-dragging him across the yard. Twenty feet from the truck, Blake flung the torch and then picked Saif up bodily, carrying the dazed leader like a sack of flour. A pool of blue and yellow flame spread under the truck.

There was no hurdling the far wall with 150 pounds of extra weight on his shoulder, but Blake clambered over and then shuffle-walked as fast as he could toward the trail. One hundred feet on, Mahmoud and Khalil appeared, and together the three men carried the half-conscious leader up the trail.

They had just crested the first ridge when Blake heard the truck's fuel tank explode, a large but soft *woomph* that drowned out the sounds of the screaming women.

CHAPTER FORTY-TWO

❏ ❏ ❏

Defense Intelligence Analysis Center
Bolling Air Force Base, Washington, DC

Tuesdays at nine were a regular conference for Colonel Angela Musashi: her one-on-one with the DIA director. The general—even if she were somehow miraculously promoted to his rank, he would never be a "Ron" to her—was already well versed in Directorate of Human Intelligence topics, but he used these weekly conferences to pick the colonel's brains and get her insights: the gut feelings and intuitions too nonfactual to make it into a memorandum.

Once a month, the one-on-ones were also about the colonel's development as an officer. As the director once told her, "When you get that third star, you're very conscious of the fact the law places strict limits on the number of general officers on active service at any one time, and as you add stars, that number decreases. That does two things; it makes you appreciate what you've got, and it also reminds you that, sooner or later, you've got to get out of the way so other good people can move up. And that gets you thinking about succession planning. You're only forty, Angie. You've had combat experience, and you're smart. So I think it's well worth my time to mentor you and help you be every bit the officer you can be."

This was one of those mentoring mornings. They talked about media training, which the director described as, "Something no officers worth their salt ever look forward to, but all officers need."

Then he'd asked her, "Garj Valley—what are you hearing on that? Anything new since Reg paid us a visit?"

The colonel shook her head. "We've been doing Predator overflights two, three times a week, sir. Garj Valley is an active camp, and it appears that they are indeed training, but it looks like the regular Taliban stuff: small squads getting ready to go over and add to the irritation in Afghanistan. We'd take it out, but the administration is asking us to be judicious about our Predator strikes. This one doesn't look high-profile enough."

The director cupped his chin with his thumb. "Sounds as if there might be a 'but' at the end of that paragraph, Angie."

The colonel paused, collecting her thoughts—something her media trainer totally approved of.

"General, I don't have a shred of physical evidence to back this up," she said. "Not a photograph or even 100 percent credible witness. But as you know, better than ten years ago one of Russia's former national security advisors claimed that better than 130 Soviet RA-115s—back-packable nuclear weapons similar to our SADMs—were unaccounted for in the Russian arsenal. A couple of stories circulated; one was that the GRU had already transported them to potential targets, and the other was that they were being sold, and al-Qaeda had already acquired several."

"Neither a happy prospect," the director said. "But as you say, this was better than ten years ago."

"Sir, an RA-115 can remain viable for decades as long as its circuitry is regularly charged," the colonel said. "And we've received several reports in recent weeks—not from rock-solid sources but not from the fringe either—that two of these weapons have come into Pakistan. Another thing: we know there has been an increase in the number of North Koreans entering Pakistan on diplomatic passports, including one who matches the description of Kim Sung Chi. He's a North Korean nuclear engineer who is said to be one of their top people in the manufacture of dirty bombs. And Pakistan's nuclear program is suspected of having the ability to manufacture cesium-137. So rumor has the bombs, the stuff to convert them to dirty ordnance, and the man who knows how to do it, all in the same country. A remote hill camp might be the perfect place to do the work."

The director turned his coffee cup on its wooden coaster.

"But there's no physical evidence to back any of this up," he said.

The colonel shook her head. "No, sir."

"Then we keep our eyes open and keep listening for further word from Reg." The director got to his feet. "Good report, Angie."

"Thank you, sir." She stood as well and started for the door.

"And Angie?"

The colonel stopped and turned. "Sir?"

"Trust your instincts on this one. I do."

CHAPTER FORTY-THREE

Garj Valley, Pakistan

"And what do you think of your tent-mate's shooting now, Khalil?"

The big man looked across the crowded room. Practically everyone was there—everyone but the sentries—because for one hour each evening after the fourth prayer time the cadre allowed the diesel generator to be started, providing electricity to power the television and an older Agat computer with a big cathode-ray-tube display.

"I think . . ." the big man's Arabic seemed to have even a thicker Iraqi accent than usual, "I think his aim has improved."

Saif laughed, holding his side as he did so. Upon their return to the camp, the cook, who was also the medic, had taped several of Saif's ribs.

The night before, Saif was in much rougher shape. Blake, Khalil, and Mahmoud took turns slinging him between them in pairs, taking most of his weight as he groaned and staggered up the trail. When not carrying Saif, Blake fell back behind the other three and surveyed the trail behind them in the rising moonlight, looking for pursuers. But apparently everyone in the village lost the appetite for revenge. They were not followed.

With every step, Blake thought about the people he killed. True, it was Khalil who shot the police chief. But the man in the truck with him was obviously the policeman's ally. And the four men from the pasture had clearly grieved the policeman's loss. Blake had killed in combat before, but these five lives did not feel like assets removed from the competition. These five felt like fathers who would never return to their families. And killing them felt like murder.

"Saif," Blake finally asked when they stopped for water, "who were those men?"

"Friends of the police captain's," Saif said, smiling to hide the pain of his broken ribs. He was the only one of the four sitting, and he was half-curled, holding his side. Then he added, "Taliban."

For a long moment there was no sound, only the whisper of unfelt wind over a distant ridge. Then Khalil asked a question, "The police chief: was he Taliban as well?"

Saif nodded.

Another stunned silence.

"But our camp," Blake asked, "isn't it provided to us by Taliban? Aren't they our allies?"

Saif took a breath, grimaced, and looked at Mahmoud. "Explain it to them."

Mahmoud made a motion with his hand, and Blake, Khalil, and he sat on the ground next to Saif.

"Years ago, before the Russians fought here, the tribes in this area and in the north fought among themselves constantly," he said. "Some were arguing over land or grazing rights. Some were claiming revenge for insults so old no one really remembered who said what first. No one trusted anyone. When the Taliban took power in Afghanistan in the last decade, many of these tribes set aside their differences in the name of Islam and supported them. Eventually there were those who thought of themselves as Afghan Taliban and those who thought of themselves as Pakistani Taliban, and sometimes these two did not think the same way. But when the Northern Alliance took power in Afghanistan, Mullah Omar, who heads all Taliban, asked Pakistanis to set aside their differences and fight alongside their Afghan brothers. That is why there are camps such as ours; they are near the borders, and the Taliban have long used them to train young men for the Afghan war."

Blake and Khalil nodded to show they understood. Saif had his eyes closed, but the grimace on his face showed he was not sleeping.

"Of course, not all of the Taliban in Pakistan agree with this view," Mahmoud said. "Some feel that Pakistan should fight for Pakistan alone, impose sharia law across the country, and eliminate those Taliban leaders who insist on an alliance with Afghanistan. The men we fought tonight were such Taliban. And the policeman was the son of such a Taliban leader, a man they worked to put into his position so they could arrest and weaken those who did not agree with them. They still wish to fight America, to fight the NATO, but they wish to do it only here, and they threatened our allies, our hosts who have given us our camp. So as a show of gratitude, we agreed to do this thing."

Blake and Khalil looked at each other.

"Why didn't you tell us?" Blake asked.

Saif opened his eyes. "A good soldier follows his orders without explanation," he said, "just as you did. Both of you are my brothers, but I had to see you in a fight, to know you would obey, as you have."

He winced as he took a breath. "And besides, had I told you that you would be killing men who hate our enemies, just as we do, that could have caused you confusion. This way, letting you believe the policeman was only a servant of the Pakistani government, it was an easier kill, yes? Please forgive me if you feel I deceived you."

The news of the successful mission, of Blake's rescue of Saif, had opened new avenues in the mountain camp. Every man, even Khalil, wanted to sit next to him at mealtimes. On the range other soldiers told him they heard he would soon be part of the officers' cadre.

And that evening, while the power was on to receive the satellite feed from Al Jazeera on the television and the computer accessed the Internet from another satellite dish, the mood in the camp's company was one of celebration. There was even a full evening meal with beef. The men were happy.

Someone clapped Blake on the shoulder as he leaned with two other men to study the Arabic script on the computer screen. The Internet connection was a cobbled-together system. A satellite phone, which was normally kept on a charger next to Saif's cot, and operated with a password only Saif knew, was connected to the computer and used to send instructions—Web site instructions and page changes—to a server hundreds of miles away. The incoming pages arrived by a direct satellite feed.

It was a wash-your-feet-with-your-socks-on sort of approach. While Web pages arrived at broadband speeds, outgoing commands were glacial, sometimes taking a minute or more to execute. The system was so slow the officers did not allow the reading or writing of e-mail, either one of which would have quickly locked up the system. But they did allow the men to access and read the blogs on Internet sites that reinforced al-Qaeda propaganda. And Alia was absolutely correct: Abdul-Rassul.com was one of the approved Web sites. In fact, its new-postings page was the first one the men looked at every night. And every night Blake crowded in with them and scanned the Arabic new-message headings for *farasa asfar*: "yellow butterfly."

In better than two months there, he had not seen it. It was starting to feel as if he never would. But he scanned the headings and feigned enthusiasm for the diatribe in the blogs, looking at them each night until the electricity was cut off.

The next morning there was fresh activity in the camp. Saif and the Land Rover left at dawn, and some of the newer recruits were set to work putting up three more tents. At lunchtime four of the officers' cadre moved their belongings out to two of them.

No one explained what the change was all about, not in the talk after prayers and not at dinner that evening. The Land Rover stayed gone all day, as did Saif and Mahmoud; and when night fell, the number of sentries was increased to four from the usual two.

They arrived at midmorning the next day, two older Toyota four-wheel-drive pickups, one white and one tan, both streaked with mud, their pickup beds covered by canvas awnings held up from inside on tubular metal struts. The drivers were each accompanied by riflemen. All four wore the clothing of Taliban hillsmen, and the trucks were parked, not with the big flatbed and the jeep in the vehicle park but inside the mud-walled yard next to the command center, right up against the building. The Taliban newcomers carried small rucksacks out to one of the newly erected tents, went inside, and stayed there.

Just after midday prayer Saif and Mahmoud returned, and in the Land Rover with them were three more men—an Arab in Talib clothing, a Korean, and a Pakistani who wore boots, olive-green trousers, and a khaki shirt with epaulets. He looked as if he was dressed for scout camp.

The Arab rounded up the Taliban truck crews, who set about carrying several large wooden crates up to one of the upper rooms of the command post, as well as two steamer-trunk-size metal containers, shiny and silver in color; it took all four of them to lift each one.

At midafternoon Blake saw Khalil working with one of the younger men, putting staked sides on the flatbed truck.

"What are you up to?" Blake asked.

"We've got seven more people in camp than usual," Khalil said. "We need to resupply. Mahmoud asked for volunteers. So I said I'd go."

"You volunteered?" The journey down from the hills was hot and dusty and especially uncomfortable in the heavy truck, which jarred its passengers' spines with every bump. The supply run was one of the least popular tasks around the camp.

"I need a change of scenery," Khalil said. He smiled. "And besides, maybe there are some new women in town."

"I thought all the women where we get our supplies were over sixty . . . and even they wear bhurkas."

Khalil smiled more broadly. He had amazingly straight teeth for an Iraqi. "You have taught me to be an optimist, Grant Reinbolt!"

That night Saif and Mahmoud were not at dinner or evening prayer. When the generator came on and the men gathered for news, Blake kept expecting the camp leader to come downstairs and introduce the visitors, but it never happened. He looked at Abdul-Rassul.com and scanned for the Arabic "yellow butterfly," but again it was not there.

Blake went back to his tent still wondering what the changes in the camp meant. He was almost asleep when he heard the distinctive grumble of the flatbed truck arriving back in camp. Half an hour later the tent flap opened, and Khalil came in, but the big Iraqi said nothing. He just took off his boots and went to sleep.

CHAPTER FORTY-FOUR

❑ ❑ ❑

Defense Intelligence Analysis Center
Bolling Air Force Base, Washington, DC

"General?"

The DIA director paused in the corridor outside his office, turned and smiled. "What's up, Colonel?"

Angie Musashi glanced at the half-dozen or so people passing in the hall."May I speak with you inside, sir?"

"After you."

They walked past the entrance to the director's anteroom and went to a second door, which the director opened with a swipe card. This opened onto a hallway about fifty feet long and, at the end of the hall, another door, this one with a keypad. He punched in four numbers, and they walked directly into his office.

The general set his cover on a hat stand. "What have you got, Angie?"

"That MI6 man we met with last month . . . Chambers. He called me today. We have movement. He's showing a delivery, believed to be ordnance, arriving at Garj Valley."

"Imagery?"

The colonel shook her head. "Human intel. Their person in-country."

The general pursed his lips. "Have we confirmed with our own assets?"

Musashi shook her head again. "Electrical storms around Bagram. They can interfere with some of the UAV flight controls. All of our drones are grounded, and I'm hesitant to ask for manned reconnaissance. Everything else we use is much noisier than a drone; I'd hate to give our hand away. We do have a satellite we can reposition to pass in sixteen hours; I've asked for imagery in the full spectrum."

"Then you're doing what you can," the general said. "Keep doing it."

He pushed a button on his telephone. "Vicki?"

"Sir?"

"Could you get on Outlook and see if I can get some time with the director of National Intelligence tomorrow?"

"Certainly, General. What time?"

The director pushed the Mute button on his phone. "How long will it take to analyze that imagery, Colonel?"

"Full spectrum? Six hours, sir. Maybe seven."

The director opened the line again. "See if you can get me in for this time tomorrow, Vicki."

CHAPTER FORTY-FIVE

❑ ❑ ❑

Garj Valley, Pakistan

Blake knelt on the woven rug and went through the motions of morning prayer with the nine Muslims gathered around him. Saif was not there, but then again he was pretty sure Saif would find bending prostrate too painful with his damaged ribs. Blake was amazed the man was able to take a daylong ride in the Land Rover. And Mahmoud was not there as well. Nor had he seen the three strangers since they arrived.

Prayer ended and Blake looked over each shoulder, each time saying, "*As Salaamu 'alaikum wa rahmatulaah.*" And when he looked over his left shoulder, at the angel recording his sins, there was Saif, smiling.

"Prayer is beautiful, is it not?" The elder closed his eyes as if remembering something pleasant. "I hope to join you again here soon, my brother. But until then, could you come upstairs? There is someone I would like you to meet."

Blake saw that Saif had placed a guard, one of the older recruits, at the top of the steep stairs. There was never one there before. The three strangers were sitting at a table but rose when he and Saif entered. Behind them a large square of canvas covered some things that looked large enough to be furniture.

"My brother, my friends, this is Grant Reinbolt," said Saif.

No one offered to shake hands. But the Arab took a step nearer and looked Blake straight in the eyes.

"Tell me something, American," he said. "Why do you hate your country?"

CHAPTER FORTY-SIX

❏ ❏ ❏

Blake cocked his head. "Hate my country? I don't hate my country. I love my country."

The Arab and Saif looked at each other.

"But my government," Blake said. "My government is corrupt. We say we believe in freedom of religion, but we do not. You know, and I know, there is no God but Allah, and that Muhammad, praise his name, is the prophet of Allah. But we are prevented from sharing this truth—from using the rifle, if we must, to do so. Were it not for my brothers in Islam, I would be dead now. My life belongs to Islam. I will do anything for it. And if I can do something against the government that is tainting my country, then the life I have been given back is sweet."

The stranger crossed his arms. "Your Arabic is very good; you speak well."

He looked at Saif, who smiled.

"And on the face of it," the stranger said, "I would be inclined to believe that you say only what you wish our ears to hear. But my brother in Islam here, whom I trust with my life, tells me that you, and you alone, saved his life. I understand you are a very brave man."

Blake looked down at his feet. It seemed like the thing to do. "I have been well trained."

"And Allah be praised for that. But for what we want you to do, we need more than a well-trained soldier. We need a man who can be brave. Tell me, American, can you be brave again?"

Blake looked straight at the stranger. "If that is what Islam requires of me, then yes. I can be brave. I will die, if necessary."

The stranger smiled. "Not this time, it won't."

Saif motioned Blake to the table, and the four men sat. The Asian straightened his glasses and spoke for about fifteen seconds in Korean. The one dressed in khakis translated into Arabic.

"Are you a fisherman? Have you ever driven a boat?"

Blake nodded. "Sure."

"In the ocean?"

"I've done some offshore fishing with buddies." It was true. He'd often gone fishing during leaves from Fort Bragg.

"Do you know a place in North Carolina called Morehead City?"

This was getting eerie.

"Yes," Blake told them truthfully. "It's right near Beaufort. Small commercial port. I think the Navy had a sub base there once. I've fished out of there a few times. The Outer Banks tend to knock down the bigger seas between them and the mainland, so it's one of the best places on the East Coast to fish offshore. You're protected by the barrier islands most of the way out."

The Korean, the Arab, and Saif were all nodding at one another. Then the Korean spoke again. And again the man in khakis translated.

"When you were in Washington, you were a taxi driver, is that right?"

"That's right."

"And did you ever drive to Union Station, ever wait there?"

"I did so often. It was where my dispatcher usually told me to wait when I did not have a fare."

The Korean nodded.

"Union Station is near the United States Capitol Building, is it not?"

"It is very near. You can see it from the taxi stands in front of the station. It, the Senate Buildings: they are all quite close."

More nods all around.

"When a taxi is waiting at this taxi stand, must the driver wait with it?"

"Yes, it's required. Police keep people from parking in front of the station, and they also make sure the cabbies stay with their cars."

"Doesn't anyone ever walk away? To use the restroom? To get a drink of water?"

Blake shrugged. "You're not supposed to, but sure. The cabbies get to know one another. You need to go to the restroom, you ask another cabbie to watch your cab, to move it up if the queue moves."

"And how long could a taxi be left this way?"

Blake looked down, thinking. "Maybe ten minutes."

"What happens after that?"

"I suppose they would look for you, check the restrooms. And then, if the cab is still unattended, it would probably be towed."

"Do they keep tow trucks there?"

"No." Blake shook his head. "They would have to call one."

"How quickly could it be there?"

He thought. "We had a cab break a tie-rod pulling away from the taxi stand once. The police called the nearest wrecker. It was there in fifteen, twenty minutes."

"So if a person left a cab there, the soonest it would be moved would be twenty-five minutes?"

"At the soonest. That would be my guess. Maybe longer."

Again there were nods all around.

The Korean stood.

"This translation business is tedious." His English was impeccable. He sounded nearly American, with just the barest hint of a British accent. "Arabic is not necessary for what we have to do next. Come over here, Mr. Reinbolt."

He walked to the back of the room and whisked away the canvas tarpaulin.

On the floor were two open cases. Each was lined with a goldish metal foil, like the foil Blake saw in images of space capsules. Each had a cylinder running diagonally across it, a rectangular box in the corner with wires leading from it, and another rectangular box with what appeared to be an older laptop keyboard and a digital display. On the inside of the box was a rectangular meter with Cyrillic writing on it and a face divided into green, yellow, and red sections. The needle was well into the green. Around the outside of the case, affixed with web strapping, were a number of spheres of dull, gray metal.

"This is a nuclear munition designed to be carried by infantry," the Korean said.

"A nuclear bomb?"

"Technically yes, although this is not an aerial bomb; one doesn't drop it from an aircraft. This one is designed to be placed and then detonated."

Blake examined it, hands behind his back. "How much damage will it do?"

"By itself, it would have sufficient yield to level about a city block, maybe a little more. Buildings a block or two farther out would be heavily damaged but would still stand, and it would break every window for several miles. But it's nothing like what you chaps dropped on Hiroshima, if that's what you mean."

Blake did not reply.

"This is designed to be used on the battlefield—to take out a fortified command post or neutralize a vehicle park or an airfield," the Korean said. "Basically, a big bang. These lead spheres arranged around it, though, each contain a sealed glass vial filled with an extremely radioactive substance the human body will readily absorb, as if it were potassium. They make the device much heavier, far too heavy for a single man to carry; but they also make it much, much more effective.

"The spheres will break upon detonation, and the shock wave will immediately send the cesium, the radioactive substance, several blocks in all directions. After that it becomes wind-borne. If even a light breeze is blowing, any area downwind will be contaminated for several miles. I'm told that, on a fine summer afternoon, it is quite common to have the wind blowing steadily from the train station toward the Capitol. Everyone on the Hill will be affected by the cesium."

Blake took a breath. "How many people would this kill?"

"Immediately?" The Korean looked at the ceiling, as if the answer were written there. "Hundreds certainly. Everyone in the train station and on the street outside. Possibly thousands. Probably most of the people in the Rayburn Senate Building. The initial scale would be about that of the World Trade Center collapses. But within the next twenty-four hours, hundreds of thousands would fall sick, and thousands would be dead or dying within a week. It would cause widespread panic in Washington, possibly up and down the Eastern Seaboard. This is particularly true if we detonate the second one elsewhere a couple of weeks later, which we fully intend to do."

He held a hand out to Blake, as if showing him a new car.

"Push the toggle switch on the far left of the top row," the Korean said. "Don't be afraid. There are several safeguards in place."

Blake did that, and the digital display blinked zeros across its width and then went blank, only a colon showing in red.

"It is just like setting a microwave," the Korean said. "Using the numeric keypad, set it for twenty-five minutes, and then hit the key with the return arrow."

Blake did it. The display read: 25:00.00.

The Korean handed Blake a cell phone. "This is preprogramed. It will only dial a single phone number in the 202 area code, which is the number for the initiating device. Turn it on and press the green button as if you are making a call."

Blake did it and looked at the device. "Nothing happened."

The Korean laughed. "That is because it requires an American 3G cellular network to operate, and we are up here in the howling wilderness, many kilometers from a cellular tower, let alone a 3G network. But trust me; were there such a network, the countdown would have started by now."

He looked at his translator and said something in Korean. The translator turned to the others.

"He says the instructions are quite simple, and this man understands them, but we should train several more times, just to be sure."

The other men came over and looked at the munitions sitting on the floor. The generator was out for the night, and the room was illuminated by oil lamps. It seemed odd to be inspecting digital technology and a nuclear weapon using pretty much the same sort of lighting employed in biblical times.

"Grant Reinbolt," Saif said, "we need you to do two things for Islam."

Blake faced him. "Anything."

Saif smiled. "We will be flying you home soon, my brother. These weapons are almost ready. They will leave here soon. First by truck, then by air. And finally on a ship."

"When does this ship leave? Where?"

Saif shook his head. "That part it is not necessary that you know. But this ship will pass near the Outer Banks, and we need you to be there when it passes."

Saif waved at himself, at the Arab Qaeda standing with them. "Were men who looked like us to intercept the ship, were a Muslim of color to be there, people would be suspicious. But you—if you shave your beard and cut your hair, wear Western clothes—you will look like any of the hundreds of fishermen who go there in the fall of the year, fishing for . . ."

"For blues," Blake said. "For wahoo."

"Exactly. My brother Raheesh will help you get a boat, a trailer, a pickup truck. You will put the boat in at this Morehead City, meet the freighter offshore. Many ships pass near that area because of the Eastern Seaboard traffic; the American government would have no reason to look for just one. The fishing boat we will have for you will have a large cavity for carrying the bait, the catch . . ."

"A live well," Blake said in English.

"Exactly. And these weapons will be crated in such a fashion they will fit in that 'live well.' You will meet the freighter, the crew will off-load onto your sport-fishing boat, you will return to Morehead City, put the boat onto the trailer, and drive it all back to Washington.

"We will help you put a weapon into the trunk of a taxi cab, one Raheesh and his people have reinforced to carry the weight. You will set the timer and drive to Union Station with a ticket for the Acela train to New York. You have ridden the Acela before, yes?"

Blake nodded.

"No one will notice you going out to meet the freighter because you will look like every other fisherman," Saif said. "And no one will think it out of place when you take the cab to Union Station because the cabbies at the station all know you; you will tell them you were visiting your sick mother these past few months.

"Four minutes before the Acela train is to depart, you will leave your cab, walk directly to the gate, and get on. When the train leaves the station, you will dial the phone, and the timer will activate. By the time detonation occurs, you will be many miles away, maybe even too far to hear or see what has happened. And if they question people on the train, you will be just another American, traveling to New York, although we doubt you will be questioned. The investigation will center on Washington."

Saif smiled. "It is perfect, is it not?"

Blake looked at the case, at the gold foil, at the timer with its glowing red numerals.

"Yes," he said. "We can do this. I can do this."

And I can, he thought. *Now how do I stop it?*

CHAPTER FORTY-SEVEN

❑ ❑ ❑

Benazir Bhutto International Airport
Islamabad, Pakistan

The Boeing 757 chimed, the overhead light winked off, and Colsun Atwater unbuckled his seat belt, thankful his elite mileage status qualified him for a free first-class upgrade, something for which he would never ask the government to pay. After trips of a certain distance, it was allowed; but Colsun Atwater believed in staying low-key and in the extremely unlikely event a journalist ever got access to Agency expense accounts, Atwater wanted to make certain his records were like Caesar's wife—beyond reproach.

The first-class cabin was mostly men in suits and one woman in conservative business attire. Half an hour before landing, she went to the restroom and emerged covered head to toe in a black bhurka that exposed only her eyes and her hands. It was late afternoon, and Atwater doubted she would have a business meeting this late in the day, but he felt her choice wise. Sharia law—the strict and conservative form of Islam that, among other things, forbade the education or public appearances of women—was already well established in Pakistan's north and had its adherents elsewhere in the country as well.

Atwater had landed in Islamabad before. The airport was of that vintage before airports became shopping malls, and it could have been any American airport built back in the seventies with one exception: spaced throughout the public areas were small prayer rooms, separate ones for men and women, designed for Muslim worship.

He wouldn't see it this time, though, because as soon as he emerged from the jetway into the overchilled air of the airport, his carry-on suiter over his shoulder, Barry Iddings—CIA's Islamabad station chief—was there with two men, one a federal policeman and the other in the uniform of Pakistan immigration.

"Barry, this is Lufthansa, not Air Force One."

The station chief, short of stature, bald, and with the thickest and bushiest mustache Atwater ever saw on a government official, laughed. "The head of immigration had dinner with me last night, and when I mentioned I had an old friend visiting, he insisted."

Atwater shook his head, chuckling, and gave the immigration officer his passport, which the man stamped and returned with a curt bow. There was no mention of customs; the diplomatic passport freed Atwater of that obligation. So, with the policeman leading the way, Atwater and Iddings went through a couple of keypad-secured doors and, in a matter of minutes, were getting into a black GMC Suburban idling at the curb.

"To what do I owe the pleasure?" Idings asked as they settled back and the SUV began to move.

"I had some business in the Middle East, and this was an easy add," Atwater told him. "And I have a presence in-country I wanted to brief you on face-to-face."

"They're setting dinner for us at the embassy as soon as you've had a chance to splash some water on your face. Want to talk about it over some mint lamb chops?"

"That sounds great."

The two men settled back and visited, talking about mutual friends, family, colleagues who were coming up for retirement. The trip went smoothly until they turned off the main road about two blocks from the embassy. Then the SUV came to a stop.

"Phil?" Iddings looked up, addressing the driver. "What's up?"

"FedEx truck in a fender bender with a taxi, sir." The driver looked back and began backing the vehicle up. "Drivers are hashing it out, and I don't want us sitting in one place. I'll go around the block."

He backed swiftly to the corner, backed expertly around it, and started down a residential street in the gathering dusk. Atwater sat up, looking over the seat back at the street ahead. One of the cars parked ahead looked as if it was about three feet off the curb, sticking out enough to slow them to a crawl as they passed. And they were passing a man with a cell phone in his hand; there was just enough light for Atwater to see that.

But the man wasn't talking on the phone, and he wasn't looking at it.

He was looking at the Suburban.

"Driver." Atwater leaned forward. They were almost even with the car that was sticking out. "Back up. Now."

"Yes, sir." The SUV came to a halt, backed up five feet.

And then the world erupted in flame, smoke, and noise, and the windows blew in, and the world winked out.

CHAPTER FORTY-EIGHT

❑ ❑ ❑

Defense Intelligence Analysis Center
Bolling Air Force Base, Washington, DC

"What have you got for me, Angie?"

The colonel laid two 11x14 color prints on the conference table in front of the director, side by side.

"This image was shot last week on a Predator overflight," she said, pointing to the left-hand image. "And this one was taken by satellite yesterday at noon local, right after the satellite was repositioned."

The director leaned forward. The Predator image was surprisingly clear, but the satellite image was even clearer. It was the difference between a good TV image and high-definition. And there were other differences.

"Two more vehicles in the satellite shot," the director observed. "And it looks as if they've added two tents under that camo netting."

"Yes, sir. The report relayed from MI6, from their HUMINT on the ground, is that the munitions arrived in two Toyota pickups with canvas awnings over the backs, one white and one tan. And our photo analysts tell me the vehicles in that satellite image are definitely two Toyota trucks—one white and one tan."

"HUMINT." The director squinted at the photographs. "Human intelligence got us in some serious jams in Iraq, Angie."

"True, sir, but that was Iraqi HUMINT. This is British. First-world. Dependable. MI6 says their asset believes the weapons are about to be deployed. He is recommending we strike before that happens. He is asking to have the entire camp taken out, on his call."

"But we have no imagery of the WMDs?"

The colonel shook her head.

"No fire . . ." The director tapped the table. "But there's sure enough smoke for my book."

He stood up. "Come with me, Angie. I want you there when I brief the director of National Intelligence."

The colonel stood. "General, if you share this with DNI, it takes the lid off. He'll inform NSA, CIA . . . everybody."

"I know that," the director said. "But it's something we have to do."

"Before we take the camp out, sir?"

"That's right," the director said, grabbing his attache case. "Before we take this camp out."

CHAPTER FORTY-NINE

❑ ❑ ❑

CIA Headquarters, Langley, Virginia

Alia got to her desk at seven in the morning and began culling the news reports for the day. By eight-thirty she was on her second cup of coffee, and the Agency's computers were done scanning the reports for trigger words, but she kept the Associated Press feed up on her second computer screen, something she did every day, just in case something late-breaking arrived as she was finishing up.

Atwater's flight would have landed in Islamabad about forty-five minutes before, and, if she knew him, he would want the file with the highlights up on the server just as soon as he got into the embassy and finished dinner. In the three years she'd been working for him, Alia had learned that Colsun Atwater did not consider time zones a valid excuse for not getting his work done.

She was saving the file on her left-hand screen when the AP feed auto-refreshed on her right. There was the after-lunch summary of activity on the London stock exchange and an item saying that the Pope was planning a visit to Chile.

And the third dateline caught her eye.

ISLAMABAD (AP)—Pakistan federal police report that an improvised explosive device (IED) was detonated near Embassy Row this evening, severely damaging an American embassy vehicle and killing all three occupants. An embassy spokesperson was not able to confirm or deny the report at this time.

Alia set her coffee down, her hand shaking.

No. . . .

No.

Her phone rang, and she let it ring three times before she lifted the handset.

"Depu— . . . Deputy Director of Operations," Alia suppressed a sob.

"Alia? It's Caroline in the director's office. . . . Honey, are you okay?"

"It's him, isn't it?" Alia fought to pull herself together. "The news report. It's Colsun."

There was a long pause on the phone. On Alia's computer, there was the muted ping of arriving e-mail.

"Honey," the voice said on the phone, "I just sent you a note. The director and some other people are coming down to see you."

Alia gasped for breath. "Caroline, tell me. It's him, isn't it?"

"Alia, I can't . . . they have to come see you. Do you want me to come down as well?"

"Yes." Alia wiped her eyes with her fingers. "Please."

She hung up the phone and looked around her office as if she had never been in it before. In the closet the safe was open; she opened it when she got in that morning to get out a list of watchwords she used to double-check those flagged by the computer in the slipping files.

She remembered the envelope Colsun handed her.

How had he referred to it? A "God-forbid circumstance." That was it. And the present one certainly fit.

Alia remembered Atwater's instructions: . . . *give that to my successor and have him open it immediately. And only he opens it.*

Not somebody from the director's office. Not some administrator. If anybody tries to clean the office out between appointments, take it and hide it.

Potentially, it was a felony to remove a classified document from an Agency office.

Was it still a felony if you were ordered to do it?

Was it still an order if the person who gave it to you was dead?

Alia removed the envelope from the safe, closed the safe door, and locked it. She looked at the envelope in her hands, glanced at her purse, and rejected it as a possibility. The security guards typically checked her purse—at least a quick look inside—anytime she entered or left the building.

What do you do with it?

Folding the envelope into quarters, she lifted her blouse in back, put the envelope under the waistbelt of her skirt, in the small of her back, and tucked her blouse back in.

A minute later the office door opened, and the director stepped in, followed by an older woman with blonde hair and Caroline, his assistant.

"Alia? This is Dr. McAleavey, a counselor who's on staff here with the Agency. I'm afraid we have some bad news."

CHAPTER FIFTY

❑ ❑ ❑

Garj Valley, Pakistan

The days with the Korean engineer and his Arab benefactor became numbingly similar. Blake went through the simple sequence of setting the timer and arming the munitions. The engineer showed him where the ordnance could be lifted, what could be touched, what should not be touched.

Saif produced nautical maps of the Morehead City port area and the Outer Banks and asked Blake to show him how he would proceed out of the harbor and then through the inlets. Then Saif produced charts that were already marked and, beaming, showed Blake that his course and theirs were exactly the same.

From time to time, Blake would be excused; and, several times when this happened, Khalil went up the steps to meet with the Arab and the Korean and the translator.

Is he the one who is supposed to place the second weapon?

Blake considered that, but it sounded crazy. The cell recruited Grant Reinbolt because he looked like a good old boy, sounded like a good old boy, looked as if you could set him up with a plug of Red Man and a twelve-pack of Budweiser and keep him happy all night. Find him coming in to the docks at Morehead City, and you might check to make sure he had enough personal floatation devices on board, but you'd never suspect him of transporting nuclear weapons.

Khalil, on the other hand, stood out from the rest of the men in the camp because he *looked* like a terrorist. Central Casting couldn't have made a better choice. Even though TSA and the FBI and all the other agencies supposedly had regulations to prevent them from profiling Middle Easterners, a federal agent would have to be all the way out of his or her mind not to stop Kahlil, ask him for some ID, and maybe take him in for a little closer questioning. The man just had that look about him.

Saif never offered any information about what part Khalil had to play in all this, and Blake knew better than to ask. The Pakistani police captain episode proved that; he was supposed to follow orders, whatever they were. In the week he worked with the Korean, Blake asked Saif only one question: "When do I leave?"

Saif smiled and said, "Soon enough, my brother. We shall tell you when the time has come."

Blake was learning more, but he still didn't know nearly enough.

CHAPTER FIFTY-ONE

Georgetown, Washington, DC

Dr. McAleavey was a grief counselor. She offered Alia the rest of the day off, but Alia insisted on staying. For one thing, it wouldn't be fair to the rest of the assistants in Operations if she took off and left them to deal with the loss of their deputy director alone.

For another thing, she'd wanted to leave the Agency at five, in the rush when all the other salaried nonmanagers left headquarters. She wanted to leave in a flood of people, when Security was watching hundreds of individuals depart and not just one. She'd wanted to do everything humanly possible to avoid having someone ask, "Excuse me, miss, but what's that tucked in the back of your skirt?"

Now, finally at home in her two-bedroom walk-up, she sat on her couch and waited for men in black jumpsuits to come flying through her front door and windows with guns drawn.

Alia thought it was poetic license when novelists wrote about "trembling hands," but her hands were shaking visibly when she set the folded manila envelope on the coffee table. Her fingernails rattled against the stiff manila paper of the envelope. She undid the string and opened it, her heart melting just a little at the sight of

Atwater's slanted, all-block-letter script. Setting the envelope aside, she unfolded the legal-size paper all the way and began to read:

TO: DDO

RE: Al-Qaeda Cell, Washington, DC/Garj Valley, Pakistan

Be advised this office has placed an asset operating under the alias of Grant Reinbolt into al-Qaeda-affiliated group based Bailey's Crossroads, DC area, and he has since matriculated into Pakistan training facility based in Garj Valley (Afghanistan border area).

Asset's name is Lieutenant Blake Kershaw, USA Special Forces, officially listed as deceased military roles.

Alia stopped reading for a moment.

Kershaw. *He had a last name.* Blake Kershaw.

She went back to her reading.

Asset replaces look-alike recruited by al-Qaeda via domestic sources in response to need for operatives who do not appear ethnically Muslim. Believe ultimate use will be to smuggle and place WMD or WMDs. Fact that asset has matriculated to Pakistan leads this office to strongly believe said WMDs are being prepared and trained within Garj Valley.

The rest she knew—the surgical alteration, the code words, the disposition of the real Grant Reinbolt.

WMDs, weapons of mass destruction. That and an operative in-country were enough, she knew, for her to go to somebody—Colsun's deputy or the director or one of his direct reports—and bring it out from under wraps. Colsun's second-in-command was still on an airplane, coming back from Indonesia and wouldn't be home for a day.

She wondered if this could wait that long.

She wondered how the Agency would react.

For the first half-day after she produced the memo, Alia knew, the attention would center on her removal of a classified document. It would certainly cost her the job. It might even result in her arrest. But eventually somebody would read the memorandum. Somebody would know where he was if they had to get him out. And that would make it worth it.

She put the memo back in its envelope and just sat there, waiting for the night to pass. She turned on the television but did not watch it. And somewhere around ten o'clock, she dozed off.

She was still on the couch when her BlackBerry buzzed in her purse, buzzed loudly enough to bring her awake. Yawning, she fished it out and looked at it. It was coming up on three in the morning, and there was a message waiting.

The message was not for her. It was for Colsun. Alia had administration rights to his account; any request for a meeting was automatically e-mailed to her as well. And Colsun had not yet been removed from the director's e-mail list; that probably wouldn't happen for a couple of weeks.

The meeting request was set for very early—six in the morning—and it had a lengthy list of attendees: directors of all intelligence agencies, their counter-terrorism chiefs, operations leadership, a presidential advisor, the Joint Chiefs of Staff. And in the subject line there was a message: [ATT. DOC.].

It was something the Agency did to add another level of security to the BlackBerrys. Classified subject matter could only be placed in encrypted documents which could in turn only be decrypted with the use of an algorithm that changed several times a second. To use it Alia had to highlight the document, click on it, and then key in a pass code that activated the servers at Langley. These would decode the subject and display it only as long as she had that window open. If she changed applications, the decoded text would disappear.

The BlackBerry displayed a growing line across the bottom of its screen and then text appeared . . .

SUBJECT: DISPOSITION, GARJ VALLEY, PAK.

Garj Valley.

Alia stared at it, stunned.

Why Garj Valley? Why now?

Maybe Colsun had managed to convey to someone in Pakistan that he had Blake in-country. That was plausible. But wouldn't that sort of meeting wait for Colsun's assistant deputy to get back to Langley?

It would and she knew it would.

So what else? Was it exploratory? Had they noticed something on their own, wanted to discuss it?

No. That sort of thing would be done with a much shorter list of attendees. And it would happen during regular office hours.

So why six in the morning? And why include the Joint Chiefs?

Alia did the math. Six in the morning, Washington time, was four in the afternoon in Islamabad. Start of the day here, end of the day there for a meeting. If they needed in-country intelligence, it was plausible they would teleconference at that time.

She looked at the BlackBerry. Yes; two individuals from the Islamabad station were included.

So why include the Joint Chiefs?

It had to mean they were planning a military action. There were only two such actions Alia could imagine. The first was a force-on-force ground confrontation, storming the camp.

In which case Blake might be rescued. If they knew he was there.

The second was they were going to strike and destroy the camp.

In which case Blake would be killed.

Alia's stomach crawled. Her first instinct was to log onto Abdul-Rassul.com, enter the Arabic for "yellow butterfly," and get Blake out of there. But you didn't just leave an armed camp; if Blake did, he would be risking his life. For all Alia knew, there was a Special Forces team already heading his way to bring him safely home.

It wasn't a decision she could make without more information.

The note came from the director's office, and she responded: *Caroline, given circumstances, may I attend in Colsun's place? Alia.*

It was grasping at straws and Alia knew it. A few seconds later a reply came back: *Will try to get you seated for future events when acting DDO is not available. This time, no can do. Highly classified.*

It was a polite way to tell Alia to get back in her pay grade.

She weighed her options. She could not wait for Colsun's acting deputy to arrive. She supposed she could show up anyhow, show the memo. But all that would do is get her hauled away for questioning. They'd meet without her; by the time she got to talk to somebody, it could be days too late. There were lots of people meeting about this valley camp, and the Agency didn't bring in all hands at six in the morning unless they were planning something major.

Think.

Think.

If I act, will I be saving him? Or killing him?

A name came to her.

General Sam Wilson. Blake told her to go see him if anything happened to him, to give the General the bank documents to take to Blake's mother.

In the few minutes Blake spoke about him, he'd seemed to trust the general implicitly. Alia looked General Sam up on the Internet later that night, saw he had served at or near the top of various intelligence organizations.

One of our own is what she thought.

Now she needed one of her own. She turned on her home computer, did a MapQuest search for Hampden-Sydney College, and printed out the results. Then she grabbed her keys and headed for the door.

CHAPTER FIFTY-TWO

❑ ❑ ❑

Hampden-Sydney College, Hampden-Sydney, Virginia

General Sam Wilson parked his pickup truck, stepped down from it, and scowled at the little car parked in the Wilson Center's gravel lot. It was a Scion xD, one of those little coupes favored by city people who want something that doesn't cost much and parks easily. He didn't recognize it, and he was pretty sure he knew most of his upperclassmen's cars.

He peered at the car. There was someone in the driver's seat. A young woman. He squinted through the glass.

She was pretty. Very pretty. Tan skinned, jet-black hair. He was positive he had never seen her before.

He looked at his watch. It was not even six in the morning. The sun was still rising.

General Sam tapped on the window with his cane, and the young woman startled awake. She pushed a button on the door handle, and then she did something with the key and the windshield wipers came on. She stopped them and pushed the door-handle button again. The window came down.

"Young lady, may I help you?"

She took in his hat, his jacket, the cane. "Sir? Are you General Sam Wilson?"

He nodded. "I am. And you?"

"I work with . . . I work with Colsun Atwater."

General Sam's face fell. "I heard about that on the news. A terrible thing. Horrible."

He paused, looking at her, waiting.

"Sir," Alia told him, "I'm here about Blake. Blake Kershaw."

The general's countenance changed completely; any guard, any reserve, was completely gone.

"We had best go inside, where it is warm," he said.

"I'm sorry to just show up like this," Alia told him as she sat in his office and he handed her a cup of tea. "I needed to see you, and I couldn't find a number. I drove down and got here a little after five. I saw the sign that said Wilson Center, and I thought I would park here, wait for someone to show up. I must have dozed off."

"How is Blake?"

Alia set her cup down, put her fingers to her lips, and blinked back tears. "I don't know."

The general nodded and sat behind his desk. "Then tell me what you do know, Alia," he said. "Start with that."

It took her fifteen minutes to tell the entire story, and when she finished, the general picked up the phone and dialed a number from memory.

"This is Samuel Wilson," he said to whoever answered the phone. "Is the director available? Yes, I am aware of that meeting. It is why I am calling. Could you interrupt him? It is a matter of national security." He listened for a moment. "No . . . the name is Sam Wilson. Yes, I understand that. . . . No. This afternoon will be too late."

He hung up and turned to Alia. "New assistant in the director's office. She's slow-walking me." He looked down at his desk and then up at Alia. "Put aside what you have gained through fact. I want your intuition now. Your gut feeling. Is Blake in grave danger? Will he die if we do not act?"

"Yes." Alia closed her eyes. "That is, I *think*. But if I order him out and it turns out he could have . . ."

She opened her eyes again, and General Sam was picking up the phone.

"I think I know someone who will listen," he told her. He began dialing another number.

"Hello, Martha? Sam Wilson here." He listened for a moment and said, "Yes, she's fine. Organizing some event to buy some land for a park right now. Listen, Martha, I hate to do this, but I'm coming in, and I need five minutes of his time."

He glanced at his watch. "Three, three-and-a-half hours from now. I know it's a bother. . . . You sure? . . . I'll see you then?"

He looked up at Alia. "Are you rested? Can you drive?"

"Sure." She got to her feet as the older man was getting to his. "Where are we going?"

"Back where you came from. Back to Washington."

CHAPTER FIFTY-THREE

❑ ❑ ❑

Garj Valley, Pakistan

Blake came back from prayer that morning to find Khalil already gone from the tent. He'd put his Qur'an away and headed back to the command post where the rest of the men were filing in for breakfast. Khalil was already sitting shoulder to shoulder with one group of trainees so Blake joined another where there was still room.

Then Saif came down from the upper room.

"My brothers," he announced, "all practice, all training, is cancelled for this day. Our guests will be leaving tomorrow morning, and we must spend the day helping them to ready their things and pack their trucks. They will also require supplies for their journey, and I would like two volunteers to drive down the mountain and fetch those."

Khalil rose to his knees, hand up. The man next to him glanced at Khalil and grudgingly raised his hand as well.

Blake cocked his head. *What is it with this guy and the supply runs? This is the third he's volunteered for this week.*

"Thank you, my brothers. Part of the fight is supplying the fight. Allah honors your dedication to our cause."

Then Saif went through some other announcements—recognition of men who completed various stages of their training, reading a note of support from Mullah Omar—and the men finished breakfast. Trying not to look too obvious about it, Blake went back to his tent, hoping to run into Khalil and ask about the supply trips; the line about the local women was obviously pure hogwash. But when he got to the tent, the big man was not there, and a few seconds later Blake heard the distinctive sound of the flatbed truck starting up and heading down the mountain trail.

Blake thought, then and there, about sitting in the truck cab for two hours as it bumped and jostled over the rough trail.

Glutton for punishment.

The rest of the day was as Saif said it would be—a workday. Men with carpentry skills were put to work nailing together hardwood shipping crates while others worked under the Korean's direction, listening to his translator's orders as they wrapped the cased munitions in plastic. After midday prayers, both weapons were wrapped and set in their shipping cases. Plastic foam, like the type used for spray insulation, was shot in around them to form a tight-fitting, shock-resistant collar. Then the cases were nailed shut and carried down to the trucks. Saif detailed six men to move each one, with extra men spotting in case someone slipped.

Blake was not allowed to help at all.

"My brother, you are too valuable," Saif explained. "If you slip and break an arm, crush a hand, all we are doing here is for nought. Just watch the men as they work. You will do your share in the weeks to come."

Khalil and the supply truck came back just before dinner. Water, spare fuel cans, and food were all off-loaded into the smaller trucks. The men all washed and filed in for their evening stew. Saif, the Arab, the Korean, and the translator were all waiting there for them.

"My brothers, you have worked well," Saif told the men. "All is ready for our brothers' journey. Two of our Talib brothers will be staying here with us for the next few days, and our benefactor and his engineer will leave the camp with the trucks. We have come to tell you now because they leave tonight."

"What?" It was Khalil who spoke up. "In the dark? Down these mountains? Surely it is better for them to leave in daylight."

"A risk they must take," Saif said. "I spoke by satellite phone today with our people in Chagai. A Pakistani Army detachment is due to arrive there tomorrow at noon. We want to be through Chagai before they arrive."

"Then wait another day," Khalil suggested.

"Regrettably, we cannot," Saif said. "We have people who will be waiting for these things to arrive; they have no communication with us until that happens, and they cannot tarry long."

Dinner continued, and Blake kept glancing over at Khalil. The big man seemed to be himself, talking and joking with those around him, but the talk appeared forced, as if he was ill at ease. And as dinner concluded, Khalil sought out Saif.

Blake helped carry bowls to the galley area and paused near where the two men were speaking.

"Let me go with the trucks tonight," Khalil was asking.

"My brother, there is no room. Two of the Talib are staying here as it is."

"Let one of the drivers stay. I can drive."

Saif scowled. "Khalil, my brother, why do you ask me to change plans? I have told you what you must do. Tonight you stay here. Now go in peace."

Blake almost forgot to carry his bowl to the galley. While Saif was in charge at the camp, it was rare for him to put his foot down.

And it was also rare for Khalil to make waves.

Al-Qaeda politics? All organizations had them. Blake didn't see why this one would be any different.

Still it was puzzling.

CHAPTER FIFTY-FOUR

❏ ❏ ❏

Washington, DC

"There you go," General Sam said. "E Street Northwest. Take that."

Alia was confused. She'd assumed they were on their way back to Langley, but the general told her to leave the interstate and go on surface streets into the city. Now they were in central Washington, in the crowded traffic of the latter part of rush hour.

The fountain in front of the White House was playing on her right; the Ellipse was on the left.

"Stay to your right," the general told her. "There. Take that. Executive Avenue."

Alia hit her brakes. "Sir?"

"Right there," General Sam told her. "Turn in there."

"General Wilson, that's the White House."

"And I would not have you turn here, were it not. Show the guard your Agency identification." The general had his wallet out.

"I'm not cleared."

"You are now. And give him this, as well." He handed her a White House staff ID. It was current.

He was right. The guard at the shack swiped their cards and passed them through. Alia parked in a handicapped spot near an entrance to the West Wing ("It's okay, dear, they know I have a sticker on my car"), and they were met at the entrance by a man Alia recognized from television as the Chief of Staff.

"General," she whispered as they walked. "How do you . . . ?"

"I used to work with the man," he told her, walking steadily with his cane. If he felt subconscious about walking through the White House wearing a porkpie hat and a Hampden-Sydney warm-up jacket, he didn't show it.

They walked on. Alia cleared her throat. "Are we going to the Oval Office?"

The general chuckled. "Of course not. The Oval Office is for state business."

They stopped in front of an elevator, and the Chief of Staff swiped a card and pushed a button. The general stepped in.

"Come on in, my dear," he told Alia. "We're headed up to the residence."

A Marine in dress blues met them at the elevator along with a Secret Service man in a suit.

"Is he in the parlor?" General Sam asked.

"Yes, sir," the Marine told him.

"No need for an escort then," the general said. "I know my way."

Not real, Alia thought. She was acutely aware she was still wearing the same clothes she wore to the office the morning before, she had not showered in twenty-four hours. The general smiled at her and made a come-along motion with his hand. He offered his arm and she took it.

"Sam, she looks a bit young for you."

Alia recognized the voice. Then she recognized the face.

"She's not mine, Mister President. I'm just borrowing her."

The President, in suspenders, shirtsleeves, and tie, showed them to a sofa. "Can we get you anything? Coffee? Breakfast?"

"Thank you, sir, no. Perhaps later, but I realize you are probably disrupting your schedule to see us, so I'll come straight to the point. And let me say right now that, if my instincts are wrong and we are troubling you over a nonevent, then you have my abject apologies."

"No apologies needed for a visit from an old friend." The president sat. "What is it, Sam?"

"Garj Valley, Mr. President," General Sam said. "What's happening with that?"

"How did you . . . ?" The President shook his head. "I should have learned years ago not to ask you that." He glanced at Alia. "Sam, maybe you and I should excuse ourselves."

"She's the one who brought it to my attention, sir."

The president half-smiled. "I'm pretty sure I'd be breaking a law."

"In word, perhaps, but not in spirit, sir." The general set his hat on a doilied end table. "Sir, this young woman is Colsun Atwater's right-hand . . ."

"I'm sorry about your loss then."

"Yes, sir," the general continued. "Colsun was running an asset in Pakistan. Good fellow. Decorated war hero. Hampden-Sydney man, one of our best. I fixed him up with Colsun myself. And he is operating subrosa in that camp in the Garj Valley."

The president's jaw dropped a fraction of an inch. "Oh, for . . . Sam, your instincts are spot-on. We have a strike going into that camp. UAV; we're taking the entire thing out. Today, just a few hours from now. I signed the order after breakfast this morning."

Alia gulped.

The president put his fist to his chin.

"General, I can't call off that strike. The threat is too large." He reached for a phone. "I can inquire as to the exact timing. Do you have a way of getting information to your asset?"

The general looked at Alia.

"Mr. President . . ." She took a breath and looked at her watch. "I need to use a computer. One with an Internet connection. Now, sir. Please."

CHAPTER FIFTY-FIVE

Garj Valley, Pakistan

Blake fell into a habit during prayer. He'd memorized hundreds of Bible verses over the years, and as he went through the motions of Muslim prayer, even as he was speaking aloud in Arabic, he recalled his Bible readings, chapter and verse.

Usually he would recall dozens of verses over the prayer time. But this time he could only think of one.

Whoever is not against us is for us.

Where was that from? It wasn't even a complete verse. He was pretty sure of that. He tried to remember the rest of it.

Whoever is not against us is for us.

That was all he could come up with. The context he knew . . . some of the apostles found a man working miracles in the name of Christ, and they told him to stop. But Jesus told them to let him continue.

Whoever is not against us is for us.

He was pretty sure it was one of the Gospels. But he couldn't for the life of him remember which one. It had been a long time since he'd read a Bible.

Prayer ended, and he was still trying to remember the rest of the verse.

The trucks left before prayer time, Khalil waiting at the wall, watching them go. And when the electricity came on for its one hour, the big man joined everyone in the common room, but he did not join in the banter, and the few jokes he made fell flat.

Blake joined the younger men looking at the blogs on Abdul-Rassul.com. They were the usual terrorist diatribe, nothing new. Then he sat and watched Al Jazeera with the officers.

Mahmoud looked at his watch and stood.

"Brothers, it is time," he said. "I am going to turn off the generator."

"But I just refreshed the page," one of the younger recruits complained. "It hasn't come up yet."

"Then pray it does soon." Mahmoud laughed. "I am cutting off the generator."

"Here it comes," the young man said as Mahmoud left. "There's a new post. Wait . . . *farasa asfar*?"

Blake froze.

"'Yellow butterfly?' Why would someone head a message like that?" The young recruit read the message. "It looks like a note on local prayer times in London. And it says . . ."

The computer and the television went dead, along with the overhead light- bulb. The room was bathed with the flickering yellow light of oil lamps.

"It was probably just a typo," the younger recruit was saying.

"You'll find out tomorrow," one of the officers said. The other men laughed.

Blake wiped his neck.

He was sweating.

CHAPTER FIFTY-SIX

Bagram Air Base, Afghanistan

Senior Master Sergeant George Vapreszan looked up at the sky. Just a few stars were showing beyond the glare of the work lights set up on the tarmac—a moonless evening, perfect for a night sortie.

Vapreszan had been readying United States Air Force aircraft for combat for more than twenty years, and in those two decades of service, one of his greatest moments of pride had always been the handoff; when he relinquished a perfectly prepped aircraft to the man or woman who would fly it into harm's way. There was something almost holy about that moment when he would shake the hand of the pilot and Vapreszan's airplane would become the other person's airplane. His wife once saw a video of him performing that transaction, and later that night she told him, "You know, I believe you give away those airplanes with more hesitation than my own father showed when he gave me away to you at the altar."

"Course I do," Vapreszan told her. "Your daddy knew I wasn't gonna perform some fool stunt and fly you into a mountain."

Over the years only five of the aircraft Vapreszan and his team readied had not come back. But he could go to sleep every night knowing he gave those pilots everything in his power to give. Their aircraft were combat readied and perfect, and the losses were ground-to-air missiles and, in one case, bird strikes—circumstances well beyond his control.

In all five of those cases, Vapreszan was the last man to look the pilot in the eye, the last man to shake the other's hand before he met his Maker. Those were moments he took seriously, moments he would always remember.

Which was why he was always disgruntled now when he performed that handoff with a Dell Latitude E6400 XFR ruggedized laptop computer, wirelessly linked to a proprietary military broadband network.

But that was what he was about to do right now.

Most Americans even casually acquainted with network news are familiar with the MQ-1 Predator UAV, an unmanned aerial vehicle used extensively for aerial surveillance and airborne attack. Capable of cruising at eighty to one hundred miles per hour for better than forty hours, the Predator drone has a wingspan of just under fifty feet and can carry two missiles—the hard points will accept either Hellfires or Stingers—to reach out and touch someone. And with fewer than two hundred Predators in the air force inventory, it is a fairly rare bird.

But Senior Master Sergeant Vapreszan was secretly pleased to note that the dull gray aircraft he just ran the checklist on was even rarer. With a sixty-six-foot wingspan, a two-hundred-mile-per-hour cruise, and transcontinental range, the MQ-9 Reaper UAV made the Predator look like a Model T.

This bird earned its name: for this mission Vapreszan's armorers equipped the Reaper with four AGM-114 Hellfire missiles and two GBU-12 Paveway II laser-guided bombs—more than enough armament to, if aimed judiciously, take out a medium-size nuclear aircraft carrier. And while the Reaper did not carry a human pilot, it was an extremely rare bird; there were fewer than thirty Reapers in the whole world.

The senior master sergeant got into a Humvee full of electronics—he never did this without pondering the fact that this one vehicle probably cost more than the entire Montana ranch he and his wife hoped one day to retire to—and followed the Reaper as it was towed to the blue marker lights designating the beginning of the taxiway. The tow vehicle was removed, and the drone sat alone on the tarmac, with only a small "shore power" unit umbilicaled to it.

"We're go."

In the truck behind him, a sergeant flipped switches and keyed in codes as she went through the Reaper's engine-start sequence. A whine was audible through the closed windows; black smoke coughed from the turboprop exhaust, followed by a puff of white, and then a shrill whine that was nearly a scream. Anticollision strobe lights blinked brightly from the wingtips, the tail. The aircraft's prop became a translucent disk in the dark, whirring behind the Reaper's tail as a crew rushed to disconnect the umbilical.

"All readings optimal," the sergeant reported.

"Go taxi," Vapreszan told her.

In the next moment the twenty-million-dollar aircraft became the world's largest remote-control toy. The sergeant steered it down the taxiway with a joystick and a throttle knob, getting her bearings by looking over Vapreszan's shoulder. She steered to the hold-short line, applied brakes, and ran the turboprop engine up, looking for fluctuations in the display. After thirty seconds she made the turn onto the runway, stopping on the numbers with the drone's nose aimed at the opposite end.

"All go," she said. "Ready for launch."

"Roger go for handoff." Vapreszan typed a short command into his laptop and hit "Enter." Confirmation came back five seconds later, and the Reaper's engine went up to full power, the airplane moving slowly at first and then more rapidly, its wingtips lifting slightly as the Humvee chased it down the runway, a spotlight trained on the drone.

Vapreszan watched it go.

He missed his handshakes.

CHAPTER FIFTY-SEVEN

❑ ❑ ❑

Creech Air Force Base, Nevada

Most days First Lieutenant Timothy Hildebrand went into combat wearing Teva sandals, Columbia cargo shorts, and a Reyn's Hawaiian shirt. The walk from the parking lot into the command center of Third Special Operations Squadron was enough to drench a standard uniform in sweat most days; the high desert was not exactly the most temperate spot on the planet. And because some UAV missions could call for pilots to be in their seats several hours at a time, the dress code in the control center was usually considerably relaxed. Even the headset he wore had only a single earphone; Hildebrand generally looked like he was a telemarketer working in a call center.

Not today.

Today Hildebrand wore an olive-drab uniform jumpsuit, little changed from what many Air Force pilots wore in Vietnam. He got the heads-up before he reported; he had an audience today—a suit who looked to be some sort of intelligence agency or another, one Air Force brigadier, and one Army major general. The officers standing off to the side, watching him, their covers tucked under their elbows, the farts-and-darts and scrambled eggs on the brims clearly visible.

"The lieutenant is now in command of the aircraft, but the takeoff is being closely audited by our people on the ground in Afghanistan, gentlemen," the brigadier said. Hildebrand half-listened without taking his eyes off the GPS and heads-up video displays on his four-screen console. His commander continued, "From the time we input a command here to the time the control surface or throttle responds on the aircraft is a little under 1.3 seconds. At altitude that's not an issue; we've got plenty of wiggle room. But this close to the ground, if we get a wind gust or a bird strike, the chase vehicle can override us and abort before we put the aircraft in greater jeopardy."

Hildebrand pushed a microphone button on the console, which looked like a light gray, multiscreen version of a video game, a console with one large display in front of the pilot, two smaller touch-screen displays side by side beneath it, another larger display angled to the side, a keyboard and a joystick that looked as if they could have been part of Microsoft Flight Simulator.

"Reaper Two-One, rotate." And with that he pulled smoothly back on the joystick. On the heads-up display before him, the runway dropped away. Stars appeared with the glaring brightness typical of a night-vision image. Below them was jagged darkness—distant mountains. On the screen angled to Hildebrand's right, a small aircraft icon began tracking on what appeared to be an air-traffic-control screen with a topography underlay. His head was turned, watching the ground-tracking display.

"You don't need to see where you're going?" It was the intelligence man, the suit, who asked.

"No, sir," the brigadier told him. "This is better than using the HUD. With the onboard cameras we can see details ten, fifteen miles ahead in a narrow cone—bit less when we're using an augmented image like this. With the ground-track display we know where everything around the aircraft is for two hundred miles in every direction. Actually, we can see father than that if need be."

"Excuse me, son." The brigadier reached over Hildebrand's shoulder to point at a number on the screen. "We're already at fifteen thousand feet, gentlemen; that's better than ten thousand feet above ground level. Our weapons load is maxed out; we're carrying as much ordnance as the aircraft can accommodate when we're armed with Paveways. But we don't require a full fuel load for this mission; we only fueled half full, and the only reason we have that much is just in case Bagram gets weathered in and we have to divert for landing. So she climbs pretty good. We'll go to service ceiling."

"Which is?" The suit again.

"That's classified," the brigadier explained. "Sorry, sir, but we don't throw those numbers around, not even in here."

Hildebrand monitored his readouts and began keying in the latitude and longitude of a series of predetermined waypoints, getting the autopilot ready to take over for the translation.

"Senior Airman?"

An enlisted man hustled over. "What can I get you, sir?"

"Nothing for me, Jimmy," the pilot said. "But can you hustle up some chairs for these gentlemen? It's gonna take us a little over forty-five minutes to get to the job site, and they might want to take a load off."

CHAPTER FIFTY-EIGHT

❑ ❑ ❑

The Garj Valley, Pakistan

Yellow butterfly.

Blake lay on his cot, listening to the odd quiet of the Pakistani night. The evening outside the tent was still, not even the sough of wind to disturb the silence.

An attack was imminent; he just didn't know when. And whatever way it came, whether by missile or aircraft or a Special Forces team, he knew he would not hear it coming.

He forced himself into the deep rhythm of a sleeping man's breathing and listened for Khalil to do the same.

If he's not asleep in five minutes, I'm going to have to just kill him and leave. Blake didn't like the thought of that. Clandestine or not, he had fought alongside the gruff, outspoken man; and, much as he hated to say it, he felt something of a bond to him now.

Besides, Khalil was a big man, strong. Blake couldn't be certain he would die either quickly or quietly. Lying on his side, the sleeping bag pulled over his shoulders, Blake watched the far side of the tent through half-closed eyes.

A shadow rose on the other cot.

This is getting worse. He's not falling asleep. He's getting up.

Blake watched, wishing there was enough light to see more than shapes. But it was a dark night: very dark.

Perfect for attacking a camp.

The other man bent forward, pulling on boots.

Heading to the latrine?

But no. Khalil was getting dressed: a vest, his purgee, a coat. He rose to his feet, and Blake saw him look Blake's way—look right at him, as if thinking about something—and then silently lift something from the floor and put it on his shoulders.

A pack. He's leaving the camp.

Khalil walked slowly, methodically, silently to the tent flap. He lifted it, stepped outside, and was gone.

Blake heard the crunch of gravel outside. It receded, and then the night was silent again.

Odd.

There was no time to ponder mysteries. Blake sat up, shed his sleeping bag, and opened his own boots. Stopping for a moment, he took the insoles out and emptied the Krugerrands into his hand, transferring them into his coat pocket, where he could get at them more readily. Pulling on his boots, he dressed as Khalil dressed, in his warmest clothes. Standing, he thought about readying a pack, some spare socks and rations.

Forget it. Something big and bad is on the way. You do not have the time.

His passport was somewhere up in the officers' quarters; Saif requested it when he first arrived. No matter. He wouldn't need a passport. He hoped.

Slinging his Kalashnikov over his shoulder, Blake slipped from the tent into a night only marginally less black. He needed to put distance between the camp and himself, and he needed to do it quickly.

The vehicles.

Had Saif left the keys in the Land Rover? Blake was not there when it was moved and parked. He couldn't be sure. But if he could steal a vehicle—any vehicle—and disable the rest, he could leave quickly and probably evade pursuit.

Hunched to present as little profile as possible, he walked with the quiet, rolling gait—heel, outside of foot, ball of foot—he learned stalking in the woods back in Virginia. When he stepped out from under the camouflage netting, the ground around him became marginally more distinct. He wished for night-vision goggles. Then he wished he was elsewhere. And finally he moved on toward the supply shack where the vehicles were parked.

A metallic creak brought him to a halt. Blake froze—looking, listening.

It was Khalil. The big man had the hood up on the flatbed truck, and he was standing on its front bumper, bent over the engine compartment. Blake heard the big man grunt softly, straighten up, and toss something off into the darkness, where it landed with the barest whisk of sound on the dirt.

Khalil moved to the Land Rover and lifted its hood as well. It creaked, the sound preternaturally loud in the night.

He's pulling the distributor cables. Disabling the vehicles.

Blake needed one of them.

Using the rifle would wake the entire camp. Slipping nearer to the vehicle park, Blake reached to the ground, felt near his feet, and found what he needed.

The Mark I rock: earth's oldest weapon. Picking up a smooth, brick-size stone, Blake was just about to sprint when he heard the metallic chick of a rifle being chambered.

"Put your hands up!" The command was in Arabic. "Do not move."

Blake froze. One of the camp sentries was approaching Khalil, rifle leveled at him. Behind Khalil, Blake could barely make out a second sentry approaching silently, his rifle at quarter-arms.

"My brother," the big Iraqi said, "you are just in time. Someone has been at these trucks."

Blake saw Khalil's hand move behind his back, the faint glint of a knife-blade, hidden from the approaching sentry.

No! There's one behind you.

"Khalil?" The sentry asked. "Is that you, my brother?"

"Yes. Come look at this mess."

As soon as the first sentry was within reach, Khalil stepped forward. His arm thrust up and out, and the sentry dropped with a gurgle, the knife jutting from beneath his chin.

The other sentry, the one behind Khalil, broke into a run.

So did Blake.

Khalil was just turning when the second sentry swung his rifle, the butt-stock connecting with the big man's head.

Khalil dropped.

The second sentry brought his rifle to his shoulder, chambered it, pointing his muzzle at the man at his feet.

Leaping from six feet away, Blake swung the brick-size stone and brought it solidly into the sentry's temple, felt a sensation like crockery breaking in a leather sack.

The night became quiet again.

Breathing through his open mouth so he would not rasp, Blake felt around in the Land Rover's engine compartment. Spark-plug wires were hanging loose, and the top of the distributor cap was bare.

This one's not going anywhere.

That left only one vehicle sitting there: the Russian Ural motorcycle with the sidecar. Peering in the darkness, he felt around on the engine; all the wires seemed to still be connected. And there was a key in the ignition.

Blake looked to the ground. Both sentries were dead. But Khalil's chest was rising and falling.

The ninth chapter of Mark, verses 38 through 40—the verses that had half-come to him as he went through the motions of prayer the night before—came to him again, only fully this time: *"Teacher," said John, "we saw a man driving out demons in your name and we told him to stop, because he was not one of us. Do not stop him," Jesus said. "No one who does a miracle in my name can in the next moment say anything bad about me, for whoever is not against us is for us."*

"For whoever is not against us is for us." Blake bent over, grabbed the big man by the wrist, and lifted him in a fireman's carry. Shuffling over to the motorcycle, he slid the man into a sitting position in the sidecar.

Blake slapped the big man's face lightly.

Nothing.

He pinched his ear, again without result.

Concussed.

It looked as if he was on his own. Glancing around at the darkened camp, Blake felt beneath the gas tank, found the metal bar on the fuel petcock and turned it open. He groped near the carburetor, located the choke, and pulled it out. Then he pushed open the pedal on the kick-starter and cycled it three times, slowly. The engine sighed as the pistons moved through their strokes.

Blake hoped someone had been taking care of this thing. He switched on the key, rose up on the kick-starter, and dropped on it with all of his weight.

Someone had been taking care of the old Ural. It clattered to life, not with the deep, throaty rumble of a Harley but certainly with enough noise to wake the camp, if not the dead. The headlamp came on at the same time, its beam piercing out the darkness like an arrowhead of yellow light, pointing straight back at him.

Over the sound of the engine, Blake heard a distant shout.

Time to leave.

To his south lay the tents and the headquarters building where the cadre slept. There was no hope of running that gauntlet. Pulling in the clutch lever, he lifted the foot-shifter peg with his toe, felt the old Russian motorcycle clunk into gear.

More shouts.

Blake twisted the throttle, eased out the clutch, and then, as the Ural began to move, gave her the gas. The back tires, both the one beneath him and the one outboard of the sidecar, spun, spitting gravel and dirt into the darkness behind him. The headlight illuminated the path up into the firing range, and he took it, shifting gears, the ancient motorcycle gaining speed.

He couldn't hear the shouts over the sound of the engine anymore, but he could hear a popping behind him.

Gunfire.

CHAPTER FIFTY-NINE

❑ ❑ ❑

Creech Air Force Base, Nevada

On the screen the icon representing Tim Hildebrand's Reaper came to full brightness, and the display automatically contracted to the hundred-mile range. He leaned forward and keyed in an instruction. The heads-up display gradually lightened and displayed a high-resolution video image, rendered in gray tones.

"Generals? Sir? We're about ten minutes from engagement," he said, and the five men sitting behind him stood and formed a semicircle behind his chair.

The senior Air Force officer looked over his pilot's head at the screen.

"General, sir, normally at this point we could bring in a look-down satellite image on the upper display: much better resolution on those. They have a system that digitally corrects for atmospheric distortion." The brigadier shook his head. "But these people we're after are pretty smart; they built their camp in a narrow valley that runs north-south, and the hills around it are steep enough we'd only get a few minutes of satellite image per pass. So we've vectored the Reaper to come in from the south. The valley has a slight incline, south to north, so we should have a good view of the camp once we get the intervening hills out of the way. The display you're looking at is infrared—heat sensitive—rendered on top of a night-vision image."

"From the south," the suit repeated. "So that puts us well into Pakistani air space. Were they briefed on this mission?"

"They always are, sir," the brigadier said. "Although we keep the information need-to-know and generally don't share until just before we enter. But trust me; if we didn't say anything, they would never know we were there. Even if they had eyes on that camp, they'd be hard-pressed to know where the attack came from. You can't hear this bird when it's at altitude, you can't see it during the day under most conditions, and right now over there it's dead of night. We're a shadow in a coal chute."

The brigadier went to the next console over, pressed a keypad, and a large monitor came alive with a full-color, high-resolution video of the terrorists' mountain camp. You could clearly see the turbans on the men walking from one mud-walled building to another. The image was sharp enough that you could catch glimpses of people walking from tent to tent under the camouflage netting.

"One of our Predator pilots in the Fifty-Third Wing shot this just before noon local time yesterday," the brigadier general said. "We do assessment footage to determine target value and judge the risk of collateral damage, which in this case is absolutely zero. We overflew for two hours and then analyzed after, and every individual we got a clear shot of yesterday was armed. It's all good. No sheepherders, no school kids. Just armed males. One hundred percent, wall-to-wall bad guys."

Hildebrand keyed his microphone. "Reaper Two-One passing fifty kilometers to objective Alpha. Commencing run at twenty kilometers. Confirm flightpath clear . . ." He listened for a moment. "Roger. Path confirmed clear."

He adjusted the contrast on the live infrared heads-up display: a gradual progression of gray hills and ridges.

"This place is out in the boonies," he mused. "Not even a goat out for a midnight stroll. Usually, we'll see a village or a camp on the way in. Not here."

He zoomed the image in, then zoomed all the way back out again.

"That call the lieutenant just made was to one of our E-3s flying a racetrack pattern over the border region," the air force general explained to the civilian visitor. "Same asset that was giving us the airspace data earlier. He just called to make sure we don't have any aircraft entering the space between us and the target before we go hot. We don't, and now he'll be turning off his transponder and his marker beacons."

Hildebrand leaned forward and hit two rocker switches.

"The transponder responds with an identifying code when radar interrogates it," the brigadier said. "The Reaper is not completely stealthy, but it is low return. Engine noise is low, we're at high altitude, not showing a light; unless somebody has extremely sophisticated radar, we are now pretty much undetectable."

On the heads-up display, a ridge disappeared into the bottom of the frame, and gray rectangular shapes appeared. One was white in one corner. Beyond were six gray domes, three of them each contained one or more white dashes.

"Camp coming up," the brigadier said. "The nearer building analyzed as a command post, officers' quarters. They've got a stove going; that's the white signature in the corner."

"And the white spots in the tents," the suit said. "Those are . . . ?"

"The opposition," the Air Force general said. "Sleeping."

"We're missing two vehicles," the Army officer observed.

"How's that?" It was the suit.

"The Predator imagery showed two trucks outside the command post. Gone now."

"You gotta be . . ." The suit crowded in close enough that Hildebrand was about to say something when the brigadier reached over and pulled the man back.

"It is what it is," the brigadier said. "We'll complete the mission now, worry about the after-action later."

The Reaper's cameras picked up four other heat signatures: two lying on the ground next to the vehicles, and two, close together, heading away from the sentry at the two o'clock position, moving up and to the right.

"Got two that seem to be sleeping outside here," the brigadier said. "We'll get them, no problem, when we take out those two trucks. Those two on the move, if they get much farther, maybe not."

"What are they on? A bicycle of some kind?'

"It's emitting heat, but the engine is partially obscured. Motorcycle. With a sidecar, is my guess."

Hildebrand moved the joystick and worked with his left hand on one of the touch screens. Small crosshairs with alphanumeric code were superimposed on each of the two buildings. Then he placed another marker in the center of the area where the tents were pitched and one on the truck in the walled yard. A tone sounded after each crosshair appeared.

"The Reaper now has four on-board lasers designating four different targets, one for each Hellfire," the brigadier explained. "The procedure is we fire the Hellfires at seven kilometers out and drop the Paveways at five kilometers, maybe twenty seconds later. Our pilot will kill the two outermost lasers as soon as we have missile impact. The bombs will select the buildings. If you watch the infrared really close, you might even see the bombs; they'll look like small fish swimming away, very quickly."

Hildebrand took hold of the joystick and pressed a button at its base. The infrared video image jiggled a little and then smoothed out as he took the Reaper off autopilot. He keyed the microphone.

"Reaper Two-One homing Alpha, ten kilometers and closing." Four new tones sounded from speakers next to the display. "Missiles tone. Laser lock."

The video image rose in the frame as the aircraft nosed down.

"Nine kliks." Hildebrand said. "Eight . . . Seven."

He pressed a button on the side of the joystick four times in rapid succession. The infrared image jiggled again. Four starbursts appeared on screen, streaking toward the target, their trails glowing behind them in the heat-sensitive image. "Missiles away."

"They can hear us coming," the suit said.

"Not possible," the brigadier told him.

"But look. The tents. They're evacuating."

The camp dropped out of the bottom of the screen, the image jumped again, and then the camp came back into view. The images leaving the tents appeared to be running. Other bodies left the larger building but did not run; they stood there, near the doorways.

"Bombs away," Hildebrand said.

Sparks of white appeared next to the images leaving the tents. The Reaper pilot scowled and zoomed his display in slightly.

"They aren't running away," Hildebrand said.

"How's that?"

"The men from the tents, sir. They aren't running away. They're chasing the two on the motorcycle."

The suit leaned closer. "How do you know that?"

"Those little white flashes," Hildebrand said. "They're small heat signatures."

Nobody said anything.

Hildebrand glanced back at the suit. "That's gunfire, sir."

CHAPTER SIXTY

❑ ❑ ❑

The Garj Valley, Pakistan

A trail of dust spurts erupted on the trail before the motorcycle and walked away from it in the yellow headlamp beam.

Automatic weapons fire. Getting close.

Boulders, big enough to wreck the bike at this speed, flashed by as Blake gunned the engine up the trail. There was no chance of swerving to throw off his pursuers' aim. His only hope was to get out of range. Already going much faster than he was comfortable with on the rough trail, bouncing up and off the seat over and over as the bike dipped through washouts, he opened the throttle even further and hung on. In the sidecar next to him, the big Iraqi flopped like a rag doll, head lolling from side to side, unconscious but moaning.

Blake glanced back, gauging his distance. He was moving away from the camp but still within rifle range. Blue-white muzzle blasts punctuated the darkness from a half-dozen different sources. Beneath his hands, the handlebar felt as if it had just been struck with a hammer, and a bullet rang off into the darkness.

Lord, Blake prayed, still glancing back, *I've done what I can do. It's all up to you now.*

And as soon as he'd thought that, the mountain camp behind him erupted into four separate orange-white fireballs.

CHAPTER SIXTY-ONE

❑ ❑ ❑

Creech Air Force Base, Nevada

The heads-up display went momentarily black, then came alive again, the image showing more contrast now that four fires were burning in the ruins of what was once the camp. At the bottom of the screen, two small black shapes fluttered in like darts missing part of their fletching. White destruction bubbled up when they impacted, the two explosions considerably larger than those caused by the missiles, although the screen stayed alive this time, the camera's iris already stopped down.

The four men in the control center saw concussive shockwaves radiate out from the two explosions. One overtook the fleeing motorcycle, turning it sideways on the trail and knocking the rider off. For twenty seconds, both the motorcycle and its rider just sat there. Then they saw the rider stand up, remount the bike and drop, restarting the engine. The motorcycle and its sidecar continued up the trail.

"We need to take everyone out." It was the suit. "No escapes. You got guns, a cannon on that bird?"

"No, sir," the brigadier told him. "The Reaper is fast for a UAV, but it's no fighter. If a MIG engages with us close up, we don't dogfight;

we just die. All we have is missiles and bombs, and we've already used every one of those. We've got plenty of fuel, though, and they're headed toward Afghanistan. Follow them, Lieutenant."

"Yes, Sir."

The Army officer walked over to the wall and picked up a phone. Glancing back, Hildebrand saw him key in a series of numbers.

"Griffin here," he said into the phone. "Our coalition outside Chagai can start up the trail. No hurry; the camp has been neutralized . . . that's right: no defenders left on site. We still have that Special Forces team just over the border, waiting on that trail we reconned?"

He listened for a moment. "Tell them that we have two coming their way. On a motorcycle. Lat-long at present is . . . General?"

The brigadier read the number's off the Reaper's heads-up display, and the major general repeated it into the phone.

"We have eyes on, and we will keep them in sight," the Army officer said. "We'll update when they are nearing contact. Tell the team to monitor the Reaper pilot's frequency."

For the next forty minutes, the four men watched the look-down image from the Reaper: the rider, his passenger, the engine, and the exhaust registering white in the heat-sensitive image as the motorcycle labored up and down mountain switchbacks and over passes on the crude, unimproved trail. More than once the rider stopped and got off to clear larger stones from his path. Twice he inched the motorcycle around obstacles, the machine tipping so far it appeared almost side-on in the aerial image.

"That boy's tenacious, I'll give him that," the army officer remarked.

"Has to be," the brigadier observed. "He's not going back where he came from. This is his only chance."

Five minutes after that, an alphanumeric code crawled across the corner of Hildebrand's display.

"Crossing the border," the brigadier said. "The Reaper has just entered Afghani airspace."

Hildebrand keyed his mike. "Subjects crossing border. On your side, Special Forces."

"Roger, Reaper." The response, coming from speakers above the pilot's console, was eerily crisp, despite the fact it came from halfway around the world. "No visual here."

Hildebrand moved a slider on his touch screen, and the Reaper's camera zoomed out. The motorcycle, its rider, and its passenger became a single white dot. At the top of the screen, a smaller cluster of dots appeared, arranged in a crude semicircle.

"Special Forces, be advised: subject is ten kilometers east your position and closing. ETA fifteen, possibly twenty minutes."

"Roger, Reaper." Again, the voice on the Special Forces team's satellite link could almost have come from the room in which they were standing. On the screen two of the dots separated from the cluster and began slowly moving east, down the trail.

Hildebrand kept adjusting the zoom, keeping the motorcycle and its riders at the bottom of the heads-up display, the Special Forces soldiers at the top. As the minutes passed, the image gained enough magnification to resolve the motorcycle's passengers into two distinct smears of white light. The two Special Forces pickets came together in the center of the trail and then separated to either side of it.

"They can hear him," the Army said.

Hildebrand keyed his mike. "Special Forces, confirm contact."

Thirty seconds passed. The speakers on the console clicked.

"Contact."

CHAPTER SIXTY-TWO

❑ ❑ ❑

Eastern Afghanistan

The shockwave from the bombing of the camp hit Blake like a sheet of steel plate; he ached all over. He had no goggles, and he coughed as he rode and tried to blink more moisture into his eyes.

The Ural's engine sputtered and then caught again as the trail changed angle, moving the gas around in the tank. Blake wondered how much gas he'd begun with; the ancient motorcycle had no gauge. Not that it mattered all that much; he was heading west by northwest into Afghanistan, actually *in* Afghanistan if he was estimating correctly, and the nearest cities where he could be certain of contacting a consulate, an embassy, or the American military were Jalalabad or Asadabad. As the crow flew, the Ural could probably make it on a tank of gas, but if you added in all the mountain switchbacks and gains and drops in elevation, they were both hopelessly out of range.

So sooner or later he would be walking. And the big Middle Easterner in the sidecar was still drifting in and out of consciousness. Blake could carry him; he already did that once. But he couldn't carry him far.

He wasn't even sure why he'd brought the big man along. Yes, he'd been escaping the camp at the same time as Blake, but that didn't necessarily make him an ally. Maybe Khalil got cold feet and was smart enough to know, this far into it, al-Qaeda was not going to just let him walk.

But Blake wasn't about to let someone who was not opposition die in the attack on the camp.

So would he let him die in the mountains?

He might have to.

Holding the throttle open with his right hand, Blake reached into his coat pocket with his left.

His heart sank as soon as he touched it; it was ripped, torn in his fall from the motorcycle.

The Krugerrands were gone. Every last one of them.

So there was no hope of buying assistance from villagers, shepherds, or passersby.

Blake gritted his teeth, rolled his aching shoulders, and kept riding into the night.

In the yellow-white headlamp of the motorcycle, nothing moved. There was not even a blade of grass to quiver in the wind. It was just rock in various sizes, dirt, and dust. Lots of dust.

Blake gunned the engine to crest a rise.

Lord, he prayed as he crested it, *I am trusting you to get me—or us, if it is your will—where we need to go. I can't do it on my own. I am trusting you to take us to safety.*

He had just finished praying that when, for the first time since fleeing the camp, he saw movement. Something came arcing out of the darkness and dropped onto the path illuminated by the headlamp: something green and round, with the butt of a tube protruding from it.

It took Blake nearly a full second to recognize it for what it was.

Grenade.

It detonated, loud and bright, the light of it illuminating the rocks and ground around him like an extremely large camera strobe. He turned away from it when it went off, so he was not blinded by it; and as the bright flash lit up the night, he saw several palm-size green-and-tan rectangles on the trail ahead of him, wire running from one to another. He squeezed the hand brake, and as he did, the trail ahead of him erupted in orange fire, smoke, and dirt. The motorcycle dropped as if he was riding it off the edge of a cliff. And then Blake was flying through the air, crumpling into the ground.

CHAPTER SIXTY-THREE

❑ ❑ ❑

Blake awoke to the feeling of his face being slapped. Slapped hard.

Flash-bang. That was his first thought. The thing he saw tossed onto the trail was a flash-bang, the sort of grenade used to disorient enemy forces when storming a small, enclosed space, such as a house. The things he saw on the trail, the blocks of material wired together . . . C4: plastic explosive. Daisy-chained together. To form a cratering charge.

A standard technique.

He had used it himself.

In Special Forces exercises.

He fluttered his eyelids open and dimly saw the Ural lying on its side, its engine and headlamp dead. There was pain in his arms; someone was kneeling on them. He felt the prick of a knife tip under his chin, and whoever was on him used the knife to steer his face upward, so he was looking straight up at the man kneeling astride him.

The night was still moonless and dark, but even from the silhouette, Blake could see the man on top of him was wearing fatigues and a helmet, his night-vision goggles flipped up and away from his eyes.

"That's right, boy, look at me." Blake's ears were still ringing, but the man's voice sounded eerily familiar. The man poked the knife-tip just a little harder. "I've been waiting years for this. You've hurt and killed a lot of good men, and you hurt me, and now it's my turn. Tell your Allah he'd better make him some room because we are going to be sending a boatload of you boys to join him."

That voice.

Blake blinked. "Harry? Harry Chee?"

CHAPTER SIXTY-FOUR

❑ ❑ ❑

Water. Eyedrops. Ibuprofen. An MRE. All of these helped Blake begin to feel half-human again as he sat on the ground against a boulder, surrounded by the Special Forces team. To the east the clear sky was just beginning to take on the slightest tinge of gray.

"Well, I'll tell you one thing right now, Kersh," Chee was saying. "You owe me 179 bucks."

"I do? Why's that?"

"Flowers for your funeral, man. I was a freaking pallbearer." The Navajo scowled. "Whose body was I carrying, anyhow?"

Blake shrugged.

"And another thing." Chee poked Blake in the chest with his finger. "That letter I wrote to your mother when I heard about the chopper going down? Don't you ever let me hear about you reading it. That clear?"

"Flowers and letters," Blake mused. "What are you going to do next? Ask me to the prom?"

He flinched. "Don't hit me, man. I'm sore. Besides, you'd be striking an officer."

Chee squinted at him and offered his canteen. "How's that work, anyhow? You still get to keep the commission after you're dead?"

Blake shrugged again and took a drink.

The team's captain came over and squatted next to Blake. He was muscular and African-American: no one Blake ever met.

"How are you feeling?"

"Better, sir. Thank you."

"Sorry about the reception."

"Don't mention it. You thought I was al-Qaeda."

The captain's brow furrowed. "So what are you, anyhow? Chee tells me you're supposed to be buried at Arlington. You Agency?"

Blake nodded. "And I'd appreciate it if you and Harry kept my identity between us, sir."

"Understood." The officer cocked his head. "Normally, I'd have you in cuffs until we can get this goat-roping straightened out, but Chee's vouching for you, so that's good enough for me. Just don't take any walks away from the team, okay? We've got a couple Blackhawks coming in for the dust-off in . . ." he checked his watch, "twenty minutes, and we'll sort this all out back at Bagram."

Blake took another drink. "If you don't mind me asking, sir, what brings you up here?"

The captain peered at him a moment and then sat back. "Sensitive-site exploitation. After-action survey—photograph anything recognizable and tally up a body count, bag DNA samples. And if you're Agency, we've got one of your boys along, and he brought a Geiger counter and a hazmat suit."

The captain looked up. "Mr. Cooper? Could you step over here, please?"

A lean man in unmarked BDUs ambled over.

The captain nodded toward Blake. "Man here says he is CIA. You know him?"

Cooper peered at Blake, then turned to the captain. "No, sir, but that doesn't mean much of anything. It's a big agency, and there's lots above my pay grade."

He turned back to Blake. "Who do you work for in the Agency?"

Blake rested the canteen on his knee. "Colsun Atwater. Deputy Director of Operations. You know him?"

"Atwater? I know I've heard the name. Wait . . . wasn't he killed in Islamabad a couple days ago?"

"What?" Blake nearly dropped the canteen.

"Car bomb. Took out some embassy personnel, including our station chief. And Atwater. Sorry, man; guess you didn't know."

Blake sat back, sagged.

"What about him?" The captain nodded at the moaning Khalil, who was having his blood pressure taken by the team's medic. "He agency, too?"

Blake shook his head. "I don't know who he is. But he was leaving camp at the same time as me, so I brought him along."

"Doc?" The captain was speaking to the medic. "Any way of bringing that one around?"

"He's concussed pretty good, sir. But I have epinephrine in my kit; it's the same thing as adrenaline. If I give him a shot of that in the chest, it might bring him around. He's got a pretty good BP; I think he can take it."

"Do it."

The medic exposed the big man's chest, swabbed it with alcohol, and opened a syrette with a long needle.

"Keep an eye on him as he comes to," Blake cautioned. "Might not be friendly."

The captain nodded and unholstered his pistol.

When the medic jabbed the epinephrine syrette into the man's chest, the effect was like jumping a dead battery. The big man's head came up, eyes open. He was staring at the medic.

"You're Americans," he said.

Blake gaped. The man had just spoken, not in the thick Iraqi accent he used for the last four weeks, but in an urbane London accent bordering on posh.

"We are," the medic nodded. "Green Berets—Special Forces."

The big man touched his head gingerly, then he looked at his chest, where the medic was removing the syrette and its long needle. "My name is Commander Graham Ghannon, Her Majesty's Special Boat Services. I am on assignment with MI6, and I have crucial information I must get to a British embassy just as soon as possible."

"What sort of information?" It was the Special Forces captain who asked.

"There are two WMDs that pose a danger to a Western power," Ghannon said. "They left the camp I was in. But I know the port from which they will be leaving. And I know when they will leave."

Then he noticed Blake sitting there. "Reinbolt?"

Blake grinned. "No, Captain. The name is Kershaw. And I'll tell you what, sir; if you know the name of a port and a date, this thing here just might still be in play."

CHAPTER SIXTY-FIVE

The Arabian Sea

Strapped tightly into the high-back seat, squeezing its hand-grips, Blake glanced forward past two rows of similarly heavy-duty, high-tech seating, the canvas-roofed cabin illuminated only by the starlight through the windows. His first thought was that this must be what it was like to be shot into orbit on the Space Shuttle.

Then the craft leapt upward, Blake went weightless, and the craft dropped, jarring his spine despite the shock-mitigating seat. His head thudded back, and despite the fact the seat back was heavily padded, he was glad for the plastic helmet he was wearing.

Blake revised his estimate. He was pretty sure the Space Shuttle didn't get this rough.

The navy chief next to him chuckled. "First time in a Mark V, Lieutenant?"

The eighty-one-foot, fast-attack boat lifted clear of the sea once again and slammed back into it.

"This," Blake half-shouted back, "is the first time I've ever been in *anything* like this."

The chief laughed again. Under his helmet he wore, as all the team wore, a black balaclava hiding everything except his eyes. But Blake could tell from his eyes, even in the dark cabin, that the man was grinning. "This here's the Mako. New, improved version, Lieutenant. Carbon-fiber hull. Regular Mark Vs have aluminum hulls. Don't give as much when they hit. Hard on the SWCCs." He pronounced the acronym "swicks."

"Broken backs?" Blake asked as they dropped again.

The chief shook his head. "Broken and sprained ankles mostly. A few ruptured disks. You join the SEALS, you get shot at once in a while, spend maybe 1 percent of your working time around people who really want to hurt you. But you join a Special Warfare Combatant-Command crew, and you get to do this . . ." The boat went airborne and crashed to the sea again. ". . . every single day."

The big boat heeled into a turn, skipping heavily in the rough seas.

"And people say you've gotta be nuts to join the SEALS." The chief laughed as the fast-attack vessel boomed and shuddered.

Ten minutes later the diesel engines began to drop in tempo. Looking forward, Blake could see the row of six windows that formed the craft's windshield. Beyond them was the sharp snout of the boat's long bow, phosphorescent spray breaking over it. The bow dipped, and Blake could see the tiny white stern and mast lights of a distant freighter.

Had Blake taken a guess at what port the munitions were being flown to, he would have said, "Karachi," and he would have been wrong.

Ghannon—Blake still thought of the MI6 man as "Khalil"—identified the port of embarkation as Gwadar, a town in Pakistan's Balochistan province and a place Blake had only seen on maps. Then, during the briefing at Bagram, it all became clear: Gwadar was a modern, deep-water port built early in the twenty-first century and brought up to operational levels in 2008. It could accommodate vessels of literally every size but was not watched as closely as the more traditional, long-established ports.

It had an international airport, easily capable of handling heavy jets, just nine miles north of it—an airport at which incoming domestic freight would barely merit a glance. And it was built with heavy investment by the Chinese and was even overseen by PSA International, the oversight authority of the Port of Singapore.

That was the central problem.

Over months of eavesdropping and volunteering to carry written communications, Graham Ghannon deduced that the nuclear devices would be leaving Gwadar on the fourth morning following their departure from the mountain camp. That placed both weapons in a known location. But when Blake and the CIA acting station chief suggested seizing them there, they'd hit a stone wall.

"Absolutely not," the State Department representative said during the hastily arranged meeting in a windowless briefing room at Bagram. "I've spoken with our ambassadors here and in Islamabad, and they both agree: we can't risk an incident. Not with the Pakistanis and particularly not with the Chinese." She tapped her finger for emphasis. "This could be seen as provocative."

"It's defensive," the acting station chief insisted. "We have intelligence that these weapons are going to be shipped to the Eastern Seaboard of the United States."

The woman from State peered over her reading glasses as she listened to him. She hadn't touched the coffee in the mug next to her legal pad. She hadn't even uncapped her pen.

"Intelligence on WMDs doesn't go too far in diplomatic circles these days," she told him.

Blake leaned forward. "With all respect ma'am, this isn't hearsay. I saw these."

"And identified them from file imagery as Soviet RA-115s," the acting chief added. "We have probable cause."

"This isn't a drug bust in the barrio," the woman from State replied. "What you are proposing is the disruption of a foreign port. Even if Pakistan gave us the go-ahead to do such a thing—and that's a mighty big if—Beijing could interpret it as critical of their presence here."

Blake leaned back in the government-issue chair, making its pedestal creak, his mind racing. His instinct was to contact Atwater, get some muscle in his corner. But Atwater was dead.

"Ma'am . . ." He kept his voice under control. Just barely. "We know the target. It's Washington. Does the secretary of state know you're about to let al-Qaeda ship a nuke to her doorstep at Foggy Bottom?"

The woman did the looking-over-the-reading-glasses thing again. "Lieutenant, I wouldn't try to play hardball if I were you. The only reason you're in here is that the Green Berets vouch for you and you delivered a code word, verified by your voice print, I know that means to give you full cooperation, but don't push it."

Blake was tired. He spoke his mind. "Then cooperate, ma'am. Does the secretary know?"

The woman huffed. "The secretary has been briefed on the matter. She has consulted with the Security Council, and based on their advice, the president has authorized interdiction at sea. There's part of a SEAL team, with fast boats and a C-17 to transport them, on *Diego Garcia* right now. We've arranged permission to land them in Karachi."

She nodded at Blake. "Lieutenant, you, and your MI6 counterpart, have been cleared to accompany the SEALs. There are only three freighters scheduled to leave Gwadar on the morning in question."

She looked at a sheet in front of her. "They are the *Sultana*, registered in Jordan; the *Tigris*, Pakistani registration; and the *Anesidora*, registered in Greece. You may interdict all three once they have passed into international waters. You know what to look for, so look. With due caution and regard for the safety of those on board, of course."

The acting chief shook his head. "Tracking a ship at sea is a tricky proposition, even with radar and satellites. You take your eye off one for even a minute, you might not see it again until it arrives at its destination."

"Then I suggest you all keep your eyes on them," the State woman said. "This order comes straight from the president."

The diesels were throttled down to an idle. The Mark V began to wallow slowly in the long rollers of the Arabian Sea. Along with the men around him, Blake unfastened his seat harness and moved back, out from under the canvas canopy, to the open deck behind.

The moonless sky was sprayed with stars, and the freighter, the *Tigris*, now lay about a mile off the port bow.

"Can they see us on radar?"

"Doubtful," the chief said as they untied the eight-man inflatable boat secured just ahead of the sloping afterdeck. "Carbon-fiber is fairly stealthy, plus we're pretty low to the water. If they had the gain turned high enough to see us, they'd be getting a lot of sea return as well. Here we go—be sure to hop in before we hit the end of the ramp."

It was like starting a bobsled run. The eight men pushed the small Combat Rubber Raiding Craft down the short, slanted launch ramp, jumping in just before it hit the water. Fifteen seconds later, a well-muffled outboard motor was running, and the little boat was running across the dark water, spray showering the men as they closed on the *Tigris*. They pulled ahead of the 760-foot ship, and then the SEAL running the outboard slowed it to a crawl.

"Other half of the team launched off their own Mark V same time we did," the chief explained. "Two of our guys are jumaring up lines to reach the deck. When they get there, they'll fix four caving ladders, let us know when those are in place."

The radio earpiece under Blake's balaclava clicked.

"That's the signal," the chief said as the outboard throttled up again. "We're hot."

The small boat closed on the freighter, moving alongside and then closing in. Blake could just make out two pairs of Cymalume sticks, glowing a soft green and marking the bottoms of two ladders about four feet apart.

"We're first up," said the chief. Following his lead, Blake reached up, grabbed an aluminum rung of the steel-cable ladder, and began to pull his way up the side of the ship.

It was just past midnight, and the men did not clamber over the top of the rail. Rather, they slid under it and began moving in a combat-crawl aft, toward the pilothouse, rifles slung across their backs, pistols in their right hands. In his earpiece Blake heard a series of clicks as each member of the platoon indicated he was on board and moving into position.

He kept crawling until he reached the deck just below the pilothouse. Two members of the other platoon were already there, and Blake could tell by the size of one it was Ghannon.

"Got two guys heading down to the engine room to heave us to, just in case these boys aren't cooperative," the chief whispered. "Wait for their signal."

It came—three clicks in the radio headset.

"Remember," Blake cautioned the others. "There's a chance these people are just carrying machine parts. We may not have the ship carrying the weapons."

The other three nodded, and then they split into two teams, each going to a different side of the ship.

The hatch to the starboard ladder well was open, light spilling out. Blake and the chief slipped in, blinking under the relative glare of a forty-watt bulb in a protective cage. They climbed the stairlike ladder, dropping to a crouch as they neared the top.

The hatch to the pilothouse was shut. The chief reached up with his left hand. "One . . ." he whispered, "two . . ."

On "three" he threw the hatch open and Blake stepped in, shouting in Arabic, "United States Navy!"

The man at the wheel was wide-eyed with fright. Behind him an older man was frozen in the act of lighting a cigarette. The match burned to his fingertips and he startled, dropping it. The other hatch opened, and Ghannon and the other SEAL came in as well.

"Do you speak English?" Blake asked him.

"Badly," the captain replied, his Pakistani accent thick. "What business you have on my ship?"

"We need to check your cargo for contraband," Ghannon told him.

"Certainly," the captain replied. "Here. Let me just get manifest."

He opened a drawer.

When he turned, time seemed to slow down. The first thing Blake saw was the Type 77, the old Chinese police pistol, in his hand. It was a gun that could be cycled with one hand, and the slide was snapping forward, chambering a round. At the same time the wheelman slapped a button to the side of the helm, and a klaxon began to sound.

"Gun!" Blake shouted as he raised his M9.

The three Americans and the Englishman all shot at the same time, and the captain dropped without getting off a single round.

The helmsman raised his hands, and for a moment they all stood there, the smell of cordite thick in the air of the wheelhouse. Then the windows ahead of them shattered, and the helmsman shuddered as the four platoon members dropped prone on the deck. Kalashnikov fire rattled from the deck below, answered by the higher-pitch reports of the SEAL FNs. The helmsman fell, bleeding from several wounds.

On the wheelhouse deck Blake was looking straight into the face of Ghannon. He could only see the Englishman's eyes, but he could tell the big man was grinning.

"Brother," Ghannon said, "I don't know about you, but I think we've found the right ship!"

They crawled to the hatch, where Blake froze just as a member of the freighter's crew appeared, a Slovakian K-100 pistol gripped tightly in his right hand.

Reaching up, Blake twisted the pistol out of the man's grasp and back-handed him hard in the solar plexus. The crewman fell, gasping, and Blake secured his hands behind his back with a zip strip.

"Intel puts twenty-eight officers and crew on board," Ghannon said as he zip-stripped the man's ankles. "Three down, here—odds are getting better by the minute."

They stepped into the ladder well, small arms fire echoing up from beneath them. Two explosions, hollow and loud, sounded from below. Even without his recent experience, Blake would have recognized them as flash-bang grenades. There were three more short bursts of FN fire, and then the ship fell silent.

"This is Hawkins," the chief radioed from the wheelhouse. "I got two dead opposition and one prisoner up here. Hagleigh's got some cuts on his face from when the hadjis shot the glass out of the wheelhouse. Nothing bad. Other than that, we're good."

"Army and the Brit here," Blake checked in—the acting station chief asked them to not use names before sending them out with the SEALS. "No damage."

All around the ship the rest of the platoon checked in, and Blake kept a count. Altogether, seven opposition were dead and twenty-two captured, and only the SEAL with the glass cuts was injured.

Blake paused and did the math again. "You said twenty-eight officers and crew on board, didn't you?"

Ghannon nodded, "And our mates just accounted for twenty-nine of the opposition."

The radio clicked. "Army? UK?"

"Army here," Blake replied.

"Come on down to the first mate's cabin, Lieutenant. Got something you need to see."

Blake looked at Ghannon.

"Captain's quarters are generally just below the wheelhouse," Ghannon said. "First officer is aft of or below that. On this design I'd say below. Follow me."

"Got a dude in here not dressed like the rest," the SEAL ensign said as they got to the open bulkhead hatch on the deck below the captain's quarters. "Watch your step when you come in."

Blake stepped over the footwide pool of blood just past the hatch. A man wearing a dress shirt and Dockers was lying face-down in it, a laptop computer in his left hand. Ghannon reached down and turned him over, and both he and Blake stood up straight.

Blake looked at the ensign. "Did we find any Asians aboard?"

The SEAL shook his head. "All look to be Pakistani, maybe some Afghani. But no Asians. Why?"

Blake nodded at the dead man. "Last time we saw him, he was translating for a Korean nuclear scientist. Guess he had other skills as well."

He leaned over, picked up the laptop, opened it, and pressed the power button. The computer fan came on, the screen flickered, and the password box came up. Blake powered it down.

"The Agency should be able to get past the password without a problem." He looked at Ghannon. "Let's check the hold. My guess, we start with the hatch nearest the deck crane."

CHAPTER SIXTY-SIX

❑ ❑ ❑

They were only ten minutes into the search when a senior chief radioed that he believed he'd found something.

"It's not all that far above background levels," he said as Blake and Ghannon came down the ladder into the *Tigris*'s dimly lighted hold. "But every time I get near this one crate, I get a small spike."

"Show me." Blake edged sideways down the narrow walkway between the blocks of crates tied down in the hold.

"Here," the senior chief handed him a ruggedized iPaq handheld computer. "Detector's bluetoothed to the handheld. You'll see the bar lift when I get near the crate."

The senior chief leaned between two big plywood boxes stamped in Arabic to get to a crate near the bottom of a large pallet of freight.

"Right here," he said. And as he did, the bar jumped up on the handheld: still in the safe zone, but the ionizing radiation was definitely higher near the crate.

"Let me have a look, Senior Chief." The SEAL moved to the side, and Blake edged in, extended an LED flashlight into the gap between boxes, and looked at the corner of the crate—the only part he could see.

"Could be one of 'em." He turned to the senior chief. "Can we get that deck crane going, dig this one out?"

The senior chief peered at the open hatch above, then at the pallet.

"Twenty minutes," he said. "We'll have it up on deck for you."

Nineteen minutes later the cargo above it was shifted, and the crate was brought to the deck in front of Blake, Ghannon, and the SEAL team captain.

"Do I have to worry," the SEAL officer asked, "about this thing going Hiroshima when we try to open it?"

"No," Blake told him. "I was there when we crated them. If this is one of our weapons—and it sure looks like the crates we used—they're shipped in standby mode, and there's nothing in there with them but foam."

"Okay, then." The SEALs removed the lifting straps and cut the inchwide metal bands binding the crate. Someone found a prybar in the freighter's engine room, and they worked their way around the top of the crate, ten-penny nails screeching in protest as the top was pried up.

The eastern sky was beginning to lighten ever so slightly, a blue-black less deep than that directly above. Blake guessed it was coming on 0500, and although half the platoon was still searching the hold, no one had called out that they had found the other weapon.

The top was lifted away from the crate, revealing a plane of hardened orangish-tan spray insulation.

"If we take the sides away as well, we can cut the insulation off," Blake said. "It's in a pretty tough case. Titanium alloy, I think they said."

The wooden sides of the crate were pried away, and then three SEALs began cutting the foam away with eight-inch tactical knives. When they finished, it was the same sort of case Blake saw every day during his training in the high camp. He opened it, half-expecting to find it empty. But the weapon was there, a diode glowing dimly up at him.

"It's here and the circuitry is still charged."

"Not for long," the SEAL captain said.

Two members of the SEAL platoon went to work on the weapon, one reading instructions from a handheld computer while the other worked with screwdrivers and needle-nose pliers. Five minutes later he was holding up a cylinder about the size of a soda can.

"Battery's out," he said. "It's inert."

"One down," Blake agreed. He looked at the SEAL captain. "No sign of the other?"

"Negative." The officer shook his head. "And our people have been through this hold twice."

"So it's on one of the other two ships that left yesterday morning."

The captain nodded. "The *Sultana* is about ninety miles south of us. Too far away to chase in a Mark V, but we've got Seahawks I can scramble off a carrier in the Gulf. I'm gonna have 'em send two down with a skeleton crew to take this tub up to Bahrain, some weapons folks to further secure this device, and a couple naval intelligence people to have a go at that laptop we found and see if they can get anything off it. They'll aerial refuel en route, pick us up, and we'll go drop in on that second freighter."

"Sounds like a plan," Blake agreed. "What do we do about the *Anesidora*?"

"Pray it's not the one."

Blake looked up.

"*Anesidora* is smaller and considerably faster than this one or the other," the captain said. "Command tells me radar lost it in traffic somewhere near the mouth of the Gulf of Aden. It may have entered the Gulf, or it might have gone down around the Horn of Africa. They're shifting satellites to try to find it, but that takes time, and even when they're shifted, we're talking needle in a haystack. Small needle. Big haystack."

CHAPTER SIXTY-SEVEN

❑ ❑ ❑

The navy MH-60R Seahawk and the Army UH-60 Blackhawk are both variants of the same Sikorsky helicopter, and the web seats and cramped after-cabin were familiar to Blake, who'd ridden Blackhawks more times than he could count.

Ghannon was next to him, head back against the throbbing bulkhead, asleep, and around him half the SEAL platoon was either napping or simply sitting with the in-neutral faces of men who had been awake all night. It was coming up on nine in the morning, broad daylight and absolutely the worst time of day to be mounting a Special Ops mission, but as the SEAL captain told him, "We've already lost track of one of these tubs. Better go get the other while we still have some idea where it is."

The helicopter tilted into a steep bank and began to climb and make a turn. Across from Blake, the SEAL captain leaned forward.

"We're close. Almost close enough for a visual. So the pilot's making his approach high and from the east, keep us in the sun from the freighter's perspective for as long as possible."

Blake nodded. It made sense, and it was one of the few advantages the SEAL platoon would have; they had eighteen half-exhausted men—the sixteen members of the platoon, plus Blake and Ghannon—versus a freighter crew of twenty-eight, most of whom would be well rested.

Around the crowded cabin, men began to stir, checking closures on their webbing and pulling on gloves. Blake did the same.

"We're first aboard," the SEAL captain shouted as the helicopter's side doors slid open. "Other bird's right behind us."

Blake looked up over the shoulders of the pilot and copilot. Through the windscreen, he could see the bridge of the *Sultana*, head-on, people gesturing inside.

"Pilot's got the refueling probe extended," the captain shouted. "Looks like a gun. Keep 'em concerned. Here we go."

Four lines were dropped to either side of the helicopter, and eight men dropped out at a time, not rappelling but simply sliding down the thick lines like firemen sliding down a pole, controlling their descent with their gloved hands. Blake went in the second wave, rushing forward toward cover the instant his boots touched the deck.

Ghannon was one the last man out of the helicopter, and as soon as he reached the deck, the helicopter banked and lifted away. The big Englishman raised a bullhorn to his lips.

"United States Navy. Heave to and muster your crew on deck. Now."

He repeated the order in Arabic and rushed forward to join Blake, flat against a steel bulkhead. Then the second Seahawk dropped in and deposited the second half of the platoon. Twenty seconds later the second helicopter also lifted away, heading off to rendezvous with its tanker.

"Don't shoot," a man shouted in thick English. "We come."

To either side of the *Sultana*'s superstructure, men emerged, their hands raised. One carried a broomstick, to which he had tied his white undershirt as a flag of surrender.

The SEALs, rifles to their shoulders, herded the crew to the center of the deck and had them sit. Blake did a quick head count.

"Twenty-eight," he told Ghannon. "All compliant."

"The last lot fought us like it was bloody Armageddon," the Englishman observed. "What does that tell you?"

Blake lowered his rifle. "We aren't going to find anything on this ship."

CHAPTER SIXTY-EIGHT

Checking the freighter's hold took less than half an hour.

"Manifest shows 221 Royal Enfield Standard motorcycles, manufactured in Chennai, plus spare parts and dealer tools," the ensign said. "That looks like what we've got. Half the hold's empty; they were in Gwadar to offload, not to take anything more. None of the crates are big enough to contain what we found on the *Tigris*. We're searching the rest of the ship, but . . . looks like a dry hole, captain."

Blake nodded, and the captain turned to a senior chief. "We have comms established? Up on the bridge? Good—let's call this in, figure the next step."

Blake walked to the rail, looked out at the Arabian Sea. The morning sky was virtually cloudless, the deep water rolling with low, deep blue swells. The sea was beautiful, spectacularly so. He kept his eyes open as he whispered, *"Heavenly Father, I don't believe you brought me this far to fail. Father, our enemies are working to destroy us. In the name of Christ Jesus, I ask you to prevent this. Use me, Lord, in any way you see fit; but please, Father, prevent them."*

"Lieutenant?" The SEAL captain was calling from above, from the fair-weather bridge.

"Sir?"

"Can you come on up? Commander Ghannon, if you can come, too."

Blake and Ghannon climbed the steep, stairlike ladder to the wheelhouse and stepped inside. The captain was looking down at handwritten notes, and the senior chief was monitoring a radio headset.

"*Tigris*, last night's freighter was bound for New York, according to its log," the captain said. "That jive with what you know?"

Ghannon shrugged. "All I knew was departure and that the weapons were headed for the East Coast."

"It could jive," Blake said. "I was supposed to intercept a freighter off the Outer Banks. Wouldn't know which one until I got there. But ships upbound from Miami to New York often pass near the Outer Banks. It's a busy freight route. Would make sense to ease into that, draw less attention. We can't be sure that was the ship I was supposed to meet, though. Could easily be the *Anesidora*."

The SEAL captain nodded. "How about the name, 'Grant Reinbolt'? That ring a bell?"

"That's me. The identity I assumed."

The Navy officer nodded again. "I guessed as much. Our intelligence people got into that laptop we seized. E-mails received early last evening say the organization in Washington is expecting Grant Reinbolt to arrive on a British Air flight at Dulles tonight at twenty-three hundred Eastern. Nothing went outbound on that laptop, Lieutenant. No distress call we know of. So if the missing freighter is the one you were supposed to meet, we might still have a shot at this."

The men fell silent, a muted beep from the weather radar the only sound on the small bridge as Blake did the math. "Twenty-three hundred in Washington. That's twenty hours from now."

He looked at Ghannon. "They still think it's on? But they haven't heard from the camp in better than forty-eight hours. They've got to know something's up."

Ghannon shook his head. "The satellite phone played up a couple of times before you got there. One time it was out for ten days. Both times they didn't hear from us until we resupplied, and we resupplied just before the attack. So we probably have two, three days, maybe even a week before they suspect anything's up at the camp."

"So I've got twenty hours to get to Washington? From here?"

Ghannon looked at the SEAL captain. "What's your nearest dependable point to put our lad, here, on a fast jet to DC?"

The Navy man pursed his lips. "Iraq, I'd imagine. *Diego Garcia* is too far in the wrong direction, but we have aircraft at Balad that could do the job. But to put him on a chopper, arrange the refuel, get him up there? That's gonna eat up some time."

"Where are we?" Ghannon asked. The navy officer showed him on a chart.

Ghannon turned to the senior chief. "Have you a satellite phone I can use? Yes? Perfect."

Ghannon stepped out onto the fair-weather bridge for a better satellite link, squinting in the brilliant sunlight. From the relative shadow of the bridge, Blake watched while the Brit made his call.

Finally Ghannon stepped back inside. "Call your helicopter, Captain. If we can put the lieutenant, here, on a Seahawk within the hour, I can have him in Iraq within three."

The SEAL scowled. "How are you doing that?"

Ghannon pointed at the chart. "We're here, off Oman. Masirah Island, here, is just forty kilometers away. It has an airbase capable of handling light jets; I've flown into it before. MI6 has located an RAF HS125—same thing as a small corporate jet—that is flying a vice-counsel from Cairo to Nashik. I've arranged to divert it to Masirah and leave the vice-counsel on the ground for the time being. Diplomatic Corps is going to scream bloody murder, but it's done. We fly the lieutenant, here, to Masirah on the chopper, the jet takes him to Iraq, you have something fast waiting there, and—Bob's your uncle—we can have him in DC with hours to spare."

The SEAL shook his head. "Doubtful Oman is going to let a United States Navy chopper land on their airbase."

"I know. The relationship with your administration is strained . . . the human-trafficking issue. But while Oman was never a colony, the sultanate has been close to the UK over the years, and some of the royal family have been educated in England, so we're tugging on some old-school ties. Bring your helicopter in. They'll look the other way while the lieutenant here and I land on the taxiway at Masirah, and the RAF will get us safe and sound to Iraq. Unofficial channels, but gets the job done."

Blake looked at Ghannon. "You're coming with?"

"That's what London said. As far as Iraq, I am. That way, no troubles in Oman. It'll work."

The SEAL captain looked at Blake. Blake nodded.

"If I wind up in a court-martial over this," the SEAL captain said, "I'm depending on you two to bust me out of the brig."

He turned to the senior chief. "Call in a Seahawk. The lieutenant and the commander, here, need to be outbound soonest."

CHAPTER SIXTY-NINE

❑ ❑ ❑

Alia was just sitting down at her desk with coffee when the phone rang. She set the cup aside and picked up the handset.

"DDO," she said.

She listened to the voice on the other end for a moment and began crying.

"You are alive," she said, gasping. "We received notice the codeword was given at Bagram, but since then we haven't heard a thing. Where are you? . . . Iraq? Are you okay? Are you coming home?"

She listened for a moment.

"Back with them? Haven't you done enough? Couldn't we send . . . ? Oh. I see. I'm sorry. Yes. Let me get a pen."

She began to take notes.

"Yes. Those are all clothes we can find in the DC area, no problem. Describe the bag to me again? All right. And we can get you some running shoes you would have been able to find in London. I understand. Andrews at eight this evening, twelve hours from now. We'll arrange transport."

She listened for a few more seconds.

"Yes," she told the phone. "I miss you, too."

CHAPTER SEVENTY

❏ ❏ ❏

Balad Airbase, Iraq

Blake hung up the phone in the airbase commander's office and turned to Ghannon. "We're on. Agency is meeting me at eight tonight at Andrews. They're getting a bag of clothes that will match what I took to Pakistan, British Air luggage tag on it. Shuttle to CIA, then Dulles, and we'll put me through a side door so I come out of Immigration with everyone else."

"The SEALS and I will be about twenty-four hours behind you. We're flying into Pax River."

Blake looked the big Brit over. Like Blake, Ghanon had gotten both a shave and a haircut from the base barber. He looked like a different man. Blake extended his hand. "Thanks for getting me here. I owe you one."

"Actually, it's I who owe you two, lad. Between the captain of police's house and the camp attack, I make it twice you've saved my life in the past month."

"Okay." Blake smiled. "You owe me, then. Three steak dinners, restaurant of my choosing."

"Done." Ghannon cocked his head. "Three? Who's the third for?"

"My girl."

Ghannon laughed. “Legally dead and out of the country for what—four, five months? And you’ve still got a girl? My hat’s off to you, lad. Listen . . . you’ve got a plane to catch. Off with you. I’ll see you in DC.”

They shook hands again, and Blake stepped out into the corridor.

“Lieutenant Kershaw?”

He turned. An Air Force enlisted person—young and pretty, with dark hair pulled back to either side—was standing there with a duffel bag next to her. She had a brilliant smile, and she reminded him of Alia.

“Yes?”

“I’m Senior Airman Davis, sir. I’m here to get you dressed.”

Blake felt his eyebrows rise.

The senior airman laughed. “Not dress you myself, sir. Just show you what goes where and do the safety inspection once you’re finished.” She lifted the duffel. “G-suit, helmet—it can be a little complicated unless you’ve done it before. Ready room is just down the hallway, sir.”

“Oh. Sure.” Blake took the duffel and walked with her.

“Listen,” he said as he walked, “I’ve never flown in anything like this before. Anything I need to know?”

The senior airman looked up at him. “Where are they ferrying you to sir?”

“Washington.”

“Andrews?” She nodded. “That’s a haul. That’s about as far as you can go.”

“And that means?”

“Last thing before you get in that airplane, sir? Hit the men’s room. Pee for all you’re worth. Trust me. You’ll be glad you did.”

“You in good shape, physically, Lieutenant?”

The voice, coming from four feet ahead of Blake, could have been coming from the North Pole. It sounded electronic in the helmet speakers. In the Afghan night, blue taxiway lights were crawling past them in the predawn gloom as they rolled out to the runway.

"I was, Captain. Right now . . . well, sir, I've been blown up twice in the past seventy-two hours. Little sore, sir."

"Good to know. We'll keep ourselves within three Gs." The pilot spoke to the tower, the engine ran up and then died back down, hydraulics hummed from somewhere behind Blake, and the airplane made the turn onto the end of the runway.

"Okay, Lieutenant. Here we go."

The takeoff felt like what Blake imagined it would feel like to be shot out of a cannon. Past the pilot's head all he could see was dark-blue sky, a few clouds. In one minute brilliant sunlight was entering the cockpit, and Blake had the briefest glimpse of snow-capped mountains, peaks so white it hurt to look at them, before they turned and headed west.

"Your first time in an E, lieutenant?"

"'E,' sir?"

"F/A-15E. Strike Eagle. We're the dual-role version of the F-15."

"'Dual role,' sir?"

"Air and ground attack both. If it's up, we shoot it down, and if it's down, we blow it up. We can pull Mach 2.5, but fuel economy sucks if we do that, so we'll be flying about Mach one-and-a-quarter most of the way. In ferry mode we'll be refueling about once every eighteen-hundred miles. We'll have a tanker meeting us over the Med and two more over the Atlantic. Anything you need to know?'

Blake rolled his shoulders as much as he could. The Balad ground crew had strapped him in so tightly he felt an inch shorter.

"This thing recline?"

"Only if I go ballistic, Lieutenant. "Enjoy the ride."

Blake wasn't sure how much later it was when he felt the plane begin to descend.

"Are we landing, sir?"

"Not for hours. We cruise at forty-thousand feet for better fuel economy, but the tanker is down at twenty-five. It's a good show. You'll like it."

The KC-767 Global Tanker—big, gray, and virtually windowless—was dragging a refueling boom that reminded Blake of a stingray's tail. The Strike Eagle wobbled down through the tanker's wake and then settled in steady air just below and behind it. The refueling boom came nearer and nearer to Blake.

"Sir? You're not planning on putting that in the seat with me, are you?"

The pilot laughed. "Just about. Refueling receptacle's in the root of the port-side wing."

Blake watched as the boom, looking very big and very heavy from just a few feet away, bobbed slightly in the air next to him. It didn't take a lot of imagination to picture it crashing through the canopy. It settled into an open cavity at the base of the wing. He could feel a metallic THUCK, and the fighter flew in tandem with the big tanker for several minutes. Then there was a softer click, the boom lifted away, and the fighter rolled to its right and began climbing.

"And back upstairs we go," the pilot said. "Catch some zees, and I'll wake you for the next one."

"Thank you, sir, but if it's all the same to you, I'll just sleep through it."

The pilot laughed all the way to forty thousand feet.

The senior airman was right. By the time they landed at Andrews, there was only one burning question on Blake's mind. And he never had to ask it.

"Porta Potties right at the end of the flight line, sirs," the airman told them as he helped them out of their ejection seats. "Two units. No waiting."

"Good," the pilot groaned. "I'd hate to pull rank."

CHAPTER SEVENTY-ONE

❏ ❏ ❏

The McDonnell Douglas Explorer helicopter crossed Georgetown Pike, swooping low over darkened ballfields and trees, and settled toward the CIA helipad in a misting rain, fans of white radiating out from the floodlights surrounding the pad, a square of white at the edge of a parking lot. From his place in the right-hand seat, Blake could see a young woman in a rain jacket and hood waiting in a golf cart, and his heart leapt up. Then the rotor wash blew her hood back, revealing blonde hair.

Not Alia.

Blake's heartbeat settled back to normal. He was still in the air force flight suit, still dressed as he had been at Andrews when he'd walked into the ready room and a stocky air force enlisted man had approached him with a sheet of paper, folded and taped shut.

"Message from Bagram, sir. I was instructed to deliver it to the lieutenant who was passenger on the ferry flight."

"That would be me. Thank you, Senior Airman."

Blake had waited until the man left and then opened the note. There were only four lines and a name:

POST-OP ANALYSIS OF DEVICE SHOWS NO TIMER.

WAS DESIGNED TO DETONATE UPON RECEIPT OF

CELL-PHONE SIGNAL. JUST IN CASE YOU WONDERED;

THESE PEOPLE DEFINITELY NOT YOUR FRIENDS.

GHANNON

Blake tore the message into strips and deposited them into two wastepaper baskets, one on either side of the room.

The helicopter set down, the pilot nodded, and Blake opened the door and stepped out into the gale under the idling rotors. He latched the door behind him, hunched, and ran to the cart.

"Welcome to CIA, sir," the young woman told him. "Or welcome back. I understand you're one of ours, although I was instructed not to ask for ID."

"Wise advice." Blake half-shouted to be heard over the dark blue helicopter as it lifted off behind him. "I don't have any."

"We have the bag and clothes you requested." The young woman nodded over her right shoulder at a carry-on bag in the space behind the seats.

Blake glanced back. The bag was difficult to make out in the low light, but it looked exactly like what he'd left Washington with, nearly half a year earlier.

"I'm taking you to the Headquarters gym," the young woman explained. "You can change there. Shower, too, if you want."

"I want," Blake said. "But I can't. The people picking me up think I just flew steerage from the Middle East. I'd better show up just a little funky."

The driver took the cart right up a pathway to a doorway.

"Gym's inside on your right, sir. When you leave the men's locker room, take two rights to get to an exit that leads to a portico. We'll have a car waiting there to take you to Dulles."

A shower was out of the question, but Blake took advantage of the sinks in the empty locker room to clean himself up as much as he figured he could have done in an airplane lavatory.

The clothes, he noted with satisfaction, had obviously been washed a few times to give them a more aged look. Even the running shoes were scuffed around the soles. And Alia had provided him with a toilet kit containing European toothpaste, European shampoo, and English deodorant.

Semi-refreshed, he got dressed, left the flight suit in an empty locker, and took the two rights out of the locker room to find the exit, where a Chevy Malibu with government plates was waiting. An army sergeant got out of the driver's seat and opened the back door, and Blake immediately regretted the lack of a shower.

Because waiting in the back seat was Alia.

"Welcome back, Lieutenant." She nodded toward the driver's seat, where the sergeant was just getting back in. *Not in the know; don't say anything confidential.*

"Miss." Blake settled in next to her and, as the sergeant glanced out his window, reached over and gave Alia's hand a squeeze. She squeezed back, smiled, and drew her hand back.

"Transit will take a little under half an hour, sir. Take a nap, if you'd like."

I.e., *no conversation until we get there.*

"Thanks," Blake told her. "I think I will."

He closed his eyes and pretended to sleep for what seemed like the longest twenty-eight minutes of his life.

Through slitted eyes, he watched as they drove on an expressway, then pulled onto an access road, and then crossed a secure checkpoint, where he pretended to awaken as the car crossed onto the airport tarmac. Five minutes later, they pulled up next to a plain metal door in the side of the terminal. Alia got out, keyed a number into a door-side pad, and opened it. Then she nodded at Blake.

Blake got out of the car, overnight bag over his shoulder, and crossed the few feet of chilly night air to the door, his tongue feeling thick in his mouth. He stepped inside. They were in a short, carpeted hallway—just the two of them.

Blake set the bag down. Opened his arms.

She came to him, a perfect fit. For a long moment they just held each other, wordlessly. He lifted her chin, brought his face down to hers.

She stopped him.

"I . . . I might get lipstick on you. And that door . . ." She indicated the only other door in the hallway. ". . . leads to the cleared side of Customs. If somebody is waiting for you, they'll probably be just outside."

She handed him a British Airways ticket envelope with a used boarding pass. Then she handed him a slim stack of currency.

"Nine hundreds and five twenties. In case you need money to bolt."

Blake nodded.

"We have a contact number at the Agency that's easy to remember." She gave it to him. "When it asks you for an extension, push 1-3-7-9—the four corners of the keypad. That will ring straight to me, and if I don't pick up within four rings, it will forward to my mobile. And the FBI will have the Morehead City marina under surveillance."

Blake thought about how easily he'd picked up the FBI tail in Washington. He shook his head.

"No," he told her. "No close tail. These people will be way too spooky, this late in the game. Have the FBI wait at the Coast Guard station at Fort Macon. I'll call you just before we head out and they can track us, scramble a cutter, and arrest us all once we get to the ship. Less chance of tipping our hand that way; the Coast Guard is a fairly common sight in those waters."

Alia looked up at him, thin-lipped.

"Okay," she finally said. "But as the slightest sign of anything going wrong, call in and push '1-3-7-9.' All right?"

"Okay." Blake nodded. "Got it."

There was a faint buzzing sound, and Alia looked at her BlackBerry.

"Your flight has deplaned, and the passengers are just entering Immigration. If you go now, you'll leave Customs just ahead of them."

"Okay." Blake didn't move. He was no longer holding her, but she was close.

"I thought . . ." She put her arms around him again. "I thought I would never see you again."

He tried to smile. "I had to come back to you. You told me to."

She looked up, eyes damp. "Then I'm telling you to again."

Blake kissed the top of her head, smelling vanilla-scented shampoo. Then he picked up his bag, and stepped out the door at the end of the hallway.

The Customs hall was huge, long lines of people shuffling bags to inspection booths, and he was on the exit side. People were passing through frosted glass doors that slid open as they approached.

Blake joined the throng of exiting passengers and stepped out into the terminal. There was Qasid, waiting beyond a set of ropes, a big grin on his face.

Blake remembered Ghannon's note: THESE PEOPLE DEFINITELY NOT YOUR FRIENDS.

He stepped to a trash can, pretended to throw something inside. Then he walked around the end of the rope barricade, his arms open.

"Grant Reinbolt, my brother," Qasid thumped him on the back and nearly lifted him off the ground. "You had a good flight?"

"I had a long one," Blake told him. "It's good to be back."

CHAPTER SEVENTY-TWO

❑ ❑ ❑

The little bedside alarm clock chimed and Blake awoke. It was like deja vu. He was in Saif's nephew's apartment, back in the bed he slept in before he departed. His Qur'an was next to the alarm clock, and he got up and went through the sham of Muslim morning prayer.

There were no snores from the next bedroom. Apparently the nephew was away. Possibly taking a vacation from his unemployment.

Blake showered and shaved, nicking himself once because he had shaved so little over the last half year. He stuck a bit of toilet paper to the cut, got dressed, peeled the toilet paper off slowly, and put on a Windbreaker that had sat unused in the closet for all those months. Then he walked the few blocks to the Starbucks.

"Ah, yes! Here he is!" Saif stood, beaming.

The ringleader looked less like his brother—now his dead brother—than Blake remembered. This man looked softer, a city person. And he was dressed completely in Western clothes: loafers, slacks, a button-down shirt, and a sport coat.

"Raheesh sends his greetings." Blake hugged the thin man. "He sends his apologies. The satellite phone was not working when I left. The man who drove me was supposed to get parts to fix it, but they had not come in yet when we got to the village."

"Such is life," Saif told him. "It is not like here, yes? Here you have only to make a call, and you can get anything. Ah, sit, my brother. Qasid is getting you some coffee and a scone."

They sat and Saif asked him about the camp, Blake answering truthfully except for the part about the air strike.

The coffee came, and Blake sipped from the cup with its cardboard hand guard.

"And my brother tells me you saved his life," Saif exclaimed. He looked at his cohort. "I tell you, this man is a hero!"

And yet you are still ready to kill me to make your statement. Blake shook his head. "It was a team effort."

"And modest!" Saif clapped him on the shoulder. "Today you relax, my friend. No taxi for you today or this week. Tomorrow, though, Qasid will take you to buy clothes."

Blake sipped his coffee. "Clothes?"

"To look like the fisherman," Saif told him with a wink. "We leave for North Carolina on Friday."

CHAPTER SEVENTY-THREE

❑ ❑ ❑

Morehead City, North Carolina

The truck was a two-year-old F-150 pickup, the boat a twenty-two-foot Trojan American powered by a single large Mercury outboard, sitting on a trailer with four wheels. It was a little smaller than Blake used on his leaves, going fishing with friends from Fort Bragg, but it made the driving easy. It was almost as if the boat was not back there at all.

He was by himself yet not by himself. To keep up appearances, Saif told him to drive alone while Saif, Qasid, and another man—a big bruiser Saif introduced as "Hassan, our brother from New York"—rode behind in a Lincoln Town Car. They separated driving past Baltimore, and Blake used the respite to pull into a truck stop and buy a prepaid cell phone, which he stashed in the overhead console of the truck.

It almost felt like he was going fishing. Rods and reels lay in the deck of the boat, and he had a big tackle box Qasid spent a small fortune on at Outdoor World, complete with plugs and spoons appropriate for fishing this late in the season, when an angler would have to venture nearly forty miles offshore to get to the west wall of the Gulf Stream.

It was, Blake had to admit, nearly the perfect cover for a rendezvous with a freighter, far out at sea.

Now he was passing sights familiar to him from his days in training: the overpass, Olympus Dive Center, where they had the deck gun to the *U-352* bolted to the patio outside.

The Lincoln was close behind him now, and he pulled into the Sanitary Restaurant.

"It is an odd name," Saif said as they walked in from the parking lot.

"It's clean and they don't serve alcohol," Blake explained. "So they named it 'The Sanitary.'"

"Almost halal, huh?" All the men laughed.

All four of them were dressed like middle-class fishermen, although only Blake truly looked the part.

They went inside and ordered, all four ordering burgers, which didn't raise so much as a look from the waitress, even though the Sanitary was known for seafood.

They were just getting dessert when Saif's iPhone rang.

"Perhaps it is the *Tigris*," he said to Qasid in Arabic. "They are overdue in calling."

Then he looked at the phone. "No. It is an international number."

"Hello," he said in English. "Then, looking up at Blake, he switched to French. *"Merci, bien. Comment allez-vous?"*

Blake pretended to stare absently out the big picture windows. Grant Reinbolt, after all, did not speak French.

But Blake Kershaw did.

In three minutes' time, he had it all. The *Anesidora* was bound for Baltimore and due to dock there late in the evening. Saif concluded his phone call, and then he engaged Blake in conversation about the fishing—how the plugs were used, which fish fought the hardest.

"It sounds fascinating, my brother," he said. His eyes twinkled as he spoke, his sincerity sounding absolutely authentic, not like the man who was less than a week away from killing a million people. "I wish I was coming with you, but . . ."

He laughed again.

Blake rubbed his arms.

"Is it chilly in here to you?" He looked at Qasid, who shrugged. Blake rubbed his arms again. "I'm a little cold. If I'm going to have ice cream, I'd better run outside and get a jacket. Would you excuse me?"

He left the restaurant and crossed the street to where he'd parked the truck and boat, double-checking to make sure he was out of sight and no one followed. Then he opened the truck and got out the cell phone, dialing the contact number and then the four-digit extension.

Alia answered on the first ring.

"Do you have a pen?" Blake glanced at the restaurant again. "I have to be quick. The vessel we are looking for, the *Anesidora*, docks in Baltimore tonight. The opposition still thinks the Tigris is coming; that's the freighter we're suppose to meet. So tell the FBI they can take us now, here in Morehead. I don't know who is making contact with the *Anesidora*, so it's best if we seize it while everything is still on board. Let the deputy chief know and then call MI6. Their man, Ghannon, is with the SEAL team at Pax River. They're our best bet for making the seizure. Can you read that back to me?"

He listened for a moment. "Perfect. I've got to go. . . . Yes, I'll be safe. Just tell the FBI to move it."

He switched the phone off, grabbed his Windbreaker, locked the truck up, tossed the phone into a trash can, and went back inside.

"That's better," he said as he sat, rubbing his arms for theatrical effect.

"We got you some more coffee," Saif said, pushing a cup toward him.

Blake looked at the cup. "Cream and sugar?"

Saif laughed. "Qasid made it for you. Drink it down so you don't hurt his feelings."

Blake finished the cup in two draughts, and then the four men ate dessert, Saif still making a show of talking about fishing.

They were on their way out of the restaurant when Blake staggered. He stopped, hand to his head, and Hassan put his arm about him and kept him moving.

"My head," Blake said thickly. They got to the Lincoln, and Hassan lowered him into the back seat.

"I received a call while you were out at the truck," Saif told him. "My brother Raheesh had heart problems a few years back. A cardiologist must check him every year. One of our people took the doctor up to the camp, and they found it destroyed and full of American soldiers. The doctor was captured, but his guide got away. And the people in the village below told him they heard explosions up on the mountain a week ago on Wednesday."

"Wha—?" Blake could barely sit up.

"You were scheduled to leave a week ago on Thursday, Grant Reinbolt. The day after the camp was destroyed. How is that possible? No—do not try to get up. What we put into your drink will make walking quite impossible. Now we must get you somewhere. Someplace where you, Hassan, and I can have a little talk."

CHAPTER SEVENTY-FOUR

❑ ❑ ❑

Patuxent River Naval Base, Maryland

"What do you mean, the FBI is claiming jurisdiction?" Graham Ghannon was aware his voice was several decibels too loud for indoors. He didn't care. "We know what we're looking for. Send us in."

The base commander swiveled in his tucked-leather, wingback desk chair, and shook his head. "It's not just FBI, Commander. Coast Guard, ATF, Port Authority, everybody and their brother is claiming jurisdiction. Except CIA; they've expressly ceded authority to us."

"Then move on that."

"It's not that simple." It was a Naval Intelligence Service officer who spoke up. "These folks all have to live with one another afterward."

"That's just the point." Ghannon's voice was loud enough it threatened to shake the oaken bookcases. "If these people have offices near the waterfront, they may not be able to live together."

"Port Authority has people watching the vessel," the intelligence man said. "So far only some of the crew have gotten off. Nobody is carrying anything large enough to be the device. It's under control."

"Under control? You have terrorists with a nuclear weapon, docked at the center of a major port, and you call that 'under control'?"

The Navy officers looked at him blankly, and Ghannon stormed out of the stately room.

CHAPTER SEVENTY-FIVE

❏ ❏ ❏

New Bern, North Carolina

The home was huge, with six bedrooms and five baths, one of the coastal rentals people buy for their retirements and then rent out through agents in the meantime, the rentals paying for mortgages and upkeep while their New York City owners awaited their turn in the sun. It was high on a bluff overlooking the inlet, and Blake was in the family room, where he would have been admiring the view, were it not for the fact he was kneeling, barefooted, his wrists tied behind his back to his ankles with telephone cord. He had been kneeling in this fashion for the better part of a day, and now he had company.

"Where is your passport?" Saif asked him.

"I threw it away after I left Customs. Raheesh told me to. He said not to risk having two sets of identification here in the States."

"I saw him throw something in the trash can," Qasid S from the side of the room.

"Maybe," Saif allowed. "How did you get from the camp to London?"

Blake did the math. His return would have had to have been more rapid than his trip in. "By light plane. And then by airliner. Once we had reached an EU country."

"Which EU country?"

Blake hesitated. Instantly, the bare soles of his feet stung as if he had stepped on a high-voltage line. He grunted and felt the cords of his neck bulge.

Saif knelt next to him. "A wire coat hanger, my friend. You get them free from the dry cleaners. Who would know that, in the hands of one such as Hassan, they could inflict such pain? Now . . . which country?"

"Italy," Blake said quickly. His feet roared with pain again. He wondered if the FBI was searching for them. Probably in Morehead City, forty-five minutes away.

"We will get to the bottom of this," Saif told him. "We have all day."

CHAPTER SEVENTY-SIX

❑ ❑ ❑

Patuxent River Naval Base, Maryland

"Admiral, do you have family in Baltimore? Anywhere along the Chesapeake?" Graham Ghannon tried to keep his voice modulated, his demeanor as near to calm as possible.

"I know what you are getting at, Commander. No sale." The two men were walking along the water, the sun setting.

"Admiral, we have agencies engaged in a spitting match all over Washington while nearly a kiloton of explosives sits on that ship."

"We think it sits on that ship. And that's the point, Commander. Nobody has come to claim it. If they do, we'll take them out."

Ghannon walked a few feet further. A gull screamed in the distance. "'We?' Who's 'we,' Admiral?"

The flag officer stopped walking. "Trust me. I'm just as frustrated as you, Commander. And yes. To answer your question, I do have family in Baltimore. And I trust our SEALs to take care of the situation. But I have to get a green light to do that."

"Admiral," Ghannon said, "I hope it comes soon."

CHAPTER SEVENTY-SEVEN

❑ ❑ ❑

New Bern, North Carolina

"Drink, Grant Reinbolt." Qasid rotated the American into a sitting position and was holding a cup to his lips. "It is only water."

You bet. The same way that the coffee in Morehead City was only coffee. Blake took a mouthful, held it, waited until Qasid's back turned, and then let it slowly dribble out of his mouth and onto the carpet.

"I don't understand what is going on," he told Qasid. "I am here to serve. I am trained to serve. If the freighter carrying the device I was to use has not come, then let me be the one to use the device on the other."

"What do you mean, 'use the device'?"

"Take it where it is needed."

Qasid shook his head. "But Grant Reinbolt, it is already there. The timer was set on it while they were far out at sea. Tomorrow at noon, it will detonate in the harbor front, right where it sits now."

Then Qasid glanced at Blake nervously, as if he had said too much.

Blake felt cold. Of course: Washington had no port—a weapon would have to be transported into the city. But Baltimore's port was in the heart of a major metropolitan area. Whichever way the nuclear plume drifted, it would kill thousands.

He strained against the telephone cord. It was standard, plastic over copper wire. And copper stretched. Marginally. He flexed his arms against the tension of the cord. Was it looser? Perhaps—marginally. But it was going to take time.

CHAPTER SEVENTY-EIGHT

❑ ❑ ❑

Patuxent River Naval Base, Maryland

"Ghannon."

It was the SEAL captain. Graham Ghannon, stretched on a cot fully clothed, sat up, awake. "What is it?"

"We're a 'go.' Choppers are warming up on the pad."

Ghannon got to his feet and grabbed his gear. Through the window, light was beginning to break. "Washington finally get their heads out?"

The captain shook his head. "This is the admiral. Pretty sure he's acting on his own. But I didn't ask."

"Wise," Ghannon said. "And your admiral is a brave man. How many are we taking?"

"One platoon."

Sixteen men. Plus Ghannon would make seventeen.

"It's enough," he said.

He stepped into the hallway, which was filled with the sound of pounding feet, of men heading off to war.

CHAPTER SEVENTY-NINE

❑ ❑ ❑

New Bern, North Carolina

At 5:45 in the morning, Blake finally worked his thumb free of the phone cord. He spent ten minutes working the rest of his hand through and then flexed the freed hand, urging feeling back into it. He brought it before his face, and the wrist looked as red as raw sirloin.

Behind the family room was an open kitchen, and he crawled in there, using his freed hand to pull himself along. He got to his knees, also raw, and peered over the counter.

A block of butcher's knives was against the far side of the counter. He reached for it.

No good. At least eight inches short.

Blake slid open a drawer, found a soup ladle. He extended it, hooked the knife block and pulled it toward him, working slowly so he would not knock it over and alert anyone who was downstairs.

Closer.

Closer.

He got it within reach and slid the largest knife out, used it to cut his other wrist free from his ankles. His legs complained as he straightened them, but he ignored the protest and bent to cut his ankles free.

Done. He still had phone cord around one wrist and two ankles, but his limbs were free.

He tried getting to his feet. His legs would not respond. They felt like wood, all except for the soles of his feet, which were sending a dull and escalating signal of pain.

The counter had stools at it, and he used one to reach for the phone, wiggle it off its hook, hold it to his ear.

Nothing. Either unplugged or not connected to begin with.

Downstairs a door opened and closed. Men's voices. Arabic.

Stand up. Blake urged himself, commanded himself. Nothing happened.

Stand up. He got to his knees. That was it.

Footsteps on the stair.

Blake walked on his knees back to the knife block, got the paring knife and, butcher's knife in one hand and paring knife in the other, hobbled to the refrigerator, next to the stairwell.

"Grant Reinbolt, I have brought you foo—"

Qasid never got the last word out. Flat on his stomach, Blake drew the butcher's knife hard across the man's nearest Achilles tendon. That dropped Qasid to the ground, and Blake, trained in ground combat, quickly flipped his head back and drove the paring knife upward. When it hit the brain stem, the man collapsed.

"Qasid?" It was the big man, the one from New York. "Did you fall?"

Blake struggled to his feet and tottered as the big man walked in. But when Blake tried to step forward, his leg nearly collapsed.

Hassan looked at the dead man at his feet, roared, and then launched himself at Blake, pinning him to the wall, knocking both knives to the floor. He got his hands to Blake's throat.

The room began to darken.

Lord. This—your enemy. Help. Now.

Blake pushed with all his might. The big man staggered back against the counter, and Blake shoved again.

Hassan tripped over Qasid's body, pinwheeled his arms. Blake stooped to reach for one of the knives, and the sound of shattering glass filled the room.

Blake looked up. Cool wind was blowing in the open window, bits of sash dangling.

He staggered to the window and looked down.

Hassan's body was on the deck, three stories down, a halo of blood growing around his head.

CHAPTER EIGHTY

❑ ❑ ❑

Baltimore Harbor

SEALs poured off either side of the Seahawk onto the deck and ran, ducked low, toward the superstructure of the *Anesidora*. The helicopter lifted away and was replaced by another, which deposited its eight warriors and then lifted off as well.

Ghannon and the captain ran up opposite sides of the deck and climbed to the bridge.

It was empty.

They stood still listening to their radios as the team reported in:

"Engine room, clear."

"Mess, clear."

"Galley, clear."

So it went, around the ship. No one in the officers' quarters, no one in crew's quarters. *Anesidora* was empty.

"No watch?" Ghannon looked at the SEAL captain, hand up.

"They left a few at a time," the captain said. "Everybody assumed there were still some left, but . . ."

"So they just ran off and left their weapon?" Ghannon shook his head. "Why do I feel this is nearing the fan?"

He looked at the instruments on the bridge: radio off, radar dark. The freighter had been completely shut down.

"Commander Ghannon?" It was the radio headset. A woman's voice. No one on the team.

"Ghannon, go."

"Pax River here, sir. We have a code word communication coming in on a cell phone, sir. Says most urgent."

"Put it through."

"Graham?"

Ghannon straightened up. "Lieutenant? Where are you?"

"North Carolina. Listen. The delivery on the device on that ship is not the same as it was for Washington. This one is staying put. And it's armed already. It's set to go off at noon."

Ghannon felt his stomach crawl. Noon. He looked at his watch. Five-and-a-half hours.

"Sounds as if we had better find it, Lieutenant." He moved to the open window. Men had opened the cargo hatches and were gesturing.

"What is it?" He called down.

"The cargo. It's pistachio nuts. In twenty kilo bags. There are thousands of them. It's going to take hours to sort through this."

CHAPTER EIGHTY-ONE

❑ ❑ ❑

New Bern, North Carolina

"Prepare to make way! Stat! Cut those lines! We have to get this thing downbound. Now!"

Blake held the cell phone to his ear and listened to the commands being given on the freighter.

"Smart move," he said into the mouthpiece. "I'll be back in touch as soon as I can."

The car keys were in the same place Blake found the cell phone: Hassan's pocket. The big man's shoes were too big for him, but he found some washcloths in the bathroom and put them inside as extra insoles. They gave just enough cushion that he could walk, albeit painfully. He got down to the car and looked around.

No Saif.

Blake calculated miles in his head. New Bern to Baltimore would take . . . forever. He dialed the agency, then Alia's extension.

"Good. You're there. Listen: I need a Blackhawk, fully fueled, with crew, at the Coastal Airport at New Bern, just as soon as they can get one there from Bragg."

He listened. "Yes. I'm fine. A little beat up. But the second weapon is active. It's on the ship, and Ghannon is trying to take it down the Chesapeake to open water. He might make it, but we need to start evacuating people. Maryland, Delaware, anyplace that might get windblown fallout from the Chesapeake."

He listened again.

"Alia, I've got to do this. And you have to get that evacuation order out, stat. Please. Get me that helicopter."

He started the car and began to drive north as fast as he could safely go.

"Safely" seemed a shaky proposition.

Half an hour later he was at the New Bern airport, the distant thunder of a helicopter sounding from the horizon, a rent-a-cop telling him he couldn't leave the car where he was leaving it. Running as best he could on mangled feet through the airport, Blake shot past a set of metal detectors and some startled TSA part-timers, and then ran out onto the tarmac.

Two men in uniforms came out the doors after him, just as the air began to swirl around him. He looked up at a Blackhawk helicopter dropping out of the sky.

"Need a code word, sir," a crewman shouted from the open door.

"Yellow butterfly."

Strong hands reached down, grabbed him off the tarmac, and pulled him into the helicopter. They lifted off, leaving the two astonished security officers gaping skyward.

CHAPTER EIGHTY-TWO

❑ ❑ ❑

Over the Chesapeake Bay

On both shores traffic was bumper to bumper, slowly moving north, a hundred thousand windshields reflecting sun up at the helicopter, five thousand feet above the broad water.

On the Chesapeake, boat traffic had disappeared, all except for a flotilla of pleasure craft, all racing northward as fast as their engines would push them.

"Lieutenant? We have comms with your team on the freighter. Go when ready."

"Graham," Blake shouted to be heard over the rotors. "What's your sit?"

"Just cleared the bridge, Blake. We're headed for open water. Lads are heaving pistachio nuts over the side, digging in all four holds. Going to be a row at your EPA when they hear about this. Wait . . . they found it. It's not in the crate that it left the camp in. It's just the device, in the shipping case, unlocked."

"Great." The bridge was coming up, and Blake could see a ship, about a mile beyond it. He looked at the pilot. "How's the wind?"

"Offshore about ten knots."

Blake nodded. "We have a winch?"

The pilot nodded. "Easier to deploy if we're on the deck. The bridge approach looks clear. I can set down there."

"What will it hold, weight wise?"

"Five hundred pounds."

"That'll do," Blake said. "Make it so."

He keyed his mike. "Graham, we have about forty minutes left. We're setting down on the bridge to rig the winch. We'll come in, lift the device off the ship, carry it out to deep water, and drop it. NOAA will have a cow, but underwater's the safest place for this thing to go off."

"Have a better idea. How about we pull the battery, same as the last one, and render it inert?" The Brit's voice sounded surprisingly calm on the radio.

The helicopter was settling on the bridge. Blake could just make out the ship, a low rectangle on the horizon.

"This one wasn't meant to be transported, Graham. Best just to pitch it."

The crew began rigging the winch.

"You'd never get clear. Not in the time we have left. Besides, one of our lads has it open, Blake. Says it looks fairly straightforward. Thinks he can . . ."

The ship disappeared, replaced by a sphere of glowing white-orange, bright as the sun. Blake blinked and turned away. When he looked back, a ball of cloud was boiling up, the water around its base dished, white and rushing outward.

Then the shockwave hit, Blake was knocked off his feet, and the world went black.

CHAPTER EIGHTY-THREE

❑ ❑ ❑

Walter Reed Army Medical Center
Washington, DC

Alia. General Sam. Two doctors. A man in a suit Blake didn't recognize.

"How many dead?"

They looked back at him in the hospital bed.

"The weapon," he said. "How many did it kill?"

"All the men on the freighter," the man in the suit said. "I'm Amos Phillips, Colsun's assistant deputy. "We have another two hundred fatalities and about a thousand casualties from flying glass and overturned vehicles on shore. But the plume blew to sea. No fallout on occupied land."

Blake nodded slowly, thinking.

"Grant Reinbolt," he finally said. "I guess its curtains with that identity for me; is that right?"

"Yeah," Phillips agreed. "That identity's 'burned,' so to speak."

"Then what about the real Grant Reinbolt? We bring him back?"

Phillips looked at General Sam, then Alia, and then Blake. "That could be difficult," the assistant deputy director said. "While his abduction was technically a Mossad op, you were involved, and that puts CIA operating on domestic soil. Half-truths get out on this, it could reflect badly on Colsun's memory. And then there's the fact that Reinbolt's been held better than half a year without charges, that we'd have to reveal sources to prosecute. . . . Can of worms. Even if we do all that, all he does is go back to jail, anyhow. And he's not going to have friends in jail. Not this time."

Blake tried to sit up, groaned, and settled for a half-prop against the pillow. "I stole this guy's life. I'd like to give it back. If there are consequences for the bad decisions he made, then that's probably the way it should be. But I'd rather see it done on the up-and-up, even if it comes back to bite us. Even if it comes back to bite me."

Phillips looked Blake in the eye. Blake had the feeling he was being studied.

"All right," Phillips said. "I'll see what I can do."

Blake nodded and allowed himself to slide back onto the pillow. He felt himself getting tired.

"My mother," he said, mustering the effort to speak. "Since we've burned the Reinbolt cover, have we told her . . . anything?"

He saw General Sam and Alia look at one another, then at Phillips.

"Blake," Phillips said, "you're a pretty unique asset right now: a trained operative with field skills and no identity. Rare thing, this day and age. We'd like to keep it that way. For a while, at least."

Blake looked at the doctor. "How soon until I'm up?"

"Hobbling in a week, walking a week after that."

"Okay." He turned to General Sam. "Then I'd like to ask a favor."

EPILOGUE

❏ ❏ ❏

Farmville, Virginia

The Hitching Post restaurant was exactly what it sounded like: a roadside shoebox of a building with a decor tending toward utilitarian and rustic, and a gravel parking lot in which Alia's Scion xD seemed to cower among all the pickup trucks, one of which had dog cages anchored in the bed.

"What's good here?" Alia asked as the waitress left to get coffee.

"Everything," Blake told her. "Came here a lot when I lived in town. Mostly breakfasts but the dinners are good, too."

He glanced out the window where a car was arriving in the autumn evening. People got out, dressed in Carhartt jackets and flannel.

Nobody he recognized.

On the television in the corner, the evening news was on, and a commentator was talking about the *Anesidora* attack, just as the evening news commentators had every night for nearly a month.

". . . shocking lack of security that allowed al-Qaeda to bring a nuclear weapon within thirty-five miles of the nation's capitol, telling the world that its preeminent superpower is impotent to . . ."

Blake clenched his fist, opened it. Alia put her hand on top of his.

"They don't know what they're talking about," she whispered. "They're empty suits, looking for ratings."

". . . ineffective leadership and execution in the military and intelligence quarters . . ."

A man in a hunting jacket walked over to the television and turned it to ESPN.

"Thanks, Phil," the waitress said.

"Lost a good bunch of men on that ship," the man said. "Saved a lot of lives. Nobody talks about that."

Alia squeezed Blake's hand. "You see? Some people understand."

"Wish they were the ones with the broadcast licenses." He looked up at her and smiled. Then he glanced at his watch.

"They'll be here." Alia said.

"I know they will. Order for the two of us, could you? The waitress was here when I was going to Hampden-Sydney. Pretty sure she'd recognize my voice."

"Sure."

Blake left the table, walked into the men's room, and locked the door.

He stood at the sink, put a hand on either side of it, and looked into the mirror. There were few mirrors at the camp, so it still surprised him when he saw his face; even the general shape of it seemed foreign to him. He had heard stories of Civil War mothers finding their bandaged sons in hospitals after battles, recognizing the men they'd raised simply by looking at their eyes, even when the eyes were virtually all that was visible.

He leaned nearer to the mirror. In his eyes, the dye the surgeons implanted was beginning to fade from the irises. But they still appeared darker than he'd grown up with.

Blake splashed some cold water on his face, dried with a paper towel, and left the men's room, pausing outside the door long enough to watch the waitress write on her pad at their table and then leave. He walked back and rejoined Alia looking at the waitress as she walked away.

"What are you thinking?" Alia asked him.

"That waitress . . ." Blake nodded in her direction. "Her name's Sue. Had a son in Iraq, a Navy hospital corpsman attached to the Marines. Killed in a firefight in 2006. I used to come in here, arm in a cast, and she asked me what happed. I told her, and she sat down, let me know about her son. Cried her eyes out. And I said guys like me owe a lot to guys like her son. That knowing somebody can patch you up is a real solace in battle. Sue and I . . . we opened up, you know?"

Alia nodded slowly.

"And now," Blake said, "she doesn't recognize me. I'm nobody."

Alia cocked her head, ever so slightly.

"You're not 'nobody,'" she told him. "To at least one person here"—she wagged a finger at herself—"you're *everybody*."

"I'm glad you came," he said.

"Me, too."

He sat, and she reached across the corner of the table and took his hand again.

"Soon," she told him.

Blake smiled. But even as he smiled, his mind kept drifting back to something he'd read once—it might have been in a magazine at the surgeon's office, back when they were working to save his arm.

The article was about people in the Witness Protection Program. And it said a sizeable number—it might even have been a majority—failed, and dropped back into their old lives within five years, even though they had financial security and even if they had their families with them.

The reason, the magazine said, was *identity*. He even remembered one line from the piece, word for word.

"Identity," the article said, "appears to be an necessary to life as air, or water, or food."

Blake and Alia were just getting their dinners when the three of them came through the door: General Sam, the surgeon who worked on Blake after his battle injuries . . . and his mother.

She looked radiant, younger than he'd remembered. Her skin seemed to glow, and she had an almost girlish grace.

"She looks," Alia whispered, "like she's in love."

Blake turned to Alia. She looked exactly the same way.

"I hope you're right," he whispered back.

Blake ate his meal without remembering it. It wasn't hunger; it was just an operative doing what operatives are trained to do—blend in, maintain cover, don't stand out.

He could only hear snippets of what they were talking about. His mother was thanking General Sam for the college's thoughtfulness in creating a "Blake Kershaw Library Wing" at the Wilson Center.

"It was only right," Blake heard General Sam tell his mother. The general's baritone carried better across the crowded restaurant, and Blake could make out every word. "Your son suffered wounds on the battlefield for this nation. Then he gave his life preparing to defend it. Now, more than ever, it is apparent we need examples such as his."

"Amen," the surgeon said.

And when the meal arrived at their table, all three—Blake's mother, General Sam, and the surgeon—bowed their heads in prayer. That reassured Blake, reassured him as much as the simple one-stone engagement ring his mother wore.

He found himself looking at Alia's hand, once again in his. There was no ring on her finger.

Blake paid their check, but he and Alia lingered over coffee. Then, when General Sam and his guests rose, Blake and Alia preceded them to the door. Blake held the door open for Alia, and then he stayed there, as any Virginia gentleman would, and continued to hold the door open for the other three.

His mother was the first one through. Close enough he could smell her perfume. Close enough for her to brush her arm against his.

"Thank you, sir," she said to him. She looked in his eyes as she said it, and there was a glimmer there that bordered on recognition. Then she walked on and her surgeon, her fiancé, followed her.

The old man was the last one out.

"Thank you, General Sam," Blake whispered as he passed.

The general shifted his cane from one hand to the other, gave Blake's shoulder a squeeze, and walked on.

Then Blake closed the door, walked through the chilly evening air to the little Scion, and got in—inside with the woman he loved.

ABOUT THE AUTHOR

❑ ❑ ❑

LTG (Ret.) William G. "Jerry" Boykin spent thirty-six years in the United States Army, many of them as an original member of Delta Force, the world's premier Special Operations unit. Today he is an ordained minister and SVP at the Family Research Council. Virginia is his home.